THE CRIMSON CHILD:
THE INDESTRUCTIBLES BOOK 5

by
Matthew Phillion

The Crimson Child: the Indestructibles Book 5

Lost Continuity Press
P.O. Box 1044
Salem, MA 01970

Printed in the United States of America

ISBN-13: 978-0-9979165-1-5
(also available in eBook format)

Front cover design:
Sterling Arts & Design

Five books for five heroes.
For Lucas, Adelyn, Nick, Callan, and Joey

From the author

Book 5. What a long, strange journey this has been.

When I sat down to write the first Indestructibles book, I was looking for an escape—I wanted to write a story without worrying about a special effects budget, and I wanted a place where I could put everything I loved about storytelling in one place. Aliens and cyborgs. Magicians and werewolves. Knock-down, drag-out street fights and tiny little moments between friends. I didn't know if anyone else would want to explore this weird little comic book world I set out to build.

But I am so glad you all did.

The Crimson Child is officially the place where I've gone beyond my game plan for the Indestructibles kids. From Day 1, I knew what would happen in the first four books. I knew the growing pains they'd through in *Breakout*, and the dark future they'd face in *the Entropy of Everything*, and I even knew the crazy maneuver Kate would pull off at the end of *Like a Comet*, even if I didn't have a title for that book until it almost went to the printer.

But with this book, the gang's in uncharted territory. They've grown up a lot, and they've come to surprise me with the things they do and say. It's a lot of fun as a writer to travel past the known boundaries of the world you were planning on building.

I hope you enjoy the view. I sure had fun discovering it myself.

As always, a huge thanks to the folks who are willing to be my test subjects during the writing process—Stephanie Buck, Christian Hegg, and Colin Carlton, thanks for helping me figure out some key character moments this time around. And Christine Geiger, I can never thank you enough for the work you do as editor on these books.

Sterling Arts & Design has helped shape the Indestructiverse with each new cover, and once again, they've come through with something beautiful and dark.

I owe a special debt of gratitude to Peter Sarno and PFP Publishing. While our partnership came to an amicable close this year, this series could not exist without your support. You changed my life taking a shot on a first-time author, and I'll never forget that.

And now I invite you all on the latest adventure of the Indestructibles, their most personal, dangerous journey yet.

Matthew Phillion
Salem, Massachusetts
June, 2019

PROLOGUE:
THE TOWN THAT SIMPLY LEFT

They named her Alice, because her mother loved Lewis Carroll. Her mother always called her Alice properly, but her father called her Lissie, because, he said, Alice was a name she should grow into. But Alice also knew he called her Lissie because her mother preferred that he didn't, and for that reason, it became a secret name they shared. She had a father-name and a mother-name, and she always felt very lucky to have both, even when she grew old enough to see how much the nickname frustrated her mother.

They loved each other, her parents, but Alice always knew there was something missing, some rift between them they never spoke about, a sadness without a name.

She would hide from that sadness, conjuring up imaginary friends to join her when she hid in lonely places, where she couldn't hear her parents talk in that soft way they did to pretend they weren't arguing. Her imaginary friends would disappear when her parents found her. They were never angry that she hid, but pulled her from dark closets, or beneath tablecloths, or beside the small vernal pool that formed in their backyard, apologizing as they carried her to the kitchen for dinner or to the car to visit her grandmother. It was always her father who took her to grandma's house, and she knew, without the words ever spoken out loud, that her father needed a place to hide as much as she did. She was wise beyond her years, and she knew, if you were lucky, your family will let you hide.

But in all, she grew up quiet and peaceful in a quiet and relatively peaceful home, despite the sadness, despite the quiet worry. Her imaginary friends stayed with her, the teddy bear who came to life when no one was looking, the fairy with the pink skin and eyes black as night, the shadow that pried itself off the floor and watched over her like a protector, the unicorn the size of a small dog. Other things, creatures beyond description, out of storybooks, out of dreams. She had so many friends. If only they were real, she'd think.

Perhaps, in another life, Alice might have realized that these were not imaginary friends. But the gifts she had that allowed her to bring these creatures—bear and fairy, shadow and unicorn—to life were not the sort of aspects ordinary parents, distracted by ordinary parent things, would have noticed. And Alice's imaginary friends were very good at hiding. They did not want to be banished, you see. They knew they were not of this world, and they knew that the wrong person—someone with gifts like Alice's, who knew how to control them, who knew how to make use of them to change the world—they could chase Alice's imaginary friends away.

And so, they stayed imaginary, hiding when proper, coming to life when their protector, their conjurer, their little magician needed them.

They weren't vindictive spirits, after all. They were little creatures called up from the other side of reality, happy for an escape from their ordinary existence, and they enjoyed watching over Alice.

Or rather, they enjoyed it until the day the rift in the world opened up.

They sensed it, the rift. Magic has a way of being everywhere at once, and if a rift opened in London there was no reason a spirit in a sunny town in America would not sense it if they were paying attention. All four of Alice's protectors looked up in unison as it happened. Alice asked them why they stopped playing, and the bear looked to the fairy and the fairy to the shadow, whose hand had gone protectively to the multi-colored mane of the unicorn.

But then, like a sudden draft, it was gone. The bear cuddled into Alice's chest and the unicorn pranced and the fairy flittered onto her shoulder. Only the shadow remained worried, looking off in the distance. Perhaps it was because he was made of darkness, and like calls to like when magic is involved. Perhaps the shadow-creature was simply a worrier by nature. But he knew something had joined them on this side of the veil that did not belong here, and he knew, somehow, that it would find its way to their conjurer.

Eventually the shadow turned his attention back to Alice as well, and all went back to normal, for a little while. Or at least as normal as things can be in the home of a child no one knew was a magical savant. Magic can be mundane, sometimes, too, with tea parties and late night gossip. Magic tends to steal innocence from those who encounter it. For that reason, for many who practice magic, for many who live and breathe it like the bear and the fairy, the shadow and the unicorn, innocence is utterly sacred. It is something to be cherished, and protected, to be guarded with the very fiber of your being. Perhaps Alice was too old for imaginary friends. But lonely children find joy where they can, and these were no ordinary imaginary friends she had.

It took some time for the thing that crept through the rift to find her. It was a peaceful stretch. Alice, who was Lissie less and less now, grew up a bit. She began to question her imaginary friends. She began to feel something other than ordinary. But she never had the chance to figure out what that meant for herself.

Then her twelfth birthday arrived. The day her father had a small heart attack and was rushed to the emergency room, Alice's birthday cake still sitting on the passenger seat of his car. The day her mother raged at an airline attendant two thousand miles away that she had to get home, that her only daughter was turning twelve and she'd promised she'd be home in time. A day incredible thunderstorms raged down on the City like the tears of a heartbroken goddess. On this day, something… some *thing*… came for Alice.

The bear and the fairy and the shadow and the unicorn became their true selves that moment, the forms they'd hidden away in toys and imagination, to defend their conjurer, their master, their Alice.

The battle was short. And in the end, Alice disappeared.

And her entire town disappeared with her.

CHAPTER 1:
ONCE, IN THE DESERT

Jane touched town among the sandy dunes, the relentless heat of the desert sun hot against her shoulders, as if the sun itself came too close to the Earth here. She needed it, though, she thought, luxuriating in the solar energy her cells soaked up. She'd forsaken her uniform as Solar of the Indestructibles in favor of a tank top and shorts, the sort of summer clothing that should leave any normal human being burned to a crisp here in the desert.

But Jane was no ordinary human. She was the solar-powered girl, and here, in this place, she felt more powerful than ever.

Well, that's a lie, she thought to herself. I almost feel like my old self. Not long ago, in the cold reaches of space, she'd expended every bit of stored up energy she had within her to stop an alien spacecraft from reaching her world. The act had nearly killed her, left her wilted and half-dead in orbit. But the sun, in the end, always provides, and she'd taken full advantage of being here under the desert sky to renew herself. She felt strong, she felt healthy, and, hearing the bickering of her friends on the other side of the dunes, she felt at home.

Jane kicked off her hiking boots to feel the heat of the daylight through the soles of her feet. Again, a mere mortal would be catastrophically wounded by the temperatures. But not the solar-powered girl. This act was just one more way to take in as much power as she could. For her, this was as comforting as a tucking her feet into the sand on the beach.

Not so for her friends, who were wrapped in khaki, with balaclavas protecting their necks and faces from the blistering sun.

"That doesn't go there! That goes *there!*" yelled a man's voice, sounding less angry than put upon.

"I know exactly where it goes! You showed me yesterday!" said a young woman's voice. She did not sound angry either. In fact, she sounded like she was deliberately infuriating her companion.

Jane crested the dune to see a large piece of spaceship drifting in the air. Her eyes, with her senses amplified by all the sunlight she'd taken in, could just make out the glimmer of a bubble surrounding the component as it hung in the air. A minute figure in gigantic goggles and a sky-blue balaclava stood below, holding that piece of spaceship up with her mind, one hand outstretched lazily to hold it in place. Entropy Emily, the girl who could control gravity, sort of. Emily's hand was sheathed in a mechanical gauntlet, a smaller, more streamlined version—though certainly improvised by the look of it—of the gloves given to her before the great space battle that nearly killed them all. They were given to her, in fact, by the man she currently argued with.

That man was Henry Winter. He looked like a cross

between an aging movie star and a parody of an explorer in his khaki outfit. One leg was framed by a sort of exoskeleton brace, a device Winter had created to compensate for a long-injured leg that had left him limping and relying on a cane for years. Former high-tech hero, former billionaire, a man previously thought dead by the entire world, Henry had temporarily given up a job with the government agency dealing with super-powered threats to the world to be here, in the desert, working with Jane and Emily and the others on a task he considered even more important.

They were rebuilding the Indestructibles' base.

Half-buried in the sand, a blocky space craft jutted out, blackened in places, shattered in others. The ship was still called the Tower by Jane and her teammates, because, when they first encountered it, the craft had been hidden, embedded on top of a skyscraper in the City. But it had been nearly destroyed in the space battle, used by one of their other teammates as a battering ram to destroy an enemy attack vessel. None of them thought it would fly again, that it would be any use at all, but here they were. Henry Winter's expertise, alongside some very specialized help by the ship's former Artificial Intelligence, Neal, had been able to get many of the craft's functions working again. Things like a food-generator, an air temperature moderator, lights, and many of the ship's communications devices. Still, it looked like a small child had pushed a complicated Lego creation off the table and onto the floor, with square-ish pieces scattered and sticking out of the sand like the bones of a great mechanical beast.

Jane chose not to interrupt, but rather to listen to the banter and assess whose side she might have to take. She had very little doubt Henry was right in this case. Emily had a telltale tone to her voice when she was being deliberately antagonistic.

"This goes over there," Emily said. "You said it goes over there."

"Then why are you bubble-of-floating it over here?" Henry said.

"Because my gut instinct says you're wrong," Emily said.

"I—which one of us is the scientist here?"

"I am a certified genius," Emily said. "That has to count for something."

"I'm a MENSA member," Winter said. "I have six Ph.Ds. How many doctorates do you have?"

"Those are just pieces of paper. I believe in the school of hard knocks."

"Will you please, please put the alien moisture generator somewhere it will not be buried in a new pile of sand overnight?"

"How about over there," Emily said.

"You know what? I don't care," Henry said.

Behind him, a machine that looked like a wheeled trash can joke struggled through the sand to join them. Inside that wheeled trash can was the sentience that had once embodied the Tower itself, the AI Neal. Neal survived the Tower's demise by escaping into the portable body he now inhabited. Jane thought he must find it very frustrating and limiting after living in the body of a spaceship for generations, but the AI, ever patient, seemed unbothered.

"If I may interject," the AI said.

"Oh, Neal," Emily said. "We really need to upgrade your body. I hate seeing you living in a bucket."

"I would not dissuade you from providing an upgrade," Neal said. "But I must admit this framework is a fine temporary solution."

"It's been months, babe," Emily said.

"Months is a relatively short time span for me," Neal said.

"Don't be a martyr," Emily said.

"Neal," Henry said. "Will you please tell Emily here to put the moisture generator somewhere safe?"

"Follow me, Designation: Entropy Emily," Neal said.

Emily bopped along behind him happily. She yanked her mask down low enough to stick her tongue out at Henry before following the wheeling AI inside a broken gap in the Tower's armored hull.

"You're killing me," Henry said.

As Emily approached the hole in the hull, someone else emerged, pulling a protective hood up over a neon-orange mohawk. The newcomer was as much machine as human, with both legs gleaming metal below the knee, one entire arm and the other from the elbow down also replaced with cybernetic parts. Her right eye was a glowing green piece of robotic hardware. Still, despite the alarming amount of artificial parts she wore so proudly, the cyborg known as Bedlam looked better than Jane had ever seen her. Henry Winter had helped her improve the parts that had been installed sloppily by the evil organization who had done this to her, and while much of her was obviously, as Bedlam often joked, "not off the shelf," those parts looked more and more natural, streamlined, and human than ever before. She loosened her over-shirt a bit and Jane caught sight of the gleaming power source embedded in Bedlam's chest. Once an Indestructibles adversary, Bedlam had changed sides to join them, and her no-nonsense personality had quickly won over Jane. The cyborg woman spotted the solar-powered girl on the dune and strolled up to join her.

"You're back," Bedlam said.

"Just got here," Jane said. She nodded to where Emily and

Henry had just been. "They've been at it all day?"

"Hours and hours. I don't know how they get anything done. And it's worse when they have an audience."

The young women walked back down toward the ship and followed the perimeter so that Bedlam could walk in the shade while Jane stayed in the sun.

"What's the latest?" Bedlam said.

"No word from Billy," Jane said. Billy Case, the Indestructible known as Straylight, had gone to Saturn with others like him—heroes from across the universe sharing their bodies with aliens known as the Luminae. They were building a new home base on Titan. The very idea of it felt unreal to Jane, who had seen so many things in her young life that almost nothing should seem impossible. And yet a race of symbiotic aliens building a new home world on one of Saturn's moons… that seemed a step beyond the pale. And yet that was where their friend had disappeared to.

Jane studied Bedlam's reaction to the news. The cyborg felt out of place almost everywhere—which was the reason, really, why she stayed in the desert helping to rebuild the Tower. Billy had promised to bring her to Titan as soon as it became habitable. *She is so uncomfortable she wants to leave Earth to start over,* Jane thought. She wished there was something she could to fix that.

"And Kate's in the City, holding down the fort, so to speak," Jane said, referring to the ballerina turned vigilante known as the Dancer. Kate had been different since they stopped the alien invasion. They'd all been different. Nearly everyone on the team had faced down their own mortality in that final battle, and Kate had been the one to drive the Tower into the attacking armada, a suicide mission she never expected to come home from. *Naturally, she's different,* Jane thought.

I'm different. Emily is different. None of us are the same.

But Kate… They'd never been the warmest of friends, but there had always been something between them, a shared understanding. The vigilante had become more closed off than ever. Jane worried about her.

Jane worried about everyone, if she were honest with herself.

"What about the hairball?" Bedlam said.

"Titus is up to something," Jane said, almost smiling. If everyone on the team had pushed the limits of survival during the space battle, the werewolf Titus Whispering had looked death in the eye and won. But unlike the others—Kate's closed-off behavior, Billy disappearing, Emily loudly putting on a brave front, Bedlam's hiding, and even Jane's own quiet melancholy—Titus came back better. The shy, unconfident boy who went into space always seemed to have a plan now. He gave Jane hope. She always knew that if something happened to her as the de facto leader of the team, it would have to be Titus who stepped up. Whatever he was doing right now, she could tell it was to be better prepared for whatever happened next.

"And the old guys?" Bedlam asked.

"Doc sent Korthos back into space to take care of something or possibly to keep him busy and out of trouble," Jane said. "I don't know what. And Doc said he'll be back soon. He's following up on something weird he got wind of on the… however magicians communicate with each other."

"He scares me a bit," Bedlam said.

"He should," Jane said. Doc had long been her mentor, her guardian, her hero. He'd saved her life and she'd saved his. But no matter how close they were, she always knew: those who touched magic brought danger with them wherever they went.

Magic, Doc Silence taught his students, is the most dangerous thing they'd ever face.

"One last question," Bedlam said, unhooking a canteen of water from her belt.

"Shoot."

"Can you get your friend the sentient hurricane to stop by and dump a nice big storm on us? I'm so sick of sweating."

"That'd destroy the ecosystem," Jane said. "But I can fly you home any time you want to."

A bang erupted from inside the ship, followed by incoherent arguing between Emily and Henry.

"I just might take you up on that," Bedlam said.

CHAPTER 2:
THE CITY AFTER THE FALL

Not long ago, monsters fell from the sky.

These alien invaders plummeted to Earth and began a brief reign of terror, symbiotic warriors cultivated from across the universe as soldiers for a planet-eating symbiotic species.

It seems ridiculous now, Kate Miller thought, perched on the edge of a building as she looked out over the city. But the invasion was real. And it targeted her home. From her vantage point here, she could still see the scars. The invasion was over quickly, a multi-generational cadre of heroes—and even some villains alongside them—driving back the darkness and saving the world.

But in the brief time they were here, the monsters did unspeakable harm.

There were places in the City where smoke still bubbled up from fires that never seemed to go out. Buildings lay in ruins where alien ships crashed, the damage too extensive for the owners to afford. There were more homeless now in the City, though the local and federal governments had worked hard to try to find homes for the displaced. But the City, Kate's city, wore the battle scars of a place that had seen war. Because it had. Just a blink in the eye of time, shorter than any war humans had waged on each other, but it hadn't taken long for the invaders to devastate the City.

And this was why Kate Miller, the vigilante known as the Dancer, stayed here while her friends and allies went to the desert to rebuild their spaceship, or went to the stars to build new homes for another kind of lost aliens. She stayed here because this was her city, and someone needed to watch over it.

There was less crime now, Kate realized soon after returning. People seemed too tired, too scared. Yes, there was petty theft, but overall, surviving the invasion had left the City's residents disinclined to take from each other. She knew that would fade with time—human nature was not altruistic or kind by default, she believed. But for now, the City didn't need an avenging guardian the way it had in the past.

She also found herself doubting her old tactics. She'd been angrier when she first started her career, and hadn't ever considered the reasons why someone might turn to theft or other non-violent crime. She'd always preferred to hunt down the violent, those who did harm to others, but looking back, she felt a strange sense of guilt and embarrassment. So, blinded by her own need for revenge, she abandoned empathy and embraced the darkness. It had served her well for a while, but now, that anger felt like a burden, and one she still struggled to let go of.

But in a city with little crime for a crime-fighter to address, Kate Miller found another way to watch over her home town.

Many people went missing during the invasion.

Some would later turn up dead, of course, crushed under fallen buildings, victims of alien monsters, accidental casualties as ordinary people made mistakes of incaution as they tried to escape. Others disappeared for other reasons—a chance to leave behind a life they didn't want, a chance to run away from who they were. And others, of course, were taken. And so, in the absence of people to punch or kick, the Dancer opened herself up to another kind of heroism. She prowled the City looking for the missing.

She'd been unsuccessful tonight, pursuing the trail of a teenaged boy she had begun to suspect, based on the clues she'd found so far, had simply run away from home. His family worried about him, but Kate saw the signs in the things he'd left behind, in the words he'd used on social media, that the boy had, like so many others, seen the invasion as a reason to disappear.

She'd wanted to disappear herself sometimes. She understood the instinct. But the family wanted some sort of answer, and Kate promised she'd find one. Whether that answer would be something the family would want to hear, that was another question entirely.

She slipped down the building's fire escape and returned to street level. In the shadows of an alleyway, she removed the mask she used to hide her identity and wrapped herself in a long coat to camouflage her costume, turning up the collar against the first hint of snow falling from the sky. She unpinned the bun tightly holding her hair in place and let it fall to her shoulders before stepping out into the street.

She wouldn't find the boy tonight, but another lost soul was on his way home and she'd promised to meet him at the train station.

Titus Whispering had already arrived when Kate strolled up

to the station gates. He smiled at Kate so warmly it made her forget, for just a moment, just how angry she was with him.

Titus looked better than the last time she saw him. He'd suffered the most during the battle in outer space against the parasitic aliens, his body badly burned in an explosion. Titus was a werewolf, and very little could do a werewolf permanent harm, but even his powerful healing abilities still hadn't quite fixed the baby-pink look to certain spots on his face and neck where the worst of the burns were still healing. He had cut his hair all the way to the scalp not for fashion but because it had been burned away in patches in the battle, and it still grew in unevenly, though Kate could already tell that damage was getting better as well. The hair that did grow back, though, turned more silver than dark, matching the color of his fur when he transformed. In a year or so, Titus had told her, it would look like none of this ever happened. But she knew he was wrong about that. He might heal, but some scars would remain. There was a haunted look to his eyes, the sort of ghostly presence someone who came so close to dying can't hide.

I almost got him killed, Kate thought. It was my suicide mission into space. My idea. I'm the one who knew it would be a one-way trip.

Titus walked up to her, dropping his duffel bag at his feet to pull her into a ferocious hug. She stiffened, her frustration bubbling up again, but then there he was, the one person she cared about more than anything else in the world, and the words weren't there anymore. She wrapped her arms around him and held him tight. He felt so small, she thought. He might be a three hundred-pound werewolf when they needed him to be, but when he was not, there simply wasn't much to him.

The two of us. It's like we're barely ever here, she thought.

"I don't like what you're doing," Kate said before Titus could say anything.

"I didn't know hugs were a bad thing. Who doesn't like hugs? I mean other than you," he said, letting her go.

"You know what I'm talking about," Kate said.

Titus scooped up his bag and together they walked outside into the snow. With the Tower sitting in the desert, Kate had set up an office in an apartment downtown as a makeshift headquarters. They headed that way.

"I have to do this," Titus said.

"This," the thing Kate was so upset about, was magic. He'd gone to see Leto, the ancient werewolf shaman who had mentored Titus early on in his transformation, to learn more about the sort of feral magic she practiced. It was not so different than the more classic magic Doc Silence knew, but Titus had chosen not to go to Doc for training.

"No, you don't," Kate said. "Doc has always said magic is the most dangerous thing we'll ever face. I don't know why you insist on making it your job to learn it."

"Because Doc won't always be there," Titus said. "And when he's gone, someone has to know the things he knows."

"Why you? You have a job. You're our monster," Kate said.

"That's very kind of you," Titus said.

"You know what I mean," Kate said. "You're already putting your life on the line, physically, every day. Why should you add all of this mystic garbage to the weight you're already carrying?"

"I'm the shaman on the hill, Kate," Titus said.

She glared at him as he pulled a knit hat down over his stubbly scalp. He's trying to grow a beard, she noticed. This ridiculous boy.

"You sound like a lunatic when you say that."

"It's what Leto said I was born to be. It's what the Whispering werewolves are. We're the shaman on the hill. We keep the monsters at bay. It's my job, Kate. I was born to stop the things that go bump in the night."

"You are a thing that goes bump in the night."

"So are you."

"True," Kate said.

Titus paused. The snow caught on his coat and gleamed like stars. He seemed so far away, Kate thought. Standing next to me, worlds apart.

"Why does this bother you so much? You're the last person to tell anyone they're taking on too much of a burden. That's all you do, take on other peoples' burdens."

Kate chewed her lower lip for a moment, letting the silence grow heavy and belligerent between them. Snowflakes danced in yellowy streetlights.

"You're barely human, Titus," Kate said. Titus opened his mouth to speak, but Kate cut him off. "No. No, I never talk. Let me talk."

Titus nodded and waited.

"You're not human, not really. You're something else, you're something more. And every time you go away, every time you go north to learn more about what you are, you come back a little less you, and a little more whatever it is you're becoming. And that's your right, Titus, that's what you are and that's what you deserve to be and I will not ever, not ever try to stop you."

She stuffed her hands in her pockets and looked away.

"But magic makes people even less human," Kate said. "Look at Doc. Look at the Lady. They're barely here anymore.

They exist… it's like they exist in two places at once. Above and below. And I am just a person, Titus. I am just a pile of scars and bad decisions and nothing more than that, and I'll never be anything more than that, and every time you… You're…"

"Kate," Titus aid.

"I don't want you to become someone I can't talk to anymore," Kate said.

"I'm still here," Titus said. "I'm not going anywhere."

"This is why I don't talk," Kate said. "I'm bad at it."

"We don't have to talk anymore tonight," Titus said.

"Good," she said.

And so, they walked, vigilante and werewolf, silent but together, as snow fell on a broken city that still needed them both.

CHAPTER 3:
THE LOW ROADS

The sun splashed warm, golden light across the Plaza de Espana in Sevilla, the grand circular construction looking more like something out of a fantasy film than a modern city. Doc Silence, one of the world's last remaining magicians, did not look the way one would expect from a man of his career. No pointed hat or wizard's robes, the magician wore a long dark coat over a tee shirt and jeans, his eyes—which, when unhidden, glowed with an indigo light—covered by red-lensed glasses. He had let his beard grow since the battle against the alien invasion, and he'd been unhappy to discover that hair that had once been supernaturally silver-blue had begun turning white.

Time, he thought. Time is catching up to me.

Aging didn't concern him, though. Wizards had a way of living past their expiration date anyway. What worried him now, and what brought him here to this beautiful structure in Spain, was a series of clues that indicated that something was wrong in the shadow world where magic ran parallel to the ordinary one. He'd found hints across the world, traveling the low roads where distance was a suggestion and reality bent and warped in ways only the mystical would allow. He'd talked to seers in Louisiana and exorcists in Rome; monster hunters in London and demon-trappers in Tokyo.

Something wasn't right, and no one was quite sure what it was. The magical world was sick. And it would take a doctor to fix it.

I never meant to be the last man standing, Doc Silence thought, enjoying the warm Spanish sunlight, listening to the voices of tourists and locals. Bells rang in the distance. He loved this place. He'd spent one good week in Seville before he'd become the accidental superhero he'd eventually grow into. Back when he had friends who were ordinary in the wonderful way people who aren't like him are. Some of his last conversations as a normal person happened here, before he learned that nightmares were real, before he began a career sealing up monster-holes in closets and driving off evil spirits and stopping blood-cults from raising elder gods.

One week, one summer, drinking coffee out of tiny porcelain cups with people who knew his real name. Doc Silence gave up his real name to become a magician, as all magicians do. There were days he couldn't call it to mind without trying.

But he wasn't in Sevilla for the memories. He'd sensed the threat, the wrong-ness, had passed through here, something that didn't belong on this plane of reality, and he'd followed, a hunter chasing prey that knew it was being stalked. He didn't feel as though he were in any sort of danger—no, strangely he felt as if the presence was afraid of him. But the closer he got to the thing he sensed, this intruder in the realm under his protection, the more he sensed something else. Some second shadow, an underlying scent. Whatever it was he found himself chasing along the low roads, it didn't come into this world alone. And whatever parasitic thing followed it across the void…

That thing, he knew, did not fear Doc Silence in the least.

And then there was the other problem. The problem he'd had his entire career, really. The problem known as the Lady Natasha Grey.

It wasn't hard, in his investigation, to figure out that the Lady was somehow involved. Natasha was one of the few magicians left in this world more powerful than Doc Silence, and she moved in a part of the magical community he did not, trading in power and favors, collecting artifacts and curses like currency. Magic, though, is like a fine art—everyone's work is unique, and if you are an expert, a collector, if you will, you can spot another artist's handiwork easily enough. Whatever this wrong-ness in the magical demi-world was, Natasha Grey had a hand in it. Doc would recognize her mystical fingerprints anywhere.

He was shaken from his reverie by a small boy staring at him from near the great fountain dominating the historic site. Doc tilted his head at him, and the boy pointed to a shadowed archway nearby. Before Doc could speak to him, the boy darted off, but Doc knew well enough what was happening. He went to the archway and waited.

"The amount of guilt you walk around with, Doctor, you could have been a priest," an old, familiar voice said. Doc turned to see a silver-bearded man dressed all in black step from the shadows to greet him.

"Arturo," Doc said, extending his hand. The old man shook it. "It takes a priest to know one, doesn't it?"

Arturo nodded, gesturing to his clothing. He was dressed as a Catholic priest, black suit and white collar. An old Jesuit, Arturo was a friend, if Doc could call anyone such a thing, both a man of religion and a student of the arcane. They'd known each other a very long time.

"You set off all sorts of mystical warnings when you arrive in town, you know," Arturo said. "Just because you're one of the good guys doesn't mean the world is unaware you bring trouble with you."

"I'm chasing trouble this time, my friend," Doc said.

"I thought as much," Arturo said. "I know what you're looking for."

Doc leaned in. This was the first time he'd encountered a witness, or at least one who knew what he'd seen.

"Tell me," Doc said.

"There's a girl," the priest said. "New to this world—you know what I mean by this?"

"A traveler," Doc said.

"Yes. And not even remotely human, despite the shell she wears," Arturo said. "She travels in the company of two dogs that are absolutely not dogs."

"Guardians?"

"Some sort, yes," the priest said. "Though I'm not sure what their true form was. I'm not you, Doctor. I couldn't take the risk."

"You took enough of a risk just looking," Doc said.

"I'll be honest, she did not seem dangerous," Arturo said. "Lost, out of place, perhaps, but not dangerous. But I'll tell you, Silence, that she had riders."

Riders. A nice way of putting it, Doc thought. Sometimes creatures traveled between the planes of reality—Doc had done it himself many times, most recently when he and Lady

Grey had become trapped on the higher mystical planes and needed Jane's help to get home. Often, travelers between planes would seek out the guardians of the ones they visited to announce themselves, but not always. The travelers were rarely the problem, though. The dangerous thing was when they were incautious. Because when you traveled between worlds, you opened a door. And like any open door, sometimes unwelcome things slipped through behind you.

"She had a lamprey," Doc said, using an old, gritty slang for a creature that followed a magical traveler between planes.

The priest nodded.

"It was with her when she arrived here," Arturo said. "And it was not when she left."

Doc sighed and rubbed his eyes.

"Don't look so tired," Arturo said. "Didn't you save the world a few months back? Putting down some parasitic demon should be a vacation for you."

"Is it ever?" Doc said.

The priest laughed.

"I…" Arturo began, but then stopped short and looked up.

Doc felt the same call—both men immediately looked to the West as if magnetized.

"I don't know what that was," Arturo said.

"Something awful," Doc said. It had felt like a stab through his chest. Something had gone very wrong, very quickly, and the ley lines had cried out. Ordinary folks would say this sort of thing felt like someone had walked over their grave. But for the magically gifted, it was a clarion call, a warning signal that struck them deep in their hearts.

Doc shook off the ghostly feeling and prepared a teleportation spell. He nodded to the priest.

"Thanks for your help, my friend," Doc said. "Let's not go

so many years without speaking again."

Arturo put a hand on Doc's shoulder.

"If there's anything I can do to help," he said.

Doc shook his head.

"Just keep your eyes and ears open," Doc said. "Find me if you hear anything strange. Or if you see the traveler again."

"I will," Arturo said. "Be safe, Doctor."

"I always am," Doc said. A portal opened beside him in greenish gold.

"You were always a liar," Arturo said.

Doc smiled and stepped through the portal.

"But I lie for good reasons," Doc said.

And then he disappeared.

CHAPTER 4:
HE RETURNED FROM THE STARS

From a distance one might mistake him for a shooting star.

Billy Case, the hero known as Straylight, burned bright as he passed through the Earth's atmosphere, his body surrounded by and emanating his signature blue-white glow.

After months in the depths of space, the Earth's atmosphere felt both strange and familiar—the weight of gravity, the taste of real air, all the things he'd left behind out there near Saturn, where the Luminae were building their new home.

And what a home it was. Cobbled together from derelict spacecraft and pieces of technology the other Luminae had dragged across the galaxy, the improvised station had become a castle in the sky, with illogical wings and twisting spires, a patchwork of mismatched metals to mirror the mismatched alien hosts to Luminae from across the galaxy.

It was a strange brotherhood there. Almost none of the hosts had ever met before the battle for Earth just a few months ago, so their personalities, their names, were as remarkably new as the anatomies the different aliens bore. Tentacles and tusks, hands and claws, none of these were as different as simply learning about each other.

But at the same time, it was a grand homecoming. The Luminae themselves are all but immortal. The hosts had changed, but these beings of light who gave each host his or her power, those symbiotic creatures were the same who left their doomed home world millennia ago. And some of them had not seen each other since the day they first parted.

And so, the Titan base—which would need a name eventually, though with more than a dozen species sharing even more languages, choosing a name would be harder than building the construct itself—was a cacophony of noise, machinery and construction, strange languages, the sort of bizarre half-talking Luminae hosts catch themselves doing as they speak with the bodiless creature who shares their mind.

Despite all the noise, and the new faces, despite the opportunity to learn about aliens from across the galaxy, Billy found himself lonely quite quickly. Not only had life on Earth not particularly prepared him for the scope of the universe, but he was significantly younger than many of the other hosts. He felt like an outsider in a club he actually belonged to.

Which was why, he knew, Suresh told him to go home.

Suresh was another Luminae host, the only other human here. Known on Earth as the hero Horizon, and partnered with Billy's predecessor, Nigel, Suresh had saved the world a thousand times over, only to give up on humanity and disappear into the cosmos. Until Billy found him, and until he knew his planet needed him again. The old man, with his stark white beard and wild hair, had pulled Billy aside, sensing something was wrong.

"You should go home, kid," Suresh said. They were near what would eventually become the engine room for the base, and nearby, the reptilian Seng bickered quietly with a creature who looked like a massive centaur over how best to rework some contraption or another.

"You guys sick of me already?"

"Believe it or not, Billy, some of these guys actually like you," Suresh said. "Not me, of course, but some of the others."

"Thanks, grampa," Billy said.

"Whatever," Suresh said. "Look, you're relatively useless here."

"Two for two."

"But there's still things you can do on Earth," the older man said. "Just because we defeated the Nemesis fleet doesn't mean Earth should be without its Luminae. One of us should go back, and you know I hate people."

"True enough."

Dude, Billy's symbiotic partner, chimed in, his voice as always audible only to Billy himself.

He's right, Dude said. *Once this base is constructed, many of these Luminae will go back to the worlds they watch over as well. They're here to build a haven and to send a signal to the other Luminae out there waiting who don't know the enemy has been stopped. But we still have a job to do.*

"Moneypenny is agreeing with me, isn't he," Suresh said

Just once I'd like to meet a human who calls me something respectful, Dude said.

"You sure you don't need me for anything?" Billy said.

"Come back in a month or three," Suresh said. "And bring

me Oreos and rice wine and any good sci-fi movies we can't get streaming way out here."

"I can't bring you sake," Billy said. "I'm underage."

"Have Doc buy it for you," Suresh said, grinning wickedly. "Now get home. Go see your friends. Be young. You'll have plenty of time to save the universe. Take care of the world for me."

And thus, Billy Case said his goodbyes to his newfound brothers and flew back to Earth. The journey became less tedious every time, he found; Dude explained that, now that he was growing accustomed to interstellar travel, his body was adjusting to the flight, going into an almost meditative state as they moved at speeds the human mind and body weren't quite prepared to experience. Billy joked that Dude gave him the power to travel at light speed, and Dude, being Dude, informed him that if they could travel at light speed they could get to Earth from Titan in seventy-nine minutes rather than many hours. Dude also liked to point out how much time he wasted traveling by dragging Billy's organic body with him, since he could, without a host, literally travel at the speed of light, and Billy's carcass—that's the word Dude used, of course, "carcass"—slowed them down considerably.

Billy drifted and daydreamed until the Moon passed by on his left like a great gray beach. And then they were home.

He flew right for the remnants of the Tower, the late-day desert heat baking through his uniform until Dude's powers kicked in, regulating his body to a safe temperature. The sky was a brilliant blur of purple and pale pink, the sand gleaming gold and orange below him.

"They're making some progress," Billy said. From the air, he could see the shape of the Tower finally fully emerging from the dunes, though it still looked like a throwaway piece of set from Tatooine rather than the magnificent hospital starship it really was.

They've restored power, Dude said. *Impressive, given their lack of true understanding how the vessel works.*

"I bet Emily's taking all the credit for it," Billy said. He smiled at the thought of his diminutive best friend taunting their adult compatriots about just how much of a contribution she made to the state of things here.

But it wasn't Emily he saw first. Instead, a shock of neon orange hair and the faint glint of metal drew his eye to see Bedlam sitting on the roof of the fallen spaceship, looking up at the sky.

Something twinged in Billy's chest when he saw her. It was strange, he thought, to feel like this. The first time they'd met Bedlam punched him into the next area code and since then Billy joked that it was love at first sight for him, but they'd gotten to know each other after the battle with the Nemesis fleet and…

You feel afraid, Billy Case, Dude said. *That's unusual.*

Billy swallowed hard and smiled. I don't know how to put this into words, Dude, Billy thought, knowing the alien could hear him. What is happiness and fear at the same time every time you look at someone mean?

Some human poets might argue that the word you're looking for is love, Dude said.

Let's not go getting ahead of ourselves, Billy thought. If love is defined as being terrified at every moment you're around someone that you're going to say the wrong thing and they'll leave, love sucks.

Perhaps it's just severe anxiety, then, Dude said. The alien's disembodied voice sounded as if he might be laughing.

Bedlam didn't stand up when she saw him, instead waiting

patiently for Billy to land. He did, and stood beside her awkwardly for a minute before even more awkwardly sitting down next to her.

"Hey, stranger," Bedlam said. She had a crooked smile, accentuated by her mismatched eyes. "You smell like outer space."

"I don't even know what that means," Billy said.

"Smells like a race track," she said. "Hot metal and fumes. Just a hint of burnt steak."

"We haven't seen each other in months, and this is the first thing you say to me," Billy said.

"I was going to point out that it's hysterical I see you in full-body spandex more often than regular clothes, but this felt less awkward," Bedlam said.

"That's really awkward."

The smell she's referring to is in part created by dying stars, Dude said.

"Dude says I smell like dying stars," Billy said.

Bedlam threw her head back dramatically.

"I forgot how weird it is we're never actually having a private conversation," she said.

"I'd say you get used to it, but I'm still not used to it," Billy said. Sorry, Dude, he thought.

I'll be ignoring you for a while, Dude said. *Try to behave.*

"How's… the thing going," Bedlam said, pointing to the sky.

"Getting there. I'm useless," Billy said.

"Not like you'd be much good here," Bedlam said. "Neither am I. I mostly keep Emily and Henry from killing each other when Jane's not here."

"I'm kind of surprised you're still here," Billy said.

"Where would I go?" Bedlam said. "Mercenary work? Hard

to go back to that line of work after you've helped save the world. Feels counterintuitive."

"Yeah," Billy said. He looked at her too long, and he knew he looked at her too long, and of course Bedlam called him on it.

"You're looking at me too long," she said. "What are you doing?"

"I'm just… really happy you're here," Billy said. His stomach twisted on him again. He smiled uncomfortably. Billy felt panic rising in his guts.

Take her hand, Dude said in a whisper.

And he did.

Bedlam looked down in shock, and then back up at Billy, her face pale, her eternally confident look absent for once.

I think I made a mistake, Dude, Billy thought. You are the worst Cyrano de Bergerac ever.

How do you even know who Cyrano de Bergerac is? Dude said.

Stop talking, Billy thought.

Bedlam started to speak, but in the end, they were both saved by the arrival of Entropy Emily.

"I am wounded, Billy Case, I am absolutely wounded," Emily said. Dressed like someone out of *Dune,* Emily flung back her hood to revel her signature bright blue hair, which she'd hacked into a pixie cut, seemingly without any help from a hair stylist or even someone with particularly good vision.

"Hey, Em," Billy said.

"Don't you 'Hey, Em' me, Billy case," she said, bubble-of-floating herself up from the ground below up onto the surface of the Tower. "I'm your best bro, you jerk, and you're up here making moon-eyes at Bedlam instead of coming to say hi?"

"I just got here," Billy said.

"I can tell. You smell like a gas station got doused in

overcooked burgers," she said.

"I told you. You smell like outer space," Bedlam said.

"I really don't smell it," Billy said.

"Whatever," Emily said. First you leave us here—us, your best bud and the girl of your dreams…"

"Emily!" Billy and Bedlam yelled at the same time.

"Both of whom are desperate to check out the solar system, but no, you leave us here sweating our butts off in the desert, doing all the hard work," Emily said.

"I'm helping build a space station!" Billy yelled.

Helping is a bit of a stretch, Billy Case, Dude said.

"You need to follow instructions to use Legos," Emily said. "How much help can you possibly be?"

"I'm very helpful!"

"Whatever," Emily said. "You two want some time to make out, or do you want to see all the amazing things I've fixed on this ship?"

"*You've* fixed?" Billy said.

"I fixed. Neal and Henry helped a little bit," Emily said. "But mostly me. I really am a genius."

Billy looked at Bedlam, who nodded.

"We should talk later," she said.

Those four words sent Billy's already unsettled guts into a whirlwind.

"Okay," he managed to squeak out.

"Let's go, lovebirds," Emily said. "Come see the majesty my massive brain hath wrought."

"By majesty she means the fridge is working," Bedlam said.

"And the interwebs," Emily said. "Don't sell me short, Gobot."

"I wouldn't dare, Ewok," Bedlam said.

Great, they have pet names for each other, Billy thought.

Do you regret coming home? Dude said.

Billy glanced down at his hand still entwined with Bedlam's, and smiled at the fact that for the first time in months his ears were being assaulted by the best friend he had in the entire universe.

No, Billy thought. I'm so glad to be home.

CHAPTER 5: DREAMLESS

The woman made her way through the streets of Manhattan, catching eyes and turning heads wherever she went. But no matter who looked at her, no matter whose attention she caught, this woman, small and unassuming, with a shock of punkish hair and eyes with irises so black they absorbed light more than reflected it, no one ever really remembered her. They would look at her, and then, seemingly for no reason, they would recall their most vivid dreams—silly or scary, epic or nonsensical, sensuous or painful. Those memories would come bubbling up in their minds, often dreams unrecalled for years and years, and they'd forget the strange woman, devoured by their own reverie.

She was accompanied by two dogs, big like Rottweilers but square as bulldogs, with broad chests, thick limbs, and large, white teeth.

For those who saw her, though, even before she faded from their memories, she was hard to place. There was something incredibly familiar about her, as if she were exactly where she belonged; but simultaneously, she could not be more foreign, more unfamiliar and more out of place.

All of this seemed to matter not at all to her.

She shopped; she stopped in cafes and bakeries, in restaurants and bars, sampling much but finishing almost nothing. If one were to follow her all day they would notice she rarely had the same item twice, though themes emerged, as she adored coffee and never found a flavor of ice cream that did not capture her heart, and found almost childlike wonder in candy.

Men would approach her, sometimes threateningly, sometimes gently, but none stayed long. The lucky ones simply found themselves forgetful or uncomfortable in her presence; the unlucky ones drew the attention of the two beastly dogs, who established a safe perimeter around their mistress.

She stayed in a luxurious hotel on the very top floor, where no one seemed to notice her animal companions, or truly notice her at all. Staff held the door for her and promptly forgot about her, lost in their dreams. Management found the room perpetually paid for months in advance but could never remember to investigate their mysterious guest.

Sometimes movie stars would stay there as well, and she would chat with them, and always tell them they looked familiar, that she'd seen them before, but couldn't place them. Some were offended, others highly amused; more than one fell in love with her. She liked them, enjoyed spending time around them, because she'd seen them before, in other peoples' dreams and fantasies and memories. Movie stars were the few things she encountered in this world that reminded her of home.

Home, she thought, returning from an excursion with ice

cream for herself and a bag of expensive treats for her dogs. The canines jumped up onto the enormous bed and settled in lazily; the woman went into the palatial bathroom to wash her face.

The image in the mirror did not match the body she wore. This was something very few could detect. One woman in a public restroom Uptown saw it and her hair turned white instantly. An old homeless man saw through her in a storefront window. He asked her if she were God.

"No," she told him, "I'm not God."

"You must be something, then," the homeless man said.

"Would you like to know?" she asked.

He smiled, his teeth surprisingly white, his smile unexpectedly warm.

So, she whispered in his ear a poem perhaps only two or three people in this entire world had ever heard.

"Have you heard of the Lady Dreamless?
Promised to a nightmare Prince,
Raised to the sounds of the songs of the Damned,
Queen of the Citrine Tower, Heir to an empty throne?

Have you heard her story?
Trapped for a millennium in a black gem,
With only the whispers of passing nightmares
To keep her company?
Have you heard of her escape?
How she crossed the black and starless paths
Of faded lands, armed with only her wits
And a wisp of fire to guide her?"

"You are a goddess," the old man said.

"No," she told him. "I'm something else."

"You're made of dreams," he said.

"I'm made of dreams, but I can never have my own. That is why I'm here, you see. I wanted to see the waking world."

"It must disappoint you so," the man said.

"On the contrary," she told him. "I think you're all so beautiful."

She let sweet dreams wash over him, so that memory and joy would bring him a few moments peace, and left him standing in the street.

This strange and ugly world, she thought, remembering the homeless man as she drew a bath. She let the water run and walked into the living room to look out over the city, purple and gold and black and chrome in the evening sun. They all dream of everything other than what they are. This world is full of pain.

And she wondered, not for the first time, if she should go home. But tomorrow would be something new. Tomorrow always held such great promise.

CHAPTER 6:
JUST A LITTLE BIT OF MAGIC

Titus dreamed in his wolf form.

This wasn't an entirely new development; he dreamed this way sometimes before the invasion, certainly, and the pull of the wild was never deep beneath the surface for him. But since the Nemesis fleet—since Titus almost died in space, saved only by the relentless resiliency of his werewolf blood and a little bit of magic lent to him by Doc Silence—Titus dreamed in his wolf form almost every night.

They were feral dreams, raging across the countryside, hunting, stalking, howling at the moon, wordless stories from a primeval dreamscape.

Titus knew why this happened. He'd talked with Leto about it, the mysterious werewolf shaman who had long been his mentor.

You almost died, she said. And that experience damaged the veil between yourself and the wolf.

The veil, the rein, the thing that let Titus control the wolf when he transformed. He'd gained so much power over his monstrous form since first joining the Indestructibles that moving back and forth between human and werewolf had become second nature to him. But since his near-death experience, his control over the beast when he let it emerge was less than before. It made him anxious. Yes, he could still keep the werewolf from, say, eating random civilians, but the transformation felt like driving without brakes—that at any moment the whole thing could go sideways, and people would die.

He knew he had to let himself transform more, to regain control. But it was his nature to worry. And so, he worried.

He was startled from a particularly vivid dream about taking down an elk with his bare teeth by Kate's hand on his shoulder. Titus bolted upright in bed as if being attacked. When he registered where he was and who he was with, he laid back down. Kate just crossed her arms and waited for him to settle. She was in full Dancer armor, ready for action.

"What? Is something wrong?" Titus said. He waved his hand and muttered a few arcane words and a small globe of light appeared in his hand. He touched the globe lightly and it drifted up above the bed like a lamp.

"What is that?" Kate said, her tone horrified.

"It's a light spell," Titus said. "Look, I need to practice these things. It's harmless."

"You just casually cast a light spell and there's a lamp right next to your head," Kate said. "That's ridiculous."

"I… Whatever," Titus said, flipping on the light and dismissing the globe. He slid out of bed and started looking for his shoes. "Where are we going."

"I got a tip on one of my missing persons cases," Kate said. "It's in a part of town particularly damaged by the invasion. Thought you'd want to back me up."

"Of course I want to back you up," Titus said, pulling his signature hoodie on over a tee shirt. "Where are we headed?"

***

Twenty minutes later they were downtown, standing

outside an abandoned warehouse that was earmarked to become, before the invasion, a loft apartment complex. Instead, a piece of a Nemesis ship had sheared off a section of the building, putting an end to construction temporarily. The area still smelled vaguely of smoke and rot. That rotten smell would never fully leave Titus's mind; it reminded him of those final few moments in the Nemesis ship he'd detonated in space, organic and cruel, alien and earthy.

The front door had long ago been chained shut, but Kate took one look at the padlock and shook her head.

"You want me to break it?" Titus asked.

"There's an entire wall missing on this building," Kate said, heading toward the corner of the building. Titus followed, and together they stepped over crumbling stonework and piles of damaged bricks into the warehouse.

Kate took lead, and as always, Titus couldn't help but admire the grace with which she moved. Never making a sound, she drifted like a living shadow from vantage point to vantage point, eternally cautious, always ready to fight. Titus had none of her grace—it was a long-standing joke between them that he couldn't be trusted on stealth missions, because he walked like an elephant with knee problems—but he could tell by scent that the building was empty now. Another curse of being a werewolf, he thought. Olfactory precognition. He told her so.

"Kate, we're alone here," he said.

Her body tensed for a moment, then relaxed. She stopped sneaking and resumed a more casual, but cautious, walk. She snapped on a police-style flashlight.

"I can cast a…" Titus started.

"No," Kate said.

"Okay," Titus said.

They turned down a hallway and then into a large open area that might have been intended to be a sort of foyer or communal space for the apartments that would now never be built. The center of the space had been cleared out, and by the marks left in the dust on the floor, this had happened recently.

"Someone was here," Kate said.

"Yeah, I…"

Kate held up her hand, then turned her flashlight to a stone bench near something that looked like it would have been a food court or dining area. Emblems had been etched into the bench.

"Those look fresh," Kate said.

"And they're sigils," Titus said. Kate shot him a dirty look. "I swear I'm not turning into one of those people who only talks about my new hobby. Those are symbols I've seen Leto and Doc use."

Kate grimaced, and then let her shoulders sag in resignation.

"You're going to make me ask if you know what they mean, aren't you. I'm not too proud to ask."

"I don't know what they mean, exactly," Titus said. "I just know they're mystic in nature. Hang on."

He closed his eyes and tried to remember the words for a spell he'd just learned from Leto. Kate groaned.

"Don't you dare."

"It's barely a spell," Titus said. "It's… watch."

He spoke the words and made a symbol in the air with his index finger. A pale red light settled over the bench.

"What was that?" Kate said.

"Just a spell that tells you if anyone has used magic nearby recently," Titus said. "I swear, that's all it does."

"Tell me 'red' means 'no magic,'" Kate said.

"Now you're asking me to lie to you is what you're saying," Titus said.

Kate rubbed her eyes, clearly frustrated.

"What's the deal with this case?" Titus said.

"You know I've been running down missing persons," Kate said. "This was just… some have been harder to find than others. Kids who are a typical runaway age, in particular. This was one of those. There was a rumor that this place was being used as a crash pad by a lot of kids avoiding going home after the invasion."

"I don't need magic to tell you nobody's using this place as a flophouse," Titus said. He inhaled deeply. Dust and chemicals and rot, yes, but none of the smells you'd expect from squatters, no food or body odor or urine. The place, in fact, smelled strangely sterile.

"Kate, someone should be hiding out here," Titus said. "It's ideal for runaways or the homeless, or even someone just looking for a place to drink or do drugs without getting caught. But it smells… dead. It smells vacant."

"So, something is going on here," Kate said.

"Just not the something you'd expect," Titus said. Kate's shoulders sagged again. "You okay?"

"I just got used to finding people," Kate said.

"And this is a lot worse than going missing," Titus said.

"Yeah," Kate said. She smiled at him weakly. "But I guess vacation is over. Couldn't last forever."

CHAPTER 7:
NEW MANAGEMENT

There is a hidden floor in one of the tallest skyscrapers in Los Angeles.

It exists; it's a real floor, with windows and an elevator, like any other; but one needs to know it exists to get there, needs to know the right people, the right things to say, the right passwords. If you are an ordinary person, the elevator simply flows right past it as if it isn't there. It's been decades since anyone walked the entire length of the stairs in the building, and the businesses above and below it have particularly stringent, if less clandestine, security, and so the wealthy owners and their well-paid staff never notice the mysterious floor betwixt them.

Currently, there was one living person on this mysterious floor. He stood in an elegant boardroom, looking out massive, crystal-clear windows at the stained orange California sunset, made hazy and eerie with smog. The man wore an expensive suit, jet black, but no shirt underneath the coat, so that his bare chest, covered in tattoos written in old, arcane languages, was plainly visible. His feet were bare. He wriggled his toes in the room's expensive carpet. The man was both intimidatingly physical while also having an uncomfortable feeling of death around him, both hotly vital and cold as the grave. His head had a skull-like quality to it as well, the skin taut across his hairless face and scalp. His eyes had no irises or pupils. They were black as crude oil.

He may have been the only *living* person on this mysterious floor, but he was not alone. All around the elegant, polished wood table that dominated the room, corpses that were only recently still among the living sat in different states of shock, surprise, and fear. A few bodies also lay on the floor between the table and the glass door of the boardroom, as if the souls that not long ago inhabited those corpses had tried to run away.

Some of the bodies were worse off than the others. Many simply looked like they died of fear, but a few had been gutted by unseen blades or claws. The man at the head of the table had been tidily decapitated. The walls of the boardroom were painted a gentle cream color, but much of that surface was now spattered with blood, arterial spray and hand prints, and other things, including what appeared to be holes left by suction cups, like those on squid tentacles.

The shirtless man seemed entirely unbothered by this. He stepped over one of the prone bodies to a fancy decanter and poured himself a perfect cup of black coffee in a dainty porcelain mug. He looked at the headless man at the head of the table and considered pushing him out of his seat, but then changed his mind. Best to leave everything as it was, for maximum effect.

The phone rang, the sort of digital sing-song alert the man

hated about the modern world. He missed phones that rang with bells. He did not fear the future; he just sometimes longed for things that had become lost in the past.

He answered the phone. Instead of a receiver, connection came through a laptop in front of the headless man, sending the audio signal through a black disk at the center of the table. The caller himself appeared on a large screen along the back wall, where, in another situation, it might have appeared that a giant had taken a seat at the end of the table.

"Oh, my God," the caller said, seeing the carnage. He was a youngish man, with an expensive haircut and a shockingly blond beard. His bright blue eyes seemed to double in size as he looked through the monitor.

"Mr. Keppler," the man in the abattoir said.

"I don't understand," the younger man said. "I don't understand this at all. This can't be real."

"Please, Mr. Keppler," the mystery man said. "I need you to be very clear-headed right now. Are you listening?"

"I… yes. Yes, I'm listening," Keppler said.

"You worked with this team on occasion, I assume," the man said.

"I swear, only tangentially. Whatever they did wrong I had nothing—"

The man made a calming gesture with his hands, palms downward.

"Please," he said. "I need you to understand that if I wanted you dead, you would have been in this room."

Keppler nodded slowly, his eyes glassy.

"Do you know who I am, Mr. Keppler?" the man said.

"You're…"

"I am called King Tears," the man said. "You may have heard rumors about me. Those rumors are, for the most part, true. Do you understand?"

Keppler nodded again.

"The Los Angeles team. Did you know about their role in the Nemesis invasion?"

"Only after the fact, sir," Keppler said. "They had so many of us fooled, I just…"

"They had all of us fooled, Mr. Keppler. As did half the London office, the majority of the New York office, and an alarming number of key players in Hong Kong," King Tears said. "Many did us the great service of getting themselves killed during the invasion, and others were outed during the infighting just prior. Suffice it to say it appears that anyone who bought into the cult of stupidity that led to the organization's involvement in the invasion has been dealt with."

"The whole Los Angeles office was in on it?" Keppler said.

"Not all," King Tears said. "But enough that the few who didn't figure it out on their own forfeit their lives—too stupid to live, really."

"I didn't figure it out," Keppler said.

"No, but you're running our Vancouver office with a skeleton crew, and only met these idiots a few times a year. That can be forgiven," King Tears said.

"Forgiven," Keppler repeated.

"With this many high-level leaders dead, and even more murdered by these fools prior to the Nemesis invasion, do you know what we're left with, Mr. Keppler?"

"We're essentially crippled," Keppler said. "Sir. I'm sorry, but that was what this call was about. We're coming apart at the seams."

"I see this as an opportunity, Mr. Keppler," King Tears said. "We have a global infrastructure. We have manpower.

And now we've cut off not only the sickly part of our organization who wanted to sell the planet out to aliens, but the bloated parts as well. They did a us a great service in cutting down a great number of men and women who had, perhaps, been in charge too long, allowing the organization to stagnate."

"I… forgive me, sir, but from your reputation, I didn't think you were… Oh, God, how do I say this. I didn't think you were a stakeholder?"

King Tears laughed. Keppler looked as though his bladder gave out on him.

"That is a very polite way of saying it," King Tears said. "I wasn't a… I do like how you phrased that. I was not a stakeholder. I was a partner, and an interested party, but no, I did not hold a seat on any board. I was not one of these petty bureaucrats. I simply liked the chaos the organization sowed, and I liked the way I could profit from it."

"And when we fell apart, you stepped in," Keppler said.

King Tears pointed at the screen, smiling proudly.

"Now, this is why I didn't kill you, Mr. Keppler," King Tears said. "I looked into the tea leaves, and they told me you'd be useful."

Keppler's face went slack again, the shock catching up to him.

"So, tell me, Mr. Keppler. I will need a few useful people if I'm going to save this organization," King Tears said. "Would you like a job?"

Keppler's eyes watered. His mouth moved silently before he answered.

"Yes. Yes, I would," he said.

"Good," King Tears said, laughing deeply. "I have such great plans, Mr. Keppler. You're going to love them."

CHAPTER 8:
A WHOLE NEW MAN

Emily walked down a corridor inside the Tower she'd walked countless times before, amazed, as she had been every time she'd set foot in the ship since it crashed, by how unfamiliar everything felt there with the battle damage. It's just a hallway, she thought. Same plain white walls, same floor, and now—with the success she, Henry, and Neal had getting the power on—the same running lights along the ceiling illuminating her way.

But the walls were scorched and blackened; the floor marred by scratches and dotted with piles of sand and debris. She walked by a room that had once been a storage closet. The door hung by a thread on its hinges. She pushed it, and the entire door fell off.

"Oh, man," she said.

"You okay?" Henry said through the earpiece she wore. Emily rolled her eyes.

"I'm good," she said. "Just breaking stuff."

"Stop breaking stuff."

"We live in broken stuff," Emily said.

"Did you find it yet?"

"Almost there," Emily said. She turned a corner and found a hatch, already partially detached, which she unfastened and dropped to the floor. She flipped on the flashlight she had in her hand and looked around inside.

"Got it," Emily said. It's funny, she thought, moving cables out of her way until she found the switch she'd come here to locate. A couple of years hanging around an alien spaceship and I'm just, like, pulling panels off the wall and fixing things like I'm just checking the fuse box back home.

"Warn me before you—" Henry started to say, but Emily flipped the switch anyway. "Emily!"

"You dead?" she asked.

"No!"

"Then calm down," she said. "How's it look?"

"Come on back. I think you'll be pleased."

She meandered back down the hallway, wondering if they'd ever get the ship airborne again. The least we can do is get it out of the sand, she thought. Henry had talked to the Department about setting up some sort of landing pad for it but no one really wanted the government involved—they all agreed, including Henry, who had run the Department briefly—that fixing the Tower was a family affair they wanted to do themselves. And it was moving along okay, she thought. Electricity, the alien machines that could generate food and water at the touch of a few buttons, the ship's hilariously effective internet connection, and of course the air conditioning function so they didn't die of heat exhaustion, the bathrooms, of course… all the basics so far. But nobody really wanted to work on the engines just yet. Henry and Neal were confident in their abilities to fix a lot of things (the pair had done quite a bit of reverse engineering, they told Emily, back in the good old days when Henry worked with Doc as the hero Coldwall). But the engines, which had been capable of sustaining flight indefinitely before the crash… that was a project that made everyone nervous.

I really don't want to drop our base on a small town, Emily thought. She actually had confidence she could, with a bubble of float, carry the ship somewhere else, but that was so far above and beyond what she'd pushed her powers to in the past that she let the others talk her out of it.

So far, at least.

She found the others—Henry, Neal in his little trashcan body, Billy, Bedlam, and Jane—hanging out in a room that used to be their training facility. And in an alcove next to that training room was the objective of this little project.

A machine Emily had barely touched since she first arrived at the Tower now hummed with energy, its surface dotted with glowing buttons and screens.

"The costume generator," Jane said. "You fixed the costume generator!"

"We figured we'd go for a little victory," Henry said, tossing aside a spanner and brushing his graying hair back out of his face. "Try to get a little bit of normalcy back in your lives."

"Let me tell you," Billy said, hopping off the countertop he'd been sitting on and walking toward the machine. "My costume survived that battle, but do you know how hard it is to get Nemesis ship fuel out of a white costume? I look like one big stain."

"Truly the story of your life, Billy Case," Emily said, pushing right past him toward the generator.

"Hey," Billy said.

"I fixed it, I go first," Emily said.

"We fixed it," Henry said.

"I believe, Designation: Coldwall, I did most of the fixing in this case," Neal said.

"Whatever. We fixed it," Emily said. "I go first."

"You lost your Doctor scarf in the fight, didn't you, Em?" Jane said.

"Lost is a relative term," Emily said. "I think it's in orbit somewhere. But I got a replacement one at Comic Con."

"Then what are you making?" Jane said.

Emily tapped a few buttons, examined the screen, then activated the generator. A slim, black leather coat emerged, with up-pointed lapels. She threw it on over her dusty desert clothes and checked herself out.

"You made… a leather coat," Billy said. "That you could have found at the mall."

"A leather coat made with an alien machine," Emily said. "So, no cows had to die for this jacket. Can't find that at the mall, Billy."

"Hang on—you guys had a machine that magically just… 3D printed your costumes this whole time?" Beldam said, stomping over to join them. "I'm wearing yoga pants because they'll fit over my robo-legs. Show me how this machine works. Right now."

Jane joined Emily and folded her arms across her chest.

"Costume change, Em?" Jane said

"Yeah," Emily said. She looked up at Jane and wrinkled her nose. "I thought it was time."

"I don't get it."

"That is a replica similar to the coat worn by Christopher Eccleston as the Ninth Doctor, Designation: Solar," Neal chimed in.

"Holy heck, our AI watches Doctor Who and I never knew this," Emily said. "How did I never know this? How have we not talked about this, Neal?"

"You never asked, Designation: Entropy Emily," Neal said. "If we can activate the ship's archives, I have recordings of the original series all the way back to the beginning."

"No. Way," Emily said. "Even the missing episodes?"

"Yes, Designation: Entropy Emily. Even the missing episodes."

"This is amazing," Emily said.

"Okay, but… help a non-Whovian out here," Jane said. "Why the coat? Isn't the scarf your thing?"

"There was a war, Rose," Emily said, putting on a pitch-perfect imitation of the actor's northern accent.

"I don't get it," Jane said.

"Never mind," Emily said. "I'm just going through a dark period, okay?"

"That'll do," Jane said. "Carry on."

Emily turned her attention fully on Neal and pointed at him aggressively.

"And you," Emily said.

"Uh-oh," Neal said.

"I have been having thoughts about your situation, buckethead," Emily said.

"This is a cause of great concern for me, Designation: Entropy Emily," Neal said.

"No. I have an idea. Hey, Henry?"

"Uh-oh," Henry said.

"You have extra Coldwall suits, right?" Emily said.

"I have… quite a few of them, actually," Henry said. "I'm one hundred percent sure I'm going to regret asking why you want to know."

Emily gestured grandly at Neal.

"Our loyal friend has been stuck in a metal tube for months," Emily said. "Could we set up one of your suits to be his new home, so the poor guy can at least have arms and legs?"

"I have never actually had arms and legs, Designation: Entropy Emily," Neal said nervously. "I really do not feel any sense of loss that I don't have them now."

"Shut it, robot, I'm trying to do you a solid here," Emily said.

"He's going to need a lot of things that aren't in the suit already," Henry said. "The suit's not made to be an independent entity."

"The technology I require is relatively small, Designation: Coldwall," Neal said. "I am, as Designation: Entropy Emily has so cruelly pointed out, currently housed in a cleaning robot's body."

"Listen to the Roomba, Hank," Emily said. "Plus, if you're not in the suit, there's a whole lot of extra room in there, right?"

"You…" Henry paused, looking up at the ceiling as if making calculations in his head. "You are…"

"I'm a genius, yo," Emily said.

"Let's not get ahead of ourselves," Henry said. "But you are definitely on to something."

CHAPTER 9:
THE TOWN THAT ONCE WAS

Doc Silence stood in an empty street, looking out over three miles of nothingness.

The patterns were still there; he'd arrived by air, carried through the sky on waves of magic, where he could see the shapes of streets and sidewalks, property lines, dirt where parks and yards once stood.

But the town that once stood here was gone.

The emptiness was almost pretty, in a way; the sunset splashed the blank landscape with pink and gold watercolors; a nihilistic, abstract painting.

He hadn't had time to check the name of the town, but rather followed the hidden trails known only to magicians like him and other creatures of the night, places in reality where time and space bent and twisted. It took him hardly any time at all to travel across the globe the minute he sensed the disturbance, but still. He was too late.

He landed next to the town's sign. Welcome to Westwick.

A nowhere town, of which there are so many just like it. He took off his red-lensed sunglasses and looked the world with eyes burning with violet light. He paid a price for those eyes when he was young, in blood and in spirit, but they were the eyes of a wizard, and they let him see things no mortal could.

What those cursed eyes showed him caused a sharp intake of breath.

The town was covered in black, oily spinnerets, a nightmare maze like a spider's web gone all wrong. The tendrils formed a sort of dome around the town, an opaque, protective sphere. They radiated malice and a sickly heat, and gleamed as though covered in fever sweat.

"What happened here," Doc said, replacing his glasses. Once seen, the tendrils were visible through his glasses. The lenses had always served as a negligible barrier against the outside world anyway, Doc knew. And he had to look away to get his heart rate to return to normal.

He saw a car driving toward him in the distance. Doc waited for it to arrive, knowing who it might be.

An unmarked black vehicle pulled up beside him and the passenger door opened. An old friend emerged: Sam Barren, current acting head of the Department of What, looking simultaneously older and spryer than Doc had ever see him. The old man's eyes were gleaming blue; his silver moustache still brilliantly maintained. He wore an old fedora and a tidy brown suit. Doc smirked as he spotted argyle socks when Sam stepped out of the vehicle.

"So, we got a call an entire town just went invisible," Sam said. A lifelong special agent said, shaking Doc's hand. "Wasn't sure if I should call you or just assume you'd be here."

"I sensed it happen from six thousand miles away," Doc said.

"That why the kids aren't here?"

"No time to go get them," Doc said.

"So—alien, scientific, or…" Sam said.

"Magic," Doc said. "Definitely magic."

"I hate magic," Sam said, rolling his eyes. "Why didn't you ever let us recruit a couple of magicians to the Department, Doc?"

"There are no magicians you could recruit to the Department," Doc said, looking back at the empty town. "You think we're all out there looking for work, filling out our magician resumes?"

"Probably better that there aren't too many of you running around," Sam said. He took off his hat and scratched nearly-bald head. "I can't believe I'm asking this out loud, but is the town there, or gone? Like, is it just invisible?"

"It's not here, but it's not gone," Doc said.

"You literally just said yes to both options," Sam said. "This is why I hate magic."

Doc gestured at the empty space.

"This town familiar to you? Did anything ever happen here? The name is ringing a bell," Doc said. "But I don't know why. I feel like I should know something about this place."

"Not at all. Hang on, my assistant gave me some talking points on the way over," Sam said, grumpily tinkering with his smartphone. Doc smirked.

"Look at you, joining modern society."

"I hate this thing," Sam said. "And it's not because I'm a technophobe. I just hate being connected all of the time."
He tapped the screen a few times and made an ah-ha gesture with his hand.

"Here we go," Sam said. "Westwick, California. Population eight thousand, two-hundred and seventeen last census.

Bedroom community. Commuter town. Most notable factoid I can find is they refused to allow an Apollo's Coffee in town because it didn't fit with the plans for the town. Snobby."

"Didn't take you for an Apollo's apologist, Sam," Doc said.

"I begrudge no man the right to get a cup of coffee to make it through the day," Sam said. "Life is hard enough."

Doc couldn't help feeling as though he'd forgotten something. Why did this town feel familiar? Why did this feel purposeful? The architecture of the spinnerets looked familiar, but they could be anything—a time spider, a plague demon, even some old god stumbling back up the ladder of reality.

Sam's phone rang. The old man sighed. Doc eavesdropped.

"Sam Barren. Yeah. Really? Okay. Yeah. Yeah, we're on our way," Sam said. "Warn them I'm bringing Doc Silence. Don't want to freak them out."

Sam hung up. Doc raised an eyebrow.

"Well, we have a resident who wasn't in town when everyone disappeared," Sam said.

"That's a start," Doc said. "Where is she?"

"She's at the airport," Doc said. "I have agents holding her. She's furious."

"Tell your driver to meet us there," Doc said.

"Oh no, no you're not," Sam said.

"We can't waste time in a car, Sam," Doc said.

"I am not letting you teleport me anywhere," Sam said.

Doc waved at the driver, a confused young agent in a deep blue suit.

"Meet us at the airport," Doc said.

"What?" The driver said. "Why?"

Doc made a series of gestures with his hand, opening a portal beside him, a glowing purple sphere of light.

"I'm too old for this," Sam said, right before Doc dragged

him through the portal and they both disappeared.

CHAPTER 10:
WHERE YOU GO TO BE FORGOTTEN

Kate could tell Titus was uncomfortable. Anyone else, she thought, would be uncomfortable for the wrong reasons here—a village of tents beneath the interstate that ran into the City, providing a huge, artificial archway as a roof for the homeless. Kate knew about this place long before the invasion. She had a friend, a dancer like herself as a child, who had fallen on hard times. Kate tracked her here, with the arrogant thought that she might bring her home, but back when the young woman was not ready for someone like Kate to force help upon her. That trip made the then-newly anointed vigilante more aware of the city's homeless youth; who wanted her help, and who wanted to help her by being her eyes on the street. Since that first year she'd often received anonymous tips from the residents of the tent city, asking for her to step in, or sometimes to warn her about a bad situation.

She felt relaxed here, but could feel waves of discomfort flowing off Titus. It had nothing to do with judgment or disgust; it was sensory overload. He could see and smell and hear infinitely better than a normal human being, and the sights, the scents, and the sounds in this place were a cacophony even for Kate's normal senses. Titus was being battered by the input.

"You going to be okay?" Kate asked.

"I just need to adjust," Titus said. "I couldn't walk through a mall if I hadn't learned to adjust to situations like this."

She glanced over. His face was pinched, and his eyes squinting. He'd pulled his hood up as a barrier for his ears.

Kate saw a familiar face, a girl with eyes so green they seemed to glow in the dark.

"Mara," Kate said, and the girl turned her attention their way. Kate knew "Mara" was a fake name, but this was a place where you called yourself what you needed to be, not necessarily what you were born with.

"Hey, Dancer," the girl said, sidling up with comic swagger. She looked taller than the last time Kate saw her. She's grown, Kate thought. She's been on the streets since before she finished growing. "Who's your sidekick?"

"Partner," Titus said. "Why does everyone think I'm the sidekick?"

"This is my bloodhound," Kate said.

Mara pointed at him and smiled.

"No way, this is the werewolf dude?" Mara said.

"Everyone knows all of our codenames except mine," Titus said. "I'm always the werewolf dude."

"That's because you keep changing your codename," Kate said. She handed a photograph to Mara, who hesitated.

"You know we respect privacy down here, Dancer," Mara

said.

"I wouldn't ask if I didn't think something bad happened to him," Kate said. "You know that."

"That's the only reason I'm looking at this photo," Mara said. She scanned it. "Yeah, I think I've seen him. Follow me."

Mara led Kate and Titus deeper beneath the bridge, where it grew so dark they had to rely on sound and feel to move around. She could hear voices in the darkness. Sighs of sadness and pain, but also laughter between friends, the chatter of storytelling. This is the part of the City nobody talks about, Kate thought. Maybe I should change that.

Mara flagged down a pair of teenagers, a boy and a girl, and gestured for them to come over. They both hesitated, and Mara chided them.

"Come on, it's fine, don't be so sketchy," Mara said. "This is the Dancer and her sidekick."

"Partner," Titus said again, sighing.

The pair joined them. Mara introduced them as Bobby and Jackie, but didn't specify which was which.

"You were hanging out with this kid, right?" Mara said, showing them the photo.

"Little bit," the girl said.

"He disappeared for a while. Think I saw him earlier, though. I said hi, but he ignored me," the boy said.

"It happens," Mara said to Kate. "Sometimes people just change. They move on."

"I get it," Kate said. "Where did you see him?"

The boy scanned the tents, thinking. He gestured to follow.

"Not like he'll still be there, but I saw him over near the riverside," the boy said. The far side of the tent city bordered a river that flowed into the city parallel to the interstate. The Longfellow River had once been too polluted to swim in, but

City officials had made it a priority to make the river useable again, and in the past decade, people had begun sailing and fishing in it. A fringe benefit meant that the residents of the tent city could bathe in it without worrying they'd grow a third eye.

The ground along the water was a dicey blend of mud, swamp grass, and sand. The tents themselves stopped a good ten to twenty feet or more from the water to avoid getting wet, so when they reached the end of the makeshift housing, they had a clearer view of the area. Moonlight created a bluish half-circle where the sky leaked in. Out on the water, Kate could see a few straggling private boats making their way up the river, and beyond that, city lights like fireflies in the distance.

"Hey," the younger girl said, pointing. "There he is. What's his name? He never told us his name."

"Kevin," Kate said.

"Hey, Kevin!" the girl yelled. "Hey, you okay?"

Kevin was hunched over by the water, squatting on his haunches, the hood of a dark sweatshirt pulled up over his head. The white piping of his sneakers gleamed in the dark. He didn't respond at first, and appeared to just stare into the water.

"Weird," the girl said. "He was pretty nice before."

Kate and Titus exchanged a worried glance and started walking to the water's edge. Kate put a hand lightly on Mara's shoulder, asking her silently to stay back. Before Titus could do the same to the others, though, the boy broke out ahead of them.

"Hang on," the boy said, trotting toward the figure by the river. "Kevin? Is that you? Remember me? I'm Bobby, we were talking the other day—"

Kevin looked up from the water then, and the face that hid

beneath the hood was no longer remotely human.

His skin was raw and reddish; one eye, gleaming yellow, was larger than the other. His mouth was a hard line of grimacing pain.

"Kid, get back!" Titus yelled, but it was too late. Kevin lashed out with a hand. From the sleeve of his sweatshirt, a tendril uncoiled, tipped with a single, bone-colored claw. It raked across Bobby's chest, knocking the boy backward. Kate caught him with one arm and lowered him to the ground.

"I'm okay, I'm okay," Bobby said, clutching his chest. His hands came back bloody.

"Can you stand?" Kate said, looking over her shoulder as Titus charged past them.

"I can," Bobby said. Kate helped him to his feet and gave him over to Jackie and Mara.

"Then run. All of you. Go!" Kate said.

At the water's edge, Titus transformed, fluidly changing from unassuming young man into massive werewolf. It always looked like torture to Kate—watching his face elongate, huge fangs bursting forth, fingers stretching into long claws—but this time, she was glad for it. Kevin lashed out with the tendril, which hooked into the meat of the werewolf's shoulder. He roared in pain, but immediately slashed the fleshy tentacle with his claws, separating it from the rest of the lost boy's body. The limb twitched, splattering blood everywhere as it dropped to the ground.

Titus closed the gap between him and the boy; Kate ran toward them both, suddenly realizing that Titus was not going to pull his punches. Don't kill him by accident, Kate thought, don't kill him…

But before Titus could get to him, Kevin jumped into the river, body moving with grotesque, serpentine motions as it plunged beneath the water. By the time Kate reached the water's edge, Titus was knee-deep in the river, his massive head turning left and right searching for the boy.

"Down, boy," Kate said. Titus whipped his head around at her, his eerie golden eyes seemingly not recognizing her. Her heart skipped a beat; it had been a long, long time since she'd seen such an unrecognizable look in that monstrous face.

"Titus, it's me," she said. "Come on back."

The werewolf huffed, moving with almost comical daintiness as he clamored back onto the shore. He began to shrink, muscle and fur disappearing silently in the moonlight. A moment later, Titus looked down at his now soaked pants and torn shirt, the wound from the tendril already nearly fully healed.

"So, we found Kevin, huh?" Titus said. "Is the kid okay?"

"Let's go find him," Kate said, walking in the direction Mara and the others ran. The tent city had grown eerily quiet. During the fight, she'd not noticed the denizens fleeing en masse, but they were survivors, all of them—they knew how to get out of a bad situation fast. "You okay?"

"Yeah," Titus said.

"You didn't seem okay for a second there."

"I got fish-hooked by the hangnail from hell," Titus said. Kate nodded.

"Any idea what that was?" Kate asked.

"You're not going to like my answer," Titus said. "But if we found evidence of magic in the flophouse…"

"I don't want to call Doc," Kate said.

"We should call Doc," Titus said.

Kate looked out at the black waters of the Longfellow River, looking for signs that whatever Kevin had become was still alive. She wrinkled her nose.

"We're going to have to call Doc," she said.

CHAPTER 11:
THE LAPINES, FORMERLY OF NEW ORLEANS

Doc dragged Sam out of a magical portal just outside the arrivals gate at the airport. For some reason, two grown men appearing out of thin air didn't attract that much attention from travelers and their families; one woman in a particularly loud dress looked at them as if they'd said something offensive rather than teleported in from nowhere.

"You can't just magic us into the airport!" Sam said. "This is how I get in trouble. There's rules about these things."

"As far as I know the TSA has never acknowledged the existence of magic," Doc said.

"How would you know? When was the last time you took a regular flight?" Sam said. "You just poof yourself around the world, no respect for things like borders or passports…"

"Where are they detaining her?" Doc said, cutting Sam off.

"The resident? Hang on," Sam said, rummaging inside his

coat to pull out his ID and badge. He flagged down the nearest police officer and flashed his credentials.

"Oh, you've got to be kidding me," the officer said.

"Trust me, you want us here," Sam said. "We're going to make sure we keep the weirdness off the property."

"If the Department is here, I already know the weirdness is on site," the officer said. "I used to be a beat cop. I've seen you guys before."

"Then you probably want us out of your hair as soon as possible," Sam said. "Can you radio us in?"

The officer got on his walkie, summoning two plainclothesmen who led Sam and Doc through the gates and deep into the bowels of the airport proper. They buzzed them through multiple security checks until they found a very drab, off-white corridor. One of the plainclothes officers knocked on a door. It opened. Inside was a man in a suit—either an administrator or another plainclothes officer, Doc couldn't tell—and a middle-aged woman, road-weary and bedraggled, sitting at a table clearly intended for interrogation and not comfort. But she had been given tea and a blanket to drape over her shoulders; a tray of uneaten food sat pushed aside. This was a woman who was here because she had nowhere else to go.

She turned her attention to them and her demeanor immediately changed, from a woman defeated to a woman enraged.

"You," she said.

Sam almost back-peddled out of the room, but bumped into Doc.

"Um," Sam said. "Hello. I'm—"

"Why am I still here?" she said. "I need to get home. Do you know what I just found out? I found out my husband had a heart attack a few hours ago, while I was in the air. I'm just finding this out now, and this means my daughter is out there alone and I don't know where she is and my husband is in some hospital—"

"Mrs. Lapine, we're here about your daughter," Sam said. "We weren't aware about your husband."

"What do you mean you're here about my daughter," she said. "Where is she? Who are you? What is this?"

"Ma'am, my name is Sam Barren. I'm the director of the Department."

"The Department of what?" she demanded.

Sam looked at Doc with tired eyes.

"This is why we need a damned acronym," Sam said. Returning his attention to the woman, he continued. "My department investigates super-powered and supernatural activities primarily in the United States. We have reason to believe something of that nature has occurred in your town. What have you been told?"

"They told me that it wasn't safe to go back to my house," she said. Her voice cracked. "What does that even mean? That's all they told me, that it wasn't safe."

Doc brushed past Sam and sat down at the table across from the woman. He put his hands on the table's surface.

"I'm going to be blunt with you," Doc said. "More blunt than I should be, but you seem like someone who doesn't need to be lied to. Am I right about that?"

"Is my daughter okay? Who are you? Wait, I know you, I've seen you. You're…"

"Yes, I am," Doc said. "I'm one of those guys. My name is Doc Silence. And all we know is that something very strange has happened to your whole town, and before I go in to look for everyone, I need to get some idea of what I'm walking into.

Tell me, was there anything strange going on in town before you left?"

The woman wiped her nose with a cheap paper napkin.

"No. Nothing. We live in the most boring town in the world," she said. "We moved there because it was boring. What do you mean strange though? A gas leak, or were people sick?"

"Anything out of the ordinary at all," Doc said. "Anything you can recall."

"No," she said. "But I'll be honest… I don't like my neighbors. I don't really talk to anyone. We're all kind of in our own heads, my husband and daughter and me. I know it's not flattering to say, but that's just how it is."

"I understand," Doc said. "I can relate."

Doc rubbed his eyes beneath his sunglasses then looked over at Sam and shook his head. I've got nothing, he tried to say. Sam got most of it.

"Okay," Doc said. "Let's get you on the road to your husband, at least. Someone from the local police can get you there right now."

"Thank you," the woman said. "You'll look for my daughter?"

"I will, and I'll bring her back," Doc said. "What's her name, Missus…?

"Lapine," the woman said. "I'm Becca Lapine. My daughter's name is Alice."

Doc felt a creeping tingle run down his back. The name. Alice Lapine. He knew that name. But it couldn't be, he thought. Not here. How old would the girl be now, anyway?

"Mrs. Lapine, you said you moved to Westwick?" Doc said. "Where did you live before, if I could ask?"

"Becca," she said. "And we lived in New Orleans when

Alice was little, but it's too much city. We wanted something quieter. I got a job in California. We thought this would be better."

"New Orleans," Doc repeated. "Thank you, Becca. We'll tell the officers outside you're ready to see your husband now, unless you have any questions for us."

"Find my baby girl, Doc Silence," she said. "That's all."

Doc's heart ached at the request. It wasn't the first time someone had asked him to find their lost daughter. It would not be the last. Doc and Sam stepped out of the room and Sam relayed to the nearest officer that she could be taken where she needed to go. Then Sam focused on Doc.

"You know something," Sam said. "I know that look. Why did you ask if they moved from somewhere else? New Orleans meant something to you when she said it, didn't it? I could tell."

Doc took off his glasses and rubbed his eyes again.

"I think I screwed up, Sam," Doc said. "I think I really screwed up."

"How?" Sam asked.

"I need to check my files in the Tower's archives," Doc said. "Hopefully Henry and Emily have those up and running. Come on."

Doc opened another portal. Sam hesitated.

"No," he said. "You're not dragging me over international lines when I don't even have a change of underwear."

Doc gestured impatiently for Sam to step through the portal. Sam trundled forward.

"I'm only going because you admitted you screwed up," he said.

"Relax," Doc said. "Emily fixed the air conditioning."

"My relief knows no bounds," Sam said.

CHAPTER 12:
THERE WERE ALWAYS OTHERS

Jane sat on a countertop and watched the surreal comedy show that was Emily and Henry. The oddball pair stood arguing in front of one of Henry's old Coldwall armored suits, which was opened up to the guts with wires and cables hanging out. Between them, the sad figure of Neal, trapped in his little trash can of a temporary body, seemed to stare up at them as if they were arguing parents.

"You're limiting your thinking!" Emily yelled.

"I'm thinking like an engineer, which I am, because you can't just make things up as you go along!" Henry yelled back.

"You're just saying this because you're afraid of things you don't understand," Emily said.

"No, I'm saying that we shouldn't install anything into the suit I can't fix, because it's just taking up space that would be better used with things I can actually work on to improve his functionality," Henry said. "Why would I put technology into the suit I can't actually do anything with?"

"Because Neal can," Emily said. She turned to the AI. "Right, Neal?"

"If you install the bio-processors and memory gel-packs into the framework, I will be able to connect the two myself, Designation: Entropy Emily," Neal said. "It's not dissimilar to how I integrated myself into the Tower when I first found it." Henry stared at Neal, then at Emily.

"You two are conspiring against me," he said.

"I'm just asking you to expand your horizons," Emily said.

"You know what? Maybe you should build Neal's body."

"I don't know how," Emily said.

"Well you sure act like you do!"

"Man, you are such an infant," Emily said.

"You're deliberately making me question my sanity," Henry said. He looked over at Jane. "She's doing this on purpose."

"She does this to everyone, Henry, you should know this by now," Jane said. The conversation was interrupted by a chirping noise through the ship's comm system. Emily scooted over to the nearest console and booted it up. The screen flickered but didn't turn on.

"Hello?" the familiar voice of Titus said.

"Hey, fuzzball!" Emily said. "Miss you, Chewie."

"Miss you too, you lunatic," Titus said.

"You're the werewolf. I think you own the term lunatic. I'm more of a generalized insanity," Emily said.

"Won't argue that," Titus said. "Is Jane with you?"

"Sure is," Emily said. "Want me put her on?"

"I don't know how much you guys have working there," Titus said. "Can you kick me to a private line?"

"Oh, keeping secrets," Emily said. She yelled over to Jane. "Hey sunbeam, the room to your left has a functioning communications system. I'll send the call in there."

Jane shook her head in disbelief at how weird it was to see Emily embracing her mad genius, but complied anyway. She entered the adjoining room and closed the door behind her. A screen on the wall lit up when she entered. Titus's face appeared, grainy and faded.

"Hey, boss," Titus said.

"Hey yourself," Jane said. She tried not to wince at the sight of him. She hadn't seen him in a while, and had forgotten how much damage he'd taken during the Nemesis attack. The healing scars on his face hurt her heart. "The buzz cut suits you."

Titus scratched the silvery stubble on his head and laughed.

"Yeah, I can't wait to grow it back," he said. "But it's still not growing in quite right, y'know? So for now I've got a whiffle."

"Could be worse. You could have a lumpy head."

"Small miracles," Titus said. "Hey, you know where Doc is?"

"He's running down a lead on something," Jane said. "He didn't mention much about it. Why?"

Titus sighed.

"Kate and I were working a missing persons case here in the City, and we came across something… we think there's some magic involved."

Jane grimaced.

"Great," she said.

"Yeah. Yeah, it's not good," Titus said. "I won't go into the gory details right now, but this was pretty bad, what we ran into."

"I'll try to find him for you," Jane said.

"Thanks."

"Hey," Jane said. "How's Kate?"

The Dancer, more than anyone else on the team, had withdrawn after the Nemesis attack. She'd never been much of a talker, but Jane worried that the things she'd seen and done were weighing on her, and being Kate, she wouldn't ask for help if she needed it. At least Titus is back in the City, Jane thought. If nothing else, she's not completely alone.

"She's Kate," Titus said, smiling sheepishly.

"She can hear you, can't she," Jane said.

"She's not here, but I never assume she's not listening somehow," Titus said. "Always best that way."

"I do the same thing," Jane said. "Be careful, Titus. I'll get Doc on the line as soon as I find him."

"Thanks," Titus said. "Hey Jane?"

"Yeah?"

"I should let you know I'm… I'm learning a bit about magic."

"I assume you don't mean pulling a rabbit out of a hat or how to sneeze a handkerchief out of your nose," Jane said.

"If only," Titus said. "By the way—the rabbit thing, that's a teleportation spell. That's way harder than it looks."

"Can I ask why you're learning magic?" Jane said.

"One of us has to," Titus said. "Might as well be me."

Jane studied the battered face on the other side of the camera. They all carried burdens, every one of them. But sometimes she thought Titus was determined to carry even more of the weight of the world on his shoulders than even she did herself. More than all the Indestructibles, she knew that she and Titus were similar in ways the others didn't understand.

"Well," Jane said. "Be careful."

"Always am," Titus said.

"Don't let Kate throw you out of any windows," Jane said.

"Can't promise that," Titus said. "Talk soon."

"Yeah," Jane said, terminating the call.

She stepped out into the hallway just in time to hear the very clear sounds of Sam Barren complaining loudly just out of sight.

"Every time you teleport me around like this it is a violation of my rights!" Sam said.

"How else were we going to get here this fast?" Doc said. "And when did you become such a complainer?"

"I've always been a complainer," Sam said. "You just have those stupid rose-tinted glasses on all the time. It messes with your perspective."

Doc. Great, Jane thought. She trotted down the hall to find the pair bickering in the same room where she'd left Henry and Emily.

"Hey Jane!" Emily said, wearing a devilish grin. "Look what the cat dragged in!"

"Next time we take a helicopter," Sam said.

"A helicopter is a thousand times more dangerous than teleportation," Doc said. He saw Jane enter the room and smiled. "Hey, Jane."

"Doc, just the man I was looking for," she said. She noticed he had a set of files tucked under one arm in a manila folder.

"And you are just the woman I'm looking for," Doc said. He found a clear space on a countertop and started flipping through the files.

"Those are my files," Sam said. "You just teleported into my office and took my files."

Henry's interest had perked up as well now, stepping away from the Coldwall suit to look at what Doc had brought.

"Those are my files," Henry said. "You gave those to me."

"These are my files," Doc said. "Which I gave to you

before we went into the alternate timeline with Anachronism Annie."

"Oh, no," Henry said. "Those are *the* files."

"With all this buildup, if those aren't the actual X-Files and Mulder and Scully don't teleport into this room in the next three minutes I am going to be profoundly disappointed," Emily said.

Doc sorted through the dense papers, setting aside small bundles. Jane picked two up that he'd placed side by side and gave them a quick scan.

"Atlantis is real?" Jane asked. "There's some Atlantean princess out there running around? And… wait, Amazons are real too?"

"Amazons are real?" Emily said, all but leaping across the room to steal the file from Jane's hands. "This is a boy. This file is about a boy. Why is a boy an Amazon? He's a very good-looking boy but he's… I think a boy Amazon is an oxymoron."

"Put that down," Doc said, still rummaging through the paperwork. "And yes to all of your questions."

"Why do we not have an Amazon or an Atlantean princess on our team?" Emily said. "Not that I don't like our team. But I'm just saying. One can always become more badass."

"They turned me down," Doc said absent-mindedly. "You should meet them someday though. Echo and Artem are heroes in their own rights. You'd like them."

"Which one is Echo and which one is Artem?" Emily said.

"Clearly they're not the ones you're worried about right now," Jane said, sensing an edge of worry in Doc's voice she didn't like.

"No," Doc said. He pulled the file he'd been looking for out of the folder and handed it to Jane. "This is the one I'm worried about."

The file read: Alice Lapine – the Crimson Child. It gave a date of birth that made her maybe twelve years old. The file listed a location in New Orleans, and in Doc's strangely arcane handwriting, the term: magical adept.

"What's an adept?" Jane said.

Doc exhaled heavily.

"Most magicians, like me, acquire our abilities through practice," Doc said. "You have to want to be a magician. Magic is hard. It's dangerous. And you don't just drop out of magician school—as a general rule if you can't cut it, magic kills you. It tends to weed out the weak. But some people are born with magic inherent in their blood. Sometimes it's just a sensitivity to it; sometimes it's an aptitude. Sometimes they're just natural spellcasters. Usually it means there was some tinkering in the family history—a demon or warlock in the family tree or whatever."

"Like when one of your parents is a really good athlete," Emily offered.

"Close enough," Doc said. "The magic world calls them adepts.

"So, this kid is an adept?" Jane asked.

"I think so," Doc said. He rubbed the bridge of his nose. "You know before we formed the Indestructibles I had been monitoring a number of young people with special abilities."

"There were others?" Emily said.

"There were always others," Doc said. "Partially I looked out for them to build a roster for the team. But also, because untrained children with superpowers are walking weapons and it's good to know where those weapons are."

"She was on your list," Jane said.

"Right," Doc said. "And I left her alone, because she was

far too young to recruit, and also because her powers hadn't manifested themselves yet."

"I was pretty young when you recruited me," Emily said. "What's the difference?"

"The difference is you started throwing cars full of people around by accident," Doc said. "Your powers kicked in and we went and got you before you killed someone."

"Which you did right in the nick of time," Emily said. "I sometimes see the look on that police officer's face in my dreams when I accidentally bubble-of-floated his cruiser into the air…"

Jane waited for Emily to trail off before chiming in again.

"So, her powers have manifested now," Jane said.

"I don't know. That's my theory," Doc said. "Because her family moved to California and now their entire town has disappeared."

"Her… entire town disappeared," Jane said.

"It's more complicated than that, but, yeah," Doc said. "And it's my fault. I lost track of her."

"We've been a little busy," Jane said. "You can't be expected to monitor every strange thing in the world. I mean, we've saved the planet a few times lately. That's a valid excuse."

Doc shook his head.

"This is the equivalent of losing a magical nuclear bomb," Doc said. "It's my fault. I'm going to find her and help her."

"We'll help," Jane said. "We'll suit up."

Doc put a hand on Jane's shoulder.

"Can't punch our way out of this one, Jane," Doc said. "But I'll explain what I'm doing and we'll get through this. I promise."

Emily raised her hand. Henry and Sam sighed

simultaneously.

"Go ahead, Emily," Doc said.

"The file says she's called the Crimson Child," she said. "Why?"

Doc bit his lip.

"You know on a meteorological map how different colors show the different intensity of a weather pattern? Green is mild, yellow worse?"

"Oh no," Jane said.

"Yeah," Doc said. "Her code name is the Crimson Child because if magic is weather, she's the hot spot; at the center of a hurricane."

CHAPTER 13:
THE LADY AND THE KING

The Lady Natasha Grey had taken up residence in a penthouse apartment in Las Vegas, because the world is strange and full of wonder, and after a year on the coast of Spain she wanted to experience something a little more bizarre. She had views of casinos like castles and historical monuments, and enjoyed watching the sun sweep over this desert city each day. She wandered the streets at night to watch humanity at play, engrossed by the gamblers and the players, the interweaving of vice and desire and desperation and exhilaration around every corner. Nothing felt real here, and that amused her. In some ways, Las Vegas was the most magical town in this reality, because nothing felt truly real here to her.

I won't stay long, she thought, swimming in a pool on the top of the hotel. I'll return to the Old World soon. Europe is a better fit for me. But this place feels like the circus, and deserts, all deserts, are inherently awash in magic. Deserts are where demons are born and dragons sleep and phoenixes fall and die. Magic loves extremes and abhors the ordinary.

She climbed from the pool, ignoring the long glances of another patron, a movie star with too much time on his hands and not enough tact to look away. It's been a while since I ruined a mortal's life for fun, she thought. It might be entertaining to make a bargain with him and watch him fall.

But she decided against it. Too much time around Doc Silence, she knew. His inherent kindness was rubbing off on her. She found it irritating and terribly boring.

She returned to her room, a vast expanse of overpriced luxury she paid for with currency laundered through dark dealings with monsters both mortal and not. She showered off the pool chemicals and dressed in clothes too expensive to be casual, and looked out over the city as the sun began its descent in the West, bathing the world in red light.

A knock came at her door. It gave her pause. She'd cast spells and set wards here to make sure no one knew she was here. The hotel staff all but forgot the room existed while she stayed there. Anonymous and invisible until she wanted to be. That was how Natasha moved through this world.

Still, someone knocked. She answered.

She hadn't seen the man in the hallway in longer than she could remember. Tall and striking, he wore a dark suit without shirt or shoes, his body, where visible, marked with magical sigils and symbols. He gave off a sense of both infinite vitality and something deathlike, the way certain magical beings do. And he smiled at her like an old friend.

Which, Natasha thought, might once have been true.

"The King of Tears," Natasha said.

"The Lady of the Grey," the man said. "May I come in?"

Natasha gestured for him enter, and he strode in

confidently, but strangely respectfully, as if acknowledging he had entered her sanctuary. Magicians have a funny way of doing this, she knew. We don't like our spaces entered, but we also don't like entering each other's spaces. They fill up with the strange energies unique to each spell weaver, and those patterns and wards create a disconcerting hum to those sensitive enough to pick up on it.

"This doesn't seem like your kind of town," King Tears said. He found the minibar and poured himself a drink without asking, but was polite enough to ask if she wanted to join him. Shrugging, she said yes. Might as well, she thought.

"I'm retired," Natasha said. "Consider it a vacation."

"People like us never retire, Lady Grey," King Tears said. "You'll take a few years off, and then you'll grow bored and start meddling in the affairs of mortals again. We always do."

"You've been quiet of late," she said. "I thought you'd retired yourself."

"As I say. Took a few years off," King Tears said. "Though I started doing some consulting for some mutual friends of ours."

"Oh really," Natasha said, accepting a glass of golden bourbon from him.

"Really," he said. "And they've gone and put themselves in a bad spot. So I've decided that perhaps I could step in and…"

"Rebuild?"

"Take advantage of an existing infrastructure that is going to waste," King Tears said. "You know I hate to see something die that can be resurrected and put to good use."

"That always was your favorite game," Natasha said. "What brings you to my door?"

"I'm looking for something," he said. "And I think you know how to find it."

Natasha felt a gnawing at the pit of her stomach. She'd never trusted King Tears, but then again, most magicians don't trust each other by nature, and for good reason. But she watched his body language, the way he looked around the room, and knew, instantly, that this was not a friendly visit.

"And what exactly are you looking for?" Natasha said. "I've been retired for a little while now, but I did have my hands in the magical artifacts business for a while. Buying and selling."

"Queen of the bargains, you were," King Tears said. "Don't be so modest. No one made better deals with devils and men than you did."

"A good dealer keeps a low profile," Natasha said. "So, tell me about this thing you're looking for."

"It's not a thing," King Tears said. "It's a who."

The Lady Natasha Grey did not become a renown bargainer of the arcane by not having a good poker face, and her expression held. But her pulse spiked, just a little.

"I didn't really deal in people," Natasha said. "I did quite a bit of work with soul stocks, but those aren't really 'who.' And you know who most of those get traded between. Not usually your style."

King Tears smiled. He looked like a happy skull.

"Lady Grey, I know you helped something through the veil," King Tears said, and though his tone was jovial, his tone was not. "I want it, and I intend to have it."

"That sounds vaguely threatening, Tears."

The magician threw up his hands dismissively.

"There's no need for threats, Lady Grey. I know the way to make you agreeable isn't to scare you. It's to offer you a deal you can't refuse."

"You're asking me to betray a client," Natasha said.

"You can't tell me you've never done that before."

"Oh, of course," Natasha said. "But that just means the price goes up."

King Tears laughed, a deep, sonorous sound.

"I knew I could bring you around," he said. "Now I wouldn't ask a master bargainer deal unprepared. Think it over. You know I have the resources. Tell me what it's worth to you, and we'll strike an accord."

He finished his drink and smiled his ghastly grin again.

"I want that creature, Lady Grey. And I'm willing to pay for it."

"It almost sounds like you're asking me to take advantage of your generosity," Natasha said.

"To be honest… I'm spending someone else's currency these days, metaphysically and literally," King Tears said. "I can afford to be generous on someone else's tab."

He moved to the door and paused as he turned the handle.

"I'm looking forward to hearing what you want in return," King Tears said. "If nothing else, I know you always make the most interesting bargains."

The magician touched an imaginary hat brim and left, closing the door behind him. Natasha stood very still, letting the magical guards she had over the suite tell her when he was no longer nearby.

She steadied herself on the arm of the nearest sofa.

"And I just wanted to retire in peace," she said. "Damn it."

CHAPTER 14:
AMONGST THE STARS

Two familiar shapes drifted high up over the desert sky, one a streak of blue-white light, the other like a shimmering soap bubble, visible only when the light hit it just right.

It's good to be home, Billy thought, but he didn't feel it in his guts. Dude knew it, too.

You're lying to yourself, the alien said.

So? I lie to myself all the time, Billy thought.

And in no situation is it ever beneficial, Dude said. *But if you must.*

Must is a strong word for it, Billy thought.

"I love that you're gone for months, living among other Luminae hosts just like you, and you still can't help but do the stupid face when you're talking to Dude in your head," Emily said.

"Maybe I was just daydreaming," Billy said.

"That was not a daydreaming face. You were moving your lips and kind of drooling."

"Did I mention how much I missed you?" Billy said.

"No," Emily said. "And I can tell you didn't."

"What?" Billy said, indignant.

"Oh, don't get your spandex all twisted up, Billy Case," Emily said. "Why would you miss us? You were building a space station for galactic heroes. Coming back to Earth would bore my brains out."

Billy slowed up and came to a stop mid-air. Emily joined him.

"It mystifies me that you're so perceptive," Billy said.

"That's because you're self-absorbed for real," Emily said. "I only pretend to be self-absorbed so that people let their guards down so I can analyze them."

"I am not self-absorbed," Billy said.

You're self-absorbed, Dude said.

"Shut up, you," Billy said.

"I assume that was directed at the alien," Emily said.

"Yeah."

"Anyway," Emily said, pirouetting in her bubble of float, showing off how not-abysmal she'd become at controlling her powers lately. "You can't wait to go back, can you."

"I actually am not looking forward to going back," Billy said, and meant it. He was so much younger than the other Luminae hosts, and so inexperienced compared to them considering how far they'd traveled and how many different alien cultures they'd encountered, that he felt more than a little lonely among them. They treated him like an equal, but he still felt like the only child at the kiddie table at Thanksgiving.

He didn't say all of this to Emily, and of course she picked up on it anyway.

"You don't fit in out there, do you," Emily said.

Billy folded his arms across his chest.

"No," he said. "I mean I'm one of them. They treat me like

I'm one of them, but…"

"But with training wheels?"

"Sort of," Billy said. "I mean, I just don't have their vocabulary yet. Also, some of them are a little afraid of me."

"You are less terrifying than our dog," Emily said. "And he's ten pounds. Watson is fine, by the way. I think he likes your parents more than you now."

"As long as he likes me more than you I'm okay with that. And it's the time travel thing," Billy said. "Remember how Dude and I absorbed so much of his energy from the alternate timeline? How we had to split it off?"

"Yeah. You glowed for like weeks."

"I told them about that," Billy said. "So, some of them think I'm some sort of… like a super-powered Luminae. And others feel like I abandoned one of ours in the future by leaving Dude's spinoff Luminae in the future with Jessica."

"But now that you're back…"

Billy sighed. It did feel good to be home. To be among friends—particularly among friends who were his equals and not his superiors. But still, he…

"I feel really disconnected," Billy said.

"That's because you're an alien," Emily said.

"See you're teasing me, but that's kind of how I feel," Billy said. "I've lived amongst the stars for a while. Everything here feels… zoomed in? Maybe? I don't know. I feel a little bit claustrophobic. And also, a little bit agoraphobic, because everything's so magnified. Earth's got a lot of information it throws at you, all day, all the time. But mostly I feel… I mean disconnected is the best word I can come up with. Detached."

"You didn't look disconnected sitting with Bedlam earlier."

"We were holding hands, for crying out loud, Emily, I swear if you shame me for holding hands…"

"Relax, captain," Emily said. "I'm just teasing. I think she's lonely too. I'm happy the two of you have something, whatever it is."

"And it is very much a 'whatever it is' right now, Emily," Billy said.

"So, you're not planning a wedding."

"We have done exactly not one thing normal together the entire time we've known each other," Billy said. "I'm thinking a few dates might be more appropriate first."

"Not doing anything normal together sounds like my dream relationship, honestly," Emily said, scratching her chin. "Who wants to do normal things?"

"I just spent a few months on one of Saturn's moons," Billy said. "Trust me, normal is underrated."

"Which is exactly why you're going to get me up to that space station, Billy," Emily said.

"It's not that easy. You can't survive in the vacuum of space. I can't just float you up there."

"Buzzkill," Emily said.

"You're living in a broken spaceship in the middle of a desert with a talking robot and a mad scientist," Billy said. "I cannot figure out what you have to complain about."

"You know I bore easily," Emily said.

"True."

"And also that I've always wanted to go to space."

"Whinging isn't going to get a spaceship here for you any faster," Billy said.

"Will it make it slower?" Emily said.

"Probably not," Billy said.

"Them I'm going to whinge," Emily said.

"See, this? This I missed," Billy said.

"Still feeling disconnected?" Emily said.

"Little bit."

"Then I shall whinge until you feel better," Emily said. "Whinge, whinge, whinge."

"So helpful."

"This is why I'm your best friend," she said.

CHAPTER 15:
A MATTER OF OWNERSHIP

Kate sat in front of the not-quite-of-this-world laptop she'd taken from the Tower when she went back to the City without the rest of the team. It wasn't really a laptop, more like a small portable alien computer masquerading as a laptop, but it had buttons and a screen and she didn't know what else to call it. It also had access to the Tower's databases and could connect with resources online without appropriate security clearance, the latter of which was always something that Doc had suggested they never mention to anyone working for a government, anywhere, ever.

Today, though, the information she hunted for online was a matter of public record: building ownership.

She surfed through public records, building inspector filings with the City, and any references she could find about the building where they'd found the evidence of magical foul play. Titus was out tracking the mutated boy, Kevin, in that disturbing way he always did, by scent. She didn't understand why the… otherness of Titus worried her so much lately. She felt weirdly judgmental for having the thoughts running through her head. But she knew the reason, really. It was own humanity. She could forget sometimes, keeping up with the super-powered allies and friends she had, about her own fragility, but something about Titus surviving the explosion in space—a powerful realization of how much more than human he was, it made her feel distant. It wasn't the same as knowing that Jane was invulnerable or Billy could fly. Titus was meat and bone like her. And yet always, always more.

She shook off the wandering thoughts and returned to the task at hand. The building on the outskirts of town had changed hands several times over the years, always some bland, nebulous business name and description. Mostly packaging or storage. Finding nothing out of the ordinary, she started tracking those businesses as well. All of them were defunct, sold off for parts over the course of decades. Strange that none of ever really amounted to anything, she thought. The City has a way of being loyal to its local businesses. If they were part of the pastiche of the City, they would have survived somehow— a square named after the family owners, a random street name, some shopping center the locals refused to call by a new name. But nothing. It was as if the building were inhabited by ghosts.

So she started looking at what else these companies owned, starting with the most recent and working backwards. Most owned other buildings in the City. More than half had properties they owned across the country. A handful were international.

But none of the companies that ever owned the derelict building still existed.

"Oh, come on," she said out loud.

"I was thinking the same thing," Titus said, striding into the office looking miserable.

"No luck, then," Kate said.

"Or too much luck," Titus said. "Kate, something bad is coming. I thought I could track him because—I mean seriously, he's a tentacle monster, that should be pretty unique to track, right? But the whole City smells like…"

"Please don't tell me the City smells like tentacle monsters."

"It smells like bad magic," Titus said.

Kate gave him a long, dirty look.

"What," Titus said.

"The magic thing. Please don't turn into a melodramatic would-be wizard."

"I don't plan on it," Titus said. "But Kate, there's a pallor hanging over this place. It's like a fog."

Kate rocked back in her chair and brushed the hair back from her eyes.

"What are you working on?" Titus asked, intrusively looking over her shoulder at the computer.

"Trying to track down who owns the building we investigated," Kate said. "I'm getting a lot of nothing."

"Lots of companies bought and sold," Titus said. "That's sketchy."

"That's what I was thinking," Kate said. "But public records are limited and I'm not exactly a hacker here."

"There are ways we could get around that," Titus said.

"Don't say magic."

"I wasn't going to say magic."

"What, then."

"You know who I would ask to do a search for us," Titus said. "Neal."

Kate grimaced. She'd felt guilty around the AI ever since she crashed the Tower, feeling—irrationally, she knew—as if the harm done to the ship was actually harm she'd inflicted on Neal himself. The AI had flat out told her, in his usual cheerful way, that he understood her actions and was simply relieved he'd had time to transfer his consciousness into the mobile robotic unit he now lived in. But still, it bothered Kate to be around him. She felt personally responsible for crippling the ship that had been Neal's body and home for longer than even Doc could remember.

"Don't make that face," Titus said, picking up on her mood.

"I'm not making a face."

"He forgives you," Titus said. "More than forgives you—he doesn't even consider forgiveness a requirement. You know he's just happy you both didn't die up there."

"I screwed him over, Titus."

"Kate, Neal is incapable of lying," Titus said. "If he hated you, he'd tell you. Well, I mean he'd say it in a really nice way, but he wouldn't lie."

"How do you tell someone you hate her in a really nice way?"

"Designation: Dancer," Titus said, in his best Neal impersonation. "I feel a sense of overwhelming resentment and anger toward you for your actions. I do not feel as if this response mechanism will subside."

"That was creepy, and if you ever do it again I will break your face," Kate said.

"Are we heading out to the desert?" Titus said.

"Don't sound so excited," Kate said.

"What can I say," Titus said. "I miss everyone."

Kate wrinkled her nose, refusing to acknowledge the flutter she felt in her gut that seemed to maybe, possibly hint she might miss her friends as well.

"Fine," Kate said. "But I'm driving."

CHAPTER 16: THROUGH THE LOOKING GLASS ALL OVER AGAIN

Jane watched Doc size up an empty space in front of him like an art critic studying a painting. Beyond him, a blank wasteland that had once been a town stretched out, empty and silent. Behind them, Sam Barren hovered around a Department car. He'd tagged along to make it official—it was an entire town that disappeared, after all, and the Department had to be involved—but Sam's distrust of the mystical made him grumpy.

We've been here before, Jane thought. Doc going off to some other plane of existence and leaving us here without him. Of course, last time we weren't ready, she thought. We've all been through so much more now. He thought he could trust us then, but he knows he can trust us now.

Still, she didn't like him running off on his own.

"You sure I can't come with you?" Jane said. "I'd feel

better if you weren't going in alone."

Doc exhaled. He looked over his shoulder and smiled at Jane.

"I'd feel better not going in alone myself," Doc said. "But if there's one thing I've done wrong, Jane, it's that I never taught any of you how to really stand up against magical threats. None of you are truly ready for this. And that's my fault."

Jane opened her mouth to speak, hesitated, then changed her mind.

"Titus is learning," she blurted out.

"About magic? I know," Doc said.

"See, I should have known better than to assume he could keep that from you," Jane said.

"His mentor Leto ratted him out," Doc said. "Professional courtesy among magicians. She thought I should know one of my... I was about to say students, but really, you're not anymore, are you? Any of you. You're well past being students. But one of my former students had taken up magic."

"In case you wanted to stop him?" Jane said.

"It's just good to know what sort of magic is living under the same roof," Doc said. "Think about it like what chemicals you store under the kitchen sink. It's good to know you don't have anything that shouldn't be mixed together there."

"You explain magic so mundanely," Jane said. "You really could have been a teacher."

"Always thought I was one," Doc said, smiling. "But yeah. I know. I'm happy he's doing it. He's got the right nature for it. Titus has always been a good combination of cautious and curious. Too much of one and you'll never learn enough about magic to make it worthwhile; too much of the other and you'll live a very short life."

"Why not bring him with you, then?" Jane said. "We could

teleport to the City and be back in ten minutes."

"Because you'll need him here, for one," Doc said. "And because if anything goes wrong, he might be helpful for you to bring me back."

"We've done this once already, Doc," Jane said. "If you could not get trapped on another existential plane that would be wonderful."

"I thought about that," Doc said. He smiled broadly and reached into his long coat, pulling out two long knives, each sheathed in ornate leather.

"I thought you only had one of those," Jane said, recognizing the weapon immediately. During their first great battle, Doc used one, a planar knife, to cut a hole in reality and disappear, dragging their biggest threat with him—a self-sacrificing move Jane never quite forgave him for. She brought him back later by finding the same planar knife, cutting another hole in reality, and dragging him back through. It feels like a lifetime ago, she thought. Her first and last experience with real magic.

"Well, I found another one," Doc said. "Last time I needed to get trapped, so that the Lady couldn't find her way back either. This time I'm bringing one with me so I can get home easily. I hope."

"And the second one is for me," Jane said.

"In case I need you to come help," Doc said. "I hope that isn't the case, but I'm not taking any chances this time."

"And how will we know if you need us to come get you?" Jane said.

Doc handed one of the knifes to Jane and then pulled out a pair of objects from his pocket, small, round mirrors the size of his palm. He gave Jane one of these as well.

"Sometimes I feel like you actually live in a Lewis Carroll

story," Jane said.

"Some days it feels like Lewis Carroll, other days it feels like H.P. Lovecraft," Doc said. He held his mirror up to his face. "Look at yours."

Jane lifted the little mirror up in front of her. Instead of her own reflection, she saw Doc's bespectacled face.

"My beard is coming in nicely," Jane said.

Doc laughed.

"In case you were wondering, wizards invented video chat thousands of years ago," Doc said. "It became a cheap magic trick right around the time the first silvered mirrors were created, but wizards have been calling each other through polished stones or still water for thousands of years."

"Thanks for the history lesson, Doc," Jane said, raising a sarcastic eyebrow. "This is glass. Can I break this?"

"Magic glass. You'd have to try really hard to break it."

"So don't let Emily touch it."

"Do not let Emily touch this mirror, no," Doc said.

Jane wagged the still-sheathed planar knife around in the air.

"And this thing? Last time you gave me crazy instructions for finding you with it," Jane said.

Doc shook his head.

"The place I'm going to is… to put it simply, it's layered on top of this space right here," he said, gesturing at the empty place where the town used to be. "If you cut through with the planar knife, it'll be like peeling back the skin of an orange. Where I'm going is just one layer down."

"That makes no sense, but okay," Jane said.

"This is why I never got around to teaching you much about magic," Doc said.

"Your job is basically entirely based on nursery rhymes and

fairy tales, isn't it," Jane said.

"Yeah," Doc said. "Now you know why there are so few people with my job anymore."

He reached out and put a hand on Jane's shoulder, but she pushed past him and grabbed him in a hug instead.

"You call the minute you need help," Jane said.

"I will."

"Don't catch a cold."

"I won't."

"Call and check in," Jane said.

"I feel like our roles have been completely reversed," Doc said.

"Your job is the weird stuff. My job is to keep the whole world safe," Jane said. "That includes you."

Doc hugged her back, then stepped away and drew the planar knife from the sheath.

"See you soon," he said. With an upward slash, he cut a man-sized hole in the air. Reddish light filtered out, like an aggressive sunset. He stepped through, and the wound in reality sealed up behind him.

"These things never go according to plan," Jane said.

CHAPTER 17:
THE PICTURE OF CAUTION

Titus stared out the window, head pressed against the glass as they circled the half-buried wreckage of the Tower, searching for a landing spot. In a rare spot of luck, Kate had taken one of the small vehicles that had always been stored in the Tower's landing bay—the flying crafts that looked like something out of Buck Rogers that Emily had dubiously dubbed the Indestructicars—and left it parked outside her apartment building before the battle with the Nemesis fleet, so they had one fully functional and undamaged transport to rely on. The others weren't completely destroyed, but nobody was willing to take an alien flying machine for a test drive without knowing if it would crash or not, and none of them were even remotely confident they'd know how to fix it if they found a problem. So the others remained, knocked around like broken toys, in their home inside the Tower.

Luck, Titus thought. Well, better than not being able to get back and forth from the Tower to the City, but he hated flying, and Kate was… well, she wasn't a bad driver, but if it were possible to ignore speed laws while flying an impossible machine, she did. He white-knuckled it every time he rode with her in this contraption.

Our poor home, he thought, looking at the battered outline of the Tower. This was his first trip back since they'd first all assembled here, when Doc found the crash site. It looked better than it had then. Clearly Emily and Henry and Solar had been busy.

But still. The starship looked like it would never fly again. Not like before. He suddenly regretted all the times he complained about living in a flying base.

Kate picked out a particularly flat space in the sand and set the craft down. Titus popped the hatch-like door beside him and stepped out. The air hit him immediately, the way his overpowered senses always did—the dry, mysterious scent of this place, the heat rising off the ground, flowers in the distance, and of course closer, the sharp tang of broken machinery and hot metal from the Tower wreck.

Kate strode ahead, not giving him time to soak in the new sensory input. He rushed to catch up. They entered through a doorway that had become the makeshift main entrance. Inside, the air was cool—they've got the HVAC running, Titus noted, smirking—and the lights were bright, though they flickered a bit, as if still indecisive about how they felt being operational.

Kate stopped just inside the doorway, but Titus pushed past her, following his nose toward the rest of the team.

They found Henry and Emily bickering over a pile of cables, Billy and Bedlam sitting hand in hand, watching the fight. The moment Billy saw them he leapt to his feet.

"My man," Billy said, crashing into Titus with a bear hug. "You look like hot garbage!"

"Better than being dead garbage," Titus said, laughing as he hugged him back ferociously.

"True that. I am so happy to see you," Billy said. He gestured with his thumb over his shoulder at Emily and Henry. "Maybe you can get Rosencrantz and Guildenstern to stop arguing."

"Did you seriously just make a Shakespeare reference?" Bedlam said.

"Why is it surprising I know who Rosencrantz and Guildenstern are?" Billy said, looking offended.

"Because you play up your reputation as being an idiot," Bedlam said. She nodded at Titus. "Good to see you again, wolf-man. Hi, Kate."

Kate nodded solemnly at the cyborg. She put a hand on Billy's shoulder.

"Welcome back to Earth," she said, not without warmth.

"That's Kate's version of giving you a hug," Emily said, stepping away from her argument with Henry to push Billy out of the way and hug Titus herself. "I missed you. I need someone to tell Henry I'm right."

"You're not right!" Henry said. "I… why am I arguing with you? Hi, Titus."

"Hey," Titus said. "What are you two doing, anyway?"

"Trying to put Humpty Dumpty back together again," Emily said.

That was when Titus noticed what all those cables they were arguing about were attached to: the garbage-can-like body Neal now inhabited.

"Oh, buddy! What are they doing to you, brother?" Titus said, running over to kneel in front of the chassis.

"Designation: Whispering," Neal said. "It has been too long since we spoke. I long for rational companionship."

Titus looked over his shoulder at Kate.

"He's happier to see me than you were," he said.

"Birds of a feather," Kate said. Emily jumped up to plant a loud kiss on Kate's cheek. The ballerina vigilante all but ignored it.

"Well, Neal, we came all this way to see you, buddy," Titus said.

"I am wounded, Titus Talbot," Emily said. "Wounded."

"Me too," Billy said.

"I didn't even know you were back on Earth," Titus said.

"Nobody ever visits me," Bedlam said. "How do you think I feel?"

"I flew seven hundred and forty-six thousand miles to see you," Billy said.

Bedlam stared at him for a long moment. Billy stared back.

"I think that's what they call a romantic gesture," Emily said. "Or possibly a humblebrag. Could go either way. Maybe both."

"Definitely both," Bedlam said.

"Not to put a damper on the family reunion," Henry said, plugging one of the cables into Neal's robotic frame. "But our boy here is a little tied up at the moment. Hope whatever you came here to ask him to do doesn't involve… y'know. Moving."

Kate waggled a portable drive in her hand. She threw it to Titus.

"We're looking into a couple of mystery locations in the City," Kate said. "I hit a wall in my research. Hoping we could take advantage of Neal's brain power to help us out."

"I'm guessing you don't get great Wi-Fi out here," Titus said.

"Designation: Coldwall was able to get our satellite uplinks working quite well, Designation: Whispering," Neal said. "I should be able to provide you with your research needs without changing my physical location right now."

"What's this 'Designation: Coldwall' business?" Emily said. "Designation: Entropy Emily busted her butt getting you that satellite uplink."

"You flipped several switches which were fundamentally helpful, Designation: Entropy Emily," Neal said. "Thank you."

"That was sarcasm. Was that sarcasm?" Emily said. She pointed at Neal then looked at Billy. "Did Neal just bust on me?"

"Neal just busted on you," Billy said.

"Every single one of you is out of your mind," Bedlam said.

"You say that like it's a bad thing," Emily said.

Kate sighed.

"And to think, for a brief moment, I regretted not working alone," she said.

"Designation: Whispering—find an appropriate port and grant me access to your research. I will do run an extended scan for you," Neal said.

Titus looked around until he found a matching port and plugged the portable drive in. The socket lit up.

"You can see ownership records, correct, Designation: Dancer?" Neal said.

"I… yes. How did you know that?" Kate said.

"Data is like fingerprints," Neal said. "I can see where you've looked before."

"I am so glad the crazily powerful AI is on our side," Bedlam said.

"One moment," Neal said. The AI went silent. So did the rest of the room.

"So," Titus said, filling the awkward silence. "Billy, how was outer space?"

"It was…" Billy started to say, but Neal chimed in immediately.

"I have found the previous ownership records you seek, Designation: Dancer," Neal said.

"Holy crap, Neal, you just startled the heck out of me," Emily said.

"My apologies, Designation: Entropy Emily."

"Can you like, cough or something before you do that next time?" Emily said.

"Perhaps if you did not make such prodigious use to our food generation device creating coffee to a nearly toxic level, you would be less easily startled, Designation: Entropy Emily," Neal said.

"Dude, don't make me regret advocating for you to get a better body," Emily said.

"He's getting a better body?" Titus said.

"Hush, precious. Neal has something to tell you," Emily said.

"Long story," Henry said.

"Neal," Kate said, interrupting. "Please ignore our bantering colleagues and let me know what you found."

"I have traced ownership to the buildings in question back to a single, suspicious shell company: Innsmouth Canneries, Designation: Dancer," Neal said.

"Oh, come on," Emily said. "That's not even remotely creative."

"Shell companies don't really have to be, right?" Titus said. "Any information on who owns Innsmouth Canneries, Neal?"

"This is where the trail becomes interesting, Designation: Whispering," Neal said. "I traced the shell company back to a familiar source: The Children of the Elder Star."

Emily and Kate unleashed a storm of quietly uttered but vicious swear words. Billy simply muttered: "Are you kidding me."

"They can't… they don't still exist, do they, Neal? I mean they collapsed because of what happened with the Nemesis fleet a few months back," Titus said.

"My search indicates that there is new activity in the Children of the Elder Star's holdings, Designation: Whispering," Neal said. "It appears the organization is not as dead as we presumed."

"What were they doing at these buildings you were investigating?" Billy said.

Titus and Kate exchanged looks.

"I think they're experimenting on runaways and homeless children," Kate said.

"We had a run-in with… something horrible," Titus said. "A runaway who had been mutated."

Bedlam hopped out of her chair, her cyborg feet hitting the floor with a metallic clank.

"I'm coming with you," Bedlam said.

Titus nodded to her. Bedlam's condition was the result of experimentation by the Children of the Elder Star as well. They'd taken her body, which had been destroyed in a car crash, and used it to build her into a weapon. It was only through the Indestructibles intervention she had been set free.

"I understand," Titus said.

"I won't let them do what they did to me to anyone else," Bedlam said. She looked at Kate, who was frowning. "Don't say no, Kate."

"After what we saw in the City, I won't turn down help," Kate said. "I'm happy to have you. I'm just thinking."

"Thinking about?" Bedlam said.

"Where we go next," Kate said.

"Designation: Dancer," Neal said. "I have a list of additional locations currently still in the possession of shell companies owned by the Children's organization."

"Then there's our next move," Bedlam said.

"I'll come too," Billy said.

Kate shook her head.

"We need you as backup, and what we're doing… we need to keep a low profile," Kate said. "You're a comet, Billy. You'll give us away."

"I have four robotic limbs and a glowing eye," Bedlam said.

'Which we can hide with an oversized hoodie and some sunglasses," Kate said. "We've been hiding a werewolf for years. We can help you stay incognito."

"I want to help," Billy said.

"Me too," Emily said.

"Billy, the speed you fly at you can be at our side in minutes," Titus said. "We'll call you in if we need a big gun."

Billy scowled.

"Fine," he said. "I guess I'll stay here and help fix Neal."

Emily laughed, loudly. Billy shot her a dirty look.

"Let Solar and Doc know what we're doing," Kate said. "We'll keep you posted."

"Be careful," Henry said. "I know you've dealt with them before, but the Children have always been more dangerous than they ever let on."

"Look at us," Titus said. "We're the picture of caution."

"A werewolf, a ballerina vigilante, and a cyborg literally named Bedlam," Emily said. "Yup, when I look at the three of you, 'caution' is totes the first word that comes to mind."

CHAPTER 18:
SAGE ADVICE

Billy wandered around the Tower's wreckage alone after Kate and her group left, or at least as alone as he could be with Dude chiming in every so often. They'd been connected long enough now that Dude felt more a part of him than someone he shared mental real estate with. He guessed the bond would only get stronger the longer they were paired up.

The problem, of course, was that Dude could sense his moods and knew he was pouting.

You're being irrational, Billy Case, Dude said.

I'm not being irrational, Billy thought. In fact, I think I'm being super rational.

"Super rational about what?" Henry Winter said, turning a corner to meet him.

Billy looked around, confused.

"You said that out loud," Henry said. "You can't remember if you said it out loud or not, can you?"

"It's insane how often that happens," Billy said.

Henry waved a hand in the air.

"I'm used to it. If you didn't know about their powers, Suresh and Nigel seemed certifiable," Henry said. "They'd talk to each other while simultaneously talking to Horizon and Moneypenny and then to each other again, and since the Luminae could talk to each other silently, there was a whole additional layer of conversation going on, too."

"Did you just call Dude Moneypenny?" Billy said.

I hate all of you, Dude said.

"It's what Nigel called your partner," Henry said.

"I'd heard," Billy said, sensing Dude fuming in the back of his mind.

"So, you look miserable," Henry said. They walked together into the galley, where Henry had a pot of coffee brewing.

"I'm… Y'know, I'm feeling kind of useless," Billy said.

"Don't tell me you're bummed out there isn't a world to save," Henry said. "Take a vacation, kid."

"No, I mean—I'm here, and there's nothing I can do to help. Can't help you and Emily fix Neal."

"Emily is not helping fix Neal as much as she thinks she is."

"Can't help Kate and Titus. Can't help… whatever Doc's working on. But back on Titan I couldn't help build the base— the other guys have traveled the galaxy, they know things I don't. So I came back here to be less useless, but somehow I'm even more useless."

"Kid," Henry said. "Not every problem needs a hammer."

"What?" Billy said.

"You guys, you're a toolbox. Kate's a scalpel, small and precise. Titus is a hacksaw, low-tech but effective. You're the hammer. Sometimes that means you stay in the toolbox. Don't worry about it so much," Henry said. "Because in our line of work, don't you worry, there will definitely come a time there's a nail that needs fixing."

"Good job with the hokey dad advice," Billy said. "Doc's never useless."

"Doc inserts himself into every problem," Henry said. "Also… he's sort of the Swiss Army Knife. Lots of options, none of which is perfect but most will do for now."

"Yeah," Billy said. "Well. I could go back, maybe. To Titan. Stay out of the way."

Tell him about the girl, Dude said.

"I'm not telling him about the girl," Billy said out loud.

"Everybody knows about the girl, William," Henry said.

"This is what I get hanging out with a bunch of fellow Luminae hosts for months," Billy said. "I've lost the ability to be subtle about this."

"What's the problem with the girl?" Henry said. "And by girl I assume you mean that intense young cyborg you've been keeping company with."

Tell him, Dude said. *I've never figured out your bizarre human mating rituals. You need to speak to an adult human.*

Dude, I swear, I'm begging you, never say 'mating rituals' ever again, Billy thought. Ever.

"It's better when you answer him out loud," Henry said, pouring himself a cup of coffee. "When you speak silently it looks like you've swallowed your own tongue."

"Okay. Fine. There isn't a problem," Billy said. "I just worry I'll screw it up. We barely know each other, and stuff keeps happening to keep us from getting to know each other, and I'm worried I'll disappoint her."

"You will," Henry said.

"What?" Billy said.

"You'll disappoint her. She'll disappoint you. It's how you

handle those disappointments, what you do to be better or what you learn about the limits of how much disappointment you can tolerate that will determine whether you make it together or not," Henry said. "And for crying out loud, you are kids. Don't put so much pressure on each other. Go to the movies. Have fun."

"Oh, gawd," Emily said, entering the galley dramatically. She wore onesie pajamas in the shape of a videogame anime rodent, complete with an electrical bolt tail. "Did I just hear you giving him relationship advice, Henry?"

"Where did you get a onesie in the desert?" Henry asked, incredulous.

"Costume generator," Emily said.

"That is such a waste of resources…"

"Why shouldn't he give me relationship advice?" Billy said.

"Because he's been divorced three times!" Emily said.

"Hey!" Henry said. "First of all, don't judge a person's life by their failed relationships unless you were there when they happened. Secondly, how did you know I was divorced three times?"

"The internet," Emily said. "C'mon, Henry, I learned the basics of quantum mechanics online. You think I can't find the *Entertainment Hollywood* article about the billionaire superhero's love life?"

"Why did you look that up?" Billy said.

"Are you kidding? I didn't look it up. My mom watched a lot of entertainment shows when I was little. I knew all about him," Emily said. "Your second wife was the nicest, by the way. You screwed up big time."

"I screwed up a lot," Henry said. "Which is why my third point is to say: why not let your friend learn from my mistakes so he doesn't repeat them?"

"Because it'll be fun to watch him flounder at love?" Emily said, sticking her tongue out at Billy. "I tease because I love, guys."

"I hate to interrupt," Neal's voice crackled over the intercom.

"You put Neal back in the ship?" Billy said.

"No, he's downloading some stuff—Neal, what's wrong?" Henry said.

"Jane is approaching and should be on-site in just a few moments, Designation: Coldwall," Neal said. "But I'm also picking up anomalous energy readings in the control center."

Emily, Billy, and Henry exchanged worried glances took off running—or in Henry's case, hobbling—toward the control center.

They got there just in time to see a doorway opening out of thin air, a circular gateway glowing with purple energy. Billy let his energy powers flow to his hands, which began to glow blue-white, ready to strike.

You asked for a problem you could be helpful with, Dude said.

Now is not the time for sarcasm, Dude, Billy thought.

A silhouette appeared in the gateway, tall and slender with short, bobbed hair. The figure stepped through the portal, and Billy and Emily broke into cursing.

"Not the reception I was hoping for, but I've had worse," the Lady Natasha Grey said, stepping through the portal and letting it close behind her.

"Why are you here?" Billy said.

"Where's your babysitter?" Natasha said, looking around the room in disgust. "There's so many of you running around and not a single one of you suggested sweeping this place up a bit?"

"How did you find this place?" Henry asked. We've got

satellite jammers and…"

"Magic, sweetheart," Natasha said. "Now hush. Where's Silence."

"No seriously, why are you here?" Billy asked again, incredulous. Then things got worse.

Jane chose that moment to come clomping around the corner looking for them.

"Guys, we need to talk about Doc… why is she here?" Jane said.

"I keep asking that same question," Billy said.

"What do you mean, talk about Doc?" Natasha said, her tone imperious.

"That's none of your damned business is what I mean," Jane said. She looked Billy right in the eyes. "Why is she here?"

"Why are you looking at me like this is my fault?" Billy said.

"I swear I've seen this in an Abbott and Costello video," Emily said. "Doc's not here, Lady. What do you want?"

Natasha turned her gaze on Emily as if seeing her for the first time.

"What do you mean, not here?" the Lady said.

"He's indisposed, but don't think that we can't handle you," Jane said. "Also, you owe me one, remember?"

Natasha looked the hodgepodge group and sighed heavily. She walked over to the counter and, without asking permission, took down a cracked mug and poured herself a cup of Henry's coffee.

"That's my coffee," Henry said softly.

"Well, I suppose you'll do," Natasha said. She leaned against the countertop, and Billy realized, much to his growing surprised, that she looked tired. Tired, and worried.

"You okay?" he asked. Jane shot him a filthy look, and Emily just went slack-jawed.

Natasha laughed, a quick bark of a bitter chuckle.

"Oh, if you only knew," she said.

"What do you mean, we'll do?" Jane said.

"I came here to ask Doctor Silence for his help," Natasha said. "Someone he cares about is going to be in grave danger soon, and I can't intervene."

"So what you're saying is…" Billy said.

"You need our help," Emily said. "She needs our help! Oh, this is going to be awesome."

"Awesome is not the word I'd go with," Jane said.

Natasha shrugged.

"I'm proud, but I'm not stupid," Natasha said. "Yes. Yes, you strange little creatures. I need to ask for your help."

CHAPTER 19:
EVERYONE WORKS FOR THE BAD GUYS

Andrew Keppler had always known the company he worked for was shady. It took a few years as a rising star in the corporate structure to realize he wasn't just working for a shady business, but rather, a legitimately evil one, as his rank grew and he was able to peel back layer upon layer of what the corporation did. He was promoted again at age twenty-nine and given the privilege of learning that he worked for the Children of the Elder Star, a clandestine organization pulling strings across the world to make bad people even more powerful. They had been around for centuries in some form or another, always working their evil through money and through surrogates, never through direct confrontation. They owned a portion of the world.

But it's a good job, Keppler told himself. The pay was great and they treated him better than his last job. I mean, if you want to see evil, Keppler thought, I worked in the insurance industry before this.

He flew into the City on King Tears' orders, taking a ridesharing car, driven by a kid wearing a "We Are Indestructible" tee shirt, out to the old factory building the Children owned through one of their hundreds of shell corporations. The kid looked at Keppler oddly when he got out of the car in front of what appeared to be a derelict building, but Keppler gave the kid another twenty bucks as a tip and muttered something about it being old family property. Once the car was out of sight, he went around to a side entrance, a rust-and-green metal door in an alley, and went inside.

Immediately, his head began to swim. The air felt too thick, the hallway simultaneously too hot and too cold. A smell of incense clung to the air alongside the coppery stink of blood, and other, less organic things. He thought for a moment he might pass out, but then his phone buzzed in his pocket, and the normalcy of that, the physical presence of it, jarred him back into reality. He answered.

"I take it you arrived safely," King Tears said on the other line.

"Yeah, I... what is this place?" Keppler asked. Further down the corridor, he saw what looked like a woman in a business suit walking—no, more like shuffling, he thought— toward him.

"Did you know your former employers have little hiding places like this all over the world?" King Tears said. "As if trying to micromanage the planet wasn't enough, they had to get into real estate as well."

"We... we own a lot of property," Keppler said, feeling his stomach twist again. The woman in the business suit grew closer, Keppler got a good look at her face and swore.

"I see you found one of the occupants," King Tears said on the other end of the line. "Don't worry. They won't hurt you."

"That's—am I looking at a zombie?" Keppler said. It suddenly became an effort to maintain bladder control.

"Zombie really isn't the right word, technically, but it's fine for shorthand. You can call them zombies," King Tears said.

"Wait—that's Janet from Human Resources!" Keppler said.

"You may not have known this, but Janet from Human Resources was a trained assassin," King Tears said. "And sadly, excessively loyal to the previous owners."

"You turned Janet from Human Resources into a zombie?" Keppler said.

"I turned most of Human Resources into zombies," King Tears said. "And accounting, too. It seemed like a waste of perfectly good vessels."

"I can't believe I'm seeing this," Keppler said.

"It gets better. Follow Janet, please," King Tears said.

On autopilot, Keppler did as he was told. The undead human resources director lead him down to the area that would have, at one point, been the factory floor.

The walls were covered in what looked like slug-skin. It moved as if the walls themselves breathed. Structures that looked like fleshy eggs jutted up from the floor in different sizes.

"What are you doing here?" Keppler said, his voice cracking.

"The Children of the Elder Star lost half their numbers during the Nemesis invasion. I murdered another quarter myself," King Tears said. "We need reinforcements. So I'm making them."

"Making them out of what?" Keppler said. "No, no, don't tell me. I don't want to know."

"You'll find out anyway," King Tears. "But it'll be more fun watching you figure it out."

Keppler paused in front of a large vacant space on the factory floor. It had been retrofitted with bars.

"Um," Keppler said. "What's the cage for?"

"You're going to love it," King Tears said. "I'm hunting big game, but if I can find it, this will change everything. There hasn't been a power like this on Earth in thousands of years."

Keppler had no idea what that meant, and his brain wouldn't allow him to speculate, as if the very act of imagining what King Tears considered "big game" would be too much for him to process.

"Great. This is fantastic," Keppler said, putting on a brave front while waves of nausea overwhelmed him. "But why am I here?"

"Ah, yes," King Tears said. "I sent you there for a purpose. I understand you've commandeered access to certain archives you did not have access to before."

"Commandeered is giving me too much credit," Keppler said. "Last man standing. The keys, digital and literal, fell to me when everyone else got killed."

"Wonderful," King Tears said. "I need you to locate a few things for me the Children kept in storage."

"We generally kept only the really dangerous stuff in storage," Keppler said. "Should I be worried?"

"My boy, you are about to be on the bow of the ship riding into a new world order," King Tears said. "Enjoy the show."

CHAPTER 20:
THE OTHER SIDE OF THE MIRROR

Well, Doc thought, looking at the California town that had been uprooted and transplanted to another reality. At least I found it.

From his vantage point on the outskirts, he could see rows of single-story homes, streets still paved perfectly, manicured lawns and small, polite trees. At his back, the world became nothing; flat and glittering white, like salt flats, the emptiness expanded off into infinity. The sky had an alien reddish hue, like an eternal, bloody sunset. This place is forever dusk, he thought. The clouds moved in strange patterns, serpentine and seething.

He had an eerie feeling creeping up the back of his neck that he was being watched. Not much I can do about that, he thought, looking once more back out into the nothingness behind him. There's nowhere to go but into the town.

He walked toward the nearest house, on a lovely little suburban road called Poplar Street. Its white vinyl siding had a soft pinkish glow from the permanent sunset. A modest car stood parked in the drive. As he moved closer, he immediately saw something to set his nerves on edge: growing up from the ground, black tendrils gripped the foundation of the house, pulsing like veins. These tubes seemed to pierce the walls of the house, becoming part of them, holding the building in place by force.

Doc carefully avoided the tendrils peered into the nearest window.

Inside, a middle-aged man circled the room, his body language pure panic. Waves of confusion and fear wafted off him. On the floor, a woman's body lay prone. Blood stained the carpet. The man knelt beside her and picked up her hand, holding it to his forehead.

Doc moved on to the next window. The very same woman lying dead on the floor in the first vignette was very much alive here, standing in her kitchen. Her face seemed small and fretful, like she might have appeared as a child. With her in the kitchen was a caricature of a matronly older woman, with steel-gray hair and a mouth like a grim wound. She towered over the younger woman, shouting at her incoherently like a violently disappointed mother.

Developing a hypothesis, Doc moved on to another window on the other side of the house. Inside, a young child sat curled up in the center of his bed, his blankets a cowl around his face. It was immediately clear why he had positioned himself so: a monster lurked under the bed, an apelike thing with dense black fur and teeth like needles, eyes red and malignant.

Doc had seen enough. He backed away from the house and

took a deep breath.

And then Jane spoke behind him.

"You let us die," Jane said. Doc turned to find his first student staggering toward him, her body rotting and torn by old wounds. Her eyes were glassy and large, and her usually radiant hair was instead aflame like a torch. "You failed us, Doc. You left us and we all died…"

Doc muttered a short incantation and opened his left hand. A sword appeared out of nowhere, a gleaming blade like a fairy tale knight might carry, but lighter, brighter, as if free of the physics of the real world.

And with a quick swipe of that blade, zombie-Jane's head separated from her shoulders and fell to the ground. The corpse crumbled away like ashes in the wind, and in seconds, it was as if she never existed.

Because she never did exist, Doc thought. Illusions made of fear and memory, twisted like poison. I'm in a nightmare. Somehow, the Crimson Child had created a pocket reality where everyone's worst fears held them captive. Doc stared at the empty space where not-Jane had stood a moment before. It's not a good nightmare, he thought. The fears are too broad, the illusions too over the top. They're grotesque. They lack the elegance of the sorts of nightmares that ruin you, at least to Doc's trained eye, the ones that skirt so close to reality that you don't know you're dreaming. Clearly the residents of the nearby house were not able to tell the difference.

"You're not supposed to be here," a new voice said, a tiny, melodic sound, sing-songy and cheerful. Doc looked around until he found the source.

"I knew this was going to be weird, but this is a lot weirder than I expected," he said, staring up at a fairy in a cotton-pink shift, her wings fluttering like a hummingbird's. She had a mop of candy-yellow hair and enormous eyes, her body small but proportional, like a doll.

"You killed one of the illusions. She's going to know you're here," the fairy said.

"Okay, let's get something out of the way first," Doc said. "Are you actually fey, or are you a figment?"

"I don't know what I am," the fairy said.

"Figment, then," Doc said. "True fey never pass up a chance to brag about their origins."

"I'm not a figment," the fairy said. "I'm real."

"Oh, you're real," Doc said. "But you're what, a conjuring? Where did you come from?"

"I belong with the girl," the fairy said. "But she's not herself. We failed her. We were her protectors, but she's changed. She's someone else now."

"We," Doc said. So, the girl conjured defense mechanisms at her age. If you failed her, he thought, responding silently to the fairy's words, then I failed her even worse. If she could conjure a figment to protect her I should have done more to keep her safe as well. I didn't know.

"Does she know you're here?" Doc said. "Her protectors. Does she know she brought you over as well?"

The fairy shrugged in a way that was far more reminiscent of Emily's body language than Doc was comfortable with.

"I'll bring you to them," the fairy said. "We saw you arrive. Saw you open a hole in the world. Can you bring everyone home again?"

"That's what I'm hoping to do," Doc said. "Now why don't you introduce me to your friends. You can fill me in on what this is all about on the way."

CHAPTER 21:
THE QUEEN ON HER THRONE

Queen Alice the First, she would be called.

That was the plan. If anyone ever showed up.

It had been such a great game at first, Alice thought. She'd painted the sky red with her hand like a brush. She'd created a palace with her mind, just closing her eyes and picturing walls of pearl and floors of marble. She wanted statues of dragons in the courtyard and there they were, with just a thought. Brave soldiers made of silver stood at attention throughout her castle, automatons at her beck and call, and ladies-in-waiting crafted of living silk.

She built all this, and waited. Perhaps, Queen Alice thought, now that I've built them a castle, my mother and father will be happy. When they did not come to her, she caused an entire wing filled with her mother's favorite things to grow out of the ground like a garden, and then did the same on the other side of the palace for her father. All the space they could want, she thought. Sometimes all we need is space. That will stop them from arguing.

But they never arrived.

No one did. She thought, if nothing else, perhaps some of the neighbors would walk up the marble stairs to marvel at the beautiful structure Alice had created. She could introduce herself – in her old life, the neighbors often ignored her, as did the kids at school, never maliciously, but in a forgetful way that made her swell up with loneliness – and invite them to stay. She could dole out titles, naming them dukes and duchesses, barons and baronesses.

Look at what I've made, she'd tell them. We don't have to live in that grim, old world anymore. I gave us something better.

And yet here she was, alone, except for the click-clack of her tin soldiers as they performed their patrols, the soft singing of her silk-crafted handmaidens, and the whispers of her Vizier.

She wasn't quite sure where the vizier came from. Alice thought she might have created him, the way she created the other denizens of the palace, but she had no memory of it. Dressed like a medieval peacock and wearing a face not unlike her favorite actor, the boy from the show about the monster-hunting brothers, the vizier had simply just been there from the beginning.

"I'm lonely," she told him. She tried not to pout. She was too old for pouting, and a queen now after all, but boredom and loneliness made her grumpy and impatient. Still, there was no need to embarrass herself in front of her advisor.

"Perhaps you should make some new courtiers," he suggested. His voice was hypnotic, but there was something else to it, too, something dangerous. Sometimes her mind drifted when she spoke with him, in that fuzzy way she felt when her father convinced her to take cold medicine when she was sick.

"I suppose I could," she said. "Maybe a jester, or dancers, or something."

She wondered where her toys went, her unicorn and her fairy, her bear and her shadow. She wondered if somehow the magic she'd used to bring them to life didn't work here, or that they were trapped back in the boring old world. She missed her friends.

"I think you're on to something," the vizier said. "Maybe you should go to the palace library and see what sort of characters your court should have."

"There is no palace library," Alice said.

"My queen… all you need to do is make one," the vizier said, smiling radiantly. Alice couldn't help it. She smiled back.

"You always know the right thing to do," she said to him.

"And that, my queen, is why you keep me around," the vizier said. He gestured toward the back of the palace, where, Alice knew, there was quite a bit of room to expand. "Shall we?"

"Will I need to remember every book I need for the library?" she asked.

"You are not only the queen, but the most powerful magician in all of the land," the vizier said. "Books will spring forth to fill your library fully formed. Waiting to be read."

They climbed a short staircase to a set of windows overlooking the rear of the palace. Alice concentrated, thinking in geometric patterns, and then, with a rumbling ascent, stonework began rising out of the silvery earth, creating floors and walls. A tornado filled with books spun and danced its way into the new structure, the tomes springing out to organize themselves on newly crafted shelves. Trees were uprooted and split, reforming into long, smooth reading tables. And then, with a snap like giant jaws, a roof slammed shut atop her new library.

"Amazing," Alice said, smiling to herself.

"And to think, you did it all yourself," the vizier said. "Now let's go expand our minds with some research."

He held out an elegant hand toward the steps, at the foot of which a new door had appeared, leading out to the library.

"After you, your majesty," he said.

And Alice was too distracted to remember why she wanted the library in the first place.

CHAPTER 22:
YOU'RE A TERRIBLE PERSON

The Lady finished her story, and everyone—Jane and Henry, Billy and Emily—sat in silence for a long, awkward moment. Billy broke the silence first.

"You're a terrible person," he said.

"Whoa," Emily said.

Jane found herself rubbing her eyes just like Doc would when he was stressed.

"I beg your pardon?" Natasha said, clearly offended.

"Nope, he's right," Jane said. "You're a terrible person."

"I can't believe I'm going to say this, but I'm actually offended," Natasha said. "I came here at great risk to myself to ask for your help and I'm a terrible person?"

Billy stood up and started counting off his fingers.

"You made a bargain with an immortal demon queen, one," he said. "Two, you brought an immortal demon queen to Earth."

"I was doing her a kindness, and I did it to help both your

beloved Doctor Silence and myself get home," Natasha said.

"No, you said you did it to get yourself home,' Jane said. "Doc already had passage."

"I don't see how that's relevant," Natasha said.

"And three, you brought an immortal demon queen here, but you gave her a body to live in that inhibits her from using her powers to their fullest potential," Billy said.

"That's a little messed up," Emily said.

"I did that so she couldn't… take over your slimeball little reality!" Natasha said. "Would you prefer I let her arrive at her full strength so she could cause havoc and destruction at will? I inhibited her powers to keep you little apes safe."

"Wait, did you say inhibit her powers?" Billy said.

"You crippled her?" Jane said.

"Oh for the love of… I did it to keep her safe, and to keep us safe. I didn't lobotomize her. I put a speed limit on her corporeal form here," Natasha said.

"So you crippled her," Jane said.

"I cannot believe I'm justifying myself to you," Natasha said. "I did this for the good of your world. I'm the good person in this equation."

"More like chaotic neutral," Emily said.

"I have no idea what that means," Natasha said.

Emily pointed around the room.

"Jane is lawful good. Billy's neutral good. I'm chaotic good. You're chaotic neutral," Emily said.

"You've… determined our Dungeons and Dragons alignments," Billy said. "Can we just once have a normal conversation…"

"If we're done talking gibberish," Natasha said.

"What's Titus?" Billy said, sounding legitimately curious.

"Human form, I think he's neutral good, but he's more true

neutral when he wolfs out," Emily said.

"Guys," Jane said.

"What about Kate?" Billy said.

"Guys," Jane repeated. "Can we focus?"

"Kate's chaotic good, I think," Emily said. "You'd think we would get along better."

Jane decided to ignore Billy and Emily and focus on Natasha instead.

"However she got here, whatever you've done to her… you said there's another magician who wants to capture her and use her? How is that even possible?" Jane said.

"This creature is powered by dreams," Natasha said. "And while that may sound ridiculous to mundanes like yourself, let me assure you, having access to a being who can manipulate and manifest dreams is an incredibly powerful tool."

"Manifest?" Billy blurted out, suddenly reinvested in the conversation. "Wait a… she can… do you mean she can make dreams real?"

Natasha shrugged.

"She's not granting you three wishes, little boy," Natasha said. "What she can do is use the fear or elation or emotion dreams give you to manipulate the real world."

"How is this even real life," Billy said.

"Tell me she does not spend time dressed as a clown," Emily said.

"What are you talking about?" Natasha said.

"Has she ever been to Derry, Maine?" Emily said.

Natasha glared at Emily for a long, hard moment. Henry, who had been quietly listening until now, finally spoke up.

"He wants to weaponize her powers," Henry said.

"That's a fair description," Natasha said.

"But she's not a willing participant," Henry said. "How do

you weaponize a super-powered person if they're not playing along?"

Emily and Jane swapped terrified looks.

"What," Billy said.

"Billy, you remember the alternate timeline," Jane said.

"Remember Earth-2 me?" Emily said. "Dark Emily?"

"Oh no," Billy said.

"What. What is going on over there," Henry said.

"I'm not sure I follow," Natasha said.

"Oh, nothing, just an alternate timeline created in a parallel universe where you kill Doc and a supervillain turned me into a weapon of mass destruction and a nuclear power plant all in the same adorable body," Emily said. "Thanks for that, by the way. Good job, Lady."

"Are you really holding me accountable for something I did… in an alternate timeline?" Natasha said.

"Still your fault," Emily said.

"I have lived for centuries and dealt with demons and monsters beyond imagining," Natasha said. "And you, you are the most annoying creature I have ever encountered."

"Thanks!" Emily said, smiling widely.

"Okay, okay, c'mon," Jane said. "What do you need us to do, exactly? And we're not doing this for you. We're doing this because you're telling us if he gets his hands on this creature a lot of people could get hurt."

"Of course," Natasha said. "I can't approach her. King Tears will know. But if you go to New York, you can warn her, and, hopefully, convince her to go into hiding."

"Preferably with us to protect her," Jane said.

"I honestly don't think you could handle him if he came after you," Natasha said. "But this buys us all some time."

"This entire plan gives me agita," Emily said.

"I can't imagine why," Billy said. "We've only had Doc drilling into our heads since day one that magic is the most dangerous thing in the world and we should never go anywhere near it. Let's do this. We haven't made any bad life choices in a while."

"In a while you mean, like, a few days," Emily said.

"Maybe hours," Billy said.

Again, Jane just let the banter roll past her. She locked eyes with Natasha.

"And what will you be doing while we're out risking our lives trying to save the world?" she asked the magician.

"Running interference to keep King Tears looking elsewhere," Natasha said. "I don't like you, and I don't particularly like this world, but I live in it. I'd rather keep it."

"I still don't know why you're not just working with him instead of us," Jane said.

"Because I know reckless ambition when I see it," Natasha said. "Ambition I can tolerate. Recklessness gets you killed. I don't care how powerful you are."

"Says the woman who brought a demon goddess to our world like she's got a day pass to Disneyworld," Emily said.

CHAPTER 23:
THE POWERFUL AND THE POWERLESS

Kate, Titus, and Bedlam hit up a half-dozen abandoned sites owned by the Children of the Elder Star before they found anything interesting. Mostly they found old offices, covered in dust, looking as though they were evacuated rather than simply closed. In one, a conference room was adorned with the rotting remains of a catering spread, a birthday cake collapsing in the center of the room, complete with candles.

The next site, though, things got interesting.

The building was located on the outskirts of the City, an area that had been taken over by small businesses and young professionals, where this empty structure looked like a blight waiting to be reclaimed. The trio were crossing the street toward the aging brick building when Titus picked up on the stench. Kate, of course, immediately noticed him grimacing.

"What do you smell?" Kate asked. "I am never going to get used to asking you that. I can't believe that's a thing I ask you."

"I hope you never get comfortable asking me what I smell," Titus said. He swallowed hard, wrinkling his nose. "It smells… wrong? Something is here that doesn't belong. I can't explain it. It's not rot, it's not poison, or chemicals. It's just not natural. That's the only way I can describe it."

"Well, that's encouraging," Bedlam said. "I'm going to kick the door in."

"Maybe we should enter with a bit of stealth," Titus said just as Bedlam's cyborg foot booted in the front door. "Or we can just do that. That's fine."

Kate pulled her mask, which had been coiled around her neck like a cowl, up to cover her face, and walked in. She unzipped the coat she'd used to hide her uniform. Bedlam peeled off the knit cap and sunglasses she wore to hide the robotic features of her face. Together, they entered, Kate pulling out a flashlight and clicking it on as she walked in.

"Something is not right here," Bedlam said. "My sensors are picking up all sorts of strangeness around us. The walls are warm. Can you sense that? I'm picking up a steady heat signature in the walls."

Kate placed her palm against one drably gray office wall.

"That's odd," she said. "Titus?"

Titus pushed ahead, leading the way down a corridor, passed more abandoned offices, a break room with moldy coffee still in a pot, a bathroom, the door slightly ajar, faucet dripping slowly. A dusty film seemed to hang in the air.

That unnatural stench smelled even closer now. He turned to the women and nodded for them to follow.

The corridor ended with an elevator and a spiral staircase. The trio opted for the stairs, of course, descending into a space that opened into a sort of atrium. Only this atrium was unlike anything they'd ever seen.

"What the hell is that," Bedlam said.

"It's alive," Kate said.

The center of the room was dominated by a what seemed like a Christmas tree of amorphous flesh, a conical pile of patchwork skin, pulsing with life. It wasn't until Titus took a step closer that he could make out parts within the cone. Hands, legs. Faces. There are faces, he thought. Please don't be alive. Please be dead. I need you to be dead.

One of the faces opened its eyes.

Bedlam yelped. Kate took an involuntary step back. Titus felt his lips curl back over his teeth like a dog, and found himself choking down the urge to transform. He needed his rational brain right now. Not yet, big guy, he thought. Soon, but not yet.

"Help," the face said.

"No," Bedlam said. "This is too much. This is too grotesque. This can't be real."

Kate took a step forward.

"Who are you?" Kate asked.

The face, a boy's face, a teenager's, seemed to ponder the question.

"I'm… Patrick," the face said. "I think that's who I am. I was Patrick. Now I'm not."

"Patrick, who did this to you," Kate said.

Again, the face struggled with the question, processing.

"The painted man," Patrick said.

"Can you tell us about the painted man?" Kate said, walking closer. Titus admired her cool—he was battling a fight or flight urge so powerful it was making him nauseous. In a struggle to be useful, he scanned the room, as much to look away from Patrick's mangled form as to look for clues. But clues he found: mystical glyphs painted on the walls, sigils and runes, power words, arcane symbols he couldn't translate. He took out his phone and snapped a few photos surreptitiously.

"He said he would give us power," Patrick said.

"What kind of power?" Bedlam said, her voice rising.

Patrick blinked, then shook his head awkwardly, the flesh it was embedded in impeding his movement.

"Why do we keep finding these places?" Bedlam said. "It feels like over and over again we find terrible places where terrible people do terrible things to people who can't say no."

Like you, Titus thought, watching the pain and rage twist on Bedlam's face. He knew exactly why she was angry. She'd been a failed experiment by the Children herself, and this was not the first lab they'd found since meeting her.

"Because the powerful will always use the powerless," Kate said. "This is what powerful people do. Whatever they want, because they can."

"Patrick," Bedlam said. "We're going to find a way to get you out of there."

Once again, Patrick struggled to shake his head.

"We can't be fixed," he said.

"We?" Bedlam said.

Titus closed his eyes and grit his teeth. He'd already seen the other faces. He wasn't ready to watch them all open their eyes and look at Bedlam as one. But he couldn't stop it. Titus opened his eyes and saw each face, six of them, embedded in this mountain of living matter, unable to move. Elsewhere, hands clenched and unclenched uselessly, disconnected from the bodies they once belonged to.

"Can you end the pain?" Patrick said.

Bedlam put a hand to her chest, mechanical fingers gripping her coat tightly.

"We can try to help you," Kate said, putting a hand on Bedlam's shoulder to steady her.

"There's no going back," one of the other faces said.

"I don't even remember who I am," said a third.

"Please set us free," said a fourth.

"Don't leave us like this," Patrick said.

"Don't leave us like this."

"Please don't leave us like this."

Bedlam made a fist, staring at it, her whole frame shaking.

"I don't think I can," she said.

Kate looked to Titus, who nodded. She'd do it if she could, he knew, but this was beyond Kate's abilities. *And this is why I am here. I am the one who kills when nobody else can. Red of tooth and claw. Every team needs a monster.*

"I'll do it," Titus said. "Patrick, can I ask you one last question?"

The boy nodded.

"Is there anyone we can say goodbye to for you? Any of you?"

"No," Patrick said.

"I don't remember," said another.

"No one will miss me," said a third.

"No one will ever look for me," said a fourth.

They're all ghosts, Titus thought. *Chosen for a purpose. The powerful and the powerless.*

"Stop the painted man," Patrick said. "Don't let them do this to anyone else."

"We will," Titus said, feeling the werewolf inside him surging up, ready to strike. "We will avenge you. I promise."

And then he let go, felt the claws burst from his fingertips and fangs grow in his mouth. Everything went red. It was hard to kill a living hill of flesh, but he found a way. He always found a way.

He came back to his senses sitting on a curb across from the building, Kate sitting beside him, Bedlam standing with her arms crossed.

"I'm sorry you had to do that," Kate said.

"It's my job," Titus said.

"No, it's not," Bedlam said. "And I should've been able to. I should have been able to honor that request. I'm sorry, Titus."

"I understand, Bedlam," Titus said. "Honestly, this is just…"

I'm the monster, Titus thought. I do what needs to be done.

"We're going to find this painted man," Bedlam said. "We have to."

CHAPTER 24:
THE GUARDIANS

Doc Silence followed the fairy-creature deeper into the woods on the outskirts of town. The forest itself had taken on a nightmarish quality to match the experiences of the townsfolk, trees dark and twisted in strange, threatening ways, bending and arching like hungry monsters.

Along the way, Doc sensed something following them at a distance, a shadow without a source. It seemed more curious than threatening, though, and so he left well enough alone, though never taking his attention fully away from it.

Eventually, the brush ahead rustled, and a gruff, rumbling voice called out.

"Galinda, what have you done?" it said, and a sight that under other circumstances would've brought a smile to Doc's face emerged from the woods. A walking teddy bear, one eye covered in a leather patch, wearing battered armor and wearing an oversized sword on his back.

"He's a magician, Captain Teddy," the fairy said. "He can help us free Queen Alice."

The bear's fuzzy shoulders slumped.

"I think our queen is too far gone," the bear said. He called over his shoulder. "You can come out, Silverhoof. It's safe, for now."

This just keeps getting more ludicrous by the second, Doc thought as a pure white unicorn trotted out of the darkness. Her mane was cotton-candy pink, her horn a pearlescent rainbow.

"She's not too far gone," another voice said. Doc watched as the shadow that had been stalking them coalesced into a vaguely humanoid form, a pair of pale yellow eyes glowing from its otherwise featureless face. "We just need to get her away from that wretched Vizier."

"The Vizier will never let us get close enough," Teddy said.

"But he might let *him* get close enough, Gloomly," Galinda said, jabbing a tiny hand in Doc's direction.

The shadow-creature darted forward so that he was nearly face to face with Doc.

"And who are *you*, then," he asked.

"My name is Doc Silence, and I'm here to put this town back where it belongs, and free your Alice," Doc said.

"Queen Alice," the armored bear corrected.

"She's only been Queen Alice since this happened," Galinda said. "She was our Lissie before, remember?"

The bear shrugged again in the saddest, most resigned gesture Doc had seen in ages.

"I was a pillow with legs before," he said.

"You look like you've seen combat," Doc said. "Has the Vizier been violent?"

The bear looked at him, his mouth a grim line.

"You mean the eye? A terrible beast took that. It was called a washing machine."

"I'm sorry to hear that," Doc said.

"Most horrifying experience of my life. I thought I was going to drown," he said.

"It must've been terrifying."

"I don't like to talk about it, but you look like you've seen some things as well."

"I have," Doc said, filled with a sudden urge to adopt this walking, talking teddy bear. "What can you tell me about the Vizier?"

"He is new," the shadow said.

"New?"

"He showed up a few days ago," Galinda said. "At first we thought he was like us, a… what did you call me?"

"A figment," Doc said.

"Something like that. Something our queen made with her mind, like us," Galinda said. "But he's not."

"He whispered in her ear, and gave her terrible dreams," Gloomly said. "But she didn't know it was him. She thought he was there to save her from the dreams. Maybe he'd been there all along and we never knew."

"Because we couldn't," Teddy said.

"And she became so afraid she changed everything. She made this place," Gloomly said. "We tried to fight him, but she protected him. And then it was like she began to forget everything that came before. We changed. Transformed. Became her servants."

"I swear, if we could chase off the Vizier, we'd get our Lissie back," Galinda said.

The presence he felt in Seville, Doc thought. Something entering this world and changing it. The presence had felt familiar to him, like something he'd fought before, but he couldn't quite place it. This place though, reminded him of somewhere he'd been trapped for a while with Lady Grey during their accidental banishment from their home reality not all that long ago. He'd spent time in the dream realms, and this place, with its nightmares in every house, its twisted trees, its red skies, felt like a little pocket dimension of nightmares.

He knew nightmares. He could fight nightmares.

"What does this Vizier look like?" Doc asked.

"He's pretty," Galinda said.

"No, he's not," Gloomly said. "He makes himself look pretty, so as not to scare her. But if you pay attention, you can see his true face out of the corner of your eye. The burning eyes. The fangs. He is more monster than man."

"I need to get a look at him. Maybe try to talk to Queen Alice. Can one of you show me how to get there?"

All three creatures exchanged a nervous look. Even the unicorn, who remained unspeaking the entire time, looked away sheepishly. Then, the fairy, shadow, and bear all spoke at the same time.

"I'll go," they said as one.

"We don't all have to risk our lives," Teddy said. "I'll take him."

"I found him," Galinda said. "Let me."

Gloomly darted onto Doc's shoulders, wrapping his dark form around him like a barely visible cloak.

"I'm the one they won't notice," he said. "I'll be his guide."

"If you're always as sneaky as you were following us here, you'll be able to slip away easier than the others if I'm captured, too, I assume," Doc said.

"Captured?" Galinda said.

"We don't know what the Vizier is capable of," Teddy said.

"Better safe than sorry."

"It's decided, then," Gloomly said.

Doc looked to both Galinda and Teddy, then gave an equally respectful nod to Silverhoof as well.

"If anything happens, I have friends who will come looking for me. A girl with hair of flames. A boy who can become a wolf. A few others. Help them, if they do. They'll need your guidance."

Captain Teddy snapped to attention.

"You have my word," he said.

I love this bear, Doc thought.

"Thank you," he said. "Let's got see about this queen."

CHAPTER 25:
MAGIC AND BARGAINS

The Lady Dreamless sat alone outside an elegant restaurant in Manhattan, sipping a shockingly expensive drink she did not pay for, watching New Yorkers walk by as if the wave of humanity before her was the most delightful form of entertainment she'd ever seen.

This world was, in many ways, infinitely entertaining to her. No, it didn't have the impossible variety the Dreamless Lands had, but she found the creativity this reality had despite the limited artistic materials at its disposal incredibly impressive. Like an artist who worked only in clay, she sometimes thought. Or trash. Fine art made from castoffs and scraps.

As someone who wove dreams with magic as one might wield a needle and thread, she found its crudeness delightful.

She reached down to pet one of her demon hounds, amused, as always, the way the glamour cast on them disguised the two impressive beasts as matching pair of jovial Great

Danes she called Castor and Pollux. As she scratched behind Castor's ear, she saw a stranger making a beeline toward her. People approached her often in this world, her own illusory form eye-catching and her demeanor mysterious, but it wasn't his approach that caught her attention. He, too, had a glamour cast on him, disguising his form to mortal eyes. Beneath the blandly handsome face and expensive suit he hid behind, his skin was a pallid, deathly gray, taught across muscle and bone, covered in ashy white tattoos. He wore no shirt beneath his suitcoat, displaying more mystic tattoos. His feet were bare. The ordinary humans allowed him to pass without so much as a second glance. Just another businessman in an expensive suit, nothing special or out of the ordinary in this place.

She could tell from his gaze he saw through her illusions as well, and he was not afraid.

"May I join you?" the gray man asked. Lady Dreamless gestured for him to sit. Her curiosity was piqued, in the very least, even if she had no real interest in dealing with this world's sloppy magics.

"I hope you don't plan to take long," Lady Dreamless said. She could smell blood on him. Meat magic, she thought, blood and sacrifice, necromancy. Her least favorite kind of magic. She preferred the bargaining tactics of Natasha Grey, or the way Doc Silence learned the secret names of things. There was an elegance to that which blood magic could never possess, as effective as the latter was.

"You're not from this world, are you," the man said. "Let me introduce myself. My name is King Tears."

"King?" Dreamless said. "Such a strange honorarium. I didn't think this land of the free believed in kings."

"It's more of a play on words," King Tears said. "Not a literal translation. You know magicians often sacrifice our names to learn our craft."

"And you gave yours away to be called a king."

"Others have become doctors or professors, ladies or barons or captains. Why not a king?"

The Lady Dreamless shrugged, mildly annoyed at the comment. She was, in fact, royalty in the Dreamless Realms, though she supposed her title meant little or nothing here.

"Speak to me, King of Tears. You have until I finish my drink or until you bore me."

A smile broke across the face of the man who called himself King Tears. It was a joyless grin.

"There is a power vacuum in this world right now, and I'm attempting to consolidate such power. To keep things from getting out of control, you see. Not for selfish reasons."

"Everyone who gathers power gathers it for selfish reasons," Lady Dreamless said. "And those who claim otherwise are the worst among a sea of liars. I know the hearts of men and women, King Tears. Don't think you can fool me."

"My apologies, my lady," King Tears said. "That is *your* honorarium, is it not? The Lady Dreamless, Queen of the Citrine Tower?"

"I can't say I'm pleased to hear you know my name," she said. "I'm here on vacation, after all."

"Yes, and far from the Dreamless Lands. Your magic is powerful here, but it's not what it might be if we were on your home turf, so to speak."

Anger flashed across the dream queen's eyes, so powerfully they glimmered with their true, luminescent red hue. Mortals around her took an involuntary step back, their subconscious minds sensing danger their waking eyes could not see.

"That sounds like a threat, King Tears."

"I was hoping it might sound more like an offer," Tears said. "Join with me, and you can rule over this world as unquestionably as you do the Dreamless Lands."

"I have no desire to rule this world. As I said, I'm here on vacation. I'm here to learn."

King Tears pondered her for a moment, a long finger tapping his lip.

"Did you know something followed you through?" he said. "This is no simple guest visa to our world. You brought an invasive species with you."

"I did no such thing."

"Deny all you want. But there are footprints all along the ley lines. You should never have come here, where you are not welcome. Where you are not safe."

"I've had enough of you. What is it with wizards and their petty arrogance?"

Lady Dreamless stood up smoothly. Her demon hounds rose then as well, flanking King Tears expertly.

And then Lady Dreamless heard Pollux let loose a soft, pathetic whine. She glanced to her dogs and saw that both had frozen in place. King Tears stood up as well, calmly, his hands moving dexterously as he cast a binding spell, locking her defenders in place.

"Don't worry. This doesn't hurt them. I'm sure you've used such magic before as well. They just simply won't be able to interfere," he said.

"I don't need my hounds to tear you apart," Lady Dreamless said. She lifted a hand, which began to glow from within with arcane energy. But nothing happened.

King Tears smiled at her in a grotesque parody of charm.

"I did offer a partnership, remember. But if I need to steal your powers from you instead, I'll take them by force. It isn't every day I have a chance to siphon off pure dream magic. It's so rare here after all."

"You don't know who you're crossing," Lady Dreamless said.

But then she saw the eyes of the patrons around her, the wait staff, the harmless humanity in the streets. They no longer emanated a sense of life. Instead, blank eyes stared out at her from the husks of faces, sallow, vacant, cold.

The dead turned to her, reaching out with grasping hands.

CHAPTER 26:
NOT MY TYPE

"You go talk to her," Billy said.

Jane raised a grumpy eyebrow at Billy, then closed her eyes and sighed as Emily made a grotesque sucking sound with her straw. They'd taken up position in an Ishmael's Coffee across the street from the fancy bistro Lady Dreamless was having a drink outside, and Emily was on her second venti Entropy Emi-latte with whipped cream, a coffee creation with enough caffeine in it to give an elephant a myocardial infarction. The Indestructibles had, in their first year, struck up a small marketing deal with Ishmael's, which had seen an unexpected resurgence after the Nemesis Fleet invasion. Apparently saving the world made people want to buy coffees named after superheroes again.

Of course, that meant Emily was floating on a severe caffeine high and about to become super annoying any second.

"I'll go talk to her," Emily said.

"No, you will not," Jane said.

"I mean, I'll go," Billy said. "But you're the diplomat, Jane. You'd be the best one to approach her."

They were able to find Lady Dreamless with Natasha's help, but when they finally spotted her, she didn't look they the way they thought she would. Jane wasn't quite sure what to expect, but a slender, elegant woman with dark hair and an old-fashioned movie star's looks was not how she'd pictured an otherworldly demi-goddess. Dreamless wore a simple black dress with pearls, black heels, a wide hat and oversized sunglasses, something straight out of *Breakfast at Tiffany's*. She was accompanied by two beautiful Great Danes, both completely black in color as well. She sipped casually on what Jane thought might be a mimosa.

Billy, echoing her thoughts, said what everyone was thinking out loud.

"I did not expect an Audrey Hepburn cosplayer when we were sent on this assignment."

"Well, first appearances aren't always what they seem to be," Jane said.

"You were exactly what you presented yourself as when we met," Billy said. "I've always admired that about you."

"What?"

"There's no bull to you. You just are who you are. Everyone else is full of it."

"I'm not full of it," Emily said.

"You are more full of it than anyone I've ever met," Billy said. "And that's why you're my best friend."

"I know that was meant as an insult, but I don't care," Emily said.

"Of course, you present yourself in such a hyper-stylized mess nobody really knows what to expect from you," Billy

said.

"Ah, I see you've figured out my secret plan," Emily said.

"I like to think my own façade holds up under scrutiny," Billy said. "Pretend to be the person you want them to think you are, that's what I say."

"You've never said that," Emily said.

"You're right," he said. "I haven't. I just made that up."

"Y'know, for a little while, I thought I had a crush on you," Jane said. "Then I realized you weren't my type. And I'm definitely not yours."

"I don't have a type," Billy said.

"Yes, you certainly do," Emily said.

"I beg your pardon?"

"You so have a type, Billy," Emily said.

"Well?" Billy said. "What is it?"

"You are into women who can, and under certain circumstances actually will, kick your ass."

Billy paused for a moment, a flash of irritation passing across his face, then shrugged.

"That's fair," he said. "Wait, though. What's your type?"

"Me?" Jane said.

"Yeah," Billy said. "You said I'm not your type."

"I don't mean that as an insult."

"None taken."

"Then why are you asking?"

"Because I don't remember you going out with anyone," Billy said. "Ever. I'm just curious."

"We've been saving the world. Non-stop. For, like, a long time," Jane said.

"Well, we've had some time off," Emily said. "The boy isn't wrong."

"I have more than one type," Jane said. "We're allowed to

have more than one type."

"And your type just doesn't include me," Billy said. "What's wrong with me?"

"There's nothing wrong with you. Are you insulted?"

"No," Billy said. "If I'm being honest, I'm just trying to be less of a garbage person, so if there's something about me that screams 'don't date him,' I'd love to know what that is."

"Billy, you're asking to open Pandora's Box right now. Nobody wants to know the answer to this question," Emily said.

"You don't?" Billy said.

"Oh man, I know all my flaws," Emily said. She started to tick them off on her fingers. "I'm immature. Annoying. I have a short attention span. I intentionally cause trouble when I'm bored. My pastime is antagonizing the few people who do like me. I'm a disaster. Those are just the surface flaws."

"Maybe I don't want to know the answer to this question," Billy said.

"If I'm being honest, when we first met, it was because you were simultaneously cocky and overconfident while also having a profound lack of self-confidence," Jane said.

Billy and Emily both turned to look at her, slack-jawed.

"That is the most accurate description of Year One Billy I have ever heard," Emily said. "Brava, lady. Brava."

"I'm legitimately annoying," Billy said. "All this time, I've always been legitimately annoying."

"That's not what I meant," Jane said. "Please don't take that to heart. You've grown a lot. And now, well, I just know you're not my type because we know each other better. I know I'm not yours either."

"Right," Billy said, distracted.

"I think you broke him," Emily said.

"Sorry," Jane said.

"But seriously. What is your type? Jon?" Emily asked.

"Jon?"

"Broadstreet. The reporter who's in love with you."

"Oh," Jane said. "I don't know. He's nice."

"But not your type," Emily said. "He looks kinda pretty now that he grew out his beard."

"I have more than one type!" Jane said. "And why does it… wait, what's your type?"

"I do not have a type," Emily said. "I am free, like a bird, to alight upon any branch I so choose. Nothing can tie me down."

"I've kind of always worked on the assumption you are your own type," Billy said.

Emily nodded confidently.

"I'd date me. I'm awesome," Emily said. "Fine. On three, Jane, we both point to the first person we see we think is attractive."

"Huh?"

"Here. On this street. Just point to someone you dig."

Jane sighed.

"Fine. It's not like we're actually doing anything, like saving the world."

"Good," Emily said. "One… two… three."

Jane and Emily both pointed at Lady Dreamless in her Holly Golightly outfit and sunglasses.

"Ha! I love it!" Emily said.

"Well, that just happened," Jane said.

Billy started clapping.

"All this time, we have finally found something you two agree on," Billy said. "This makes me so happy. I have never seen you two agree on anything since the day we met. You both think Audrey Hepburn is hot."

"We've always agreed that you're pretty annoying, Billy Case," Emily said. "What do you think of the guy walking up to her?"

"Which one?" Jane said.

"Can I just say, watching Lady Dreamless shoot down dude after dude who hits on her this afternoon has been, up until 'point at someone you find attractive,' the highlight of my day?" Billy said. "She's like some sort of rejection Jedi Master. Oh, this guy is definitely getting rejected."

They watched as a tall, magazine-handsome man took a seat at the table with Lady Dreamless. Jane, Billy, and Emily all sat back in shock.

"Wow," Billy said. "I wouldn't have guessed that one."

"I guess he's got a sort of... soap opera handsome thing going on there," Jane said. "I guess I like a little more character to a guy's face."

"He's boring," Emily said. "A little *too* boring."

"What do you mean?" Jane asked.

"We're stalking an interdimensional creature disguised as a human," Emily said. "Does that guy look like a human, or like someone wearing, like, a human hologram?"

"Oh, no," Billy said. "She might be right."

"We should get over there," Jane said.

"And blow our cover?" Emily said.

"You both just pointed at her at the same time," Billy said. "If there was any doubt we're stalking her, you two just totally gave us away anyway."

He stood up, tossing his coffee in a nearby bin.

And that was when people started turning into zombies.

CHAPTER 27:
THE ZOMBIES OF WALL STREET

I realize after all this time I should fully understand our combined capabilities, Billy thought, but can we tell if those people are still alive or not, Dude?

I'm sensing heartbeats, Dude said. *This appears to be, if I were to be so bold as to hazard a guess, some sort of extreme mind control.*

So they're not zombies, Billy thought.

I honestly don't know how zombies operate, but they're not the walking dead, if that's what you're asking.

Good enough for me, Billy thought.

He grabbed Jane by the shoulder as she stood up to race to Lady Dreamless' rescue.

"They're still alive," Billy said. "Those people."

"The zombies are still alive," she repeated.

"Yeah. So, y'know…"

"Maybe don't go for the brain like a zombie movie," Emily said, lifting off the ground in a bubble of float.

Jane yanked her hat off, revealing her flaming hair. Other patrons of the coffee shop began to run and take cover.

Others, of course, started taking photos with their phones.

"Basically, they're hostages and monsters at the same time," Jane said.

"Yeah," Billy said.

"Got a game plan to go along with your extrasensory perception?" Jane asked.

"I have a plan," Emily said.

Billy and Jane turned to her.

"Obliterate the creep who is clearly controlling them," Emily said, pointing at the man who had sat down with Lady Dreamless.

"On it," Billy said. Jane started to protest, but he waved her off. "You get to Dreamless and get her out of there. I've got the range to hit this guy at a distance, right?"

Jane nodded.

"Okay. Solid. Emily?"

"Yeah, boss?"

"I'm going to… try to not accidentally hit any of the not-zombies so hard I kill them. When you see an opening, bubble of float our target the heck out of there," Jane said.

"You got it."

Billy waited until Jane and Emily were airborne, flying toward Lady Dreamless, and then ran to his right to get a clear shot at the creepy guy.

Why are we not flying, Billy Case? Dude asked.

I'm going to let the girls catch his eye for just a second. He'll be looking at the young woman whose hair is on fire first, and when he's not looking… wham.

Every time I think I have given up on you, you prove you've actually learned something since we began our partnership.

Hey, Dude, I'm getting there. Remember, I'm the same guy who tried dive-bombing a giant mole monster as a "tactic."

As expected, the blandly handsome man whipped around, diverting his attention from Lady Dreamless to watch as Jane and Emily rocketed across the sky. He began to wave his hands in a way that Billy found alarmingly familiar, like something he'd seen Doc Silence do so many times. He's casting a spell, Billy thought. Can't let that happen.

Billy reached out both hands and let his light-blasts unleash at full power, hitting the creeper-magician like a tidal wave. The magician went crashing across the patio, slamming into a table, knocking over several chairs, and landing in a pile of furniture, umbrellas, and drinks, limbs askew, face buried under a tablecloth.

The zombies, however, kept on zombie-ing.

Okay, maybe the plan didn't work, Billy thought.

It was worth trying, Dude reassured him. *Perhaps it wasn't a concentration spell.*

Did you just make a Dungeons and Dragons joke, Dude? Billy thought.

…Not on purpose, Billy Case. We need to spend less time with Emily, I think.

Jane landed right next to Lady Dreamless and began knocking zombies away from her. Billy could tell Jane was holding back—the people who had been transformed, assuming they woke up from this spell at all, would feel dinged up for sure, but considering Jane was strong enough to punch a human head clean off its body, she was doing a pretty good job keeping the damage to a minimum. Billy ran toward them, watching as the creepy magician began to stir, climbing up out of the debris. Several zombie pedestrians took notice of Billy and began shambling toward him, and he fired off a few light-blasts to keep them away.

Any chance you can help me keep the "oomph" of those

blast at a minimum, Dude?

I'll do my best to scale back the power level, Billy Case. You focus on targeting.

Weird, it's almost like we're really a team now, isn't it?

Let's not get carried away.

The magician stood up, grasping a fallen table for support. He no longer looked like a catalogue model, though. His skin had faded from a perfect tan to sickly gray, now covered in pale tattoos. His eyes glowed an ugly, dark red. Once again, he began gesturing to cast a spell, seemingly unsure where to target his rage.

So Billy made a suggestion by once again hitting him at full power. This time, the magician was knocked from his feet, flying into the bistro. It was a nice enough day that the restaurant had its front windows wide open to let in the warm air, so instead of smashing through a giant pane of glass, Billy could hear instead what sounded like a grown man's body crashing into a wine rack.

Billy was close enough now to hear Jane explaining the situation to Lady Dreamless while punching and kicking zombies away from her.

"We're here to help," Jane said.

"Who—why?" Lady Dreamless said. "How did you know…"

"Also when and where," Emily said, scooping up the two Great Danes with her bubble of float.

"I don't understand," Lady Dreamless said.

"We're—hang on," Jane said, bodily tossing one of the zombie-waitresses aside and apologizing to her as the unwitting victim landed heavily on the pavement. "We're Doc Silence's students. We were sent to warn you. About that guy."

"And apparently we were about ten minutes late," Billy

said. He could see the magician struggling to his feet within the bistro, so he sent a blast of light through the open window. Billy took the cursing and groan that followed as a good sign that he'd hit his target.

"We'll explain later. Let's just get you out of here," Jane said.

Emily reached out a hand to Lady Dreamless, who looked all around her in a perfect combination of annoyance and confusion.

"One moment," she said. She muttered something in a language Billy couldn't recognize. It made him think of places he'd seen but could not remember, like a dream half-forgotten upon waking up.

The zombies, as one, fell to the ground.

"Did you just kill them?" Jane asked, her voice cracking.

"No," Lady Dreamless said. "I woke them from a nightmare."

She took Emily's hand and together they began rising into the air. Jane and Billy both took off as well. As they did, Billy saw the magician step from within the bistro.

"No, you don't," he said.

Billy shot him in the face with a light-blast again, sending him sprawling back into the restaurant.

"Let's get out of here," Billy said. "Pretty sure he's about to figure out how to start getting out of the way of those."

CHAPTER 28:
THE CASTLE OF QUEEN ALICE

Doc Silence walked down the center of what once was Westwick, the buildings and homes silent, the stores closed. He could sense eyes on him, both suspicious and fearful, but no one approached or called out as he walked north, toward the strange structure that now dominated the town's center.

The castle's design possessed an innocence, one without a sense of engineering or gravity, so that towers and spires spun off in unsafe, illogical patterns, looking more like a tree than a fortress. The stonework was reddish, like faded brick, and stained glass appeared in every window. Pepper pot turrets were covered by conical roofs in bright colors, adorned with flags in a rainbow of colors, with childlike drawings of mythological monsters appearing on each without any sense of reason or design. One massive gate stood open like a wide maw, guarded by knights in silver armor. They saw Doc approach and pointed long, jagged spears at him.

"This was not here a few days ago," Alice's shadow-man figment whispered in Doc's ear. The creature literally rode on

Doc's back, blending in with the dark material of the magician's trench coat.

"I assumed the castle was new," Doc muttered, trying to make sure the guards couldn't see his lips moving.

The guards called out to him.

"Halt! Who are you? What are you doing here? You don't have an appointment!" one yelled.

Doc held his hands out to his sides to show he held no weapon.

"My name is Doc Silence. I'm here to speak with Queen Alice."

"You don't have an appointment," the guard repeated.

"Are you sure?" Doc said. "Maybe you should double-check."

"Queen Alice has no appointments today," the guard said. "She never has any appointments. Go away."

"Please," Doc said. "I just request a moment of her time."

The two guards looked at each other, then one ran inside, armor clanking with each step. The remaining guard stared with palpable discomfort from behind his helmet, a bascinet obscuring all but his eyes.

"Pleasant day, isn't it?" Doc said conversationally.

"Silence!" the guard said.

Doc sensed a strange vibration along his spin and realized the shadow-man was laughing.

"Did that guard just yell your name at you?" Gloomly said.

"It happens," Doc whispered.

Finally, the other guard returned, but this time, he was not alone. Striding confidently beside him was a tall man, dressed in deep purple robes of state, a large gem hanging around his neck attached to a thick rope of gold. The man was ghostly pale, but strikingly handsome, with high cheekbones, jet black hair, eyes like black pearls. He smiled gently as he looked at Doc.

"You're not from here," the newcomer said. "Curious."

"I'm a traveler from another realm," Doc said.

"I'm less concerned where you're from than I am how you got here," the man in purple said. "We haven't had a visitor to Queen Alice's kingdom before."

"Then allow me the honor of being your first guest," Doc said.

The man lifted a hand, and both guards walked toward Doc, taking up position on either side of him. Not ungently, they guided him toward the portcullis. Doc allowed himself to be led without struggle.

"You must be the Vizier," Doc said as he approached the man in purple.

"I am," he said. "You know more about me than I know about you. My guards tell me you call yourself the doctor of silence."

"Doc to my friends," Doc Silence said. "And really, it's an honorary title. I can't say I completed any formal doctoral program."

The Vizier's face quirked into a brief smile.

"You'll find most of what happens in this kingdom is based on imagination far more than fact and paper," he said. "We find things work better that way."

"I'm still learning my way around this realm," Doc said.

"One might say we all are," The Vizier said. "It changes with the queen's whims and fancies. What is real today might be imagined tomorrow, and vice versa."

"Might I have a chance to speak with her?" Doc said. "I bring a message from the other world."

The Vizier stopped walking. The guards followed suit.

"And what might that message be, doctor?"

"The queen's mother is looking for her."

"And I suppose you're here to bring her home."

"I wouldn't be so presumptuous," Doc said. "I am simply here to deliver the message. What Queen Alice does with it is her own decision."

Again, the Vizier studied Doc's face. He seemed particularly put off by Doc's red lenses glasses and what they might hide.

"I'm curious," the Vizier said. "Very well. You'll have your audience. Follow me."

The Vizier led Doc, still flanked by the armored guards, up through winding staircases that seemed to make no logical sense. They turned in places they shouldn't, crossed over small footbridges that should not have been there, and sometimes went back down toward the lower levels before reversing direction again. Doc could not tell if the Vizier was intentionally leading him on a confusing journey to make it harder for Doc to leave, or if the castle simply followed the illogical whims of a child's mind.

They arrived finally in a large, open chamber. The stone floor remained uncovered, the walls lit by torches. It had a dungeon-like feel to it, but less because of its structure and more because it simply appeared so vacant and unused. Forgotten.

Doc smirked.

"An odd room to meet with the young queen," Doc said.

"I'm sorry, doctor," the Vizier said with a broad smile that indicated he was anything but. "I can't have you tainting her mind with stories of where she's been. She's here now, in the place where she belongs. I can't have you interfering with that."

"You're not a figment, are you," Doc said. The Vizier's

smile faded. "Not a demon, either. I know a demon or devil when I see one. You seem vaguely familiar, though. What are you, really?"

"I have no idea what you're talking about."

"Memory vampire? Psychic leech?"

"I just work here," the Vizier said. "Following the wishes of my queen."

"Right," Doc said.

"Anyway, I wish I could say it was a pleasure meeting you, doctor, but instead of lying, I'll simply say goodbye."

And then the floor gave out beneath Doc's feet.

He tumbled into complete darkness, banging into a stony surface that rapidly became smooth, like a slide. His descent curved rapidly, then dropped again, his stomach flip-flopping as he plummeted. His fall came to an abrupt, painful stop as he slammed into an earthen floor.

"Are you dead?" Gloomly said, invisible in the darkness.

"No," Doc said. He moved his limbs gingerly, making sure nothing was broken. Everything hurt in that unpleasant, bruising way he knew would feel even more later, but not cripple him. "Just old."

"That went really badly," Gloomly said.

"It went exactly how I suspected it would," Doc said. He muttered a few magic words and a small globe of violet-white light appeared in his hand. He released it to float beside him like a lamp. He found himself in an actual dungeon this time, the floor covered in straw, stone walls on three sides, a small, rusted metal gate on the fourth.

"What do you mean, suspected?"

"The way you and your friends talked about the Vizier, I had a feeling he was some kind of malignant creature. I wanted a look at him," Doc said. "Yes, it would've been preferable to get in a room with Alice and try to talk to her, but I knew if he got to us first, he'd block us somehow."

"By dropping you down a chute," Gloomly said.

"Okay, that part I wasn't expecting," Doc said. "I honestly thought it'd turn into a fight."

"So, what do we do now?" Gloomly said.

"Can you find your way back to your friends from here?" Doc asked.

There was a pause.

"I can go back up the chute," Gloomly said. "It might take some time to find my way back out of the castle."

"Well, you do that."

"And what about you?" the shadow-man said.

Doc stood up creakily and tested the bars on the cell door. They were mystically warded, which did not surprise him.

"I'll try to magic my way out of this room," Doc said.

"I'll pretend I know exactly what that means," Gloomly said.

"It's magically sealed. I can't just cast a quick spell to bust the lock, or teleport myself out. I need to be more careful than that," Doc said. "But it's nothing I haven't dealt with before."

"If you can't get out, does that mean…" Gloomly said.

Doc could barely make out the shape of the shadow-man, but saw a darker shape float upward toward the chute from which they'd emerged. There was a bizarre, almost wet thump.

"Oh, that makes me angry," Gloomly said. "Hang on."

"You're pure magic," Doc said. "If I can't get out…"

"Neither should I," the shadow said. "But I think…"

"What are you doing?" Doc said.

"Looking for a gap," Gloomly said. "I can fit through anything. I'm a shadow."

"Magic doesn't usually leave—" Doc started, but Gloomly

cut him off.

"Found one."

"Seriously?"

"About the size of the head of a nail," the shadow creatures said.

"Well, this place is built on imagination," Doc said. "Not the usual precision magic requires."

"Lucky us," Gloomly said. "But what about you? I can't squish you through a pinhole here."

"That's okay. We know you can go for help. But hang here a bit with me just in case," Doc said, drawing a mirror out of his pocket, relieved to see it hadn't shattered in the fall. "I'm going to make a phone call."

CHAPTER 29:
ALTERING THE PLAN

The Lady Natasha Grey returned to her sanctuary to prepare for the inevitable fallout when King Tears learned he wouldn't be getting what he wanted from her. She intended to have some time to prepare, of course. But knowing the Indestructibles, and having dealt with them as both enemies and allies over the past few years, if she'd learned anything at all, it's that they had a tendency to zig when you wanted them to zag. The mystical wards she'd set to watch over Lady Dreamless went off like a smoke alarm, and she knew she'd have a visitor soon.

Fortunately, she was prepared for that.

The doorknob to her Las Vegas suite fell off its moorings and the door creaked open, revealing a battle-battered and weary-looking King Tears. The magician's suit was ripped in places, and his face showed several healing wounds.

"You could have knocked," Natasha said, eyeing the now broken doorknob. She folded her arms across her chest and leaned back to half-sit on her desk.

"I went to speak with our mutual friend, the dream queen," King Tears said. "And a funny thing happened."

"You look like you've had a bit of an adventure."

"You could say that," Tears said. His bare feet left bloody footprints behind on her cream-colored carpet. Natasha could see shards of glass mixed in with the blood.

"I take it she didn't want to talk."

"Oh, more than that," Tears said, barely restrained anger in his voice. He walked directly toward Natasha. If I scared easily, she thought, this aggression might be worrisome.

"Tell me what happened," Natasha said. "Care for a drink?"

King Tears stopped just a few feet in front of her.

"Part of that menagerie of freaks Doc Silence put together got in my way," King Tears said. "Strange that they were just… there, isn't it?"

"You said it yourself—they're Doc Silence's menagerie," Lady Grey said. She poured herself a glass of bourbon and took a slow sip. "Silence once saved Lady Dreamless from the Nightmare King. It wouldn't surprise me if he knew she were here and had his protégés looking out for her."

"You'd know that, though," King Tears said, pacing. Natasha poured him a drink and held it out. He stared at it with distrust for a few seconds before accepting, downing the entire glass in one gulp. "You always said Silence was a rival, but everyone knows the two of you are more friends than enemies in the end. You warned him."

"I don't even know where he is right now," Natasha said. "We haven't spoken in months."

"I have no patience for liars," King Tears said.

"And I have no patience for paranoid bullies," she responded.

With surprising speed, King Tears lunged at her, one long-fingered hand clamping down around her throat. She felt his corpselike skin against hers for only a second before the smell of burning human flesh filled the room.

King Tears yanked his hand away, cursing wildly, grasping his wrist to examine the damage.

"You vile…"

"Did you really think you could walk into my home and threaten me with physical violence?" Natasha said. "I am your equal in this world, King Tears, and I have far more powerful friends than you do. Strike me again and see how much you enjoy being teleported to a random circle of Hell."

"You wouldn't," King Tears snarled.

"I'd rather not," Natasha said. "Dropping an enemy into the Pit is a bargaining chip I was hoping to save for a real emergency. I'll waste it on you if you lay another hand on me though. See how long it takes you to climb your way back up from the Abyss."

"I've never liked you," King Tears muttered.

"Not your biggest fan either," Natasha said. "So, what are you doing here, other than slinging accusations around without proof?"

King Tears plopped down on one of Natasha's leather sofas, still nursing his burned hand.

"I discovered something when I found Lady Dreamless," he said.

"Do tell."

"She's not alone," he said.

"She does have a pair of demon hounds with her," Natasha said.

"No, not them," King Tears said. "Something else followed her through. Something from the Dreamless Lands."

Oh, Natasha thought to herself. That's not good.

"Do you know what it is that followed her?" she asked.

"I came here assuming you did," he said. "Whatever it is, it stinks of parasitic energy. I think it would be useful, and I want it."

Natasha rubbed the bridge of her nose irritably and realized she was mimicking a gesture she'd seen Doc Silence do thousands of times, which made her even more irritable.

"No, I don't know what followed her through," she said.

"I don't believe you," King Tears said, his voice vaguely threatening, though there was less bark to it since his first threat.

"King Tears, you've known me a long time. What do you think is harder to believe: that I enabled some parasite to move across dimensions and I'm hiding it out of the goodness of my kind and generous heart? Or that if I knew a parasitic entity was here with street value among greedy men like you, and I didn't find a way to sell it?"

Tears pondered her last statement, then laughed.

"That's the first completely truthful thing I've heard you say in decades," he said. "You must know something."

"If it's parasitic, I don't know, maybe try to figure out what it might want to eat," Natasha said. "Don't make me do your homework for you."

"I'll remember this," King Tears said.

"And I'll remember you laid hands on me," Natasha said. "We'll see whose vengeance comes calling first."

Tears stood up, poured himself another drink, and once again downed it in one go. He stared Natasha down with his eerie, dead eyes, then stormed back out of her suite.

She gestured to the door, and with a small incantation, caused the doorknob and lock to repair itself. Then she sat down, exhaling loudly, and finishing her own glass.

She was not a lesser magician than King Tears, but it had been a long time since she'd engaged in a magical duel. The idea made her sick to her stomach. *I've worked too hard to not make enemies I can't deal with easily,* she thought, *and now this bull of a man is upsetting all the china.*

And what did those kids do with Lady Dreamless? She thought.

CHAPTER 30: WHAT THEY DID WITH LADY DREAMLESS

Jane found herself staring at an interdimensional mystical being on a rooftop in Queens, not quite sure what to say. Fortunately, Emily took care of that part first.

"So that was not exactly what we had planned," Emily said. She was kneeling beside one of the Great Danes, scratching him behind his ear.

"Who are you children?" Lady Dreamless said. She had removed her oversized sunglasses, delicately hanging them from the collar of her dress.

"Natasha Grey sent us to warn you about… well, I'm pretty sure she sent us to warn you about the guy we just ran away from," Jane said. "I guess we could've gotten there sooner."

"In our defense, we only found out yesterday," Billy said. He sat on the lip of the rooftop, the other Great Dane resting his head on Billy's knee.

"I appreciate the consideration, but I think I had that under control," Dreamless said.

"Doc would've wanted us to help you out, anyway," Jane said.

"Doc... Silence?" Dreamless asked. "Are you his soldiers?"

"More like his rehabilitation projects," Billy said.

"We're his team," Jane said, ignoring Billy.

"Doctor Silence has always been good to me," Dreamless said. "I didn't think he knew I was here in your world, or if he did, that he'd approve of it."

"I'm pretty sure he didn't know," Jane said. "And still doesn't. Lady Grey came to us looking for him, but he's, um, on a field trip, so we came instead."

The dream creature nodded pensively.

"Where is he now?" she asked.

"Y'know, funny you should ask that," Jane said. "Because he went through some sort of rift where a town disappeared. I haven't heard from him yet about how that's going."

"Unfortunate. I would've liked to consult with him about this being who attacked me," Dreamless said.

"So would we," Billy said.

"Also, clearly Lady Grey didn't do a very good job running interference," Emily said. "She told us she was going to try to keep him off your trail for a while."

"This is my shocked face that the Lady Grey didn't follow through on a promise," Billy said, waving a hand in front of a deadpan expression.

"In any event, we can't just stay here," Jane said.

"And our base is currently a wreck in the desert on the other side of the world," Billy said.

"I bet Kate has a hideout back home," Emily said.

"That," Jane said, pointing at Emily in agreement, "is a very good point."

She took out the earbud they each carried for communicating in the field and tucked it into her ear, tapping it once to activate it.

"Kate, you listening?" Jane said.

"We've got to talk," Kate said.

"I assume that means you're listening."

"We just saw the sort of thing that's going to haunt me to the end of my life, Jane," Kate said. "Save the snark. Why are you calling?"

"We are standing on a rooftop in Queens with the ruler of another dimension and we need a place to hide."

There was a long, heavy pause on the other end of the line.

"I have a flophouse in our old neighborhood," Kate said. "I'll give you the address."

***

Kate's hideout was a loft in one of the less reputable neighborhoods in the City, the top floor of an old factory with rooftop access to make her vigilante activities easier. It was also, Titus thought, painfully utilitarian.

Bedlam agreed. And she had no qualms about saying it out loud.

"Your hideout is depressing as hell, Kate," the cyborg said. She pointed to the mattress resting on the floor. "That's where you sleep?"

"I don't sleep much," Kate said.

"I'm amazed you've got sheets and a blanket on it," Bedlam said. Tell me you have hot water and that shower and sink in the loo aren't torture devices."

"I have hot water," Kate said. "What do you think I am, a masochist?"

"Don't answer that," Titus said.

Kate gave him a long, hard stare.

"What are you doing on your phone right now?" Kate said. "You can't be checking social media."

"I'm ordering you a bedframe from IKEA," Titus said.

"What?" Kate said.

"Kate, you don't need to live like this. You saved the world. Like three times. You don't have to live like you're on the run from the law."

"If a delivery truck from IKEA shows up outside my hideout, Titus, I will murder you in your sleep."

"Fine," Titus said, clicking through to save the order for later rather than canceling it entirely.

The window leading to the roof creaked open, and Titus looked up to see Emily's neon-blue haired head sticking through.

"Party time!" she said.

"Just… come in," Kate said. "I'm going to have to get a new hideout. This one's compromised."

"You live like this?" Emily said, floating down from the skylight with two enormous Great Danes, both shockingly nonchalant about flying, in tow.

"And now she's brought dogs into my hideout," Kate said.

"Your boyfriend is a werewolf," Emily said.

"Oh, come on, Em," Titus said, very close to being honestly offended.

Emily was followed quickly by Billy, Jane, and a newcomer, a woman of impossible-to-determine age dressed in elegantly casual black.

"Who is that?" Bedlam asked, her tone teetering on rude.

"This," Jane said, "Is Lady Dreamless."

"Ladies everywhere lately," Bedlam said.

"She's a… she's royalty from a mystical dimension. And she's currently being pursued by a creepy magician who can make zombies."

The woman nodded curtly.

"I understand you're all allies of Doc Silence," she said. "I'm afraid he's never spoken of you."

"Doc likes to play things close to the vest," Titus said, introducing himself, and then the others.

"It appears we've got two problems to deal with now," Kate said. She described the thing they'd found, the pile of humans merged together into a nightmarish monster.

"Zombies on the one hand, whatever that is on the other," Billy said. "Be a superhero, they said. It'll be fun, they said."

Behind them, a distinct whirling sound suddenly began. Titus knew the sound immediately, practicing with Leto and learning about mystical arts. A teleportation spell. He hoped Doc would emerge from the purplish portal that opened up in Kate's makeshift living room, but instead, Natasha Grey strode through instead. She immediately took in her surroundings and wrinkled her nose.

"That thing you found, Dancer, is called a flesh golem," Grey said. "Or the start of one. I liked your spaceship better. This place is a dump."

"Your opinion of my base of operations means the world to me," Kate said.

"Lady Grey," Dreamless said nodding. Both Great Danes moved to flank her defensively.

"Lady Dreamless," Natasha said back, not unkindly. "I'm sorry you've run into some trouble. I hoped our friends here might get to you before King Tears did."

"Back up, back up," Jane said. "First of all, flesh golem? Second, King Tears?"

"A flesh golem. Think of it as a less handsome version of your Frankenstein's monster story," Natasha said. "A creature stitched together with the flesh of the living, made to follow a magician's command. And King Tears is not his real name, much as Doc Silence is not his own nor Lady Grey mine. Magicians discard their true names. It's more of a self-chosen title."

"You guys do love to give yourselves honorifics you haven't earned, huh," Billy said.

"Do you even know what an honorific is?" Emily said.

"I read a lot," Billy said.

"Guys, please," Jane said.

"We found this 'flesh golem' while following whatever had caused some homeless kids to mutate into bizarre creatures," Kate said. "Titus and I fought a kid who seemed to no longer be in control of his own body. His limbs were twisted into something…"

"I'd call it Lovecraftian," Titus said. "Grotesque, misshapen. Hard to describe. The kid looked like he was in terrible pain."

"Blood magic," Natasha said. "My least favorite."

"Blood magic?" Bedlam asked. "Sounds like something out of a video game."

"It's a type of magic, a school of magic," Titus said. Everyone, including Dreamless and Natasha, turned to look at him in surprise.

"Well look at you," Natasha said. "The little werewolf is a novice spellcaster. I can see it now. I'm impressed, young man. Nice to see one of you children has some ambition."

Kate walked away to the small kitchenette, still within earshot of the conversation but with her back distinctly to Titus. She opened an aging refrigerator and took out a bottle of water.

"Care to elaborate, Titus?" Jane said.

"I am so here for this," Emily said. "It's like finding out Dungeons and Dragons is real."

"We already kind of know Dungeons and Dragons is real," Billy said. "Remember that board game incident?"

"I am so mad you guys made me put that game back in Doc's study," Emily said.

"I'm really not the one to explain," Titus said. "I only know the very basics. Stuff my mentor taught me."

Natasha looked to Dreamless, who made a slight gesture to the sorceress.

"Magic comes in different forms," Natasha said. "Some of it is more science than art, some more art than science. Every magician works in their own unique way, of course, but there are methods and styles. Cheats and shortcuts."

"So you and Doc are both magicians, but not the same kind," Jane said.

"Silence is a street magician. He's quite the jack of all trades. I've always enjoyed that about him, the way he steals and borrows from different magics," Natasha said. "But in the end, I know he prefers the magic of secrets."

"What's that?" Emily said. Titus was surprised by the lack of sarcasm in her voice. He could tell she was honestly intrigued.

"Everything in this world has a secret name," Natasha said. "If you call to the wind by its secret name, you might cause the weather to change. If you know the name of lightning, you can command it to strike down your enemies."

"The secret names of things," Emily said.

"What about you?" Jane said.

"I normally do not reveal my methods, but it's no mystery

that I work in bargains and pacts," Natasha said. "I trade information or value, broker power for power. I buy my magic with other magic, or artifacts, or things darker and more valuable."

Like souls, Titus thought. Leto had warned him about magicians like Natasha Grey.

"I would assume our little werewolf friend here is learning about the magic of nature. The living world has its own kind of magic," Natasha said. "And I can't imagine something as primal and raw as a werewolf tribe would be drawn to anything less pure than nature magic."

"You're not wrong," Titus lied. Leto was a very old werewolf, and had learned a great many things in her time, and she wanted Titus, the last of the Whisperings, to be as prepared as possible. But there was no need for Natasha to know that, not now.

"So blood magic is…" Billy said, his lip curling in disgust.

"Body magic. Necromancy. Twisting and sacrificing living things for power," Dreamless broke in. "It is forbidden in my land. Blood magic is worse than all others. Secret magic, pacts and deals, all of those can be done in good faith, if the magicians so choose. But blood magic always has a cost, and that cost is never willing."

"But it's a hell of a shortcut," Natasha said. "And I say that as someone who knows the best place to literally buy power."

Jane rubbed her eyes irritably.

"If he's a blood… magician? What does he want with Lady Dreamless?" she asked.

"I'm curious about that myself," Dreamless said.

"He's consolidating power for some idiotic reason," Natasha said. "And you, darling, are power incarnate."

"What exactly does *that* mean?" Bedlam said, folding her

arms across her chest.

"Dream magic is rare and incredibly powerful," Dreamless said.

Titus found himself instantly drawn in by her voice in a way he hadn't been before. It wasn't a spell, not in the way he'd begun to think of them; it was more of a natural effect, something about her voice itself, her presence, that filled his heart with wonder, even longing. I could get pulled into dangerous water by that voice, he thought.

"Dream magic can alter reality. Change the past and present. It literally makes real that which you dream in your mind," Dreamless continued. "But he couldn't take it from me. Not even in this inhibited form."

"Inhibited form?" Kate said, returning to the conversation finally. She did not make eye contact with Titus and there was no doubt in his mind that was on purpose.

"While Lady Dreamless is here in your world, she inhabits a body, a form that she asked me to create for her," Natasha said. "Her power is tied very much to the Dreamless Lands. She couldn't come here in her true state without someone noticing."

"Could this King Tears want to somehow… sacrifice that body or something?" Titus said.

"I think it's simpler than that," Natasha said. "He wants a power he could control. And having the Queen of the Dreamless Lands trapped and in his service…"

"I would sooner die," Dreamless said. "I've been enslaved once. I will not be again."

"Well, I have some good news about that," Natasha said.

"Great," Jane said. "Always with the good news."

"Something followed you through, my dear," Natasha said. "And our necromancer thinks it might be an easier target than you."

"I won't have him controlling dream magic," Dreamless said.

"Glad we're all on the same page," Jane said. "The question is, what are we going to do about it?'

CHAPTER 31:
I'VE HAD BETTER INTERNSHIPS

Keppler had no idea why King Tears ordered him to meet him in an old, long-unused warehouse in the City. It was among the various properties the Children of the Elder Star had ownership of all across the City—all across the world, really—but why it held any sort of importance, he couldn't fathom.

He hired a car, despite King Tears telling him the zombies were perfectly capable of driving him over, and stepped out in a neighborhood where he was earnestly concerned that his expensive shoes and fitted dress pants would make him a target for a mugging. A homeless man asked him for money. Keppler ignored him and he entered the warehouse.

Until recently, he would not have instantly recognized the wretched stink of old blood and opened guts, but they were familiar to him now, and he recognized them immediately. He walked with trepidation down the long corridor within the warehouse entrance and into an open space beyond.

The carnage he found there took his breath away.

A great mound of flesh had been torn asunder, limbs tossed about, innards discarded on the flood like party favors. He nearly stepped on an eyeball. Keppler began to wretch, running to a darkened corner of the foyer to empty the contents of his stomach on the ground.

"You get used to it," King Tears said, previously unseen in the shadows. The magician's white tattoos glowed in the darkness.

"What happened here?" Keppler squealed, voice cracking as he wiped vomit from the corners of his mouth.

"Someone killed my experiment," King Tears said. "Violently, apparently. These are claw marks if I'm not mistaken. I am not having a wonderful day."

"What was this?" Keppler said, struggling to not return to puking his guts out.

"What might have been a useful, dumb, powerful weapon," King Tears said. "No great loss in the end. I can always find more urchins to stitch together. Still, a waste of resources and time."

"I don't understand," Keppler said.

"That's because you're a simple tool in the service of your betters," King Tears said. "Speaking of service, tell me you found what I asked you to seek out."

Keppler nodded, cracking a briefcase he'd carried in.

"I'm almost afraid to ask what you need these for," Keppler said. "Although if I'm being honest, I'm afraid to ask why my employers had these in a vault in the first place."

"Your employers liked torture, enslavement, and greed," King Tears said, lifting a barbed whip from the briefcase. "I wish I had this in Manhattan. Not your fault, of course. I got impatient. I should have waited."

"What happened in New York?" Keppler asked.

"Complications," King Tears said. "Did you bring those files I asked you to bring me when I called as well?"

"Those were easier to find than the… stuff in that briefcase," Keppler said, handing King Tears a manila envelope. Tears tore the envelope open and began to peruse.

"Solar-powered messiah. Alien host. Mortal with a death wish. Ah, a werewolf. I wonder if he's the cause of this mess here. Sentient gravitational anomaly? That's a curious one."

"They caused problems for our organization a few years back," Keppler said. "We've apparently been keeping tabs on them ever since. And then they were involved in that… embarrassing incident."

"When half your board of directors tried to sell out the planet? The greed and stupidity of rich men, I swear to all the gods in heaven and hell, I will never understand why men like that continue to remain in power throughout history," King Tears said. "Humanity always rewards morons who say the right thing."

"Anyway," Keppler said nervously. "Our files haven't been updated since the invasion, but they were pretty extensive up until then."

"This will be helpful. Thank you, Mr. Keppler," King Tears said, gesturing with the envelope. "It defies reason why Doc Silence would waste his time being a glorified high school teacher. The man was a world class magician. Probably the strongest white magic practitioner in a century. And instead he's wasting his time training freaks and lunatics."

"I… if I may," Keppler said.

King Tears raised an eyebrow curiously.

"Yes?"

"The freaks in that envelope stopped an alien invasion. Maybe they're not… I'm sorry, but maybe underestimating them isn't the preferred course of action?"

King Tears stared blankly at Keppler for a moment, and the young executive thought he was about to be eviscerated. Instead, the magician laughed.

"You know, my boy, you might be worth keeping around yet," he said. "You're not wrong. Every tool has its uses. Maybe Silence was onto something."

Keppler tried to let the magician's laughter lessen his stress levels, but it still felt like his stomach acid was eating through the lining.

"What do we do next?" he asked.

"Well, the dream queen knows I'm looking for her, so she may be more problematic to lock down now than before," King Tears said. "Again, that was my fault. Rush to action. I should've known better. But fortunately, there's a secondary acquisition we can focus on."

"A what?"

"Someone was foolish enough to open a door between the Dreamless Lands and our world, and something slipped through," King Tears said. "I want it."

"How do we make that happen?" Keppler asked.

"I have an assignment for you," King Tears said. "I need you to scour current events. Find me the weirdest thing happening out there in the world right now. Whatever that is, I'd put money on it being where our next target is."

"That's easy," Keppler said. "An entire town disappeared out in California."

"Excuse me?" King Tears said, immediately intrigued.

"Yeah. Gone," Keppler said. "People, buildings, streets, everything disappeared."

King Tears contemplated this new information for a minute, scratching at his five o'clock shadow.

"Well then," he said. "I guess we're going to California."

"We?" Keppler said.

"There were some vaults in the Los Angeles office I didn't have time to unlock," King Tears said. "And some bodies you could help me identify while we're there."

Keppler's stomach knotted up inside, churning and roiling with stress.

"Whatever you say, boss," he said.

CHAPTER 32:
THE QUEEN AND THE WIZARD

Doc Silence traced the edge of his cell, making arcane gestures in the air, often leaving glowing traces of light behind. He muttered to himself occasionally, tilting his head to listen to voices only he could hear.

Gloomly, barely visible in the darkness of the dungeon, sat in an almost comically human fashion, leaning against the wall.

"I thought you said you were going to call for help," the shadow-man said.

"I will," Doc said. "But I need to know more about this world that's been constructed before I ask my team to come in here and risk their lives."

"I've watched you for several hours walking around in circles talking to yourself," Gloomly said. I don't know how much you can learn about the world from that."

"I'm pulling at the threads of magic," Doc said. "Not enough to destabilize the world. Just enough to… get its pulse. Or see how it's knit together. I'm getting a better idea of how it came to be."

The shadow leaned in, eyes eerily bright.

"And what have you learned?" Gloomly said. "Honest question. My friends and I were barely corporeal less than a week ago, and now the bear carries a longsword."

"Which is adorable," Doc said.

"Which is alarming," the shadow said. "The others were toys before this happened, magician. I was something else. I understood my place a little more. But this… I know I should be grateful for the life breathed into me, but I know it's not right."

"Very little in magic is right or wrong," Doc said. He waved a hand in front of him, and a few feet lit up in every direction, lines and sigils and wrinkles in reality. "These are the veins of the world."

"I don't follow."

"Something holds every world together. Science, usually, even the weirder ones," Doc said. "But this world was created wholesale. It didn't exist until Alice willed it into existence."

"Like us," Gloomly said.

"Like you," Doc repeated. "It's woven from dream magic, which is generally unstable. Dream magic is incredibly powerful, but it's fleeting. It doesn't want to last. It wants very much to evoke emotion, and then be forgotten."

"So this place shouldn't exist much longer?"

"No, that's not it," Doc said. "It's very firmly held together. I can see it in the construction. It's not pretty, or elegant— elegant isn't what dream magic does, it's more abstract art than geometry—but there is a powerful will holding it all together, and a powerful magician ensuring it remains as real as any other world."

"Alice," Gloomly said.

"That would be my guess," Doc said. "How she got access

to dream magic I haven't quite figured out yet, though I have my suspicions. But Alice is a staggeringly powerful natural magician. She has an innate ability most magicians I've met would give their left arm for."

"She's a very powerful magician, and then someone taught her dream magic, and those two things made this world?" Gloomly said.

"Working on a hypothesis on that," Doc said. Her innate ability is how she brought you and your friends to life. That wasn't dream magic. All of you are far too… forgive the term, but you're too real to be dream magic."

The shadow-man somehow, despite being made of ethereal dark matter, shot Doc a sarcastic look.

"I'm not sure if that's an insult or a compliment."

"Neither. Just a statement of fact," Doc said.

"So we're real," Gloomly said. "You're real."

"The town is real," Doc said. "The castle is not."

"The town is real?"

"Yes," Doc said. "She literally transported her world with her when she made this place. Up and transplanted her entire town, buildings, people, dogs and cats, the whole thing, right there. There's a blank space in the real world where it should be."

"Is that impressive, or is that scary?" the shadow-man said.

"Both," Doc said. "She shouldn't be able to do that. I can't do that alone. But I think that's where the dream magic comes into play. She had help."

"The Vizier," Gloomly said.

Doc nodded.

"Exactly."

"We knew there was something wrong about him," Gloomly said.

"Your instincts were…" Doc trailed off, then held up a hand. "Company. You should hide."

"Hiding is literally my natural state. I'm a shadow."

"Well, do your thing. Don't get spotted."

Gloomly melted into the darkest recesses of the cell, even his glowing eyes disappearing from view. Doc sat down lotus position in the center of the cell and waited, listening to the sound of metal armor clanking, and something else, a softer, lighter footfall.

A pair of faceless guards appeared at his cell door, eyes barely visible beneath their metal masks. They stood in silence for a moment before a third figure appeared, shorter, smaller, dressed in an impractically ornate dress of deep red.

"You're our prisoner," Queen Alice said.

Doc fought the urge to smile. Alice carried herself as one playing royalty, her shoulders back, neck tall, chin just slightly upturned. She wore goth-y black eye makeup and crimson lipstick as if to hide her age or identity, but her eyes, despite the regalia, the dark hair pulled back severely, the spikey tiara upon her brow, were those of a child.

"I am, your majesty," Doc said, remaining seated.

"It's customary to kneel before the queen, outlander," one of the guards said in a gruff voice, but Alice held up a hand, silencing him.

"You're not from here," she said.

"I'm not," Doc said. "But neither are you."

"Insolent dog," the other guard muttered, but again, Alice waved him off.

"I belong here," she said. "I made this world."

"That you did," Doc said. "But you left a world behind when you built this place."

"I don't like that world," she said. "It's lonely and cruel."

"I'm honestly not particularly proud of it myself," Doc said. "But it's ours, and it's the only one most of us really ever get, so we have to make the most of it."

"My Vizier says you're dangerous," Alice said.

Doc smiled warmly.

"Not to you. Nor this place you've built," Doc said. "I'm here to bring a message to you from home."

"Don't call it that."

"My apologies," Doc said. "But your mother misses you. And your father is going to be okay."

"My father," Alice said, her voice trailing off. "Something happened to him."

"He had a heart attack, but the doctors were able to help him," Doc said.

"My mother wasn't there," Alice said.

"And she is sorry for that," Doc said. "I spoke with her. She just wants to know you're okay."

Alice pursed her lips, eyebrows furrowing.

"I don't know if I believe you," she said.

"That's understandable. I'm a stranger to you."

"Any you're a wizard," Alice said. She leaned closer to the bars of the cell, her guards visibly tensing.

"I am," Doc said. "And you are, too. I should have found you sooner, Alice. I'm sorry for that. I could have helped you more. I didn't realize how far along you were."

"I have help," Alice said. "I don't need a teacher."

"My queen," a familiar voice said loudly from the hall. A few heavy footfalls later, the Vizier emerged into view. "I wondered where you got off to."

"We've never had a prisoner before," Alice said. "I wanted to see him."

The Vizier gave Doc a dark, malignant stare.

"Pay him no mind," he said. "That's why you have me, your highness. Let me take care of messy things like prisoners."

Alice nodded passively, allowing herself to be led away. Doc didn't miss her turn her eyes to him one last time though, a hard, assessing stare falling upon him before she disappeared.

Once their footfalls faded, Doc sighed.

"You can come out now," he said.

Gloomly did not emerge from hiding, though his eyes opened up, two glowing spots in the darkness.

"She's not well," he said.

"I can't tell if she's mystically charmed or just tricked, but neither is good," Doc said. "We're going to have to get her away from that creature, whatever it is."

"The Vizier isn't a figment like me?" Gloomly said.

"No, he's something else entirely," Doc said. "You should go warn your friends. You can leave here unseen?"

"Have I not already told you my natural state is hiding? And the spell trapping you here seems to require a physical body to restrain."

"I know, I know," Doc said. "You get going. And keep an eye out for my allies. They'll need your guidance when they get here."

"How will I know it's them?" Gloomly said.

"Trust me," Doc said. The minute you meet them, there'll be no mistake."

CHAPTER 33: MIRROR, MIRROR

Jane watched the others as they spread out across Kate's hideout, sometimes brainstorming about their next step, sometimes just killing time. Billy was having a quiet conversation with Bedlam near the windows. They were both smiling, which Jane was glad to see. She was pulling for those two to figure things out. Titus, unexpectedly, engaged in a brief conversation with Natasha, something that made everyone more than a little uncomfortable, Kate glaring particularly hard at that situation. Not that she wasn't glaring at everyone, including Emily as she bubble-of-floated herself lazily around the ceiling.

Titus broke away from his chat to join Jane by the kitchenette.

"We should consider trying to figure out who King Tears' next target is," he said. "Might help us get ahead of him."

"Yeah," Jane said. "Anything useful from Lady Grey?"

"I think she's offering to train me a bit," Titus said.

"And are you going to take her up on that?"

"I'm thinking no," Titus said. "Between Leto and Doc, I think I've got some good teachers who would not be looking for a way to sell my werewolf soul to a demon lord of the Nine Hells or something."

"Are there nine hells?" Jane asked.

"I don't know," Titus said. "It's an expression. I can't remember if it's something Doc said or if it's something I read playing Dungeons and Dragons."

"Emily would know," Jane said.

"Emily would know what?" Emily yelled from the ceiling.

"Nothing," Jane and Titus said simultaneously.

"Whatever," Emily said, drifting away.

"Speaking of Doc," Titus said. "Any word?"

"None," Jane said. "He can reach me though. If he's alive."

"You don't say that with a level of reassuring confidence," Titus said.

Jane shrugged.

"He does what he does," she said.

Kate strode over, stretching out her back and shoulders as she walked.

"We've got to do something," she said. "I don't care what it is. I can't sit here waiting around for some monster attack. Titus, we can go hunting more of those Children of the Elder Star properties. See if we shake anything up."

"I feel like splitting the team right now is dangerous," Jane said.

"We've got the numbers," Billy said, butting in.

"I'm with the Dancer," Bedlam said. "There's gotta be something we can hit."

"I didn't say it that way," Kate said.

"But it was implied, Swan Lake," Bedlam said. "I can tell what you're thinking. You want to punch something. I'm right there with you."

Kate stared, but didn't deny the accusation.

"I suppose we wait for…" Jane said, before trailing off as a muffled voice emanated from her pocket.

"Did you butt-dial someone?" Billy said.

"Nobody butt-dials anyone anymore," Emily said. "What are you, thirty? Butt-dialing is for old people."

"Stop," Jane said, wrestling the mirror Doc gave her from her pocket. She opened the protective cover to find Doc looking back at her, somewhere very dark.

"Good," he said. "You're there."

"Where else would I be?" Jane said.

"Is that a mirror phone?" Emily said, dropping from the ceiling to look obtrusively over Jane's shoulder.

Curious, both Dreamless and Natasha approached to listen in. Kate shot them both a killer glare. Neither got too close, but still stood near enough to listen.

"Well, I'm glad we established a backup plan," Doc said.

"That looks like a dungeon," Billy said.

"Doc, are you in a dungeon?" Emily asked.

"Yes, I'm in a dungeon," Doc said. "I think I'm going to need backup. I found our missing magical savant, but there's an entity here manipulating her. He… it? Seems familiar. Very skilled in dream magic, which makes me wonder if…"

"My passenger," Lady Dreamless said.

"Who's that?" Doc asked.

Jane sighed.

"That's the other reason I'm glad you called," Jane said. "Do you know someone called Lady Dreamless?"

Doc took off his glasses and rubbed the bridge of his nose.

"I'm just going to assume Natasha Grey had something to do with this."

Natasha shook her head at Jane. Jane, smirking, turned the mirror around so Doc could look right at her.

"Hi, Silence," she said.

"Hello, Natasha," he replied. "Couldn't just enjoy the trip back from the Dreamless Lands? Had to go wheeling and dealing?"

"I needed to pay my way, darling," she said. "It was your dream queen over here who requested the deal."

Jane turned the mirror to face Dreamless next.

"I just wanted to see your world for a little while, Doctor," she said. "I was curious."

Doc exhaled heavily.

"We'll deal with all of that when I get back. You said something about a passenger?"

"Something slipped through from the Dreamless Lands when I made my journey," the queen said. "My senses are different here. I didn't know."

"Well, I'm going to hazard a wild guess that I know where it is, even if we don't know what it is," Doc said. "Why are you both there? Where are you, anyway?"

Jane turned the mirror back to herself. Emily stuck her head into the frame and waved hello. Doc nonchalantly waved back.

"We ran into a complication," Jane said.

Billy stuck his head into view next.

"A guy who can make zombies," he said.

"And flesh golems," Titus said, loud enough for Doc to hear him but not bothering to get in front of the mirror.

"King Tears is making a play in the power vacuum left by the Children of the Elder Star, darling," Natasha said.

"Tears? I hate that guy."

"Everyone hates that guy," Natasha said.

"Okay, you know what? We'll deal with King Tears after we get Westwick back on Earth," Doc said. "Jane, you'll have to go where the town disappeared and use the planar knife to open a gateway like we discussed."

Natasha shuddered.

"I will never trust one of those again after what you did," she said.

"Who should come over?" Jane said.

"Everyone," Doc said. "Alice Lapine is incredibly powerful. She's able to create constructs to act as soldiers and guards. Anything that looks like it walked out of a Renaissance Faire is not alive."

"So we can hit those guys," Bedlam said.

"Yes, you can hit those guys," Doc said. "Hi, Bedlam."

"Hey," she replied.

"Anything we shouldn't hit?" Kate said.

"Anyone who looks like they're from the town itself," Doc said. "Alice basically picked up and moved all of Westwick, including its residents. And this place is infected with nightmare energy. Lots of scared people who don't understand what's happening."

"Don't hit people in blue jeans. Hit people in pantaloons," Kate said. "Got it."

"Also if you see an armored teddy bear riding on a unicorn with a pixie, they're on your side."

The entire room went silent for what felt like an eternity.

"You okay, Doc? Get hit on the head?" Billy said.

"Just… y'know, just trust me on that one," Doc said.

"Teddy bear, unicorn, pixie," Billy said. "Keen."

"Anything else we should know before we head in there, Doc?" Titus asked.

Doc nodded slowly.

"This place is powered on dreams, and nightmares," Doc said. "Be prepared for strangeness. If something doesn't feel right, it probably isn't."

CHAPTER 34: QUESTIONING AUTHORITY

Alice Lapine sat on her throne, adorned in a regal red dress, and pondered pensively.

She felt as though something wasn't quite right in her kingdom, but she couldn't put her finger on it. At first she thought perhaps the land needed some readjusting, so she called for a map of her lands and, tracing a finger over different geographical areas, created mountains and forests, a massive, placid lake in the shape of a footprint to the north. She could see the horizon from her throne room, and it wasn't hard to spot the new mountain range rising up from the earth in the distance like teeth.

But creating new places in her realm did not lift the weight in her heart, or the itch at the back of her mind.

The Vizier happened upon her during this mood, as he so often did, knowing just when she most needed his advice. He took a knee below the dais where her throne stood, but she waved off the formality.

"You look worried, my queen," he said, eyes twinkling.

"That man in our dungeon," Alice said. "Who is he?"

"Just a trespasser, your highness. Nothing to be concerned about."

"Are you sure?"

The Vizier carefully approached, slowly and respectfully climbing the stairs to join her.

"He's very lost, and should not be here,' he said softly. "Let me worry about him. I'll keep your kingdom safe. It's why you have me here, is it not?'

"Thank you, Vizier," she said, feeling a bit fuzzy headed, as if she had a cold coming on. "I don't know what I'd do without you."

"I live to serve," the man said, smiling warmly.

Alice scrunched up her nose, squinting in thought, then turned to him.

"He said something about my mother," she said.

"Perhaps you misheard him," the Vizier said.

"No," she said. "He definitely said something about my mother."

"That troubles you?"

"I'm having trouble remembering my mother," Alice said.

"Perhaps that's for the best," the Vizier said. "The mind thankfully hides bad memories."

"Should I have bad memories of my mother?" Alice said.

"I don't know," the Vizier said. "I'm afraid we never met."

Alice nodded, sitting back calmly on her throne. But in her mind, her thoughts raced, scrambling to find some semblance of a memory, something to latch onto that might tell her who her mother was.

She remembered something else, though, just a glimmer, a passing thought. A man, the sight of whom made her heart swell, falling over, clutching his chest. Right lights flashing.

Men and women wearing rubber gloves leaping to help.

"Did you ever meet my father?" Alice asked.

"I'm afraid I did not," the Vizier said. "He passed away before I came to court, sadly."

"Yes," Alice said, hesitation in her tone. "Sadly. I think you might have liked him."

"I'm sure I would have, your highness."

Alice stared dazedly at the guards who stood at the ready throughout the throne room, finding herself almost hypnotized by the echoing emptiness of the hall.

"There's so many things I don't remember, Vizier," she said. "I don't like it."

"It's the cost of your great magic, my queen," The Vizier said reassuringly. "The power alters your memories, erases things. This is your burden to bear, but it enables you to keep your entire kingdom safe."

"Is this also why I can't leave the palace?"" she asked.

"Sadly, yes," the Vizier said. "This palace is protected against a great many evils that wish to do you harm. You're safe here, but we can't protect you out in the world."

"Maybe someday I can leave?"

"Of course," the Vizier said. "It is your kingdom after all. You should walk through it someday."

Alice nodded. The Vizier bowed, and began walking down the steps away from her.

"What will happen to the man in the dungeon?" she asked, trying to mask the intensity of her curiosity.

"Let me worry about that," the Vizier said. "After all, only you have the power to build the rest of your kingdom. Leave the mundane tasks like prisoners to someone who cannot shape the world as you do."

The Vizier left Alice to look over maps and raise more

mountains. But she did not set out to work just yet. Instead, she kept turning the stranger's words over and over in her mind.

Your mother misses you. And your father is going to be okay.

CHAPTER 35:
THE WEIGHT OF THINGS

Entropy Emily was not inclined to being intimidated. Certainly not scared. She wasn't even particularly inclined to worry about things, if she was being honest.

But for some reason, standing in front of the wide-open space where Westwick, California once stood, she was all of the above.

"I think I'm going to throw up," Emily said. And meant it.

"You don't look so good, kid," Bedlam said. "You need some water or something?"

"No, I'm just… do any of you guys feel that?" Emily said.

"Feel what?" Bedlam said.

"Maybe Dude is picking up on something," Emily said, rubbing her temples. "Hey Billy?"

"What I don't understand is why you had spare costumes for all of us in your apartment," she heard Billy saying to Kate, ignoring Emily's call for attention. Natasha and Dreamless hung back away from the group, talking softly and ignoring the bickering young heroes.

"Why wouldn't I have your gear," Kate said.

"Because that meant you stole our clothes and kept them in your murder room," Billy said.

"There was always a chance you would need your costumes in an emergency," Kate said. "Our base crashed on the other side of the world. You can't just fly up to the Tower to get your pants. I plan for all contingencies."

"You had my costume in your closet," Billy said.

"You're just upset she handled your leotard," Titus said.

"You," Billy said, pointing at Titus, who was hanging back, leaning casually on that weird spear the other werewolves had given him so long ago. "You were in on this."

"I had no idea she took one of your leotards," Titus said. "I mean she has some of my alien-technology werewolf yoga pants and I'm not upset."

"You're a thing," Billy said. "It's not a bad idea for you to have spare pants at her place. Meanwhile, Assassin's Creed over here just has my suit and Jane's cape and skirt hanging in a closet."

"Which I'm happy about, by the way, so I don't have to go into an alternate dimension wearing khaki shorts and Chucks," Jane said. "Glad you thought ahead, Kate."

Kate gestured to Jane as if to say, "I rest my case."

"A reasonable person appreciates this sort of thing," Kate said.

"Billy, you're just mad because you have your suit but you don't have the right underwear to go with it and now you're all bunched up and you think your butt looks bad," Emily said with a little more anger in her voice than intended.

"Well, now I can't stop looking at how bunched up his shorts are under his spandex," Bedlam said, fighting off a laugh.

"Someday, I will get through a twenty-four-hour period with dignity," Billy said.

Emily rubbed her eyes until she saw stars in her vision.

"You okay, Em?" Billy said, all sarcasm gone from his voice.

"This place feels wrong," Emily said. "I think it's setting off something with my powers. Can you use your Dude-powers and see if there's like, a weird magnetic field or something?"

Emily felt Bedlam's hand rest on her shoulder to steady her, which she found shockingly reassuring. She looked over to the cyborg.

"Thanks," she said.

"No problem, kid," Bedlam said.

"What do you mean it's setting something off in your powers?" Jane asked, her tone deadly serious. Of course she's freaked out, Emily thought. We were together when my powers nearly destroyed the alternate timeline we saved a while back. She knows better than anyone what my stuff can do if it gets out of whack.

"I… okay, my powers are all gravity-based, really," Emily said. "And I'm used to being able to… I can feel the weight of things. Does that make sense? I always have this sense of how everything is placed in the world around me. It's like sonar, I guess."

"You've never mentioned this before," Kate said.

"It's a useless power," Emily said. "More like a side effect. It doesn't do anything, y'know? Except right now, that…"

She pointed out at the miles of open space where Westwick once stood.

"That is not anything like what it's supposed to be. And it's not just gone, or empty," Emily said. "Empty doesn't bother me. It's almost like something wants to be there but can't."

"We gotta fix this town," Titus said. "This is so bad."

"Are you going to be okay?" Jane asked.

"I feel like I'm going to projectile vomit, but if you guys can stay down wind of me I think we'll be fine," Emily said.

"Maybe it's an inner ear thing," Titus said.

"I work with gravity," Emily said. "If I have an inner ear thing, my career is over, dude."

"Are you okay to come with us?" Jane asked.

Emily nodded vigorously.

"If anything, I think I'll be better if we go to the other side," Emily said. "Let's do this thing."

"Okay," Jane said, producing the planar knife Doc had given her.

Natasha and Dreamless rejoined the group.

"Have you decided if you're coming with us?" Jane asked as the sorceress approached.

"I think I'll stay here and monitor what King Tears is up to," Natasha said. "There's a good chance he'll come looking for me, and I should be around just in case. He thinks I'm retired, so I wouldn't be dimension-hopping."

"What about you, Lady Dreamless?" Titus asked.

The strange woman tilted her head at the werewolf curiously.

"I would like to see this pocket dimension," she said. "But I worry that whatever entity you hunt will know I'm there the moment I arrive. I should like to give you time to search before I enter. Maybe by then my presence will be a beneficial distraction."

"I only have one knife," Jane said.

Natasha exhaled loudly.

"I don't usually like to give away trade secrets like this, but, as they say, desperate times call for desperate measures," she said. "Doc Silence stole that planar knife from my collection. I have several more. I can open another portal later. How much of a head start would you like, darling?"

"Twelve hours," Kate said bluntly.

"That is very specific," Billy said.

"No, it works," Titus said. "It's a town, right? That gives us time to explore, get the lay of the land, and then if we haven't found the creature by then, maybe Lady Dreamless arriving will, as she said, flush it out into the open."

"Twelve hours it is," Natasha said. "For now, I'll transport us somewhere less conspicuous. Good luck, moppets."

Natasha Grey made a quick gesture in the air, muttered a few arcane words, and vanished from sight, Lady Dreamless in tow.

Emily caught Titus moving his hand at his side, as if mimicking the gesture the sorceress had made.

"What are you doing over there, Chewie?" Emily said.

"Nothing," Titus said irritably.

Emily caught Kate's death glare—directed at Titus, not at her—and let the conversation drop.

"Okay," Jane said, brandishing planar knife. It was dagger-like, but the shape of the blade, the thinness of it, reminded Emily of a straight razor. "I'm going to, um, cut a hole in reality. Don't waste any time. Jump right through. I'm not sure how long it stays open."

"You guys bring me to the best places," Bedlam said. "My first interdimensional field trip! I'm so excited."

"On three," Jane said.

"One," Emily said.

"Two," Billy said.

"Three," Jane said, slashing downward through the open air. The blade left a glowing tear in reality, an eerie reddish-gold light leaking through.

Emily linked arms with Bedlam and together, they ran through the tear.

And then they were gone.

CHAPTER 36:
GATHER OUR ARMY

Andrew Keppler looked out the window as the rental car up to where Westwick, California used to be and whistled in shock. The government had been keeping information about the missing town under wraps to prevent panic, but even with the Children of the Elder Star mostly defunct, the organization had insider information only large piles of money could access, so he'd seen some footage not wildly available. In person, it was a thousand times more terrifying.

"The whole place is gone," he said.

King Tears sat next to him in the back of the rental, eyes hidden behind heavy sunglasses. He said nothing, staring passively out the window, until they parked. He got out without a word and walked directly up to the perfectly straight line where the street leading into town ended, as if cut with scissors.

"This is fascinating," he said, tracing the empty space with long, tattooed fingers.

Keppler rushed to catch up to him, grimacing at the dust

kicking up and sticking to his expensive shoes.

"Is it really gone? Or is it, like, an illusion or something?"

"Oh, it's gone," King Tears said. As he touched the blank space on where the town once began, Keppler could see strange symbols he'd come to understand were mystic runes glitter and disappear. "But nothing is ever completely gone. I'm reading its ghost."

King Tears stepped off the road and into the dusty earth where Westwick had been, walking barefoot through the dirt, grime clinging to his dark dress pants. Keppler begrudgingly followed.

"Someone opened up a doorway back there," King Tears said. "There's a scar in the astral plane. We won't be the first to go through to the other side."

"Go through to… we?" Keppler said.

"You didn't think I'd leave my favorite colleague behind while I traveled into the great unknown, did you?" King Tears said. He seemed to be following a path in the dirt, almost as if he could still see streets and sidewalks.

"I… I mean it's just that I don't know how much help I can be," Keppler said. "I'm just a mid-level executive, not a magician."

"While I agree there's almost nothing as useless as a mid-level executive, you've become a little bit more than that," King Tears said. He grinned at Keppler wickedly. "After all, there's no one above you anymore. That makes you upper management. And everyone knows those are the guys who cash out the best."

"I'm not sure I like 'cash out' in this context," Keppler said.

King Tears ignored him, continuing his journey deeper into the emptiness. Finally, he stopped and held out his hands to either side, again making strange gestures Keppler knew were part of a spell.

"What are you doing?" he asked.

"Every town has a graveyard," King Tears said. "If I'm going to the other side, I need to know if there are soldiers I can raise up from the dead. It appears when this town disappeared, it took everything with it, including graveyards and underground plumbing. The teleportation spell was exceedingly thorough."

"You're going to raise peoples' grandparents from the dead to fight for you?"

"It's not nearly as thrilling as it sounds," King Tears said. "Necromancy is a bit boring, to be honest. I prefer flesh sculpting."

"Like what you were doing with the test subjects back in the City," Keppler said.

"Exactly," King Tears responded. "Zombies are fine for basic tasks, but if you can create a real weapon, a true monster, one that can think and act independently, well, that's a far more useful tool in a battle."

Keppler stopped in his tracks.

"That's what that thing was? The pile of bodies in the warehouse? It was a weapon?"

"It was the start of one. Clearly it wasn't particularly useful yet. The boy we allowed to escape into the homeless community though, he was a work of art," King Tears said.

Keppler's stomach roiled. He'd worked for the Children of the Elder Star since college, offered an internship by a friendly recruiter, groomed for management in their cult-like structure. He knew much of what they did. Somehow, he'd always compartmentalized the Children's research and development departments—he had nothing to do with those brain-dead teenagers they were experimenting on, so he could collect his paycheck and not worry. He liaised between finance and marketing. He worked in budgets. He never had to get his hands dirty. It never felt any worse than, say, working for a hedge fund in his mind.

And now his new boss was talking about raising the dead and mutating test subjects as though this were the simplest thing in the world.

King Tears began walking back to the car, and Keppler again hustled to follow him.

"Are we going right now?" Keppler asked.

"Of course not," Tears said. "I want you to make arrangements to have several of our most functional mutations shipped here. We'll want to bring a show of force. Bring me a list of our inventory. I'll help assess which ones will be most suitable for the task."

"Sure," Keppler said, trying to keep the distaste out of his voice.

"I'm beginning to enjoy delegation," King Tears mused.

It occurred to Keppler, in that moment, that he'd been delegated to since he was nineteen. These are things they don't warn you about in business school, he thought.

"I assume the Children have ways of shipping live cargo quickly and efficiently?" King Tears said. "Well, live-ish."

"Those channels are still available," Keppler said flatly.

"Good. Make it happen," King Tears said. He had a disconcerting glee in his voice. He's looking forward to this, Keppler thought. Morbid old man.

"I'll get a list drawn up," Keppler said as they returned to the car. He watched the empty space behind them disappear in the distance as they drove away, feeling vaguely like it might be a metaphor for his own life.

***

Neither King Tears nor Andrew Keppler noticed an unassuming, unmarked car parked just off the road nearby. They failed to see the high-tech binoculars watching them, or the old man with a silver mustache and light brown fedora observing them as they came and went.

Sam Barren leaned back in his seat as they drove away, took off his hat, and scratched his thinning hair absently. Doc had warned him to keep an eye on the site, not just for gawkers—regular law enforcement could keep them away—but for the sort of super-powered vultures who would want a look at this sort of event to find a way to take advantage of it. Watching a man with gray skin covered in mystic tattoos walk barefoot through the town like he was dowsing for water definitely lined up with the sort of weirdos Doc had warned him about.

Sam looked at his cell phone with resignation. Doc was unreachable, of course on the other side of the veil, but he'd told him who to call if anyone like this showed up. Sam wasn't particularly happy about it, but any port in a storm, as they say.

He dialed the number Doc left him and tried to keep the annoyance out of his voice. The call went to voicemail, which ruined Sam's mood even more. Sam hated voicemail.

"Lady Natasha Grey, I was given this number by Doc Silence," Sam said. "He said you want to know if anyone showed up in Westwick…"

CHAPTER 37:
AN UNFAIR RANGE OF
EMOTIONAL ABUSE

Titus was the last one through the portal, emerging to find the others standing around taking in their surroundings.

"Well, it's a town," Emily said, still arm in arm with Bedlam.

"Why is everything so red?" Bedlam said.

She wasn't wrong, Titus thought. The sky had a reddish hue to it, bathing the entire town in a sort of perpetual ruddy sunset. The town itself, rows of simple suburban houses in bright colors spread out before them along faded streets, a small downtown area in the distance. Behind them and ringing the town was a deep forest. The forest made the wilder part of Titus' nature anxious, as if the wolf inside knew those trees weren't real. Beyond the trees, mountain ranges in deep purple jutted up like trees. And on the far side of the town: a castle. It looks like someone built it out of blocks, Titus thought, watching as bright crimson flags danced on the wind.

"Red sky in morning, sailors take warning," Emily said. "Red sky at night, sailors delight. Which one is it?"

"Why are there no people?" Jane asked.

Kate brushed by her and approached the nearest house. Titus followed her. Inside, they saw a woman staring into a mirror. There was nothing wrong with her face, but reflected in the mirror, tiny worms wriggled beneath her skin. The woman touched her cheeks with a look of silent terror.

"Nightmares," Kate said to Titus. He nodded.

"You guys don't want to look at what's happening in this one," Billy said loudly from outside the neighboring house.

"I want to see," Emily said.

Bedlam joined Billy at the window, took one look inside, then turned right back around and walked away.

"No, no, absolutely not, you do not want to look in there," she said.

"Why not?" Emily said, pushing past the cyborg.

"Oh," Emily said. "Oh, that's why."

"Did I not tell you?" Bedlam said.

"Look, we're still figuring out our friendship," Emily said. "I now know that we have a similar level of 'don't look at that.'"

"Well, listen next time," Bedlam said.

"They're not all bad," Jane said, standing by a third window. Titus joined her and looked inside. An entire family was celebrating Christmas, opening gifts, drinking cocoa, singing carols.

"Well that's curious," Titus said. "I wonder how it's determined if they should get a dream or a nightmare."

"Either way it seems like the use of dream images is controlling the population," Kate said. "Clearly it's a pacifying device."

"One family gets Christmas morning, while someone else gets maggots crawling under her skin," Titus said. "That's a pretty unfair range of emotional abuse."

"Do your powers work here?" Kate asked.

Jane held out her hand palm up. A swirl of flame appeared instantly.

"Looks like mine do," she said.

"Dude's talking my ear off," Billy said. "I'm assuming that's a good sign."

Billy started to float into the air slowly. He looked down at his feet, then at Emily.

"Em," he said. He immediately dropped the six or so inches to the ground, landing on his feet awkwardly.

"My stuff works," Emily said.

"Okay then," Jane said. "We're not helpless here. Where do we go next?"

Titus pointed to the castle with the tip of his spear.

"I'm just taking an educated guess, but…" he said.

"That looks like a clue to me," Bedlam said.

"Do you want me to scout ahead?" Billy asked.

Jane shook her head.

"I have a feeling we should probably be a little stealthy," she said. "You and I draw a lot of attention to ourselves when we're airborne."

"Have I mentioned how much I hate walking ever since I learned to fly?" Billy said.

"Are you seriously going to whine about walking a few miles?" Bedlam said, punching Billy in the shoulder playfully.

They all began to walk toward the downtown when Titus cocked his head and looked back to the forest.

"Did you guys hear that?" he asked.

"Did Timmy fall down a well?" Emily said.

"That joke never gets less offensive," Titus said. "I'm serious. I hear someone calling for help."

He changed direction to walk toward the nearest outcropping of trees. There is definitely someone calling for help, he thought.

"Maybe it's someone from the town," Titus said.

"And if so, maybe it's just someone from the town who's afraid of the woods," Billy said. "Let it go, Titus."

"He's not wrong," Kate said. "We put this town back where it came from and we'll save everyone all at once. It's more efficient than rescuing each individual person from their personal nightmare."

"Just give me one minute," Titus said. "I don't know why, but something seems really off about this."

He walked up to the edge of the forest, listening intently. The call for help seemed to be coming from all directions at once, simultaneously distant and close.

"Can any of you tell what direction it's coming from?" Titus asked, turning around.

And then he discovered he was alone, surrounded by trees, the voice crying for help still ringing out in the distance.

"Great," he said. "I fell for it."

CHAPTER 38: NIGHTMARE

The Vizier was not his true name, but it was convenient, and felt apropos, and so he allowed it to continue. It accurately summarized his role in this new reality, the creature thought.

Creatures born in the Dreamless Lands find names to be fleeting things anyway. Much is fleeting in that strange, colorful realm, where nonsense made as much sense as logic, a place where science had less place than whimsy.

Whimsy, the creature thought. No, the Dreamless Lands are not all whimsy. Some parts of it are inky and cruel, where fear and anxiety are fuel for the machine. It was in once such place he was born, a formless sentient nightmare, a predator hunting thoughts the way wolves stalk deer.

The Dreamless Realms are not a fantasy land. They are as much built on terror as joy, like all dreams are.

Nightmares like him—much of the population of the Dreamless Lands, really—were not particularly powerful. Yes, they could frighten and manipulate, but raw power, true magic, was not theirs to possess. No, much of the strength of the

Dreamless Lands lay firmly, selfishly, in the hands of their queen, the Lady Dreamless, and her eternal nemesis, the Nightmare Prince. Some mistake the Lady Dreamless and the Nightmare Prince as polar opposites, light and darkness, day and night, good and evil, but they were neither as pure as that, nor as simple. These rulers of the Dreamless Lands were more mercurial, more akin to the fey of folklore, generous when they chose to be, cruel when they desired, selfish in a way unique to creatures who hold so much power that mere mortals and lesser creatures are unfathomably alien and insignificant.

And while those two demigods held sway over their land from on high, nightmares and dream fairies, will-o-wisps and night terrors, all the beings who made up the general populace of the Dreamless Lands carried on, living lives of eternal powerlessness.

Some of them, like the Vizier, became ambitious.

Ambition was treated strangely in the Dreamless Lands. The Nightmare Prince seemed to foster it, enjoying the games it caused, up until one of his subjects became a threat, at which point he snuffed out their existence like a dream that disappears just as you wake. Lady Dreamless was all but oblivious to ambition in her people. If someone became a nuisance or a danger, she would put a stop to it, but for the most part, they were allowed their machinations and plans unhindered and ignored.

The Vizier, a minor nightmare, decided to ply his ambition in the palace of Lady Dreamless rather than his prince. He felt perhaps he might find an opening there that the more aware, more Machiavellian ruler would notice and put a stop to.

And so, the Vizier spent decades perhaps centuries, skulking about the Dreamless Palace. Time moves strangely in the Dreamless Lands. There was no real way to know for sure how long he lurked and waited.

And then one day, two strangers arrived at the gates, the man in red sunglasses and long black coat, and the woman with the eyes made of fire. The man was known to the realm, an ally of the Lady Dreamless and an antagonist to the Nightmare Prince, and owed a favor, but the woman made a bargain for the help she sought. The Vizier listened in to their conversation, creeping along the ceiling like a shard of shadow. He learned the Lady Dreamless wanted to see another realm, and that this mystery woman would open that gateway, provide her a corporeal form, and enable her to explore this newer world safely.

The Vizier bided his time, watching and waiting, eavesdropping on communications between worlds. And finally, he knew when the portal would be opened. It felt like an eternity before that moment came, but when it did, a white and purple tunnel between the worlds opening in a private corner of the Dreamless Palace, he leapt through the second after his queen entered the mystic portal.

He found himself in a drab, cold world, full of drab, cold people. But it was a new world, and his power over fear enabled him to survive, as the inhabitants of this world were very fearful of so many things.

But here or in the Dreamless Lands, a solitary nightmare only possesses so much magic.

He wandered this world in an inversion of the life of glamor his queen enjoyed. Where she traveled to the most beautiful parts, the Vizier kept to the back roads and back alleys, where nightmares belong. He made his own way, feeding off the anxiety of mortals, using them to get what he needed to survive.

And then one day he felt a presence in the distance. A

human humming with incredible magical energy.

The Vizier went to investigate.

He found a mortal child, a crimson thrum of magic thus far untapped humming from within her. She lived an ordinary life, in an ordinary place, but the Vizier could sense her boredom, her loneliness. Her fear.

A nightmare is only as powerful as the minds it controls. And thus, the Vizier searched through the girl's mind, this Alice Lapine, and found a face she would find familiar and welcome, and presented himself not as a nightmare, but rather as a friend. A someone whom she could trust implicitly.

She needed friends, and he would become her very best friend, one who would lead her out of this boring life and reach her full potential.

And all the while, the tendrils of his control leached off her magic, bleeding off the arcane energy she so naturally drew to her side.

With her raw power and his guidance, they began to build a world. One where the nightmare ruled, behind the figurehead of a young girl who happened to be an endless font of magic.

And then the intruders began to arrive. He'd sent Alice's figments away easy enough, sowing discord and distrust between Alice and her creations. The man with the red sunglasses and long black coat was easy to deal with, all but volunteering to walk into the Vizier's trap. But then the others arrived, a half-dozen beings intended to disrupt this beautiful crimson world the nightmare was helping to create.

This would not do.

He sent out tendrils of terror into the world, seeking these newcomers out, searching for their fears, for their dreams.

No one would take this world away from him. He was Alice's best friend, after all.

CHAPTER 39:
WE'RE US

With his friends gone and no immediately apparent way to get them back, Titus resigned himself to running into the forest to find the source of the voice crying for help. He held the arcane spear—it's wide, dagger-like blade adorned with ancient runes, the haft preternaturally strong, a gift from the werewolves who trained him—parallel to the ground as he jumped from rock to root to avoid stepping on leaves or brush and alerting anyone to his presence.

The forest quickly swallowed him up. Glancing over his shoulder, Titus saw that the town had disappeared, as if he'd traveled many miles into the wilderness. Okay, he thought. Reality is warped here. That makes a strange amount of sense, all things considered. He slowed his pace, creeping with a level of stealth that would almost make Kate proud. Or if not proud, at least not outright annoyed, which he usually did when they were supposed to be sneaky.

The cries for help went silent with a sickening scream. He couldn't tell anything about the person calling—male or female, old or young. They'd spoken in a language he could understand, though, so whoever it was, they were human, he assumed. Of course, here in another reality, that was really making a significant assumption.

Then he heard the chewing noises.

Titus stood up straight, no longer hunching to hide himself behind trees and shrubs. Standing his full height—which wasn't particularly tall, admittedly, but enough to see over some of the lower brush—he saw something that made his stomach twist. A massive, broad, muscular back, covered in silvery fur, cartoonish, broad shoulders leading up to a sloping neck. A short, upturned tail twitched as the creature leaned forward. Titus could easily make out the sound of rending flesh, sharp teeth grinding into muscle and bone.

I know you, he thought to himself. You're me.

The creature ceased its meal then, breathing heavily as if the effort of devouring its victim left it breathless. The monster turned its thick neck, revealing the long, wolfish snout Titus expected to see. It was covered in bright red blood almost up to the rims of its golden eyes, which flashed at him in wordless rage.

The werewolf stood up on its hind legs and faced Titus, revealing the mutilated corpse of a human behind it. The beast uttered a low, pensive growl.

"Paging Doctor Freud," Titus said, readying his spear.

The werewolf snarled and began to circle him. Titus moved with it, making sure to keep the distance between them the same. He lowered his enchanted spear at the creature's heart.

"This isn't even a little bit subtle," Titus said. "You're what I fear becoming. All I have to do is…"

Before he could finish speaking, the werewolf pounced. Dammit, I'm fast, Titus thought, the blur of silver fur almost too much for his eyes to register. He got the spear up in time and felt it bite into muscle, tearing at the werewolf's gut. A massive paw swiped at him and he felt hot weals crease his face, narrowly missing his eye. He twisted the spear and pushed backward, forcing himself out from under the beast's weight.

"Okay, that was real," he said, blood running from his cheek into his mouth, the taste warm and metallic.

The werewolf charged again, but this time Titus was ready, sidestepping and jabbing the spear into the monster's hamstring. The werewolf fell to the ground, rending the dirt and sending debris into the air as it howled in rage.

"I knew I should have dealt with you already," Titus said, blinking blood out of his eyes. The werewolf limped as it prepared another attack. "Yeah, you and I haven't been on speaking terms lately."

The wolf slashed at him with a paw, missing, but then kicking him with its one good leg. Titus staggered backward, the monster opening fresh cuts across his chest, shredding his sweatshirt. The wolf lost its balance, though, falling over as the leg he'd hamstrung gave out.

"You know why? Because I'm afraid of you," Titus said. He jabbed at the wolf with his spear, but the creature batted the blade aside easily. "I don't want you to consume me. I want to be more than just a rage-filled monster."

The werewolf tried to leap on top of him, but the damage to its leg caused the jump to go off-course. Titus dodged, but the wolf was able to catch his leg with one long arm, claws raking across his thigh. Angrily, Titus lashed out with his spear again, this time digging into the meat of the werewolf's shoulder. The blade caught on something, bone and gristle, becoming stuck. The wolf swung around wildly trying to free itself from the blade, and Titus held onto the haft for dear life, knowing he needed to use it as leverage to keep the wolf at bay.

"But this is no way to live," Titus said, his now limping gait mirrored in the hamstrung werewolf. They continued to circle each other like boxers. "I can't contain you. You can't control me. We're stuck with each other, you vicious bastard, whether we like it or not."

The wolf snapped at him. My teeth are enormous, Titus marveled absently. He'd never truly seen himself in full werewolf form, not like this, and he suddenly felt very bad for anyone who'd faced him directly. I truly am a fairytale monster, he thought.

"Okay, we're going to work this out if it kills both of us," Titus said, breathing heavily. "Fine. Fine! We're going to hash this family drama out now? Right here? Let's do it. Let's get it over with, you overbearing fleabag."

The wolf, realizing Titus was using the spear as leverage to keep him away, began to push itself deeper onto the weapon. There was a horrific popping noise as the spear burst out the other side of the monster's shoulder, and then a stomach-churning, wet slopping sound as the wooden haft entered its flesh.

"You're psychotic," Titus said, watching the wolf snarl and snap in pain, but nonetheless, grow closer and closer, pushing through catastrophic body trauma to get nearer to him.

The things I've put that body through to save the world, Titus thought. The werewolf kept him alive in an exploding alien spaceship. It suffered a million cuts at the hands of the Assassin Rose. It went to war at the end of the world. Nothing stops it. Nothing shuts it down. The monster has no desire other than to survive.

I have no desire other than to survive, Titus thought. That thing is me. It's always been me.

He held onto the spear's handle with strength he didn't know he possessed as the werewolf grew so close he could feel the heat of its breath on his face.

"I won't let you devour me," Titus said. "You aren't some *thing* inside me wrestling for control. We're the same, you and me. Not two minds in one body. Not a monster and a man sharing the same space. We're in this together. You don't get to say no to that."

The werewolf rammed itself forward, and before Titus could react, it's jaws clamped down on his shoulder, the mouth so wide, so vast that he felt its canines pierce his stomach below his ribcage. He's going to kill me, Titus thought. He's going to eat me alive.

"No," Titus said. Blood bubbled up from his guts into his mouth. "I'm not me. You're not you. We're us."

He grabbed the wolf by the thick, silvery fur on either side of its face and pulled, commanding. The beast released its jaws. Titus forced it to look him in the eyes. Face to face. Breath to breath.

He put his forehead against the monster's. It huffed irritably, then bumped it head against his, like a dog showing affection.

"We're in this together. This body, this life. You're me. I'm you. Okay?"

The wolf uttered a low, deep, rumbling sound, less a growl and more an acknowledgement. Titus felt his whole body go cold, then very hot, as if taken with a raging fever. His eyes rolled back in his head. He fell to the ground, the world growing dark and cloudy around him.

He may have blacked out for a moment. Maybe his heart

stopped. He couldn't tell. Everything hurt, inside and out. He tasted blood in his mouth. His skin was sticky with it.

His spear lay on the ground beside him. The werewolf, and the victim it had been dining on, were both nowhere to be seen. Titus reached down to pick up his weapon. Where he expected a human hand, the wide, furred hand of his werewolf form appeared, picking up the spear from the ground. He used it to push himself to his feet. Glancing down, he watched the brutal wounds on his chest sealing up quickly, knitting closed before his eyes, covered over by whitish fur.

His heart raced, thundering with the power of this immortal beast he'd always been so afraid of. I'm no longer along for the ride, he thought. It's been me all along.

He smiled, an odd sensation as it split his elongated snout. Tilting his nose toward the sky, he inhaled, sniffing the air for his friends.

"Let's see what inner demons you're all facing," Titus said, surprised at the thick, throaty sound of his own voice in this form. And with the loping gait of a top-tier predator, he sprang into action to rescue his friends from their own nightmares.

CHAPTER 40: THE MYTH OF KATHERINE MILLER

Click.

Kate found herself alone under a dark sky, a solitary streetlight above splashing a circle of white on the pavement. Her boots crunched as she took a step, grinding glass into the concrete. In the distance, she could hear the sounds of an unseen highway.

She did not have to look at the nearest street sign to know where she was, or why she was here. She turned to her right and saw the body in the street just as she knew she would.

"I know what you're doing," she said out loud. She had, after all, had this dream hundreds of times.

And that sound. *Click.* A tiny bone fracturing as her booted foot connected with the young man's head. The way she felt that click shudder up her leg into her hip, her mind trying to ignore it even as her body screamed out what she'd done.

She knew who the body would be, but she walked up to it

anyway, rolling it over with her foot. The same face, the fleshy, sneering mug of the man who had caused her parents' death. This was a memory, she knew, of the night she'd finally found him. Years putting herself back together again like Humpty Dumpty, all for one moment of vengeance, and the thing she remembers most, the part she turns over and over in her mind when she sleeps, is how dissatisfying revenge turned out to be.

She learned about the man after, about his life, about the things that led him to crime, about mistakes made and opportunities never offered. But that night, in her makeshift costume, the memory of her dead parents still hanging around her shoulders like a noose, Kate thought she knew what she wanted. She thought revenge would make her feel better, would fill up the empty hole in her heart where her parents once were, but revenge only made that hole deeper and wider and darker. All the revenge, all the heroics, all the death-defying decisions she'd make in the time that followed added up to nothing, just sand in the wind.

Click. Bone breaking. A thin line of blood running from the man's ear. The stillness of his body.

Of course, here among dreams, this would be the scene she'd find. She dreamed about it more than anything else, the memory of that night. I believed I was brave, she thought, staring at the body in the street. He didn't look real. The memory wasn't sharp enough, so he blurred at the edges, a caricature of a man with a wide mouth and dark eyebrows beneath short blond hair, one crooked incisor punctuating a ghastly grin.

That was the night Doc found her. Did he know what she'd done? Kate often wondered. She supposed he did. He knew everything back then, or at least acted as though he did. Did he hide the man's body? Magic it away? Was there some spell he cast when Kate wasn't looking, mending the man's broken bones? Did anyone know what happened that night? In a lot of ways, Kate herself wasn't sure. She never checked for a pulse. She never confirmed if he'd lived or died. She didn't want to know. It wasn't an answer she was prepared to face.

Whatever happened, happened. She thought. I can only spend the rest of my life trying to be better than that.

She walked away from the corpse, stopping in her tracks as she heard a scratching sound behind her. She turned to look back. The dead man had crawled to his feet and was now shuffling slowly toward her, one arm hanging limply at his side, head lolling to the right. She walked a little faster, but the zombie kept pace with her, shoes scraping on the pavement. Finally, she turned completely around to face him and waited until he was close enough to smell, close enough to hear the wheezing groan of his lungs struggling to draw in air.

She kicked the zombie in the chest, knocking him to the ground easily. His arms and legs struggled and strained, but he seemed incapable of righting himself. Kate shook her head and walked away.

The streets changed, gradually, moving more quickly than they should from urban sprawl to suburban ordinariness. She'd walked several blocks before she realized exactly where she was.

"No," she said, seeing her childhood home a few doors down.

It was an old, well cared-for Victorian, a wraparound porch lining the front and right side of the building. A turret dominated the left side of the building. She almost smiled, remembering pretending to be a princess there as a child, before everything went wrong. A tall dormer, bay windows, all the classic marks of the style of home, things she took for granted before becoming who and what she was now. She thought all homes were like this, when she was little.

She pushed open the gate and walked up the front steps. This dream put her here for a reason, she thought. Might as well see it all the way to the end.

The interior was warm, and lit with soft golden light. Hardwood floors, polished, dark wood banisters, a runner Kate used to dance on so her feet wouldn't make so much noise as her parents worked.

She heard voices in the kitchen.

None of this is real, she thought to herself as she walked down the hall, past the living room with its crackling fireplace. It's all in my head. This place is using my memories against me.

But still, knowing that, her breath caught in her throat when she saw her mother sitting at the bar-style countertop in the kitchen, sipping coffee from a white porcelain mug. Hair up to reveal her long neck, tiny diamond studs in her ears, Kate recognized every detail immediately.

"Hi, kitten," a man said, and Kate felt her heart harden to stone.

Her father was there in the kitchen as well, leaning in conspiratorially to her mother, the way he did when he flirted with her. They'd always flirted, she remembered, and she'd thought it so strange that an old married couple would flirt, not realizing that it was a sign they still very much enjoyed being around each other.

She could have looked at them, she could have watched them, but she was not prepared for her father to speak to her, not here. He smiled at her radiantly. He was a handsome if not pretty man, his nose clearly broken more than once, a raggedness around his eyes that belayed a roughness he otherwise did not carry. Her parents were wealthy, she knew, and enjoyed that wealth, but she knew her father paid for college with cash he won as a boxer. He told her he'd wanted to be a surgeon. But he'd taken too many blows to the head, and his hands were too scarred up from the ring, but he still found work in medicine, and never talked about how he got there in the company of his peers. He'd met her mother in school, and he always said she was a better doctor than he'd ever be, but in the end, when all was said and done, they'd both wanted to be artists and neither had the chance. Her father was a singer. Her mother played violin. The house was filled with music, always.

And Kate was their dancer.

She walked into the kitchen, biting her lip as her mother turned to smile at her. If either noticed her strange outfit, or the miles and scars on Kate's face, they said nothing. Her mother patted the seat beside her and Kate slid onto the stool. She ran her fingertips along the underside of the counter, feeling the chips and wear she'd memorized like Braille as a child.

This is all gone, she thought, listening to her parents make small talk with each other, as if nothing had changed. The house was sold, because teenaged, orphaned Kate couldn't afford the mortgage, and she didn't want to live in a place full of ghosts anyway.

She never told anyone, not even Titus, but she'd walk by sometimes, when she was done patrolling the city for the night. A family lived there, now, with three little boys, and she'd sit in the shadows and listen to them play and argue and tease each other for a few minutes before heading back into the City. She wondered if this countertop was still there, or if they'd changed everything. Her parents always talked about remodeling, but she knew despite living well, they were more in debt than they admitted to anyone, as doctors often are. Still, they'd made sure she was taken care of. Neither of them grew up particularly safe or secure, unlike many of their work peers, and they crafted an illusion of a far better life, like so many do. No one ever questioned it, including Kate, who was too young to know the difference, too innocent to hear the fabrications in their words.

She looked back to her father and saw a thin trickle of blood running down from his hairline. Her mind flashed to the night of the attack, when he'd crashed the car, the empty expression on his face as he bled out. She glanced down at her mother's hands and saw flecks of blood on her diamond wedding ring. Another detail from the crash Kate never forgot. Her mother lifted that blood-flecked hand and placed it on Kate's shoulder.

"Are you okay, Katie?" she said.

We look so much alike, Kate thought. She had her mother's face, her bone structure, but their eyes were different colors. She had her father's eyes, both in pigment, and now, after years of fighting, in the ring and out, the same scars as well. They wanted me to be their dancer, she thought. They wanted me to have the life they didn't get to have.

"I'm fine," she said, her voice rough. I must be such a disappointment to them, she thought. But no, they're not real, they're not here, she remembered. This is all a dream, a cruel trick, something to scare her, or manipulate her.

You have work to do, Kate, she thought to herself. There's no time for memories here. This is no place to be maudlin.

But still, she thought. It's good to see them again.

"I have to go," she said, angry with herself at the emotion welling up her chest, the burn of tears trying to break free from her eyes.

"You just got here," her mother said.

"You work too hard," her father said. "It's okay to be a kid sometimes, kitten."

"We all work too hard," Kate said. "But there's always work to be done."

"We'll be here when you get back, then," her mother said, and that was where the illusion broke just a little bit, a slight vacancy to her mother's eyes. She was the wittiest person Kate had ever met, and never, not once, was there ever any vacancy in her expression.

"I'm sorry," Kate said. "I'll… I'll be back."

She pulled herself slowly away from her mother's grasp, who didn't fight her departure. Her father held up a wide hand to wave goodbye, that ridiculous finger-wiggling wave that looked so out of place with his rough frame, which he'd always done because it made Kate laugh. She did laugh then, just a little, with a hint of a sob as well.

She walked out of the house, fists clenched tight, shoulders bunched up and ready to fight. She saw Titus standing across the street. He flickered like a broken hologram between his human and werewolf forms, as if he were both at once. His body was marred with new cuts and wounds, most healed over but still raw and red.

"We need to go," she said.

Titus nodded in that quiet, understanding way he always did, watching her with unnatural golden eyes.

"Everything okay?" he asked.

"I'm fine," Kate said. "This place is nothing but illusions."

"I know," he said. "I had to fight mine."

"Well, I never dream," Kate said. "So this place had nothing to use against me. We should find the others, though. Pull them out of whatever they're going through."

"Okay," Titus said. "You know this place?"

"Just some old house," Kate said. "Like I said. It was clutching at straws. I saw right through everything it threw at me."

Again, Titus nodded. He seemed to commit right then to one form, his werewolf shape taking over. Kate felt an unexpected comfort in that, the hulking monster at her side instead of the caring face of the boy who loved her despite finding herself so utterly unlovable. The wolf was easier to be with sometimes.

Together, they walked into the darkness, Titus following some trail only he could see.

Kate glanced over her shoulder one last time at the house from her memories.

And then she put her mask back on and went to work.

CHAPTER 41:
WE DON'T GET TO BE HAPPY

Jane walked alone through a cornfield brushing tall stalks out of her way as she traversed through the high growth. She knew exactly where she was. She didn't need to see the farm to recognize the place where she grew up.

But still, when she reached the edge of the field, her heart skipped a beat. The old red farmhouse stood waiting, the barn she'd burned down the day before she met Doc Silence looking as though that incident never happened. The sky was a pale and perfect blue, marred only by graceful white clouds and a thin trail of chimney smoke.

Jane made her way up the front stairs but hesitated before entering. She lifted her hand to knock, but as if on cue, a voice called out to her from inside.

"Well, don't just stand there," Doris Hawkins said. "Lunch is ready. Come on in."

Jane pulled the screen door opened and entered. The house hadn't changed at all since the last time she'd seen it, or really much in general for as long as she could remember. She ran her fingers along the darkly stained wood of the bannister in the front hallway leading upstairs, then turned right into the kitchen. Her adoptive mother, Doris, puttered with something on the stove. She looked over her shoulder to see Jane watching her and beckoned with an impatient wave of her hand.

"Well, come on now," Doris said. "I know you've always been shy, but this is your home."

"Home," Jane said. I'm dreaming, Jane thought. For some reason, I'm dreaming of home.

"Stop loitering," Doris said. "There's someone here to see you."

Doris disappeared around the corner. Jane heard the clattering of plates and went to join her. When she entered the kitchen, her guts twisted up inside. Sitting at the kitchen table, shockingly formal in her black, gold, and white uniform, was Jane's future self, the one she'd met in the alternate timeline where everything went wrong.

"Hi," Future Jane said before taking a bite of a sandwich.

"So this is what it's like to be awake during an anxiety dream," Jane said, sitting down across from her doppelganger.

"Like this is anything new to either one of us," her future self said.

They both looked around the kitchen, taking in the details, remembering the tiny specifics that made it home.

"You could just stay here," the doppelganger said.

"No, I can't," Jane said.

"See that's our problem," her future self said. "We never say no. We never stop. We put everything else first."

"Are you telling me I grow up to be resentful?" Jane said. "I've met you before. The real you. You weren't angry."

"No," the older Jane said. "No, I'm not angry."

She paused to take a long sip of iced tea.

"Maybe I should be though," she said. "Everything we do to keep this world safe and it keeps walking right back into traffic."

"That's our job," Jane said. "We're the… immune system, right? We're white blood cells for the planet."

"I feel like I shouldn't tell you this," the older Jane said. "But when else am I going to have a chance to warn you? Jane, we are never, ever going to be happy."

"You say that like I'm going to be surprised by it," Jane said.

"What?"

"I know I'm never going to be happy," Jane said. "I've never been happy. I was born unhappy. It's like the parts for happy were left out of me when I was put together at the factory, so to speak.

"God, we need so much therapy," the older Jane said.

"You think I need therapy?"

"Can't hurt," her older self said. "You could just keep saving the world every day as a way to avoid ever addressing your mental health issues, but that's a lot of work."

"I guess," Jane said.

"And can I let you in on a little secret, younger me?" the other Jane said.

"Is it a secret if I'm you and you're me?"

The older Jane cocked her head.

"It's still a secret to you," the older Jane said. "Just make sure you're careful who you share it with."

"I'll try to limit it to future versions of myself, to pay it forward," Jane said.

"That works," the older woman said.

"Well?" Jane asked.

"We can't save everyone," the doppelganger said. "And you'll try and try to save everyone and eventually you realize you're not capable of facing any number as acceptable losses. Everyone says Kate is the perfectionist, but you're the one who won't let go. The only difference is Kate already knows she's mad as a hatter. You'll drive yourself insane trying to deny it."

"You're a lot more pessimistic than the last time I saw you."

"Well," the older Jane said. "I died."

"Saving the world."

"Is that really what you want? Are you really so lonely and unhappy that you keep saving the world because you have nothing better to do?"

"It's what I'm here to do. It's my job," Jane said.

"And I'm telling you, no matter what you do, no matter who you save, someday, somehow, that job will kill you."

Jane stood up and strode over to the kitchen window to look out at the cornfield, her back to her future self.

"I really never become happy?" she asked.

"I tried my whole life, kid," the doppelganger said. She tapped her own chest, above the heart, then her head. "Something doesn't work right in here. Or up here. We don't get to be happy."

"Then it's a good thing I have a job to do," Jane said.

"There you go, letting being a hero define you. Don't do that. You're only hurting yourself when you do that."

"I don't know how to be anything else," Jane said. "Can I let you in on a secret?"

"Of course."

"I've never been happy. Not a single day of my whole life," Jane said. "And I know you're a nightmare just trying to distract me because if you really were me, you'd know that."

Her older self shrugged.

"I think you knew that the moment you saw me," she said.

Jane glanced all around the kitchen again. The ugly yellow refrigerator. The old, hand-carved table. Doris' prized super-powered mixer for the bread she loved baking but never quite got right. It felt like home, Jane thought, even though it was just a poor facsimile.

"You might be a figment of my imagination, but you're not wrong," Jane said. "I do this because I don't know how to do anything else. I don't know how to be anything else. And I don't know why that is. Nobody taught me to be this way. Nobody guided me to it. I'm just like this."

"You could just stay here," her doppelganger said again. "With mom and dad. The farm is safe."

"That's the thing though, right? They are out there waiting for me. Back home. And I need to get back to them safely. For their happiness."

"It is exhausting being this selfless," the doppelganger said. "Even now, you're trying to fix the world for everyone else."

"Somebody has to," Jane said. "Are we going to fight now? I don't really want to fight myself."

"You fight yourself every day," the older version of Jane said, smiling. "Don't need me to throw a haymaker at your face to make that happen."

Jane bit her lip, thinking.

"Tell me your best moment," she said.

"We've already established I'm just a part of you, a piece of your memories," the doppelganger said. "How can I tell you my best moment?"

"Because you are me," Jane said. "And that means you know my best moment."

The older woman paused, looking out the window, biting

her own lip in a perfect imitation of her younger self.

"Do you remember the first time we flew?" she said.

"Yeah," Jane said. "It was like every worry melted away. Just me and the sky. Nothing could touch me there."

"That was a great day," the doppelganger said. "It was almost like…"

"Like I was happy," Jane finished.

"Then everything else happened," the older Jane said.

"And it never stopped happening."

"We just kept saving the world."

"And never thought about saving ourselves."

"I wanted to let myself be tired."

"But there was no time to be tired."

"No time to be sad."

"Or guilty."

"Or lonely."

"Or lost."

Jane realized that her older self had disappeared, leaving her alone in the farmhouse kitchen. I've been talking to myself for a while, haven't I, she thought. Jane heard her mother moving around the living room, heard her father singing an old Irish folksong upstairs, the one she still knew by heart.

And though it falls upon my lot that I should rise and you should not, I'll gently rise and I'll softly call, goodnight and joy be with you all. Goodnight, and joy be with you all.

Jane walked quietly out of the farmhouse, avoiding the imagined imitations of her parents, and let the reddish gold light of the sun warm her skin. She took a deep breath, shaking off the melancholy and loneliness this dream had filled her with.

There's time to be unhappy later, she thought. We have a world to save.

And she took to the air, trying, so very hard, to hold in her memory that first flight, the weightlessness of it, and the brief joy it let her uncover.

CHAPTER 42: MOVING MONSTERS CROSS-COUNTRY

Andrew Keppler was beginning to not just resent his job but full-on hate it.

His day became an awkward series of phone calls and meetings, bribes to get around laws about moving biological matter, paying off the right people to avoid the wrong questions being asked, and in the end, finding a way to ship thousands of pounds of mutated, sometimes necrotic flesh to California undetected. Private aircraft were hired, and private air strips rented. The creatures were handled by vendors who had been loyal to the Children of the Elder Star for decades— old school crooks who could be trusted to keep their mouths shut because they expected long-term payouts for silence.

And because they worked for the Children, they'd seen worse. Well, Keppler thought, eyeing some of the more grotesque examples of King Tears' craft, maybe not worse, but certainly strange and inhuman.

I guess I can put moving monsters cross-country on my CV, Keppler thought.

They arrived in several unmarked trucks outside the town limits of Westwick. King Tears made Keppler open the doors so the mutations could slink, crawl, scuttle, or otherwise shuffle their way out into the open.

The smell was bad enough, turning Keppler's stomach instantly. Old meat, rot, strange, alien spices, and something else, darker, that caused the part of his brain that remembered being a prey animal to want to run.

The first few out were mostly human. Transformed arms or legs, lumpy, oversized things ending in bony talons or studded with ridges or protrusions, but these still looked identifiably like people.

Then the fused creatures began to exit the vehicle, built from multiple victims. Too many arms, too many legs, eyes on all sides looking in every direction at once, mouths that tried to talk in different languages, holding different conversations simultaneously. Keppler took an involuntary step away from those.

Then came the creatures who clearly had been blended with things not of this world. Most were humanoid—four limbs, a torso, a head—but they also were marred by some unearthly, one might even say demonic, sign. One had enormous bat wings. Several had black, curved horns jutting from their foreheads. One looked at him with yellowy eyes, irises vertical slits like a lizard's, and snarled at him in a language he couldn't identify but made his guts turn to hot oil.

"Is this all you could have transported to us?" King Tears asked.

Keppler swallowed hard and clenched his fists, closing his eyes to calm himself before answering. King Tears laughed.

"I'm just kidding, Mr. Keppler. This is more than enough. Excellent work."

"Thank you, sir," Keppler said.

"I'm wholeheartedly impressed with your efficiency. You have a future here, I think," Tears said.

He turned to address the menagerie of monsters next, stepping past Keppler, who subtly backed himself away from both the magician and his pets.

"My warriors, my children. You are about to do what you were made to do: conquer a world. Join me, my wondrous creations, as we step across the threshold between realities and take what is ours," Tears said.

The monsters said nothing in return, staring mutely back at him. One of the creatures with too many mouths shushed itself.

"Very well then," King Tears said. "I need a volunteer."

Again, he was meet with silence. He scanned the gathered mutations and pointed to one, a younger man with a shock of unkempt blond hair. His skin was unnaturally red, one eye larger than the other.

"You," Tears said. "What's your name?"

"I'm… I'm Kevin, sir."

Keppler was intrigued and disheartened by the tone of the boy's voice. He recognized the resignation and resentment immediately. King Tears could control them, but they were not willing subjects, Keppler knew. He filed that information away for later.

"Come here, Kevin. You are about to be a pivotal part of our crossing over to the other side," Tears said.

"I am?" the boy said.

"Yes," Tears said, putting an arm around the boy's shoulder. Kevin's left arm was completely transformed into a tentacle-covered thing, sharp barbs hanging from ruddy flesh. He was among the smallest of the mutated creatures, though there were other younger victims among them as well.

King Tears led the young, mutilated man to the edge of the pavement where the town disappeared. He gestured out across the empty, dusty space where Westwick once stood.

"You see, we need to cross the veil. To move our weapons of war across dimensions, and we need you for that," King Tears said.

"Why me?" Kevin asked. Beyond his anger and resentment, there was also a sort of dullness to Kevin's speech, as if he weren't fully in control of his actions, like someone woken unexpectedly from a deep sleep.

"Because, Kevin, I am a master of blood magic," King Tears said. "And blood magic requires sacrifice."

With a showy, deft flourish, King Tears produced a wicked, serrated knife from within his suitcoat. With his other hand, he violently grabbed Kevin's hair and pushed his head back, exposing his neck. King Tears flicked his wrist and slit the boys' throat, holding him upright by his hair as his life's blood emptied on the ground in front of him. Tears tilted the dying boy from left to right as if painting an arc with his blood.

He dropped the body on the ground. Keppler could hear the soft, quiet gurgles as the boy finished dying, splayed out beneath the California sun.

King Tears began chanting in an arcane language, making sharp, precise movements with his hands. He clapped once, harshly, and a semi-circle lit up in the air before him. On the other side of that semi-circle, Keppler could see the town they were looking for, bathed in crimson light. King Tears gestured with both arms and the portal opened wider, large enough to accommodate the biggest of his creations.

"Come, my warriors," King Tears said cheerfully. He made a disconcertingly friendly gesture to Keppler to join him. "Let us journey to this other world, and take what is ours. Isn't the acquisition of incredible power so much fun?"

Keppler allowed himself to be led through the portal. He could feel the blood covering King Tears' hand seeping through his own suit coat.

That'll never come out, Keppler thought. None of this will ever come out of anything.

CHAPTER 43:
THE ANTHILL

Billy stared out into the yawning abyss of space and wondered why this was his current predicament, considering a few seconds ago he was standing in a reasonable facsimile of southern California.

Space, Billy thought. I'm in space. I wasn't in space before. I don't really appreciate the unrequested change of scenery.

He looked around. Behind him, casting a glow of reflected distant sunlight, was Saturn, its rings close enough he could see them as the asteroids and space debris they really were, not the pretty streaks they'd appear at a distance. The base the Luminae were building when he last visited was not there, though, as far as Billy could tell. He hoped that meant he was in a dream or hallucination and not that they'd given up their construction project without telling him or Dude.

Speaking of, Billy thought.

"Dude, are you here?" Billy asked. He waited for the alien to respond. Nothing. "Dude? No? Great."

He held his hands out in front of him, palms up, and

activated the light blasts he should have been able to project. Both hands lit up in the bright blueish-white glow he was expecting.

Okay, so I have my powers, Billy thought. Dude isn't answering, but this means he's still here, otherwise I'd be powerless. Also dead and frozen solid in the cold vacuum of space.

Billy darted around to get his bearings. The planet seemed to be as vast and terrifying as it was in real life, though no matter how close or far from it he tried to fly, it always seemed to be the same distance. Frustrated, he burned downward at top speed, trying to reach the planet's atmosphere. Nothing.

Optical illusion, Billy thought. Wherever I am, it can't let me get any closer to Saturn.

And then it hit: pure, unadulterated agoraphobia.

He'd had similar attacks in the past, when he went into space to scout out the Nemesis Fleet—something about the vastness of the cosmos spread out before him had made Billy, who is admittedly relatively self-centered, feel catastrophically unimportant and insignificant. That was when he was impossibly fast and able, with Dude's internal guidance, to travel back and forth from Saturn to Earth in a few days. Dude was even able to help Billy fall into a kind of trance to keep from having a panic attack out of boredom.

But here, right now, the was no Dude, no trance, and definitely no hyper-speed travel.

Don't panic, Billy thought, as panic did, in fact rise in his guts like acid. Don't panic, be cool, this is just a nightmare, you've had similar nightmares before, oh boy, now you're panicking, this is bad…

He heard a garbled sound in his head, like a radio tuned incorrectly. The sound warbled and whined until finally,

Dude's voice came through with its usual clarity.

There you are, Dude said.

"Dude!" Billy said. "Oh am I glad to hear your voice, buddy."

You were having a panic attack.

"Yes, absolutely, I was having a panic attack. I'm still having a panic attack. Can you feel me sweating? I'm sweating."

Calm down, Billy Case. This is an illusion.

"So you know how to get us out of here?"

I did not say that.

"Well, you're no help," Billy said. "Lost in space. This is literally my recurring nightmare."

Billy sensed Dude hesitating.

"What," Billy said. "What are you holding back?"

Where are the other Luminae?

"Gone," Billy said. "We're alone out here."

Again, there was an unspoken hesitation.

"Dude?"

You said this was your own recurring nightmare.

"Yeah," Billy said. "I, like, okay, our trip into the great beyond a while back? Not gonna lie, my friend, it messed me up."

Billy realized his voice was about to crack with emotion. He fought it, as if the alien listening to him speak didn't hear all his thoughts, wasn't living in his brain, wasn't there when Billy daydreamed or went to the bathroom.

"I don't like feeling insignificant," Billy said. "I mean, I know I'm not important. I'm okay not being important. I'm just a guy. But, Dude, the universe is so big. So big. We're nothing. It just goes on and on, forever, in all directions, and we're just this little collection of cells that thinks we're important but really how important can you be when you make plans based on not missing a TV show, y'know? We're nothing."

Dude didn't answer. Billy began to panic again, afraid he'd lost him.

"Dude?"

Ants build complex homes beneath the earth. That is their world, and that world is significant to them. They do not worry about their significance to the rest of the universe, Billy Case. They worry about the home they've built, and ensuring its survival. You are not insignificant. You serve a great purpose. You keep your home safe.

"That is… bizarrely inspiring, Dude," Billy said. He still felt sick to his stomach, but the tightness in his chest began to loosen. "Although for what it's worth, usually being compared to an ant is traditionally a method of telling someone they're actually insignificant."

Sometimes it takes an alien perspective to see the bigger picture, Dude said.

"Heh. Yeah," Billy said. He scanned the blanket of stars spread out before him and sighed. "Still. Here we are. Hey, you sounded concerned for a minute, there."

Your personal nightmare is to be insignificant. But I think this place is meant for both of us, Billy Case. It draws on both of our fears.

"You're an immortal space angel. What exactly are you afraid of?"

My people are gone, Dude said. *I have waited to rejoin them for centuries. Longer. But when we finally found them again, Billy Case, we were changed, you and me. We were not the same as before.*

"How do you mean?"

When we absorbed our future selves, Dude said. *Do you remember? When we traveled to the future.*

"Hard to forget about that," Billy said. "Not every day you

get to mind-meld with someone and witness your own death. Thanks for reminding me."

The other Luminae were too polite to say it when we finally encountered them, Dude said. *But they are afraid of us. We are more powerful than any Luminae that has ever come before. And my brothers and sisters aren't sure if that makes us an abomination, or a hero, a monster, a mutation. What they do know is we make them uncomfortable, as useful a weapon as we have become.*

"Are they jealous?" Billy asked.

They are afraid. And even the Luminae are dangerous when they are afraid. And…

"What?" Billy said.

I do not want to be abandoned by my people, Billy Case. That is my greatest fear. I've been apart from them for so long. It feels unfair that when all is said and done, they might abandon me because of what we've done to save a world together.

"You're afraid of being alone and insignificant," Billy said.

Perhaps, Dude said.

"We really are a pair, aren't we," Billy said.

There is a reason I picked you above all others, Dude said. *It's not as though I didn't have other options.*

"Now you're just being mean," Billy said. "It's funny. This isn't my only recurring nightmare."

I know.

"Of course you know," Billy said. "I'm afraid of losing you, for one, you snooty old glow stick. I'm afraid of wanting to save people and not having the power to do that. I have nightmares all the time about you abandoning me. Or something happening that splits us apart again."

You will be my partner until one of us is no longer among the living, Billy Case. You have my word on that.

"See, that's super morbid and not exactly what I was

looking for," Billy said. "But I'll take it."

This is exactly what I say about you.

"Now there's the snarky old Dude I know and love," Billy said. "Okay. Good talk. How do we get back?"

Look behind you, Dude said.

Billy turned again so that Saturn was on his left. He was caught off-guard to find Titus in full werewolf form standing there with his weird spear in his hand. Titus leaned in and grabbed Billy by the shoulder.

"Wake up, doofus," Titus said, his voice a low rumble emanating from his wolfish jaws, and gave Billy a hard shake.

In the blink of an eye, Billy went from drifting in space to sitting on a rocking chair on someone's front porch back in Westwick.

"That was weird," Billy said.

"Where did you go?" Jane asked, standing next to the massive form of wolfed-out Titus. Kate was with them as well, hanging back a bit, not making eye contact.

"I think I just had a therapy session with Dude," Billy said.

"Feeling better?" Titus growled.

"Honestly? Yeah," Billy said.

"Good," Titus said. "Come on, we've got two more friends to find."

The werewolf stomped off, sniffing the air as if tracking something. Oh, Billy thought. He's literally tracking something.

You okay, Dude? Billy thought.

I am. How are you feeling?

Like I have an anthill to protect, Billy thought. Let's get to it.

CHAPTER 44:
PIECES

Bedlam held a hot cup of coffee between both hands, enjoying the warmth of it on her skin. She sat in a coffee shop, an Ishmael's, of course, because a little suburban town like Westwick would have an Ishmael's. The shop was busy but not crowded, a few people in line waiting for lattes, a tattooed man with an excessive beard working furiously on a silver laptop nearby.

I haven't sat down in a coffee shop in so long, Bedlam thought. Not since…

She looked down at her hands again and found them both as they were before her accident, before the experiment.

My real hands, she thought. Not the silvered metal of her mismatched cyborg hands. She clutched the coffee cup tighter, savoring the warmth. She could feel with her mechanical hands, they had sensors that detected temperature and touch, so she could interact with the world, but this was different. Real fingers, real flesh, real nerves.

She touched her face. The metallic parts that held her

together were gone. Bedlam turned so she could catch her reflection in the window, and two flesh-and-blood eyes looked back at her, not one gleaming robotic one beside one ordinary eye. Her usual Mohawk was a toned down but still appropriately punkish undercut. She wore earrings she remembered having as a young teenager and a sundress in pale rose pink.

This is me, she thought. This is me.

"You look lost," the man with the beard and laptop said. Bedlam glanced over at him, then looked around to make sure he had spoken to her.

"Me?"

"Yeah, you just seemed out of sorts. Sorry to pry."

"I—yeah. Right," Bedlam said. "I'm sorry. Been a while since a stranger has noticed."

"It's weird, right?" the man said. "People don't talk to each other anymore."

"That's not it," Bedlam said. "I, um. Huh. I don't get out much."

"Sorry to hear that," the man said. "I'm Rob, by the way."

He held out a hand. Hesitantly, she shook it. Warm hand against warm hand. I didn't even realize how much I missed this, she thought.

"I'm Kimberly," she said, stumbling over the urge to say the name she'd gone by for so long now. That's who I am here, she thought. I'm the old me. Before I became Frankenstein's manic pixie dream bot. "I shouldn't disturb you. You were working."

"Nothing that can't wait," Rob said. "I run a small business. Going over this month's expenses. My least favorite part of the job."

Job, Bedlam thought. Expense reports. Ordinary world

stuff. Everyone says ordinary life is boring, but when you can't go out in public without scaring people, the idea of sitting undisturbed in a coffee shop looking at numbers wasn't so bad. Bedlam never had a chance to be boring. She had no comparison by with to measure it with.

"What do you do?" Rob asked.

Bedlam had also never had a real job. She went with the first thing she thought of.

"I'm in school," she said. "I'm, um, a waitress."

"Hope you're studying something you enjoy," Rob said.

Again, Bedlam scrambled for the first thing that sprang to mind.

"I'm studying robotics," she said.

"Now that's impressive," Rob said. "I sell hand-crafted skateboards made from old recycled materials. Probably sounds ridiculous."

"Nah," Bedlam said. She felt a tickle in the back of her throat, a growing melancholy. She bit down on her inner cheek, intentionally causing herself pain. Don't you dare cry in front of this person, she thought. You don't do that. "It sounds fun."

"I mean I mostly sell to stockbrokers who are having midlife crises at thirty, but it's a living," Rob said, laughing. "Hey, are you sure you're okay? I—please don't be offended by this, but your left eye is looking kind of greenish?"

Bedlam's heart began to race. She stood up awkwardly.

"I'm going to, uh, check my eye in the women's room," she said. "Thank you or telling me. I should take a look."

"Do you want me to get help or anything?" Rob said.

"No, no, not yet," Bedlam said. "I'll just—can you keep an eye on my coffee?"

Rob nodded and smiled so warmly it made Bedlam's

stomach twist. Strangers don't look at me with kindness anymore, she thought. I don't know that they ever did.

She speed-walked to the women's restroom, relieved to find she didn't need a key or to be buzzed in. I must be having a dream, Bedlam thought. Nobody can just walk into a public restroom anymore in the real world, right? Isn't that a thing?

She closed the door behind her and latched it. Placing both hands on either side of the sink, she leaned in to look into her own eyes.

The left eye had begun to glow green from within. The eye that was, she knew, not real. Not part of her.

The porcelain of the sink suddenly crackled beneath her fingertips. Bedlam glanced down and saw that her hands, those human hands she held a cup of coffee with just a moment before, were gone, replaced not with the sleek, five-fingered upgraded models she'd acquired with the help of Agent Black and Henry Winter, but the clunky, awkward ones the Children of the Elder Star had bolted onto her body. One was just two thick fingers and a thumb, the other grotesque with exposed wiring and sloppy soldering.

"No," she said. She backed away, but her robotic hands didn't respond fast enough, still gripping the sink, yanking it from the wall. Water began to spray everywhere, soaking the room. She picked her feet up off the floor and watched as real feet of muscle and bone became misshapen, metal angles poking through the skin until the flesh gave away. Wide, stocky limbs with the look of construction equipment replaced her legs below the knee.

The transformation continued up her legs and arms, replacing all four limbs with monstrous, oversized mechanisms. The pain was blinding, as if her brain remembered the agony of the torturous transformative surgery that had been blurred out with painkillers and anesthetics. She screamed, falling backward into the bathroom door as she watched her face began to twist into a square, silver mess of steel. It caved, and she tumbled into the café, knocking over a high top. The patrons began to scream as well, running from her. She saw Rob hesitate for a moment, a look of concern turning into a mask of terror, and he ran as well.

Bedlam stomped toward the front of the coffee shop, suddenly twice her normal height, shoulders tearing through the wood and plaster of the restaurant's ceiling. She smashed through the front windows and into the street. More pedestrians ran from her, and she tripped over a car, her mechanical legs obliterating the entire driver's side. She heard a baby crying somewhere. Please don't let that baby be in this car, she thought, please, not that, I know this can't be real but I can't see that…

She felt something slam against her shins, then catch between her ankles, knocking her off balance. She fell backward, crushing a meter, coins spilling into the street like some final insult to this cacophony of injuries. She leaned backward, trying to get her awkward, slow cyborg limbs to cooperate so she could get back on her feet.

Then she felt something thump on her chest. Her entire torso was metal now, no longer even offering a semblance of humanity. She looked down to see what hit her and was greeted with the horrifying visage of Titus in full werewolf form. He set aside his spear and put a hand on each of her shoulders, somehow, despite her size, pinning her to the ground.

The wolf leaned in so close she could see the tiny serrated edges of his teeth. In a voice that was both Titus and not, the monster spoke.

"Wake up," he said.

And she did.

Bedlam woke kicking and thrashing, restrained, unexpectedly, by the oversized arms of Titus, who cradled her like a child, sitting on the pavement outside a coffee shop in the empty downtown of Westwick. The sky was red now, the same eerie red it had been when they entered the portal, and all the civilians who'd seen her in her nightmare were gone. The others stood back a few feet, outside the reach of her kicking legs. Billy had pulled the mask back from his costume and was watching with the sort of fear she would expect from someone at a hospital bedside. She calmed down, letting herself be held by the werewolf, which felt shockingly comforting, in a way.

Titus opened his eyes, gazing at her with giant, golden orbs.

"How did you do that?" Bedlam asked.

"I'm learning," Titus said. He let her go, and she sat up, but before she got to her feet, Bedlam pressed her forehead into Titus' massive, furry shoulder.

"Thanks for that," she said. "I owe you."

"You were in deeper than the others," Titus said. "I thought you might need more help finding your way home."

"I am so finding a therapist when we get back," Bedlam said, laughing and wiping tears from her eye.

"I think we all are," Billy said. "This sucks. Why can't we fight aliens or monsters or something? This is horrible."

"We're fighting ourselves," Jane said. "Doc always said magic was the most dangerous thing we'd ever face. I used to think he was exaggerating."

"Yeah," Bedlam said. "Guys, I am so glad to see you. That was really rough. Did you all have nightmares too?"

"Oh yeah," Billy said. "I had an existential crisis."

"Me too," Jane said. "I mean, it was like a literal

reenactment of an existential crisis."

"My nightmare tried to kill me," Titus said, getting to his feet and helping Bedlam stand up. She cocked her head at the strange way his voice sounded coming from his werewolf form.

"You stuck like that?" she asked.

"No," Titus said. "Just… enjoying a little more inner peace than I'm used to having."

"You kind of have a lisp when you talk like this," Billy said.

"It's the canines," Titus said, shooting Billy a cartoonish grin with his long muzzle.

"One more, then," Kate said, the first time she'd spoken since Bedlam woke up. "Where's Emily?"

Titus picked up his spear and sighed.

"I'm not going to be able to pull her out the way I did Billy and Bedlam," he said. "I may need all your help."

"Do I even want to know why," Jane said.

"You'll see," Titus said. "Believe me, you'll see."

CHAPTER 45:
ENTROPIA

Emily settled into her ornate saddle and patted her mount on the neck. She held her head high, taking a deep breath as the wind ruffled her hair. She pulled her steampunk goggles down dramatically over her eyes and nodded.

This would be the final battle for the kingdom, Emily said. We have come so far. We have battled so much. Victory would be theirs at long last.

She twisted in her saddle and her mount pivoted. His long, blue-scaled neck twisted so he could look at her with enormous golden eyes.

"Are you ready, Lord Commander?" the dragon asked, his face so close Emily could smell the ghost of flames on his breath.

"As ready as I'll ever be, Bubbles," Emily said. "You've been a brave and true companion in our war against the Laser Ninjas of Over There. I wouldn't be here without you."

"It has been an honor, fighting from Narnia to Westeros at your side," the dragon said. "If we can drive the Laser Ninjas back this day, we can finally take the Death Moon by storm and put an end to this galactic war."

"Then drive them back we shall," Emily said.

She unclipped the laser sword at her hip and held it aloft, igniting it. She looked down at her troops, gathered below, awaiting her orders. An army of short, bear-like bipedal mammals, adorned in primitive garments and armor, the mighty Fur Folk of the Planet of Trees had been her elite warriors throughout the War of One Thousand Planets, and despite their small stature and limited vocabulary, they were staunch allies and vicious fighters.

As she lifted her laser sword to them, a cacophony of barks arose, an ocean of woofs as the Fur Folks' armored corgi mounts lifted their heads to cheer. The Fur Folk joined in with their own garbled alien language, raising spear and stone club and the occasional blaster rifle overhead in excitement.

"My mighty warriors!" Emily shouted, adjusting her wizarding school uniform for maximum effect, snapping her rainbow suspenders in a display of confidence. "The undead army of Laser Ninjas think they can defeat us, but they are not prepared! They will not withstand our might, our prowess, our courage! Together, we will storm the Death Moon and put a stop to the machinations of the Dark Prince of Clowns! I swear this as Lord Commander of Dragonperch!"

Once again, her minute battalion cheered. She raised her laser sword once more, then wheeled Bubbles around, the dragon taking flight to lead the charge across an empty field. In the distance, she could see rows of ninjas ignite laser swords much like her own.

"For the kingdom of Entropia!" she shouted.

But before she could go any further, she saw the strangest thing in the middle of the battlefield: five young people, familiar, staring up at her in utter disbelief.

"Down, Bubbles. We must make sure these wayfarers are not the enemy," she said, and he dragon returned to the earth a few feet from the gathered oddities. As she drew closer, she realized she knew their names, though she couldn't figure out why they were all here.

"You really should get off the field of battle," Emily said. "I'd suggest you get out of the way so you don't get hurt. There's a war going on here."

"I have often said I wanted to have five minutes to see what goes on inside Emily's head," Billy said. "I feel like I can officially check that off the bucket list. I've now been there. I don't need to go back."

"I don't understand anything I've just seen," Kate said.

"It's like the land fan fiction threw up on," Bedlam said.

"This is amazing," Titus said. "Seriously, this is the greatest thing I have ever seen."

"Hang on," Jane said. "I get a horrific anxiety dream and Emily gets to be the Mother of Dragons and a Jedi at the same time?"

"I am not Bubbles' mother," Emily said. "He is my brave companion and best friend."

"Good day to you," the dragon said, bowing with comical grace.

"You guys deal with this," Kate said, walking away. "I'm not equipped for this. I'm just not."

"I had a legitimately panic-attack inducing nightmare," Billy said. "This is unfair."

"Hey, mine was pure body horror," Bedlam said.

"I tried to eat myself," Titus said.

"So, therapy for you too?" Bedlam said.

"I'm already in therapy," Titus said.

"Because you're a werewolf?" Bedlam asked.

"Because I have catastrophic clinically diagnosed anxiety," Titus said. "The werewolf part is just a bonus."

"We're a disaster," Billy said. "How have we saved the world multiple times?"

"By being true and brave companions," Emily said.

Billy sighed.

"I want this dream," Billy said. "Why'd I get a nightmare instead of flying an X-Wing to fight off an army of White Walkers?"

"I had an X-Wing once," Emily said. "But no starship can compare to the love and loyalty of the greatest dragon in the land."

"You flatter me," Bubbles said.

"I'm just being honest," Emily said.

"Are those… corgis in plate armor?" Bedlam said.

"Being ridden by…" Titus said.

"Yup," Billy said, throwing his arms in the air. "Yup."

"Um, guys, there's an army of ninjas with laser swords running at us," Bedlam said.

"We must defeat the undead Laser Ninjas of Over There!" Emily said. "Join us, heroes, and we will feast tonight on barbecue chicken pizza and salted caramel cheesecake!"

The army of furry aliens cheered as Emily said cheesecake.

"You know what, forget it," Bedlam said. "I want to stay here. Let's just stay in Emily's dream. This is better than any reality we can possibly go back to."

"Emily, we have a town to save," Jane said, trying, as always, to be the voice of reason. "With real people."

"The Fur Folk are people too," Emily said. "Well, aliens, but that doesn't disqualify them from fighting for their freedom. And once we defeat the Death Moon, all the great peoples of the world of Entropia will be out from under the yoke of the Dark Prince of Clowns! The mermaids of the Glittering Grotto, the elflings of the Winding Wood, the Free Robots of Trashcandar, all will finally escape their bonds!"

"The Dark Prince of Clowns," Jane said bluntly.

"He is very dark," Emily said.

"Is he also a clown," Jane said.

"That's why they all him the Dark Prince of… Clowns," Emily said. "I thought that would be self-explanatory."

"He is both a dark prince and a clown," Jane said.

"He's a prince of clowns?" Billy said. "Meaning there's a whole group of dark clowns over there?"

"This is true," Emily said. "With an army of undead ninjas."

"With laser swords," Titus said.

"Yes," Emily said.

"And are all the clowns dark, or just the prince?" Bedlam said.

"Aren't all clowns dark?" Emily said.

"I think we figured out why this qualifies as a nightmare," Bedlam said.

"I hate clowns," Billy said.

"But the prince is the very darkest among them," Emily said. "His laugh alone can turn your blood to ice and cause bladders to loosen uncontrollably."

Kate came stomping back into the conversation, hands flailing in the most spectacular display of emotion any of them had ever witnessed from her.

"Did you just say these little corgi-riding furballs are being oppressed by a cadre of evil clowns with undead ninjas?" Kate said.

"I'm glad *someone* around here is listening to me!" Emily

said.

Kate tightened her gloves and cracked her knuckles.

"We have time," she said.

"What?" Titus said.

"We're not leaving a bunch of alien teddy bears to be slaughtered by ninjas and clowns," Kate said. "I am the least sentimental person on Earth and even I can't live with myself if that happens."

"Are we really fighting undead ninjas and clowns?" Billy said.

"I'm in," Bedlam said. "Man, I am so in."

"Okay," Billy said. "Just checking. I can get behind this plan."

"This is, okay, y'know what, let's do this thing," Jane said. "Call it a group bonding experience."

"Can I have a laser sword too?" Billy said.

Emily unclipped a spare hilt from her belt and tossed it to him. He ignited it, and a massive grin split his face.

"Let's go evil clown hunting," he said.

"Does anyone else hear music from *Les Miserables* playing?" Bedlam asked.

"Titus?" Jane said.

"I'm not going to be the only one who turns down the chance to live out Emily's greatest fantasy," Titus said. "But I have one request."

"Ask it, fuzzy one," Emily said.

"I want the dragon to airdrop me into the fight like a werewolf bomb," Titus said.

"That, my dog-like friend, can be arranged," Emily said.

"All right," Jane said. "I'll take those three hundred Laser Ninjas over there."

Emily beamed down at her friends from atop her blue

dragon. She pointed her laser sword at the oncoming horde of undead ninjas, like a general gesturing at a battlefield with a saber.

"I am so very proud of you," she said. "Let's win this war. For Entropia!"

CHAPTER 45:
WHY IS OLD MAN TEDDY RUXPIN TALKING TO US

They walked from the fog of battle onto Westwick's ghostly Main Street, nary a sign of ninja or battle corgi in sight. Jane took stock of her team and saw everyone was whole and uninjured, as if the great battle for Entropia had never happened.

Of course it hadn't, she reminded herself. Nothing is real here, right?

"We will never speak of that again," Kate said, stretching her back and cracking her neck.

"We will speak of that always," Billy said. "That was the most amazing thing we've ever done."

"My dreams are the best, you guys," Emily said.

Jane sat down on a nearby bench, because Westwick was apparently one of those types of suburbs with nice benches available in its downtown.

"I just don't understand why that was how we got out of

Emily's dream," she said. "Everyone else had to overcome some sort of psychological trauma."

"We all had to overcome a conflict in the dream somehow," Titus said. "In Em's, that conflict was a fan fiction mashup battle."

"Alternately, I bet if we had convinced Emily she wasn't actually the Lord Commander of Dragonperch and had real-world responsibilities we might have also got ourselves out of there," Bedlam suggested.

"Where's the fun in that?" Billy said.

"I didn't say that was the preferable option," Bedlam said. "I'm just saying it might have maybe been an alternative one."

"Can we get back on task?" Kate said.

Jane nodded.

"First thing, we've got to find Doc," she said.

And that was the moment they realized abruptly they weren't alone.

"You are the allies of Doctor Silence?" A grizzled but friendly voice said. The entire team turned in unison to look to the source of that voice.

"Oh, you've got to be kidding me," Bedlam said.

The speaker was a teddy bear, armed for battle, one eye covered in an eyepatch. He sat astride a white unicorn like a warhorse. Perched on his shoulder was a tiny fairy dressed in a pink shift. Standing, or more accurately floating, at their side was a humanoid shadow with glowing eyes.

"Why is Old Man Teddy Ruxpin talking to us?" Billy said.

"We've been sent to help you," the bear said. "I am Sir Teddy. This is Silverhoof, Galinda, and Gloomly."

"Of course you are," Kate said.

"You know Doc?" Jane said. It had been the most absurd day of her already absurd life; somehow talking to a teddy bear with a broadsword wasn't particularly hard to roll with.

"We encountered your wizard. He was on his way to help our ruler, Queen Alice," the bear said. "He is trapped."

"We knew that part," Titus said.

"I—y'know, hang on," Jane said, producing the mirror form her pocket. She spoke into it. "Doc, can you hear me?"

Doc appeared in the mirror, still in the darkened cell they'd last seen him.

"I'm still here," Doc said. "How are you progressing?"

"We're in the, um, general area," Jane said. "Any suggestions for what to do next?"

"Here's what I know," Doc said. "Alice is being manipulated by a malignant entity. I have a few ideas about how to fix that, but I need to get out of this cell."

"Okay, storm the dungeon," Emily said.

"No, no storming the dungeon," Doc said. "Did you guys encounter your own nightmares here already?"

"Yeah," Titus muttered.

"Do I even want to know what yours looked like, Emily?" Doc asked.

"Why, specifically, are you concerned about mine?" Emily said with mock indignation.

"Because he has a pretty good handle on what the rest of us are afraid of, because he's Doc," Kate said. "None of us know what you're afraid of."

"Did the brilliant strategist just admit she can't parse me out?" Emily said.

"I gave up ages ago," Kate said, immediately redirecting the conversation. "How do we get you out of that cell, Doc? We should mention we have a talking a bear, a unicorn, a pixie, and what looks like a floating blanket with us who say they know you."

"Good," Doc said. "They're on our side. You can trust them."

"All for the good of the kingdom," Sir Teddy said, nodding sagely.

"Okay, I think we're all feeling a little freaked out and manic. The cell, Doc?" Jane said.

"The cell. I figured out how to get out. It's a very simple spell, but I need someone with at least rudimentary knowledge of magic on the other side to cast it," he said.

Kate and Titus exchanged a long look, hers annoyed, his vaguely sheepish.

"I'm here, Doc," Titus said.

"Great. This is nothing you won't be able to handle, but I'll have to walk you through it," Doc said.

The shadow-man drifted forward and bowed.

"I journeyed with Doctor Silence to the dungeon," he said, his voice strangely formal and deep. He sounded like a friendly version of Professor Snape. "I can guide you there. I should warn you that it might be difficult for the entire group to sneak in undetected, though."

"We'll go," Kate said, gesturing to Titus and herself. "This is sort of our thing anyway. We have experience with jailbreaks."

Titus let out a short laugh.

"I can't believe we really do have experience with jailbreaks," he said. "Not that the last one went particularly well."

"The other thing we need for this spell to work is for the dark entity manipulating Alice to be distracted," Doc said. "It calls itself the Vizier. It's not all-powerful, obviously, because it's acting like a parasite off Alice's magic. But it would help if the creature was preoccupied while we cast it."

"So, assault the castle?" Emily asked.

"How about we try talking?" Jane said.

"Six people here, and I'm pretty sure you're the only one who anyone would reason with," Billy said.

"So I'll go. Present myself as a traveler," Jane said. "Get them talking for a few minutes. That should be enough to confuse them, right?"

"Possibly," Doc said. "The Vizier is suspicious and paranoid, but Alice built this world and he knows it, and she's curious about newcomers. In the very least, you'll get an audience."

"We can take you," Sir Teddy said. "She has rejected us as her companions, but she'll at least open the gates if we arrive, I think."

"Are we all going, then?" Bedlam asked. "Or do the rest of us, like, hang back in reserve?"

The fairy whispered in the bear's ear, who looked up at her curiously, then gestured at the group.

"Go on, tell them, then, Galinda," he said.

"There is a group of monsters we've never seen before moving toward the castle as well," the fairy said, her voice comically musical.

"Define monsters," Billy said.

The fairy threw up her arms.

"Okay, then," Billy said. "That was helpful. Why don't I go scout out the monsters to see what we're actually dealing with."

"I'll come," Bedlam said.

"Me too," Emily said.

"No, you're with me," Jane said. "Because if I can't reach the queen through words, you can try to confuse the Vizier."

"Confusion is not one of my superpowers," Emily said.

"Yes, it is," Titus said.

"Fine," Emily said. "But can I ride on the unicorn?"

"That would be fine, miss," Sir Teddy said. The unicorn whinnied agreeably as well.

"This continues to be the greatest day of my life," Emily said. "I never want to go home."

The fairy landed on Billy's shoulder and took a proprietary seat.

"I'll guide you to the monsters," Galinda said. "We can stay at a distance. I was able to spy on them without being seen. I'll show you how."

Jane held up the mirror so Doc could see most of the group behind her.

"You okay with this plan, Doc?" she said.

"Sounds like a great plan that will inevitably come apart at the seams, as always," Doc said. "I'll see you soon."

Jane pocketed the mirror. Billy looped a shoulder under Bedlam's arm and lifted off, the fairy still perched on his shoulder.

"Well this is new and different," Bedlam said, holding onto Billy with both arms.

"We'll be like Superman and Lois," Billy said.

"Okay, Lois," Bedlam said.

As they took off, Titus and Kate began to follow the shadow-man toward the castle.

"Good luck," Titus said.

"You too, furball," Emily said, hopping up onto the unicorn's back.

"How could any of this possibly go wrong," Jane said, patting the unicorn's long, graceful neck as they started off along the most direct route to the castle in the distance.

CHAPTER 46: MIDDLE MANAGEMENT FOR MONSTERS

The graveyard wasn't particularly scary, Keppler thought. Not scary at all, really, if you could discount the fact that it was under a crimson-colored sky. Otherwise, it looked like any other graveyard a small city or larger town might have—well-manicured, tidy, with neat rows of expensive headstones and a healthy cover of green grass. The only thing scary about this graveyard, he thought, was the crowd of magically mutated creatures standing around waiting, and those guys showed up with him.

King Tears seemed satisfied by the graveyard, though, eyeing the expanse of open space and nodding.

"This will do," he said.

"This will do what?" Keppler asked.

"The creatures I created will be our greatest weapons, but we need fodder," the magician said. "Troops we can throw away in the coming fight. And what better fodder than those who are already dead?"

Keppler's stomach knotted up. He wasn't a sentimental person, but the implication Tears made had him feeling a little queasy.

"You're going to raise the dead… here?" Keppler said.

"A corpse is a corpse," King Tears said, grinning wickedly at Keppler's discomfort. "I don't see the problem."

'This isn't some medieval crypt," Keppler said. "These are real people. You're going to use someone's dead grandmother as a weapon?"

The smile faded from King Tears' face. He turned to Keppler solemnly.

"You didn't strike me as a soft touch," King Tears said. "Well, honestly, you did, but not this badly."

"This just doesn't feel right."

King Tears sighed, real exhaustion in his tenor.

"Mr. Keppler, you work for a multinational corporation that has been run with a lack of ethics that even the usual multinational corporation's lack of ethics would find appalling," he said. "You get your 401(k) and bonus package from people who spent decades experimenting on lost kids. You think the experiments that occurred most recently were dark? At least they had access to modern painkillers. The Children of the Elder Star is an old, old organization. They have literally used medieval torture techniques, and not just in the Middle Ages."

King Tears casually waved his hand this way and that, casting wordless spells like they were just off-hand gestures. Keppler felt the earth beneath him tremble slightly.

"Your employer has promoted war for profit and instability. They have destabilized economies so that some of their members could gain power and wealth. They've allowed families to starve, sometimes to save money, other times to provoke action by those who would be saviors just so that the attention of those saviors was diverted while the Children of the Elder Star engaged in some activity even more heinous they did not want to be noticed."

A hand burst free from beneath a nearby grave. Then another. Soon, the perfectly cut grass over each grave was torn asunder by the grimy, blackened skin of a zombie dressed in funeral finery.

"Your employers hired people like me to poison villages so they could obtain rights to gold or diamond mines. They hired other magicians to cause disruptive weather to kill thousands so that the land those unfortunate victims were on would need to be rebuilt, under corporate ownership. They have no interest in the sanctity or value of human life if they can profit from it. And the sad part is, they are no different than any number of other cabalistic organizations—they just have access to flashier tools, and admit what they are amongst themselves."

The zombies shambled toward King Tears now, gaits awkward and gawky, eyes empty sockets filled with dirt and decay. King Tears pointed an accusatory finger at Keppler.

"The Children of the Elder Star groomed mediocre men like you to take their places, raised you up for no reason other than they want someone just like them to continue their traditions forever and ever, waiting for whatever stupid myth or birthright they think they have ownership over. I took great pleasure in watching that belief system rot their organization from the inside out even as I took their money and gifts."

"I…" Keppler said, unsure what else to say. The smell of rot was overwhelming.

"I became a magician because the Children of the Elder

Star destroyed my home. I became a blood magician because it was the fastest and most efficient way to power. And I took the Children's contracts because it was a way to leech back what they stole from me," King Tears said. "I have no sentimentality for the dead. Everything in this world is a tool to be used. You, me, these corpses, the mutated peons all around us. There is no right or wrong. There is only those who win and those who suffer."

Keppler bowed his head, unsure if King Tears would order the zombies to tear him apart or not. He waited. Nothing happened.

"Don't moralize at me, Keppler," King Tears said. "You were a middle manager for monsters. You don't get to decide good or evil."

"Of course," Keppler said.

"That's the problem with this world. Quantifying evil. As if one kind of selfishness or cruelty is more socially acceptable than another," King Tears said. "Anyone can talk themselves into believing something selfish or monstrous or cruel is acceptable if it benefits them. If you want to get ahead in this world, Keppler, you need to accept that power comes not from finding a way to see your worst deeds as necessary for the common good, or lesser on a sliding scale of terrible things. Accept that you do evil because it benefits you and it becomes so much easier to do the things you need to do to get ahead. Consider this a lesson in an economy of ethics. Don't waste your time trying to feel better about wronging people. Feel better knowing that wronging people will make you stronger than them."

King Tears walked away, his dead and living servants following in his wake. Keppler followed as well, more convinced than ever he knew however this story ended, and it would not end well for him.

CHAPTER 47:
A WRONG OF OUR OWN MAKING

Lady Dreamless entered Westwick easily, her connection to the magic used to create the pocket dimension so strong it was as though there were no barrier between the worlds.

The transition was not without impact, though. As she stepped through, she shed the appearance she had worn on Earth, the coy movie star shell disappearing as her true form rose to the surface. Her skin faded to the color of pearl, silvery and gleaming. Her body was veined in glowing lines of red, the pattern of marble. Her hair became a shock of bright red as well, unnaturally so, not ginger but spikes of neon vermillion. Her eyes began to glow brightly from within, also red. Her fingertips elongated, almost like talons. She passed a hand over her human clothing, and they rippled as they morphed into a thin, soft tunic that fell just above her knees.

A tail sprung into existence at the base of her spine, prehensile, and tipped like a devil's.

Her demon hounds underwent similar transformations, shedding their Great Dane illusions to become hulking war beasts. Gone was the warm, slobbering wholesomeness of ordinary dogs. In its place, lantern-like eyes flickered all around like searchlights and massive jaws slathered, highlighted by massive fangs. The hounds flanked their master like an honor guard.

The Lady Dreamless reached out her hand into the open air, and where it passed, pale, sparkling light flowed through her fingers like glitter. She gathered some of this sparkling energy into the palm of her hand and examined it. She had to admire the craftsmanship; this world had the architecture of the Dreamless Realms all over it, but the power that made that possible was a raw, unrefined talent with infinite potential. The source of this power was a true savant waiting for the right guidance, Dreamless thought. She scanned the horizon, taking in the scope of this pocket dimension, and sighed. That lack of refinement showed through, with unstable areas, roaming dream storms, a permeating stink of fear that told her the balance of the dream magic was off here. That did tell her something about which of her dimension's residents had helped guide the creation of this place. It had to be a darker creature, a nightmare or night terror, something that did not understand the joy or relief dreams were capable of. They knew only pain, not grasping how much influence could be obtained with honey instead of acid.

She felt a flash of anger within her. In part at the hubris of it, that a lesser denizen of her world thought it could manipulate a power source this strong without attracting attention; but also anger at the laziness of it all. Lady Dreamless disliked nothing so much as she did intellectual laziness and a lack of curiosity.

If you're going to steal magic, do something with it worth stealing for, she thought. Don't slap together a dimension on the bones of a little town and keep all the residents under a perpetual cloud of their own anxieties.

Not only did the abuse of power bother her; the escaped dream-creature had committed the cardinal sin of being boring.

She gazed up at the strange sky, bright red above and deepening to crimson on the horizon, and wondered about the aesthetic choice the creator had made. It painted the quaint town they'd kidnapped in a bloody hue, giving the entire world a threatening feel. It piqued her curiosity. Did the nightmare decide to do this? Or was the choice a cry for help from the magician being used by the nightmare?

In the distance—not as far away as it looked, she knew, as dreamscapes tended toward misdirection and obfuscation—an impossible castle loomed, cartoonish and unwelcoming.

She stroked each of her demon hounds on the head, both looking up to her with incredible admiration and loyalty.

"Where is our betrayer, my hounds?" she asked.

Pollux turned his massive head toward the castle, staring intently.

"And where is Doc Silence, the friend and ally who gave you to me?" she said.

This time Castor turned his head, also toward the castle. Again, she thought. The cardinal sin of being boring. Lady Dreamless sighed irritably.

"I suppose we know where we're headed," she said, and began walking into the town.

She paused at a few houses along the way, looking in on the residents. Her disappointment grew as she found humans in fugue states, trapped in nightmares of their own. Some relived past trauma so awful it made her blood boil to witness. Others lived out family drama anxiety that was, by comparison, comedic in its pettiness. She understood that the subconscious mind latched on to whatever the waking mind refused to process, or was unable to process. And yet it never ceased to amaze her how humans, with their great imagination and capacity for courage and relentlessness, could trap themselves in little circles of angry parents or disappointing children, or wake in a cold sweat concerned about running late for something that mattered little in the overall arc of their lives, how they could turn simple, forgivable mistakes over and over again in their minds until the worry ate a hole in the lining of their stomach.

If I could change one thing about humanity, she thought, after spending so much time amongst them the past few months, it would be to gift them the ability to shed useless fear and anxiety. There is so much in their world, so much in the multiverse, that should truly scare you, that to waste one's life upset about something of little or no consequence was a tragedy on an epic level to Lady Dreamless.

But then, she thought, I come from a world I can alter with a stray thought. Perhaps my lesson among humans is that when you have little power over the world around you, every detail is worth fretting over.

Still, she thought, the idea seemed painfully boring to her. And this traitorous little nightmare had gone and built a whole world on that concept.

"And it's my fault the creature is here in the first place," Lady Dreamless said, admitting her disappointment in herself.

She should have known better, she thought.

"Well, my hounds," she said, both Castor and Pollux attentively listening to her voice. "Let us go right a wrong of our own making, shall we?"

CHAPTER 48: INTRUDERS IN THE QUEEN'S LANDS

Queen Alice sat on her throne watching a hologram of a beautiful airship rotate slowly above the chamber. The Vizier had helped her weave her magic to create the idea, a wonderful craft that would allow her to travel all across her kingdom so she could survey her subjects, make sure everything was in order, and see as far as the eye could see.

The airship was the Vizier's idea. Alice had become discontent and wanted to get out more, suggesting a new royal carriage pulled by a pair of winged horses, but the Vizier had suggested something more leisurely. Why tire horses and cram yourself into a buggy when you could travel the winds at your own pace far above? he'd suggested. And so, Alice began to read about dirigibles and similar ships to better understand the mechanics involved and how magic could improve upon the mundane.

She was excited to begin the process of building her new

ship, and at first, the Vizier seemed impressed by her enthusiasm, encouraging her to design, dream, and imagine a floating throne room dressed up in golds and reds.

She looked at her trusted confidante now, though, and he had a distant look on his face, staring straight ahead, in the direction of Westwick.

"You look troubled, Vizier," Alice said, turning her attention from her schematics. The hologram ceased rotating, pausing exactly where she left off.

"Something's not quite right, my queen," he said.

"What is it?" she asked, worry building in her chest.

The Vizier studied her, looking intently into her eyes in a way he rarely did.

"Do you sense it? This is your kingdom. I wonder if you can feel disturbances here instinctually," he said.

Alice closed her eyes, reaching out through the veins of magic that build this dimension, that held it together.

"We have guests," she said.

"Intruders," the Vizier said.

"Not everyone who enters is an enemy," Alice said chidingly. "Maybe they're lost. Or looking for a new home."

"What do you sense, Queen Alice?" the Vizier asked.

Alice focused her attention once again. She could feel different places in the topography of her kingdom which did not feel right, things out of place on the edge of the map.

First, of course, she sensed the magician in the dungeons. She still felt strange about that, locking the man up when all he'd done was mention her parents. But the Vizier said he was dangerous, and she trusted the Vizier more than anyone. And really, the dungeons weren't that bad, she thought.

Next, though, she felt a power surge right at the border of her kingdom, distractingly powerful. It scared her.

She began to speak, wanting to ask the Vizier about that presence, when the tendrils of her magic led her to what felt like bugs crawling across her mind. She turned her attention to this presence, and gasped.

"Someone has destroyed the cemetery," she said. "Why would someone destroy the cemetery?"

"I suspect we'll soon find out," the Vizier said, leaning in curiously. "What else do you sense?"

"Something… strange, a mind I can't understand," she said. "I don't know if it's more powerful than I am, but it worries me. It's just arrived."

"Do they seem related to you?" the Vizier said. "You can read the spells they walk with—do they feel the same, or different?"

"The scarier one reminds me of you," she said, opening her eyes, then frowning apologetically. "Not that you scare me. I just mean it's a magic that looks similar."

"I understand," the Vizier said. "And the other?"

"It's not like anything I've ever seen before," Alice said. "Not like the magician downstairs, not like me, not like you."

"Does your connection detect anything else?" the Vizier said.

She closed her eyes one more time. She felt the faintest ping of magic somewhere near the dungeons, but stray bits of spellcasting often drifted around the kingdom as she built and rebuilt her own magical constructs and mystical wards. She began to reach out with her mind for a closer inspection just to be sure, but then something caught her attention in another part of the castle. Or rather, just outside.

"My friends," Alice said.

"Friends?" the Vizier said.

"Sir Teddy and Silverhoof approach along the great road

leading to our gates," Alice said. She knew the Vizier had warned her that her companions had become untrustworthy, unsafe to keep within the castle walls, but she couldn't help herself—the idea of seeing her teddy bear once again made her heart skip a beat. She shook her head irritably, trying to remind herself that a good ruler doesn't fall prey to childlike sentiments.

"It could be a trap," the Vizier said. He cast a spell of his own, creating a circle with his fingertip. A window appeared within that circle, showing them the group approaching the main gates.

There was Sir Teddy, riding Silverhoof, looking as grim and determined and adorable as ever. Riding with him, though, was a girl a few years older than Alice with neon-blue hair, goggles perched on her forehead, and a shirt with a nuclear symbol on it. Beside them walked another young woman, dressed in a form-fitting top, skirt, and tall boots, a cape drifting off her shoulders lightly. Everything she wore was a combination of bright, primary colors. The most striking thing about her, though, was her hair—it seemed to be made of fire, flames flickering off the back as she walked.

"Who are they?" Alice asked.

"More trouble, I suspect," the Vizier said, his tone uncharacteristically short and frustrated.

"They're with my friends," Alice said.

"When you are queen, you have no friends," the Vizier said. "Everyone is out to use you. Remember that."

Alice nodded, but narrowed her eyes slowly at the Vizier, who was staring angrily at the window, watching the two new women approach.

If everyone is out to use me, Alice wondered, a nagging thought creeping up in her mind for the first time in a while, why does the Vizier help me?

She looked into the magic window at her bear, her unicorn, and wondered where Galinda and Gloomly were. She kept that thought to herself, though.

"I'd like to speak to these strangers," Queen Alice said.

"Your highness, I don't know if that's wise," the Vizier said.

"If they mean us harm, we'll throw them in the dungeon as well," she said. "But I'm bored, and I'd like to see who they are."

The Vizier watched her for just a few seconds as if to measure her seriousness. Seeing no room for argument, he bowed respectfully.

"Of course," he said. "Guards, let the newcomers in. Her majesty would like to speak with them."

CHAPTER 49:
BOLD DECISIVENESS

"Okay," Billy said. "The zombies I get. But what are those?"

Billy, Bedlam, and Galinda had found a spot on a garage roof a block away from the army of grossness making its way steadily through Westwick. They lay on one side of the garage's slightly peaked roof and glanced over the top, trying to get a read on what they were up against. Billy counted dozens, possibly over a hundred, undead creatures shambling along, which he was grossed out by but not particularly shocked, having seen this King Tears character turn baristas into mindless monsters in New York. But the other things were beyond comprehension. They were twisted human bodies, sometimes multiple bodies fused together, nightmarish monsters who all wore the expression of people who were on a miserable morning commute.

"We've seen those other things before," Bedlam said. "Titus and Kate and me. We found a massive one in that warehouse we investigated in the City."

"Are they people?" Billy asked.

"They used to be," Bedlam said. "The one we found begged for us to kill him. It. I don't know. It was a bunch of people stuck together like a giant quilt."

"They look like monsters," the fairy said, her voice somehow sing-songy and not at the same time.

"Awesome," Billy said. "Y'know, these zombies look deader than the ones we saw in Manhattan."

"Is deader a word?" Bedlam asked.

"I don't know. I think so," Billy said. "Hang on."

Hey Dude, Billy thought. Can our alien super-sensory powers tell us if those things are still alive?

It's about time you learned how to do this for yourself, Dude said, and Billy felt his vision change. The world went gray for a split second, and then became infinitely more colorful as he could suddenly see details about the marching creatures invisible to the human eye. Their body temperatures were mapped out in color patterns. He spotted the flickering twitch of heartbeats in some, but not all.

Why have I never known how to do this until now? Billy said.

You only started asking about it recently.

How many powers do we have that I don't know about yet? Billy thought.

We should have a long conversation when we get back, Dude said.

You've been holding out on me? Billy thought.

That's an ungenerous way of phrasing it, Dude said. *But I suppose I have.*

"Great," Billy sad.

"I assume you were talking to your alien," Bedlam said. "Because otherwise your eyes just randomly started glowing and then you started having a very subtle seizure."

"Yeah," Billy said. "I must've reached a new level and unlocked some abilities."

"Which are?" Bedlam asked.

"The ones that look like zombies are zombies. They're dead. The other ones are still alive."

"I could have told you that," Bedlam said.

"What?" Billy said.

Bedlam tapped her mechanical eye.

"I have imaging tech packed into this one," Bedlam said. "I already checked. Some of the big ones have multiple heartbeats, but the rotting corpses are cold and inert."

"Why did I not know you could do this?" Billy said.

"You don't ask me about my cyborg capabilities very often," Bedlam said.

"Sorry. I should be more curious."

"Actually, I find it refreshing that you don't want to talk about it," Bedlam said. "It's nice to pretend I'm not half-robot sometimes. Anyway. What's the…"

Bedlam trailed off as another figure moved into view. A tall man, grayish skinned, covered in chalky white tattoos, accompanied by a young, blond man in an expensive suit that had seen better days.

"Who's that guy?" Bedlam said.

"That's our mark," Billy said. "We ran into him in Manhattan. I was able to keep him from casting any major spells by hitting him with light blasts, but I'm pretty sure that's a trick that will only work once."

Bedlam's face darkened.

"He's the one who did that to all those people down there," Bedlam said. "The one who was altering their bodies with magic."

"I would assume so," Billy said.

"We take him out, we win, right?" Bedlam said.

Billy shook his head.

"No, he's after the magician kid too," he said. "I mean, if we could take him out, that's part of our problem solved, but we still have to deal with the other thing. Our problems are, y'know. Two-fold."

"I'm going to kill him," Bedlam said.

"I don't disagree with the sentiment, but I think that's not the wisest course of action," Billy said. Bedlam stared to slide her way off the garage roof toward the back edge where the zombie horde couldn't see her. Billy reluctantly followed. Galinda, shrugging, fluttered along beside him.

"I may not be much of a strategist, but you appear to be outnumbered," the fairy said.

"The fairy has a point," Billy said.

Bedlam clenched her fists. Billy could hear the pneumatic sounds of her cyborg fingers from several feet away.

"You didn't see what he did to those people in the warehouse," Bedlam said. "I thought I'd never see anything worse than what the Children did to me and to Valerie and to Caleb and the others, but this was… Billy, it was the worst thing I've ever seen. This guy has to die. He can't be allowed to keep doing this to people."

"Am not disagreeing," Billy said. He had the sudden self-conscious realization he was trying to rationalize with his cyborg girlfriend while dressed head to toe in spandex as a tiny fairy looked on curiously. This is what my life has led to, he thought. This is my reality.

The two of you are not sufficient to defeat that man, Dude said. *If both Doc and Lady Grey are concerned about him, he must be on their level, if not greater.*

Also not disagreeing with you either, Dude, Billy thought.

But thanks for backing me up.

"We can't let him keep going. We have a shot now," Bedlam said. "He's just a skinny dude in a suit."

"And Doc looks like an adjunct college professor with a hippy streak," Billy said. "Magicians are weird, Bedlam. Let's get the whole team together and go all in on this one, yeah?"

"If we jump him now we have the element of surprise," Bedlam said.

"Okay, so your bold decisiveness is one of the things I like the most about you, but I'm just going to go out on a limb and say a cyborg charging across a suburban lawn followed by a human glow stick will not have the element of surprise by the time we get close enough to hit him."

"Cover me," Bedlam said as she stood up and broke into a run.

"This is bad," Billy said. "Hey, fairy."

"My name is Galinda," the fairy said.

"Galinda, go get my friends. Tell them we're in trouble. The guy with the zombies is here and we're in a fight."

"Which friend should I talk to?"

"Any of them will do," Billy said. "Ideally the one with her hair on fire, but don't be picky. Just get them."

"Aye-aye!" the fairy said, taking flight and darting off toward the castle.

Billy gritted his teeth steeled himself for a fight. He took a quick look at what Bedlam was up to and saw her darting between a couple of ranch-style houses, going full speeding locomotive on the zombie horde.

"I'm going to regret this," Billy said.

So am I, Dude said.

Together, they took flight.

The accompanying flash of brilliant blue-white light was

enough to give Bedlam the distraction she needed. The tattooed magician whipped his head around to see where Billy had emerged from and started yelling, but Billy was too far away to make out exactly what he was saying. Whatever it was, he didn't get to finish it, though—Bedlam charged into the crowd, punching one zombie so hard its head unmoored from its neck to hang backward like a hood; she clobbered another one so badly it caused a domino effect, knocking over an entire column of undead as they fell over each other. Some of the more monstrous members of the nightmare parade reached for her, but it was too late—Bedlam was up in the magician's face, rearing back for a punch Billy knew would be strong enough to literally knock his block off.

Billy darted down toward the fight, then felt something heavy slam into his gut. The smell was overwhelming—blood and puss and rot, a screech that was half pain, half rage. He grabbed hold of his attacker and found that one of the mutated creatures had taken flight, lifting off on wings of patchwork flesh. Billy hammered the monstrous thing with a two-handed light blast, getting some distance between himself and the creature. It flew in closer, and he summoned a force field of glowing light around his fist and took a swing, batting it in the face.

"I feel like I'm fighting a really angry bologna sandwich, Dude," Billy said.

I wish I knew what you meant by that, Dude said. *No, I take that back. I don't want to know.*

Billy shot downward, trying to get closer to the magician and the cyborg, but he found the fight had taken a turn for the worse. Bedlam was held aloft by an invisible force, the necromancer with his hand outstretched, Darth Vader style, gripping her by the neck.

"I fell for your ambush once," King Tears said. "You thought I'd be unprepared a second time?"

Bedlam's legs kicked violently as she fought whatever mystical energy field held her off the ground, arms trying to find purchase where there was none on the invisible talons holding her neck. Billy could hear her choking for breath.

"Oh, you're one of the failures," he said. "I can see why the Children abandoned you. Goodbye, first edition."

King Tears gestured with his other hand with a yanking motion, and Billy's heart leapt into his throat as he saw electrical sparks shoot forth from Bedlam's right elbow. She screamed, in rage or pain Billy couldn't tell, and then the magician used his other hand to throw her violently away, like a doll. She smashed through a nearby house with a horrific crash.

"Bedlam!" Billy yelled, dive-bombing at King Tears full speed.

Again, his flight was cut short by the winged monstrosity, which hit him hard enough to send him careening into the ground. Billy left a ravine of dirt and grass in his wake, spitting mud from his mouth.

Shaken, he stood up, lifting is fists again to fight. The flying monster landed in front of him, and now Billy could get a good look at him—a face, once human, bifurcated and reshaped like a bat's, with long, filed teeth and wild, pain-mad eyes. Behind the bat-thing, zombies closed in on him as well. Billy stole a quick glance over his shoulder at the house where Bedlam had been so brutally thrown, but she hadn't emerged.

"Finish them off," King Tears said dismissively, already walking away. "They're just a speed bump. We have an appointment with a queen."

Billy watched as the rest of King Tears' entourage departed, leaving just enough of their forces to make life difficult for him. Great, Billy thought. It's me against bologna bat and the contents of the local graveyard.

Still no sign of Bedlam. Billy began to panic.

"Dude, what do I do," he said.

You know what to do, Billy Case.

He nodded, not quite sure if he and Dude were thinking the same thing, and unleashed a massive bolt of blue-white energy at the monster knocking it back and filling the air with the sickening stench of burned, putrid flesh.

And then he launched himself backward, darting toward the caved-in house to see if Bedlam was still alive.

CHAPTER 50: KNOCK

We're following a living shadow through a strangely tidy sewer system below an imaginary castle in a fantasy kingdom, Titus thought as they sloshed through a long, dark cavern. I guess I can't say life's ever been boring since joining the Indestructibles.

Gloomly, as the shadow-man had been introduced, paused below a metal grate above them. Kate looked up.

"This isn't a real sewer system, is it," she said.

"I get the impression everything in this castle is idealized," Titus said. "And given how powerful my sense of smell is, I'm pretty thankful for that. Should I get the grate?"

"If you don't mind," Kate said.

"I'll scout ahead," Gloomly said, disappearing up through the grate as Titus lifted it up and set it aside. Kate used Titus' werewolf height to springboard herself up through the square opening. Titus awkwardly hauled himself up last.

"Well, this is a dungeon," Titus said.

It felt like something out of a videogame—stone walls,

slightly damp, grimy enough to be creepy, but also still sort of sterile. Too clean for a quasi-medieval prison. Titus sniffed the air to try to track Doc, but Gloomly had already started down the left-hand side of the corridor, leading the way. Kate followed silently behind. Titus held back a few yards, trying to keep his stomping to a minimum.

"This way," Gloomly said.

Kate shot Titus a long, tired look that told him she was having the same thoughts about their ridiculous lives. She mouthed the words "what did we do wrong" to him, and Titus almost laughed, but caught himself. Unlike his own resignation, Kate seemed genuinely irritated that they were in a Disneyland version of a Middle Ages prison.

After a few twists and turns, Titus caught the familiar scent he associated with Doc, layers of spell ingredients and authority. The shadow-man coalesced in front of a cell and stood at attention.

"I brought them to you," he said.

"Thank you," Doc said from within the cell. Kate strode up to the bars, with Titus following closely.

"Magic prison," Kate said.

'Magic prison," Doc said. "Good to see you, Kate."

"Glad you're not dead," Kate said. "I want to go on record. I don't like that Titus is learning magic."

"I am well aware of this," Titus said.

"I wasn't talking to you," Kate said. "Will you make sure he doesn't become any weirder than you are? You are the very cusp of acceptably weird as a magician."

"I will do my best," Doc said. Titus caught him fighting a smile as well. Doc beckoned Titus over to the cell door.

"I really don't know much, Doc," Titus said.

"You don't have to know much," Doc said. "The problem

is unlocking this cell is a simple spell, but you can't do it from the inside. It's very effective for catching another magic user if that magic user doesn't have any friends."

"Good thing we still like you," Titus said.

"I'm glad I still rate," Doc said. "What I'm going to do is show you the hand gestures you'll need to do to invoke the spell. There's a secret phrase you'll need to know as well. Part of it is in a language no one speaks anymore, but that's okay, you don't have to understand what you're saying as long as you get the sounds right."

"Ancient Sumerian?" Titus asked.

"No, but close," Doc said. "I assume you're not learning classic arcana with Leto."

"It's mostly nature magic," Titus said.

"Close enough," Doc said. "I prefer spells that ask permission rather than demand the world bend to your will."

"This conversation is making me angrier by the second," Kate said. "Can we just get on with it?"

"Of course," Doc said. He began making a series of gestures with his hand, moving his fingers in a very specific order. He had Titus repeat the gesture back to him several times, then do it on his own without Doc guiding him.

"You've almost got it," Doc said. "Now let's get those words."

Titus sniffed at the air and instinctually turned toward the corridor beyond Kate's shoulder.

"We've got company coming," Titus said.

"I'll try to distract them," Gloomly said.

"No," Kate said, rotating her neck to loosen her shoulders. "I've got this. You said the guards aren't real?"

"Magical constructs," Doc said. "Not real people."

"Good," Kate said, and took off down the hall at a run.

"It's been a while since she's hit anyone, hasn't it," Doc said.

"I think she needs the workout," Titus said.

Doc began detailing the words and phrases Titus would need to cast the spell. They weren't complex, at least compared to any other spell, but it became increasingly difficult to concentrate as the cacophony of clangs, bangs, cries of pain, and other assorted chaos echoed down the hall.

"Hey, Gloomly? Go see if she needs help?" Titus said.

The shadow-man nodded and darted down the hall, barely visible in the low light.

"Ready?" Doc said.

"Yeah. Sure," Titus said, but he was interrupted as Kate slammed into the wall as if shoved, ducking down to avoid the sharp point of a pike. The blade sparked as it struck stone. She roared in frustration and used the haft of the pike as leverage to whack the offending guard off the helmet with it with a resounding clang.

"Wolf-man, the warrior-woman needs help," Gloomly said, materializing out of the darkness beside Titus.

"I do not need help!" Kate said, kicking another guard so hard his helmet and gauntlets flew off his body. Several more guards circled in, calling for help. "Just get our wizard out of his cell!"

"She needs help," Titus said.

"Go on, I'll wait," Doc said.

"Cast the spell, Titus, or so help me…" Kate said, leaping into the air, landing on another guard's shoulders, and using her legs to spin and throw him across the room, his armor clattering and unclasping like as skier losing his gear during a spill.

"Spell, right," Titus said, nodding. He held up one hand,

still fully wolfed out, and tried to say the words and make the hand gesture at the same time. While he felt more dexterous than he ever had before in this form, he couldn't quite get it right.

"Hang on," Titus said, willing himself into human form. His massive frame melted away, leaving him standing there in oversized pants and a stretched-out hoodie. The stone floor was cold against his bare feet.

"Any time now, Titus," Kate said. She'd stolen a mace from one of the guards and used it to knock two more soldiers unconscious with it. She looked at the weapon appraisingly. "Huh. I like this one."

"Last try," Titus said. He made the hand gestures—far easier with his human-shaped hands this time—and spoke the magical words as well, also far less challenging with a mouth made for spellcasting and not for hunting. He did not understand the words Doc gave him for the first part of the spell, a complicated series of sounds that did not remind Titus of any language he'd ever heard before. The last word, though, in English, he absolutely understood.

"Open," he said. And he was promptly thrown backward against the wall by a heavy gust of wind. The gate to Doc's cell swept open, and Doc walked out, legs stiff, limping a little.

"You okay?" Titus said.

"Foot's asleep. Been sitting a long time," Doc said with a smirk. "Maybe you should go help Kate."

"Absolutely," Titus said, smoothly transforming back into his werewolf shape. He bounded down the hall with a roar so loud it made his own ears ring. The guards, though, got the worst of it—one look at a three-hundred-pound werewolf charging at them and the remaining conscious soldiers turned and ran, giving up the battle.

"Sure," Kate said, catching her breath and wiping a thin trickle of blood from the corner of her mouth with the back of her hand. "I kick their collective asses, but you they just get one look at and run away in fear."

"I have good werewolf public relations on my side," Titus said, his voice once again deep and gravely in his transformed state. "Reputation matters."

"Where to now, then?" Kate said.

Doc joined them in the corridor, the glowing eyes of Gloomly hovering behind him.

"Well, if I had the spell on that cell figured out correctly, whoever cast it knows I'm free," doc said. "I suppose we should go have a conversation with him and see about setting Alice free."

"Any idea how we'll do that?" Titus said. "I don't know if we have enough time for you to teach me an exorcism spell."

Doc chuckled quietly.

"Again, if I have my theories lined up right, the most important thing we need to make this happen is Alice's trust," he said.

"Great," Kate said. "Our success is riding on a twelve-year-old magician deciding a werewolf, a creepy guy in a trench coat, and whatever you'd call me are people she wants on her side. What could possibly go wrong?"

CHAPTER 51:
BESEECHING

Everyone else seemed fairly stressed out or horrified by the entire experience, but Emily was having the time of her life here in the pocket dimension. Her own dream sequence was possibly the best thing ever, and now she found herself riding an actual unicorn toward a castle out an architect's nightmare.

"I don't understand how it doesn't fall over," Jane said, staring up at the castle. It branched out the higher it went with towers and spires spiking off in all directions, like a child had built it as a test of the stability of their building blocks.

It made perfect sense to Emily, though.

"It works like my powers," she said. "Gravity and weight don't apply. It's not supposed to make sense, and that's why it works. It can only exist in a place like this."

"I feel like it could go down like a house of cards if someone in the north tower sneezes too hard," Jane said.

"Also seems like a perfectly reasonable expectation," Emily said.

They arrived outside the massive main gate, a drawbridge

and portcullis combination that looked like something someone who had only seen castles in movies would insist upon.

The battle-scarred teddy bear patted the unicorn's neck and turned to Jane.

"This is her castle," he said.

"I assumed, it being the only castle here," Jane said. "Any advice?"

The bear and unicorn seemed to sigh in unison.

"She's quicker to anger than before," he said. "And more suspicious. I still can't believe she drove us away, her oldest friends. Proceed with caution."

"That's us," Emily said. "Proceeding with caution is our standard operating procedure."

Jane raised one doubting eyebrow at Emily and flew across the moat to knock on the gate.

"We're here to speak with Queen Alice!" she yelled, then floated back to the far side of the moat. They waited for a few minutes in silence.

"I suppose we could knock the gate down," Jane said.

"Doesn't seem diplomatic," Emily said.

"Please don't knock the gate down," Sir Teddy said.

Eventually, they heard chains rattle, and the drawbridge lowered to allow them entrance to the castle. Emily dismounted from Silverhoof and caught Sir Teddy in a small bubble of float to help him to the ground as well. The bear shot Emily an undignified look, righted his armor, and started across the bridge.

The interior was pretty, Emily thought, but not particularly detailed. In places the castle walls seemed almost blurry, as if recreated from memory rather than built, with spots that hadn't been fully fleshed out in the creator's mind. They followed a bright red carpet straight ahead, up a long staircase traced in gold. The unicorn seemed to struggle with the stairs in a half-silly, half-sad way, so Emily floated her the rest of the way.

At the top of the stairs, a vast, ornate entranceway opened to the throne room. Armored guards in red and silver uniforms stood on either side, and many more waited within the chamber. The carpet ran all the way to the far side of the chamber, where a massive, gaudy throne stood. A small figure Emily assumed had to be Queen Alice waited for them there, a girl a few years younger than herself dressed in a fanciful red dress, a crown like a geometry problem atop her head. To her left, a man who looked vaguely like a star on a TV show Emily sometimes watched waited, garbed in robes of office the color of a bruise.

"Who have you brought to me, Sir Teddy?" Queen Alice said Emily tried not to laugh at the ridiculousness of it all, the formality with which this kid talked to her teddy bear. Emily figured she probably sounded deranged herself half the time, but hearing it from someone else was a trippy experience.

"Ah, strangers from another land, Queen Alice," the bear said, bowing formally. "They seek their friend."

Emily and Jane exchanged wary looks and shrugged at each other. Jane gave Emily a tired, unconvincing smile and stepped forward.

"Queen Alice," Jane said, with more respect than Emily could have mustered. She put a hand to her chest earnestly. "We come to you for two reasons. My name is Solar, and this is Entropy Emily. We seek our friend, who came to your land not long ago, and we also bring news from home."

"You look familiar," Alice said. The advisor beside her, whom Emily assumed was this malevolent spirit they'd been warned about, was having none of it, arms folded across his chest firmly.

"We're, ah, superheroes, back home," Jane said. "You may have heard of us. The Indestructibles."

"Also there are several coffee drinks named after us. Have you ever had an Entropy Emi-latte?"

"Enough," Alice said. "You've intruded upon my kingdom, you've convinced my former friends to betray me by bringing you here… what do you want from me?"

"I'm going to be honest," Jane said. "We came here hoping we could help you, but what we've seen out there in the town are people trapped in their own nightmares and fears. And as far as I'm concerned, they're my priority. We've come to ask you to send those poor people home."

Alice stood up, her body language a mimicry of adult defensiveness.

"How dare you talk about my subjects like that. They are where they belong! I've made a safe place for them here!"

"Nope, completely terrorized," Emily said. "It's pretty rough out there. People crying, freaking out… also you took the whole town with you."

"I created this place," Alice said.

"No, you teleported Westwick wholesale," Emily said.

"You're lying," Alice said. Emily could hear a shift in Alice's voice; she'd been playing at being royalty until just that moment, but there was a vein of self-doubt, of youthful innocence, just starting to break the surface there.

"Nope. It's a parking lot. Whole thing's gone," Emily said.

"But your parents are still back there," Jane said.

"My parents don't need to be here," Alice said. "They don't need me. They have other things to worry about."

"You should talk to them yourself," Jane said. "I'm sure

they'd love to hear from you."

Alice turned her attention from Jane and Emily to her advisor, who had sat back passively watching the exchange.

"You said my subjects were happy," she said.

"They are happy," the man said. "You're going to believe two outlanders over your most trusted ally?"

Alice looked down at Emily with a sneer, then turned her attention to the teddy bear. Her face softened.

"Are they really afraid, Teddy?" she said, all imperiousness in her tone gone.

The bear stepped forward, clearing his throat.

"Many never leave their homes, Queen Alice," he said. "Some no longer speak to anyone. They see visions of things that scare them, or things they want to forget. You know I'd never lie to you."

Emily felt a trembling beneath her feet. Not an earthquake, she thought. Something else. Getting louder and closer, too.

She was the first to notice, but then others began to pick up on the tremor. Guards looked at each other curiously; Silverhoof even seemed to become aware of it, glancing at Emily with a disconcertingly human expression of confusion and alarm.

And then, from a side corridor along the stage-left side of the throne room, a cadre of Alice's uniformed guards came charging out of a smaller passageway, running for their lives.

"Monster!" one yelled.

"Its teeth are as big as my arms!" another said.

"Werewolf! It's a werewolf! Run!" said a third.

The guards already in the throne room gathered together, pointing pikes or swords at the now empty doorway. After a few seconds, a familiar face stepped calmly out.

"If you guys got to know him, you'd realize I'm the scarier

one in this partnership," Kate said, shaking her head with disdain.

Doc Silence emerged next, looking tired, hungry, and bemused, the shadow-man, Gloomly, by his side like an afterthought. Finally, a fully wolfed-out Titus appeared, ducking to avoid hitting his head on the frame of the door. Despite his monstrous form, Emily could see an almost offended look on his canine face, as if he were mildly wounded by strangers running from him in fear.

"The prisoner has escaped," the man on the dais said, pointing at Doc. "And he's brought monsters with him! Guards, seize him, now!"

Doc sighed and rubbed the bridge of his nose.

"We've got some things to talk about," Doc said.

CHAPTER 52: BREAKDOWN

Billy found Bedlam on the ground in the shattered house, one leg twitching, a trickle of blood running from the corner of her mouth. Her right cybernetic arm was hanging on by a thread, some wiring and twisted metal all that kept the limb attached at the elbow. He dropped down beside her and cradled her head in the crook of his elbow.

"Bedlam?" he said. "Please be okay, please be okay…"

"It pains me to say this," Bedlam said, her voice strangely metallic, as if tinged with static. "But I think you were right about my plan."

She opened her eyes. The biological eye was clear and alert; the artificial eye glowed dimly, then flickered and went out.

"Did you get him?" she asked.

"Not exactly," Billy said. "What can I do right now? How can I help?"

Bedlam sighed, wincing in pain.

"Unless you're an engineer, not much," she said.

"Don't you die on me," Billy said.

Bedlam chuckled. Even her laugh seemed distorted.

"You're not getting rid of me that easy," she said. "You want to know something funny? All the stuff I need to stay alive is still human."

With her left arm, which shook slightly as it moved, she took Billy's wrist and put his hand on her heart. He could feel it beating beneath his palm.

"Still ticking," she said, smiling slightly.

"What's broken?" Billy asked, trying to keep too much concern from his tone.

"Right arm's shot. Left arm, well," she said, lifting it to show how it trembled as she moved. "Something's not right there. There's something going on with my right leg, it's twitching. I think the left still works though."

"Your eye is flickering," Billy said.

"Oh that's on the fritz," she said. "What did he hit me with?"

"A house," Billy said. "And magic, I guess."

"A house," Bedlam repeated. "Help me sit up, huh?"

Billy lifted her to a sitting position so she could rest against his chest. He could hear her grinding her teeth.

"This is so stupid," she said, leaning more heavily on him than he was expecting.

Dude, can we read her vitals or anything? Billy thought.

Vaguely, Dude said. *She appears to be stable. She needs medical attention, but she'll live. I can't tell you anything about the damage to her tech, though.*

Good enough, Billy thought.

Then he heard the moaning and shuffling of feet.

"Funeral zombies," Billy said.

He saw several shambling corpses emerge from the shadows just within the walls of the house. He fired off a light blast to see what it would do, and watched as the zombie slammed violently into a nearby wall and stopped moving.

"This is so morbid," Billy thought, firing off several more shots. "Okay, I'm not really keen on mangling the corpses of peoples' relatives. New plan."

He scooped Bedlam up in his arms as gently as possible and flew straight up to where what remained of the second floor of the home still stood. He laid her down on a now-exposed twin bed, then blasted what was left of a staircase to stop the zombies from getting to them.

"Short term fix," he said.

His plan was derailed, however, by the flapping of enormous, leathery wings.

"Please tell me the flying thing didn't just find us," he said.

Bedlam looked past his shoulder, then grinned.

"It's looking right at us.

Billy stood up and turned to face the creature. He could get a better look at it now—squat-bodied, with bat-like wings the flesh of which was creepily human, its entire bulbous torso covered in eyes and mouths. They all screeched in unison.

"And what am I supposed to do about you," Billy said.

"It used to be people," Bedlam said bitterly. "Put them out of their misery, Billy."

"I don't want to kill them if they can be saved," Billy said.

"It's too late," Bedlam said. "Whatever that used to be, there's no going back."

The creature squealed at him again, raising its wings threateningly.

Billy leaned down and pressed his forehead against Bedlam's.

"I'll be right back," he said.

"I'm not going anywhere," she said, managing a brief flash

of a smile.

Billy took off in a flash of brilliant light, crashing into the Frankenstein's monster-like thing, knocking it back away from the house, and away from Bedlam. The creature lashed out with a tail he hadn't noticed before, a grotesque limb ending with a bony tip. The pointed tip tore at his uniform, scraping along his ribcage. Billy couldn't tell if he were more hurt or disgusted by the feeling.

Needing some distance, he hit the creature with blasts from both hands, knocking it away. The tail lashed out again, but this time he had the forethought to bring up the vibrant protective shield Dude empowered him to use, and the bone spike scratched against the shielding instead of opening Billy's guts. He targeted the tail this time, hitting it with an energy bolt so powerful it separated the tail from the body, sending the appendage falling to the earth. The monster screamed with a dozen mouths in simultaneous cries of pain.

I'm going to have nightmares about this for months, Billy thought.

Someday you'll have to see the gallery of creatures I encountered before I arrived on Earth, Dude said. *This is nothing compared to the tendon rhinos of Lanzo IV…*

Y'know what? I can live without ever seeing something called a tendon rhino, Billy thought. *How about some ideas on how to destroy this thing?*

I would assume basic biology would say that most of the important bits are in the torso, Dude said. *But if you have a better idea, feel free to offer a suggestion.*

Hit it in the bread basket, Billy thought. *Fine, we'll go with that.*

Billy launched a few bolts of energy, but the massive flying creature proved to be shockingly nimble, dodging each bolt with surprising ease. Billy found himself in a dogfight with the monster, trying to stay out of range enough to get a decent shot off. Somehow, losing its tail had almost benefited the creature, its flight pattern now so unbalanced and irregular that Billy couldn't predict where it would drift next.

"Oh, come on!" Billy said as he missed for the tenth time in a row. The creature bombed at him, and Billy found himself staring, horrified, at the gleaming bone of the nearest mouths as it gnashed its teeth.

More out of repulsion than combat, Billy threw a blast of energy side-armed at the creature, just trying to push it off-course and away from him.

Instead, the beam of light struck it dead center in its body.

The wings went limp, like wet rags. The bulky monstrosity began to plummet, no longer making any attempt to fly, falling to the earth like a garbage bag.

It did not hit the ground.

Instead, it became impaled on a barren tree, the thicker branches piercing the abomination's torso, jutting out like spikes on the other side. Horrific ichor dripped down the branches, sizzling as it came into contact with the bark.

"That was not what I meant to do," Billy said.

Intentional or not, it seems to have worked, Dude said.

Billy hovered above the body for a moment, waiting to see if it would arise to attack again, but it remained still, inert, and definitely deceased.

"Okay then," Billy said. He scanned the horizon to find King Tears and his menagerie. He saw that they had nearly reached the castle, having left Billy and Bedlam here to deal with the forces the magician left behind.

I hope the fairy warns Jane in time, Billy thought as he rocketed back to the house where he'd left Bedlam.

Her eyes were closed when he arrived. He landed lightly nearby and ran over to her.

"No, no, no," Billy said.

"I'm still here," Bedlam said without opening her eyes, her voice pained. "Should I be taking all of the panic in your voice as a sign you actually care about me?"

"Don't let it go to your head," Billy said, smiling as he knelt beside her. "We have to get to the castle to warn the others in case Galinda didn't make it."

"Just leave me here," Bedlam said. "I'll slow you down."

"Not possible," Billy said. "You're talking to a guy who can get to Saturn and back in a week. We can sacrifice a few nanoseconds off my top speed. I'm not leaving you behind, kid."

"If you insist," Bedlam said, opening her one good eye and winking at him. "Just try not to jostle me. I'm delicate."

"That is absolutely the first word that comes to mind when I think of you," Billy said, laughing.

"Funny you should say that," Bedlam said. "I think the same thing about you."

CHAPTER 53:
MONSTERS AT THE GATES

Somehow, along the way, Andrew Keppler had convinced himself that there is an acceptable amount of evil necessary to get ahead.

King Tears was right. Keppler knew the company he worked for did terrible things. But somehow, at every turn, he was able to justify it—their actions were good for profits, they didn't hurt that many people, if his company didn't do it, someone else would, so why not be the one who profits? And while it started out with just business decisions, as he climbed the ladder, he knew they were involved in far worse. By the third year on the job, he was well-aware he worked for super-villains.

But it beat the alternative, he thought.

And now he walked beside literal monsters, in a twisted pocket dimension, guided by a power-hungry sorcerer seeking to enslave some sort of creature so he could siphon magic from it.

What scared Keppler more wasn't the danger he was in. It

was not the morality of what King Tears had done to his test subjects, twisting them into barbaric monsters. He found himself instead thinking about what his salary demands would be when they got back to the real world. King Tears was clearly a visionary, not a manager. He needed a right-hand man. Keppler was perfectly positioned for a job in the executive suite.

I'm excited at the prospect, he thought. I know I should be disgusted with myself, but instead, I'm just thinking about stock options and summer homes.

He didn't have long to think more about his own flexible ethics before they arrived outside the castle, though. The drawbridge was up, but Keppler saw no guards, just poorly designed, impossible structure waiting to be invaded.

King Tears stopped at the edge of the moat and laughed as if entertained by the echo of his voice there.

"We're nearly there, Mr. Keppler," King Tears said. "I can feel it. The creature inside that castle will be the battery we need to power our empire."

"Figure there's more of those super-powered kids waiting for us there?" Keppler asked.

King Tears shrugged.

"Probably," he said. "But they're down two teammates. The Lady Dreamless is on another plane. The creature who created this plane doesn't know what we're here to do. It'll all work out."

"I don't want to be the party pooper here, but have we done a full risk assessment of what the possible outcomes are here?" Keppler asked.

"Risk assessment," King Tears said. "Life is risk, Keppler. Everything we do from the minute we fall out of the womb is risky. Have some guts. The reason you survived the purge of the Children of the Elder Star is because nobody thought you had the guts to be dangerous. Prove them wrong, would you?"

"You sound like my father," Keppler said. "How do we get in there?"

"That's more like it," King Tears said. He gestured at the portcullis and called forward one of the grotesque juggernauts in his employ. "Pull it down."

The flesh-monster reached out across the moat, easily crossing the distance with oversized arms. It grabbed hold of the top of the drawbridge and yanked once, twice, and on the third time, the bridge came unmoored, falling open with a massive bang.

King Tears turned to face his forces.

"Some of you can understand me. Others, well, I don't particularly care that you don't," he said. He waved a hand at the remaining zombies in their suits and dresses. "You will attack the castle guards. They don't have to live."

The zombies groaned in unison and began shambling across the bridge onto the mouth of the portcullis. He turned his attention to the smaller of his creations, the ones still mostly human-sized, some still even looking mostly human in shape as well.

"You will deal with any of these little heroes we find inside. I don't particularly care what you do to them. Just keep them away from me."

He turned next to the remaining behemoths—the one that tore the gate open, and one other.

"You will assault the castle walls. Don't tear it down," King Tears said. "Just make some noise, my wonderful monsters. I want distraction."

The two massive creatures shuffled off, shapeless and terrifying. Keppler couldn't tell which end was up or where their bodies began or ended.

"And me?" Keppler said.

"Stick close, and watch," King Tears said. "I want you to witness the ascension."

CHAPTER 54: BETRAYAL

Kate knew they'd interrupted something with their noisy entrance to the throne room. What surprised her as she assessed the situation, was that Jane and Emily had managed to cause the young magician to have doubt in the being manipulating her.

Kate could see it plain on the younger girl's face—reading intentions and moods was what Kate did, after all, and Alice was loudly telegraphing suspicion as she looked at the man in the dark purple robes, the only other person in the room who wasn't an anonymous, generic guard in uniform.

Our timing could have been better, Kate thought as she watched that doubt fade from Alice's face the second she saw Doc. Walking into the room with her prisoner in tow might have been a bad strategy for winning her over to their side.

"Guards! The prisoner has escaped!" the man in purple, whom Doc had told them was called the Vizier, called out. The guards seemed to be genuinely afraid of Titus, though, and Kate planned on using that to her advantage if they advanced on them.

Titus, however, and Doc, were both staring intently at the drama on the dais. There was tension building between the queen and the Vizier. And unfortunately, with dozens of pikes pointed at her, Kate knew she was going to have to let that drama play itself out.

Doc started talking. I hope he knows what he's doing, Kate thought.

"Alice," Doc said. "I failed you. I knew you'd be a powerful magician someday. But I wanted you to have a childhood without worry. I am so sorry someone else found you and took that away from you."

"What are you talking about?" Alice said. She sounded angry, and lost, and, Kate realized, like someone who didn't trust a single soul in that throne room. Alice whipped her head toward the Vizier.

"What are they talking about?" she asked.

"They lie," the man said. "You built this world all on your own. I am just here to give you guidance when you need it, my queen. They're just jealous of your power."

"We're not jealous," Doc said. He held a hand out plaintively. "We just want to make sure you choose what to do with it, not someone else. Alice, you'll be the most powerful magician of your generation. The only thing we want is to let you know you get to choose how to be that magician."

"You're trying to confuse me," Alice said.

"Yes, they are," the Vizier said.

"You stop talking," Alice said, her tone even angrier with him than with Doc. "Why did you tell me to send my friends away?"

Kate's eyes darted toward the bear and unicorn standing with Jane. She shook her head at the ridiculousness of it all, but

Jane caught her attention. The women locked eyes, each waiting for the other to offer a plan. Kate shrugged subtly. Jane raised an eyebrow and bit her lip, her confusion clear.

"I didn't tell you to send your friends away. You knew they were subverting your rule, and…" the Vizier said.

"I don't even remember what you said they did wrong," Alice said. "Sir Teddy, why did I send you away?"

The bear harrumphed and stepped forward.

"You said you felt that we could no longer be trusted, that we were working against you, my queen," the bear said. "Queen Alice, all we ever wanted to do was protect you. We love you. It's the only thing the four of us were created to do. We are lost without you."

Alice stared down at the bear with eyes glistening with the faintest hint of tears.

"And I told you to go," she said.

"It's okay," the bear said. "We can love you from afar as much as by your side. But when we were away, we couldn't protect you anymore. And that's why you made us. To protect you from dark things."

Alice slowly turned her head toward the Vizier, then back to the bear.

"She remembers," Gloomly said softly. Kate had almost forgotten the shadow-man was with them.

"Where is Galinda?" Alice asked. "What happened to my fairy?"

"She's with our friends," Jane said gently. "There's something else in your land, something dangerous, and she guided them to it so they could try to stop it."

Alice stood up straighter and looked down at Jane, a bit more of that imperious vibe returning to her demeanor.

"And what is this dangerous thing?" Alice said.

"Zombies," Emily said. Kate almost groaned as she said it. "I know that sounds weird, but literally, you have zombies. Heading for your castle. Right now."

"I warned you something else was here," the Vizier said. "You are beset upon from all sides, Queen Alice. I am the only one who wants to protect you."

Alice stared at her advisor with a look of annoyance Kate almost admired.

"I don't know if I believe you," she said.

Before the Vizier could respond, a tiny purplish light drifted up the stairs into the throne room. It took a moment to register, but Kate realized she was looking at fluttering, pearlescent wings. The fairy. This just keeps getting weirder and weirder, she thought, and then realized: the fairy was here without Billy and Bedlam.

The fairy drifted around the room for a moment, then dropped down onto Jane's shoulder. Why Jane? Kate thought, but then she knew: if Billy sent the fairy for help, he would always, without a doubt, tell her to find Jane. They're in trouble, Kate realized. If Billy's asking for help, things got very bad very quickly.

Jane immediately confirmed Kate's fears.

"That's my fairy friend," Alice said. "Galinda, I'm glad to see you."

The fairy bowed as she stood on Jane's shoulder. The solar-powered girl had gone very pale and very still.

"Something bad has happened," Jane said.

Doc didn't even hesitate. He stepped forward, past Kate, and pointed to Jane.

"Go. Go now," he said.

Jane nodded and grabbed Emily by the wrist, pulling her into the air as she took flight. The duo dashed out of the throne room, gone before anyone could stop them.

"Galinda, what's happening?" Alice said.

"Monsters, Queen Alice," the fairy said. "Monsters unlike anything I've ever seen before."

"There are no monsters here," Alice said. "I built this world so there would be no monsters. What's happening? Why is everything breaking?"

Doc stepped forward. Kate caught him making subtle hand gestures as he spoke, getting ready to cast a spell.

"The Vizier has been clouding your mind, Alice," Doc said. "There's nothing any of us can do to help you. But you have the power to take control back from him. That's your power. That's your right."

"They're trying to tear us apart, Alice," the Vizier said. "Don't let them do this."

"That's the first time you've called me by my name, and not queen," Alice said. "Are they telling the truth, Vizier?"

The Vizier changed, then; Kate saw it happen in the blink of an eye, as he seemed to grow taller, thinner, his eyes becoming red embers instead of the gentle grey eyes he'd had before. He stepped away from Alice and made a violent gesture with his hand, not unlike the sort of thing Kate had witnessed Doc do when casting a spell. Alice bent forward as if she'd been struck in the stomach. The Vizier pointed at Kate and the others on the left side of the throne room.

"This works so much better when you're willing," the Vizier said. "But if I have to steal your power outright, I will."

He pointed a finger, now long and tipped with a hooked claw, at Doc, who released whatever spell he'd been working on seconds before. Kate felt a barely visible shield spring up in front of her, knocking her backward onto her heels.

Gloomly darted forward like a ghost.

"Don't touch our Alice," the shadow-man said, his eyes gleaming, golden orbs as he swelled with dark power.

A burst of sickly, grimy light burst forth from the Vizier's hooked fingertip. It did not follow a straight arc, but bent and twisted like lightning. Kate watched in horror as it tore through Gloomly like paper, shredding the shadow-creature, tearing him apart at the seams.

"No!" Doc yelled, realizing too late Gloomly had left the protective circle he created. The destructive beam of arcane energy hit the shield Doc summoned and splashed against it like rain on glass, breaking into pieces and falling to the floor harmlessly.

The room went deadly quiet as Gloomly disintegrated a few inches of shadow at a time.

"I'm sorry, Alice. I tried…" the shadow-man said. And then he was gone.

"You!" Alice said, clutching her gut, her face a mask of pain and rage. "I trusted you! You killed my friend!"

"He was never real, little girl," the Vizier said, his shape still changing, growing bigger, his shoulders taking on a curved, cartoonish shape. "I saved you from your imaginary friends and showed you how to use your power to create worlds, and now, now you betray me? You could have made another shadow puppet. You could make anything you wanted to. But not anymore."

Alice stretched out her hand toward the Vizier, who looked more and more like a thing of pure nightmare than a man with each passing second.

"You let me in," he said. "I'll eat your fears and devour your magic until there is nothing left."

"Alice!" Doc said. "You can cut him off! All you need to do is will it so. That's your strength he's stealing. Take it back!"

"I can't!" Alice said.

Kate watched as Alice seemed to shrink, becoming gaunt, dark bags under her eyes. She looked sick, exhausted, drained as the nightmare creature grew in scope. We might be too late, Kate thought.

And then a new voice entered the clamor of the throne room. The voice they needed to hear.

"Not alone, you can't," the Lady Dreamless said. She emerged from a hidden passage behind the throne, one even Kate with her constant study of the battlefield had missed, the two demon hounds flanking her on either side. "But together, we can cut you free."

CHAPTER 55:
THE DEAD, WALKING

Jane didn't have to drag Emily far to find what Galinda had warned them about: they barely made it to the end of the stairs leading out of the castle before the drawbridge slammed open and the dead and twisted began pouring in.

"I think I saw this on *Game of Thrones*," Emily said. Jane let go of Emily's wrist, the two women hovering about ten feet off the floor.

"I don't see Billy or Bedlam," Jane said. "We have to…"

She trailed off as she saw a massive, misshapen creature waddle just beyond the portcullis.

"What was that," Jane said.

"And why are these zombies all dressed so nicely?" Emily said. Other creatures began to follow the standard-issue corpses, humans with arms warped into strange new shapes, or walking on legs with too many limbs, dragging spiked tails or worse.

Jane shot a glance over her shoulder back toward the throne room.

"We have to keep them from getting in," she said.

"Do we care if the zombies are mangled or not?" Emily said.

"I think they're, um, locally grown," Jane said.

"No head shots then. Gotcha," Emily said. I got this.

Emily pushed past Jane—which Jane knew was most likely to keep her from getting caught up in Emily's bubbles of float—and held both hands out in front of her, palms forward. Then she twisted her wrists like a conductor issuing instructions to her orchestra.

The zombies began to float off the ground.

"Violence is not always the solution, padawan," Emily said. She pushed forward, lifting more and more of the walking corpses with her, scooping up some of the twisted living creatures as well as she progressed.

"This is a temporary fix," Jane warned.

"Oh, I know," Emily said. "But if I pick up the zombies and drop them a mile away, I figure at the average zombie land speed, whatever's going on inside the throne room will have resolved itself by the time they get back."

"Y'know, on the whole, we've come up with worse plans together," Jane said.

"See?" Emily said. "I expect my new business cards to read: master tactician."

Emily carried dozens of zombies out of the castle gate, all of them reaching out to her or trying in vain to walk despite no longer touching the ground. Once they were outside, though, Jane saw the problem was more than just the shambling dead.

"Well those things are positively Lovecraftian," Emily said, gesturing with her chin at two living siege engines slamming massive, multi-joined appendages into the castle walls.

"Great," Jane said. "I'll take care of whatever those are.

You go find a cemetery or like, corral or something to drop the other ones in."

"Got it," Emily said. "Try to make sure the world doesn't end while I'm gone."

Emily raised her hand again, taking the pile of undead even higher into the air over Westwick and began to fly at her slow but steady speed away from the castle.

The castle itself, meanwhile, began to shake and crack beneath the heavy blows of the two stitched-together mutants. Jane flew down to the nearest, trying to figure out if it had a face to punch.

The closer she got, though, she found her answer: it didn't simply have a face. It had many, all mindless rictuses of pain.

"And I thought the body-snatching aliens were gross," she said. "Hey, I don't suppose I can talk you out of this?"

The creature didn't answer, instead smashing one of its bulky limbs against the castle wall, causing stone and mortar to crumble.

"Okay then," Jane said. The next time the creature swung its limb, Jane caught it, trying very hard not to vocalize how much the slimy texture of its skin grossed her out. The creature bucked at her grasp, so she cranked up the heat, igniting her hands with flames.

All at once, the creature issued a sound Jane would never forget, the sound of dozens of voices crying out at once.

"I'm sorry," she said, dropping to the ground with the monstrosity's arm over her shoulder like a rope. She dug her heels in and pulled the abomination away from the castle wall. It fought hard, its extra limbs pushing and dragging away from Jane.

The creature thrashed, slamming into Jane with two other arm-like parts, a fourth grasping onto the castle itself in an attempt to stop her from dragging it away. Frustrated, Jane took again to the air so the abomination could no longer use its multitude of feet to strain against her.

Jane yanked once, twice, like a tug of war, and finally she heard metal and stone break away as the creature lost its grip on the castle. Already pulling skyward, she immediately rose twenty feet or more, the unfathomable creature thrashing and swaying as it tried to find purchases.

This might be the only time I've been jealous of Emily's powers, Jane thought, the desperate, violent beast fighting against her grip. The castle rumbled again, and Jane saw the other abomination making progress in battering its way through the walls. She found her eyes drawn to the weird shape of the castle, the illogical, imbalanced geometry of it, and started to picture what would happen if one of the walls were destabilized enough to no longer be load-bearing.

It's going to knock the whole castle down, Jane thought.

She tightened her grip on the monster's arm and began to spin, using the mass of the creature as a weight, herself as the fulcrum. It was awkward and ugly, but after a few rotations she had a decent spin going. Super-strength isn't totally useless, she thought, wishing she had Kate's dance training to avoid getting dizzy.

Okay, either this is going to work, or I'm going to hit the castle and kill everyone by accident, she thought. Here goes.

She released her grip on the abomination, hoping she timed the throw right to send it flying in the right direction. Her heart skipped a beat, convinced she'd slipped or miscalculated.

The elephantine creature slammed into its twin with a vile, sickening slam. Both creatures wailed in fear or pain or both, tumbling over, their multitudes of limbs intertwining and tangling. Their legs kicked pathetically, unable to right themselves onto their feet.

Jane winced in pity while fighting off nausea. She didn't know what the massive abominations were, but she knew she'd be unhappy when she found out what made them.

In the distance, she saw Emily drifting further and further way. Okay, Jane thought. Two problems down. From the direction of the town proper, she caught a glimpse of Billy's signature blue-white light, and she sighed in relief knowing he was on his way.

Once more, she turned her attention to the castle's maw. She landed on the drawbridge and started running inside.

And that was when she saw two figures she'd missed during the fight with the undead monsters ascending the stairs into the throne room, silhouetted in the glow of flashing arcane light.

CHAPTER 56:
THIEVES OF POWER

Titus rapidly took stock of the battlefield.

In the center, Alice, confused, angry, betrayed.

The nightmare being that had once been the Vizier, now bigger, inhuman, eyes glowing from a face marred by smoke.

Doc beside him, a magical shield still held before him with one hand, his free hand preparing another spell.

Kate to his other side, arms up and ready to fight, but staying safely behind Doc's shield.

The little stuffed bear, the sword he wore on his back drawn, standing protectively in front of the unicorn, both looking at Alice with expressions both afraid and concerned.

The Lady Dreamless beyond the dais in her true form, pearlescent skin and red mystical energy. Her two muscle-bound demon hounds at her side, teeth bared, their eyes and mouths glowing with an internal flame.

The Vizier panned the throne room, lavender energy crackling around his fingers as he decided who to disintegrate next. He seemed to regard Lady Dreamless as, if not the greatest threat, the presence in the room most demanding his attention.

"You don't get to cast me out here," he said to her, his voice taking on a deep, echoing aspect. "This is my realm, not yours. You don't have the power to control me."

"You have made a great mistake, nightmare," Lady Dreamless said.

"Bold words for someone so far from home," the Vizier said.

Titus focused his attention on Alice, who looked pale, drawn, drained. He's eating away at her magic, Titus thought. He was feeding off her slowly before, but now, with nothing to lose, he's showing no restraint. The young girl wavered on her feet as if in a fever.

"Doc," Titus said, looking for guidance. "What's our play?"

"Let this play out," Doc said. "I have a feeling."

"I love risking hundreds of lives on a hunch," Kate said. "I'm going for the girl."

"Kate," Titus warned. "If you run out there you'll be obliterated like the shadow-man was."

"Not if he misses."

"You ready to take that chance?" Titus said.

Kate frowned at him, but remained in place.

"No, I don't have the power here to cast you out, not by myself," Lady Dreamless said. "But if Alice decides it's time for you to go, she does have that power."

The Vizier shifted his gaze to Alice.

"No, you don't," he said. "You might have at the beginning, but not anymore. I'm a part of you now."

"Yes, you do, Alice," Doc said. "You've had it all along. This is your world. You built every inch of it. You brought your friends to life, and you carried your town to another dimension, all by yourself. All he ever did was tell you that you had the power within yourself to do it."

Alice stared at Doc, eyes haunted and strangely old.

"Are my parents really waiting for me back home?" she said.

"Yes, they are," Doc said. "I promise."

She pointed at the Vizier with an accusatory finger. Titus could see the strength returning to her. The better she looked, the more the Vizier seemed to shrink back to human size. The power siphoning is a two-way street, Titus realized. She's taking back what's hers.

"You killed my friend," Alice said.

"You can make another one," the Vizier said. "I'll show you how."

"You don't just create friends. You don't just make kingdoms," Alice said. "They should be earned. I forgot that."

"Your mind was clouded," Doc said. "It's not your fault."

"It is my fault," Alice said. "I was greedy and childish. He told me what I wanted to hear. I've always known something was wrong, but this was… This was too much fun. All of these people suffering in fear because of me. You were imprisoned because of me. This is all my fault."

"Yes, it is," The Vizier said. He smiled, and his mouth seemed to spread wider and wider until it split his entire head, a grotesque, wide curve filled with gleaming teeth. "But we can fix it. You have the power to make the people of your town forget how this happened. They won't know who's to blame. I can make sure no one is ever mad at you for this. Don't betray me, or they'll know."

"Queen Alice," the gruff voice of the armored bear said. "It doesn't matter who's to blame. We just want you to come home."

Alice gazed down at the bear, a ridiculous sight in armor and eyepatch, but there was such unconditional love in the little character's furry face it nearly broke Titus' heart to look at it. *If you're lucky, once in your life, someone might look at you like that,* he thought. It didn't matter that it was some teddy bear the girl had accidentally breathed life into. It was a living creature now, and its heart belonged to this kid who had nearly broken the world.

"This is madness," Titus heard Kate say, but she sounded more awed than cynical.

The werewolf went back to Alice. Her eyes glistened with tears. *It's unfair that someone so young knows she's made such terrible mistakes.*

"I want to go home," Alice said.

And then her expression went from tearful to furious as she returned her focus to the Vizier.

"Get out," she said, her voice ferocious.

"My queen, you need me," the Vizier said. His power flickered.

"I've never needed you, have I," Alice said. "But you need me, don't you. You've needed me all along."

"Please don't do this," the nightmare said.

"Alice of Earth, do you wish to part with his creature?" Lady Dreamless said.

"I want him away from me," Alice said, not a shred of doubt in her voice.

Lady Dreamless flexed her fingers, and a long whip of brilliant red light appeared in her hand. She swung the whip overhead like a circus performer.

The Vizier moved fast. He cast another bolt of sickly purple energy at Lady Dreamless. Doc released the spell he'd been holding back and another arcane shield sprung up to deflect the blast.

"Titus, now," Doc said, and Titus, muttering a spell he'd learned from Leto not long ago that would help his aim strike true, threw his enchanted spear at the nightmare. It lanced through the Vizier's torso like a harpoon and stuck there, the blade emerging bloodlessly from the other side. The weapon seemed to do no real physical damage, but it was enough to distract the nightmare. Another spell fizzled in the Vizier's hands as he reached down to clutch at the spear's tip.

"No," he said.

The room flashed with a blinding red light as Lady Dreamless arced her whip down into the empty air between Alice and the Vizier. Something snapped; Titus felt it more than saw it, a sense of tension breaking, like an elastic band giving way, but on an epic scale.

Alice was knocked backward, rolling down the stairs of the dais. Both Sir Teddy and Kate ran to her—Titus, despite the shock of everything leading up to it, almost laughed at the way Kate's graceful sprint contrasted with the bear's stumpy gait. The nightmare screamed, his voice seeming to come from all directions at once.

"I worked too hard for this!" he yelled. "I waited for centuries to get away from the Dreamless Lands! I won't go back!"

"You're not going back," Lady Dreamless said. Her demon hounds sprang forward then, jaws slavering with something like lava, charging toward the nebulous, eerie shape of the Vizier's true form.

Before they could strike, though, a new player entered the room. His voice, slick and confident, made Titus' hair stand on end.

"Looks like I've arrived just in time to collect what I was

looking for," King Tears said.

Beside him, a young blond man stood shell-shocked and wide-eyed, taking in the unbelievable chaos of the room as if he were watching a film.

"I'm here for the girl's power," King Tears said. "Very convenient of you to clear her of pests before I take her."

"You don't want to be here, Tears," Doc said, his voice far more fearful than angry.

"This is why you'll always lose, Silence. You don't take the big risks," King Tears said.

The necromancer began casting a spell. Titus didn't recognize it, but he knew just enough to understand the spell was opening a connection, not unlike what had just been holding Alice and the Vizier together. He reached out for Alice, mystical energy gathering around his hand like an insect swarm.

But the spell didn't connect him with Alice. The Vizier intervened.

"You'll serve my purposes," the Vizier said, leaping between King Tears and Alice, away from the slavering jaws of the demon hounds. His body stretched out as if in a funhouse mirror, and he was sucked into the spell King Tears had begun casting. The necromancer reacted as if struck; his whole body convulsed and he let out a barking cry that sounded as though he'd been kicked in the gut.

"No, no, not you, you've ruined it!" King Tears said.

"I didn't ruin anything," the nightmare said, using King Tears' mouth. The evil magician's skin went from gray to pitch black, like crude oil. The white tattoos across his skin glowed brightly from within. When he opened his eyes, lavender light spilled out, and when he smiled, his teeth turned to filed points.

"Yes," the Vizier said from within King Tears' body. "This will do for now. Goodbye, Alice. It was almost fun playing in your sandbox. I'll miss you when you're gone."

He began casting a spell, index finger targeting Alice. Doc started calling out more magic words. Titus broke into a run, not sure what he'd do if he got there in time, but he had to do something. The teddy bear stood in front of his queen protectively, comically ineffective for what was to come. And Kate stood ready, one hand grabbing Alice's sleeve, as though she thought she yank the younger girl out of the way of the spell.

But then King Tears and the Vizier roared in pain again. The spell that crackled forth from his fingertips went off-course, tearing into the ceiling above the throne. Stone fell in huge chunks, and Lady Dreamless and her hounds disappeared in a cloud of dust and debris.

Titus saw a spike of silver jutting from King Tears' shoulder, piercing him straight through from the back.

The unicorn, Titus thought. The damned unicorn got him.

King Tears wheeled on Silverhoof violently, and with casual brutality, sent the unicorn sprawling violently across the chamber, crashing into the nearest wall. Her hoofs scraped the floor weakly for a moment, then went still.

Titus knew he needed to get the villain's attention and howled, more to distract him than as a war cry. King Tears, blood pouring from the wound in his shoulder, laughed.

"Killing a unicorn and a werewolf in the same day," the Vizier said from within the necromancer. He stepped over the prone body of his blond companion, who was crawling across the floor looking for an escape. "All we need is a dragon to finish the trifecta."

"No," Alice said, and the room grew instantly still.

Titus turned to see Alice floating above the floor, awash in bright vermillion waves of arcane energy. Power sparked from her clenched hands like sparks. Kate was to her left, but backing away cautiously, ready to move.

"You won't be killing anyone else today," Alice said. "And I'm done being used."

CHAPTER 57:
ALICE, THE QUEEN

Alice felt like a fever had just broken in her. That strange clear sensation after being sick for so long you'd forgotten how it felt to not be sick. Waves of relief flooded her limbs, her mind. Her thoughts were no longer sluggish or dulled. How long was I like this? she thought. How long was I being manipulated?

Along with clarity, power surged into her body as well. She lifted off the ground though she had no idea she could fly. She could sense the magic around her, invisible energies just waiting to be used.

The man whose body the Vizier now wore smiled at her, his old body gone, disappearing within this stranger's form. They were like overlapping evils, she sensed; malignant, powerful, greedy. They wanted her magic. That much was crystal clear. And they'd killed her friends.

The castle rumbled. She felt the structure beginning to splinter. Without her will holding it in place, the castle would not hold. Perhaps the whole dimension would not hold. But that was a concern for later. Right now, she had to face the being who had stolen her life, and another being who came here wanting to do the same.

"You've never cast a spell on your own," the Vizier said. The face he now wore smirked at her arrogantly. "You don't know how magic works without me. You need me, Alice."

"Believing that is how I got here in the first place," she said.

"And yet here we are," the Vizier said. "I thought you'd enjoy ruling a world perfectly designed to make you happy. Clearly, like all humans, you want more than your fair share. Well, it was a good run, moppet. But if I can't have your power, no one can. Not even yourself."

Behind the Vizier, the girl with the flaming hair darted in, landing a punch to his face before he could react. He grabbed her by the front of her uniform, though, and threw her with the same brutal strength he'd used on poor Silverhoof. The fire-haired young woman slammed into the wall, but instead of falling, she left a spider web-shaped indentation in the stonework.

The werewolf was circling the Vizier's new body as well, but hanging back, looking for an opening. The nightmare paid him only the slightest bit of mind.

"Alice, let's put an end to this mess. Send them all away and we'll rebuild. It'll be so much fun," he said

"You still think you can talk me into joining you after everything you've done?" she asked.

The magician in the red glasses, the one the Vizier had thrown in the dungeon, walked warily toward he confrontation, hands outstretched.

"King Tears. I know you're in there," the bespectacled wizard said. "I'd much rather reason with you right now."

"The idiot necromancer can't come to the phone right

now," the Vizier said. "He's busy."

The Vizier winked at Alice.

"I saved you the trouble of dealing with him," he said. "He came here to take your power, you know. Not like me, not to help you build a world. He was going to drain you dry and use it for himself. And you think I'm evil."

"You are evil," Alice said.

"Moralizing is so boring," the Vizier said. "Okay, then, little pet. We're going to crack you like an egg now and pour out your magic like a yolk."

With horrifying speed, the altered body of the magician lunged forward, fingers extending into long, scythe-like claws made of shadow and poison. Instinctually, Alice reacted. She did not move defensively, or step back, or call up a mystical shield. She lashed out with an arcing motion, and the Vizier's hand separated from his body above the wrist, spinning away like discarded garbage.

"How did you…" the Vizier said, staring at the bloodless stump of his hand in shock.

"You'll never hurt anyone again," she said. She clapped her hands together, then made a slashing motion downward. A bright beam of red light followed her gesture, bifurcating the stolen body the Vizier hid within. Then, she flipped her hands to that the backs were pressed up against each other. She mimicked ripping something in half.

Neither the Vizier nor King Tears had time to scream or cry out. In a split second, they were cut in half down the middle by pure magical energy, and then the body they shared was torn asunder, turning to ash before it hit the ground. The ash drifted through the room like dust in a forgotten tomb, swirling in the slight breeze.

Alice's view across the throne room was clear, now, her

nemesis gone before her very eyes. Another of the young heroes had appeared at the entrance of the chamber, a boy wearing a silver and blue uniform. He had a woman in his arms with robotic limbs, none of which seemed to work.

"What the hell just happened," he said, the puzzlement on his face readable despite his half-mask.

Before anyone could answer, the castle rumbled, shaking hard enough to almost knock the newcomer off his feet. The fire haired girl stood up, calling out to her friends.

"It's coming down!" she yelled.

The magician in the red glasses began casting spells, throwing the debris from the ceiling away to look for the elfin woman who had helped Alice break the hold the Vizier had on her.

"Run!" he said. "I've got to find Lady Dreamless. The rest of you get out of here!"

"Come on," the other young woman, the one in the dark body armor, said to Alice as she started to run for the exit. Comically, she held Sir Teddy under her arm like an indignant football, ready to carry him to safety.

"What's going on," Alice asked.

"Your hold over the castle has faded," the werewolf said. "I think this whole place is falling."

"No it isn't!" the strange, blue-haired girl said, striding into the throne room confidently, arms outstretched as if to hold the castle up with her hands. As impossible as that seemed, the building had stopped rumbling and shaking. "I can hold it for a few minutes. Get everyone out, my dudes!"

The fire-haired hero trotted past the blue-haired one toward the magician.

"Do I even want to know where you left the zombies?" she asked.

"Someone hadn't filled their pool in for the summer yet," the blue-haired girl said.

The magician had successfully uncovered both the massive dogs who had been buried. One limped along on its own, while the girl with the flaming hair picked the other up to carry it out. Beyond, the magician himself helped Lady Dreamless to her feet, and together they staggered down what remained of the dais.

"Come with us," the werewolf said, his voice surprisingly gentle despite his terrifying appearance.

"Silverhoof," Alice said, pointing to the inert form of the unicorn.

"I'll get her. You just head outside," he said.

Alice believed him. She floated rather than ran down the stairs to the exterior of the castle. As she did, she watched as her guards, hundreds of them, began to fade away like ghosts, disappearing like half-forgotten dreams.

What was real here? Alice asked herself as she left the castle, the costumed heroes close behind.

The last to leave was the blue-haired girl, backing out clumsily until she was across the moat. She yelled over her shoulder.

"Everyone accounted for?" she said.

"We're out!" the fire-haired girl said.

"Even the fairy?"

"Even the fairy!

"Okay!" the blue-haired girl said. She dropped her arms to her sides, and with it, whatever power she'd used to hold the castle together. Instantly, it began to crumble to the ground, coming apart as if it were held together with nothing but imagination.

Which, Alice knew, was true.

CHAPTER 58: THINGS FALL APART

None of this will ever make sense, Kate thought as she sat down on the soft grass outside the fallen castle. Magic. She knew it was real. She'd seen its impact. There was no doubt in her mind. But she knew only what she could do with her own body, the limitations of the physical self. And here she was, watching Doc and the goddess of some forgotten dimension triaging a dying unicorn.

The kid was crying now. She'd earned it, Kate thought. What she'd done inside that castle took an iron will. And it had cost her something, too. At some point during the final moments of the battle, Alice's hair had gone pure white, not the white of old age, but rather almost luminescent, a soft, pale glowing corona framing her face.

This place gave her whatever she wanted, and she gave it up for free will. Kate could respect that.

But now Doc was talking with her. Kate sometimes wondered if, in another lifetime, Doc Silence might have been a teacher, or a counselor, or a therapist. You sometimes hear about mentors who use manipulation or abuse to get the most out of their students, but every time, at every opportunity, she'd seen him use kindness instead. We could've done worse for a mentor, she thought.

"I can't let her die," the girl, Alice, was saying.

"We'll do what we can, but Alice, she's your figment," Doc said.

"I don't know what that means," Alice said.

"It means your mind, and your magic, gave her life. You can put her back together again. We can't," he said.

The bear—I can't believe I rescued a living teddy bear from a falling castle, Kate thought—took Alice's hand in his paw.

"I believe in you," he said. Alice nodded to him gently. Lady Dreamless took Alice by the shoulder and led her over to the unicorn, whose breathing was labored but steady, and spoke with her just out of earshot.

Speaking of broken things and magic, though, Kate thought, watching as Titus transformed back into his human form and knelt beside Billy, who had Bedlam cradled in his arms. Someone else who showed serious guts, Kate thought. She'd have to ask Billy what did such a number on Bedlam's robotic limbs.

"I can't fix them, but I'm sure Henry Winter will know what to do," Titus said, his voice gentle and reassuring.

"We can… call Agent Black," Bedlam said, straining and clearly in pain. "He's been messed up in combat before. Maybe he'll know someone who can fix me."

"For now, though, I can take away some of the pain," Titus said. "If you want. Maybe heal up some of the non-mechanical damage."

"You can do that?" Billy said. "I thought you just learned some tree magic from the boss werewolf."

"Leto is a healer," Titus said. "It was the easiest thing she could teach me."

He placed a hand lightly on Bedlam's neck as if to feel her pulse, then said a few words in a language Kate knew didn't exist anymore in the real world. Bedlam's body visibly relaxed. She leaned into Billy languidly.

"I didn't even know how much hurt until you did that," Bedlam said. "Thanks, furball."

"Any time," Titus said, standing up. He sounded wrong, and it caught Kate's attention. She waited until he walked away from Billy and Bedlam to pull him aside.

"What's wrong," she asked, trying to avoid sounding sympathetic.

"Nothing," Titus said.

"If you're going to keep using magic, you at least need to be up front with me about it," Kate said.

Titus sighed. He looked her in the eyes, and she saw a distinct look of discomfort.

"The pain has to go somewhere," Titus said. "You take it away from one place and transfer it somewhere else."

"You idiot," Kate said. "You just took her pain onto yourself?"

"Yeah," Titus said. "She's not good, Kate. She needs a real doctor soon. Or Sam Barren's healing powers, if he's willing."

"But you just…"

"Kate, I survived an exploding spaceship with burns over seventy percent of my body," he said. "This is nothing compared to that. It's okay. It's all temporary."

"Don't ever do that for me, Titus," she said.

"You going to make me pinky swear?"

"I will show you what real pain feels like if you ever do that for me," she said.

"Fine."

Kate looked at the ground.

"You're a good one, Titus Talbot."

"I try to be," he said.

Emily had been chit-chatting with the fairy, Galinda, but suddenly jumped to her feet and pointed up.

"Guys! Hey guys!" she yelled.

Kate followed Emily's point. The sky looked wrong there, unsteady, almost like waviness of heat coming off pavement in the summer.

"The sky is broken," Emily said. "Can we safely assume this has something to do with us?"

"Everything usually does," Jane said. "Doc?"

"The world is falling apart," Doc said. "Alice, it's time."

"Time for what" Alice said.

Doc gestured to the sky, and then the horizon, just beyond the town of Westwick. For the first time, Kate saw some of the residents starting to leave their homes, milling about in the streets, lost and confused.

"Time to decide," Doc said. "This world will only stay stable and whole if you will it to."

"I don't need it anymore," Alice said. "I should have never built it in the first place."

"Then you have to send those people home," Doc said. Alice's eyes went wide.

"I don't know how," she said.

"There's no trick to it," Doc said. "You have incredible innate abilities. You brought the town here to your world—not the Vizier. You did. He just gave you the idea. So all you have to do is tell it to go home. Magic is never easy. But sometimes it's very simple, if you know what to do."

Alice closed her eyes. Kate thought the kid might start

hyperventilating as she watched her breathing grow faster and faster. For a disconcertingly long few minutes, nothing happened. And then:

"Doc," Jane said. "The town."

Where Westwick once sat, a vast, empty field remained.

"I told it to go home," Alice said.

"Good job," Doc said. "And now it's our turn. Jane, you still have the planar knife?"

"Sure do," she said.

"Want to do the honors?" Doc asked.

"I have had more than my fill of magic for the day," she said, handing him the razor-thin dagger.

"That's fair, Doc said. With a deft flick of his wrist, he cut open a thin sliver in reality. The blue beyond felt familiar and welcoming after the time they'd spent under this strange red sky.

"Let's go home," Doc said.

Without asking, Emily picked up the unconscious unicorn with a bubble of float and carried it through. Billy went next with Bedlam, then Lady Dreamless and her dogs, both of whom were limping and battered but able to move under their own power. Kate shook her head in disbelief as Lady Dreamless and the hounds rippled on their way through the portal, reverting to the earthly disguises they'd shed when they came here.

As Jane was about to step through, she paused, then turned to Emily, who was close on her heels with the unicorn.

"Em, where did you say you left the zombies?" Jane asked.

"Oh," Emily said. "Oops?"

"Um, Doc…" Jane said.

"It never ends," Kate said, leading the charge as the rest of the Indestructibles ran through the portal back to Earth.

CHAPTER 59:
YOU CAN'T JUST DROP A TOWN

Jane knew they were safely home the moment she heard Sam Barren yelling at them.

"Doc Silence! You can't just drop a town… on a town!" Sam yelled. The old man was walking at them as fast as his legs would carry him, hat in one hand, the other gesturing at Doc violently.

"Hey, silver fox," Emily said cheerfully. "Good to see you too!"

"I don't even know what that means," Sam said. "All I know is I'm standing here trying to figure out how to get a warning to you and suddenly the whole town just blinks back into existence."

"Magic," Doc said.

"Whatever," Sam said, stuffing his hat back onto his head. "Speaking of which."

Sam thumbed over his shoulder to where Natasha Grey stood waiting for them, dressed in just the right ensemble to mimic one of Sam's Department of What agents.

"She's been hovering like a nervous soccer mom," Sam said.

Doc gestured for Natasha to join them. Sam's agents were all over, talking to some of the Westwick residents who had already emerged from their homes. They all looked bedraggled and exhausted. Not, Jane thought, unlike people who had been seeing their own personal nightmares on repeat for a week.

"How bad are they?" Jane asked.

"The townsfolk?" Sam said. "Confused. Scared. Exhausted. But none of them seem to think what they went through really happened. They're asking if there was something in the water, or a chemical explosion that kicked a hallucinogen into the air."

"Close enough," Titus said.

Natasha Grey joined them, patting one of the Great Danes as it looked up at her in greeting.

"I thought you were going to keep King Tears occupied if he tried to cross over," Doc said.

"I thought he was going to come threaten me again," Lady Grey said. "Clearly, and much to my undying shame, I overestimated my value to him. Where is the old scoundrel, anyway?"

"Dead," Kate said.

"I very much doubt that's a permanent state for a necromancer of his talents," the sorceress said. "But we'll deal with that later."

"What else is going on, Sam?" Doc asked.

Before Sam Barren could answer, Alice took off at a sprint. Jane saw her leap into a woman's waiting arms. They looked similar enough that Jane figured it had to be her mother.

"Becca Lapine was with my agents when the town reappeared," Sam said. "I had them bring her here. Figured you'd succeeded at whatever you went over there to do."

"Succeeded is a stretch," Billy said.

Bedlam was attempting to stand, pushing off Billy's attempts to continue to hold her. She wobbled on her feet, and when Billy hooked a protective arm around her waist for support, she didn't argue.

"What happened to her?" Sam said.

"Took one for the team," Bedlam said.

Doc was observing the mother daughter reunion. Becca touched Alice's stark-white hair curiously, but seemed relieved to have her daughter back to dwell on her transformation. Jane found herself watching him watching them.

"What are you thinking about, Doc?" she asked.

"That a mother who is on the road three weeks a month and a father recovering from a heart attack are going to have a hard time with the fact that their daughter is possibly the most powerful natural magic user of her generation," Doc said.

"Makes you wish there was a Hogwarts you could ship her off to, huh," Emily said.

"Well, there's us," Jane said.

"There's us," Doc said.

"I mean look how well Emily turned out," Titus said.

"I'm right here, Chewie," Emily said.

"We'll figure something out," Doc said.

More and more residents of Westwick filtered out into the streets. Friends embraced as if they hadn't seen each other in years. Parents held children like they could be taken away at any moment. Some wandered alone, dazed, as if looking for answers to questions they couldn't remember. Others sat down and wept openly.

"This whole town is going to need therapy," Billy said.

Sam's phone rang, interrupting his concentration as he

made a rare use of his powers to finish patching up Bedlam's physical injuries. He apologized to the cyborg and answered.

"Yeah, agent, go ahead. Yes, the Indestructibles are back too, why—a pool full of what?" Sam said. He put a hand over the receiver of his phone. "Do any of you know something about an in-ground pool full of… zombies?"

"Look, the pool was convenient," Emily said. "This isn't my fault. It was a tactical decision."

"I'll deal with this," Doc said.

"Thanks," Emily said.

"Oh no, you're coming with me," Doc said. "You're my assistant."

Emily harrumphed but did as she was told, leading Doc toward the pool she'd used as a holding pen.

"Sam, Jane, I could probably use your help on this one," Doc said.

"Me?" Sam said, indignant. "What can I do to help with a pool full of zombies?"

"Well, you are the oldest person we know," Emily said.

"I hate all of you," Sam said.

"I'll catch up, one minute," Jane said.

As Doc, Emily, and Sam raced off, Jane shifted her gaze back and forth between the conversations Alice was having with her mother and the one going on between Natasha Grey and Lady Dreamless.

"Keep an eye on them, huh?" Jane said, leaning in conspiratorially to Kate.

"Planning on it," Kate said.

"I have a bad feeling about all of it," Jane said.

"I always have a bad feeling," Kate said. "Paranoia has its benefits."

Jane touched Billy on the arm.

"You two should fly home. Don't wait for us," she said. "Have Henry take a look at those limbs."

"I'll wait for Doc to teleport us back," Billy said. "It'll be easier on her injuries."

"I can take it," Bedlam said. "Stop treating me like I'm broken."

"You are literally broken right now," Billy said. "Like that's not a metaphor. You really want to fly at supersonic speeds without a windshield?"

Bedlam winced.

"Fine, we'll wait," she said.

Jane gestured at Lady Grey with her eyebrows.

"You could ask her for a teleport," Jane said. "She owes us one."

"Absolutely not," Billy and Bedlam said in unison.

"Okay then," Jane said. "Wait for Doc it is. I'll be back after we deal with the zombies."

"Hey Jane," Bedlam called out. "If you run into any of that King Tears guy's creations and they ask you to put them out of their misery…"

"Oh, Bedlam, I don't…" Jane started to say, but Titus interrupted.

"If they ask," Titus said. "We'll take care of it."

"Mercy killings?" Jane said.

"You weren't there in the warehouse," Titus said. "If they can be saved, we save them. That may not always be the case."

"This is awful," Jane said. "I'm glad this guy is gone."

"Me too," Titus said. "Me too."

CHAPTER 60:
THE PERILS OF MIDDLE MANAGEMENT

Andrew Keppler awoke in the thin forest outside Westwick, unsure how he got there or how he survived. The last thing he remembered clearly was an explosion of light, and watching King Tears disintegrate before his eyes.

Keppler wouldn't waste any time mourning that egomaniac, but he did start to wonder where he was and how he'd get home. Staggering, he wandered back into Westwick, visible a short, clumsy walk away, and tried to parse out exactly what had happened.

The streets were no longer empty. Neighbors talking in hushed tones. A lot of people avoiding eye contact with each other, as well as with Keppler himself, as if everyone had done something embarrassing at the company Christmas party and nobody was sure who saw them do it.

Keppler checked his pockets. Still had his wallet, still had his phone. Good enough, he thought. I can do anything with those two things.

"You okay, man?" a middle-aged guy said, sitting outside a coffee shop that still had its "closed" sign hanging in the door.

"Yeah," Keppler said, scratching his hair. He found a twig stuck to his head, plucked it out, and tossed it aside. "Yeah, it was a weird day."

"Rumor has it something got into the water supply," the man said. "People hallucinating."

"Really?" Keppler said, feigning interest. "Seeing things?"

"Yeah, some folks are pretty messed up about it," the man said. "I mean, not the first time in my life I've hallucinated, to be honest, so I'm not worried, but man, but the garden club apparently is pretty freaked out."

"As garden clubs sometimes are," Keppler said.

"Yup," the man said amicably. "The funny thing is everyone said they saw one thing in common: the sky was red. That's weird, right? Mass hallucination. Maybe it was something in the water."

"Or it could've been magic," Keppler said.

He looked at the stranger with a long, blank stare. The other man began to lean back uncomfortably. Keppler burst out laughing.

"I'm just kidding," Keppler said. "Definitely drugs in the water."

"That's what I'm saying!" the other man said. "Anyway. Glad you're okay, man."

"Thanks," Keppler said. "Say. I'm from out of town. Do you know if there's a cab service here?"

"It's a pretty small town. You won't have much luck just catching one driving by. But try Patriot Cab Company. They've got a website. You got a phone?"

"I do."

"Everybody's got a phone these days," the man said. "Silly to ask. Anyway. Good luck, dude."

"Thanks again," Keppler said. He took out his phone as the stranger walked away, looked up the cab company on his browser, and called for a ride. It took the car a half hour to arrive, but sitting there in the California sun, Keppler had time to take stock of what happened, and how he survived.

King Tears wasn't wrong, he thought. Not about rebuilding. He was rebuilding wrong, and he was a sociopathic monster, but he was right about not throwing away the infrastructure the Children of the Elder Star had built. Keppler had no interest in raising the dead or commanding an army of abominations, but running a massive, cryptic, world-spanning corporation?

He could get into that. And he was pretty sure he was the only person in the world who knew where the bodies were buried and where the passwords were jotted down.

The taxi arrived, a surprisingly nice vehicle with Patriot Cab Company emblazoned on the side in red, white, and blue. Keppler held up a hand to signal the car and hopped inside. The interior was also unexpectedly high quality, with leather seats that looked barely touched. There was a distinct sea water stink to the interior, though, that undercut the leather and new-car smells.

"I need to get to the airport, please," Keppler said. He looked himself over, covered in dirt, pants torn in a few places, shoes scuffed and sloppy. "Actually, if you don't mind, I'd like to stop at a menswear place along the way. I'll pay you for your time to wait. Somewhere upscale if it's not too far out of the way."

The car pulled away from the curb, but the driver said nothing. Keppler shrugged. Maybe he didn't speak English,

Keppler thought. He figured there had to be a shop at the airport where he could buy a decent suit and get rid of this disaster.

About a mile outside town, on a flat, empty stretch of road the car pulled over. Keppler shook himself out of a daydream and watched the driver, hands clenching into fists. I wish I had a weapon, he thought. Why didn't I bring something with me?

The driver put his arm over the seat and leaned back to face him. Keppler stifled a scream.

Please let that be a mask, he thought. But then the creature in the driver's seat began to speak, and he knew he'd escaped one nightmare only to enter another.

The driver's head was shaped like an octopus, round with large, gleaming eyes set widely. Tentacles writhed like a beard below the empty space where a nose should be. These twisted and danced when it spoke, though the voice felt far more as though it came from within his head than out of a mouth beneath those wriggling appendages.

"You've been doing excellent work, Mr. Keppler," the driver said. "I've come to let you know that your efforts have not gone unnoticed by what remains of the advisory board."

"The board is gone," Keppler said.

"The board of directors is gone," the driver said. "But there have always been those who lurked just beyond, acting as advisors rather than leaders. We were disappointed in the direction the previous management, too. We thought King Tears had promise, though his means were unconventional."

"Unconventional?" Keppler said.

"It's better to work with magicians, not for them," the creature said. "Magicians are very useful, but they don't make very good executive decisions. They always either never see the big picture, blinded by their desires, or they only see the big picture, and don't have the time to make sure all the cogs are in place. He tried to skip ahead. It's a very common mistake among wizards."

"Yeah, okay," Keppler said, suddenly wondering if he had ever returned from the alternate dimension or if this was just part of an extended hallucination. "You said I was doing good work?"

"You are," the driver said. "Much was asked of you, but you somehow had the good sense to keep company assets protected from a manager who was headed toward ruin."

Keppler raised an eyebrow.

"I always did pride myself on forethought," he said.

"Well," the driver said. "We may have further use for you yet."

"I would like that very much," Keppler said.

"Then let's get you a new suit," the driver said. "Your new office will be ready for you when you arrive in New York."

Keppler couldn't resist smiling as the octopus-headed creature started the car again and pulled back on the highway.

I wonder if it's a corner office, he thought, watching the world drift by outside his window.

CHAPTER 61:
HOME

Titus sat cross-legged in front of a crystal ball back in the Tower. The old base, despite still being stuck inert in the desert, was starting to almost feel like home again. The work Henry, Neal, and even Emily had been doing made it feel livable, comfortable, and much of the technology they'd relied on for so long was back online.

This made the decision to camp out at the Tower for a week after the incident with Alice's pocket dimension a little easier. Although no one really seemed to want to leave. Not even Kate or, Titus had to admit, even himself. Something about facing their own fears so viscerally had brought the team closer than before. They wanted to be nearby. He often found himself walking the halls just to make sure he knew where the others were, and that they were okay.

Alice had remained behind with her parents, of course, which was the reason for the crystal ball. Doc had set up a scrying spell to monitor her in case her powers acted up, and they'd all volunteered to take turns watching the house for signs of danger. So far, it had remained quiet, and everyone was relieved about that.

Doc sometimes hung out while Titus took his shifts. They'd talk magic theory a bit. But more than that, Doc asked Titus his goals for spellcasting.

"A magician needs to know what he wants," Doc had said. "It's not something you keep in your pocket just in case. You need to always be aware of it, once you've started down that path. And it's okay if you decide to leave that path, Titus. Just make that decision soon, before you get too deep into the woods."

And so Titus thought about those goals. He kept coming back to something Leto and old Finn had said to him over and over again: that the Whisperings, Titus' ancestors, had not just been monsters to keep worse monsters at bay; they'd always been shamans on the hill, protecting the tribe from the dark.

If I'm going to be a shaman on the hill, Titus thought, then I need to do it right.

"Hey," Kate said, shaking him from his reverie.

"Hi," Titus said.

"Bring the ball," she said. "Team meeting."

Titus scooped up the crystal ball and followed her down a quiet, familiar hallway.

"You haven't gone back to the City in a week," Titus said.

"I'm reassessing how I handle protecting it," she said. "Every time something like this happens, I wonder why I bother. There's some vast, horrible thing waiting to destroy the world around every turn, and I can't punch or kick that into submission."

"So you do what you can," Titus said. "You change one life at a time."

Kate stopped walking.

"Did I say something wrong?" Titus said.

"No," Kate said. "It's just that… that's why I started doing this in the first place."

"Then go back to that," Titus said. "Be the thing you need to be in the world, Kate, not the thing you think you have to be."

"You're practicing that shaman thing, aren't you," Kate said.

"I am spending a painful amount of time alone with my own thoughts," Titus said.

"Let's fix that a bit," Kate said.

"I'd appreciate it," Titus said.

Jane, in a moment of boredom, had rearranged an area that had once been a rec room into a sort of communal meeting space. Kate and Titus entered to find her already there, along with Doc and Lady Dreamless. One of the demon dogs, still in its Great Dane disguise, had curled up on Doc's lap like a Lhasa Apso. Doc didn't seem to mind, though.

Titus was not pleased to see that Natasha Grey had joined them today. Unlike Lady Dreamless, who had nowhere else to go, Natasha had disappeared immediately after the battle. This was the first they'd seen of her in days.

Billy and Bedlam walked in next. Walked, Titus thought proudly. Bedlam's right arm needed extensive repairs, and Henry Winter had arranged for her to meet with a cybernetics specialist in a few days, but he'd been able to get her up and moving again for the most part. His fixes were temporary, but it was enough to get her on her feet. Billy was hilariously, and even charmingly, doting, which Titus had never expected his friend to be. Although it occurred to him that Billy had never had to take care of anyone before.

"Hey, lovebirds," Emily said, sliding into the room

dramatically. Henry limped in behind her.

"Doc, I know you have a reason for calling everyone in here, but I think Emily and I have something you'll all want to see," Henry said. He stepped aside to make room in the entranceway. Behind him, one of his old Coldwall armored suits walked in. It had been stripped down to scale back on some of the bulky armor, but otherwise, it was still impressive, a blue and silvery-white, human shaped weapon.

"Who's in there?" Billy asked.

"I am, Designation: Straylight," Neal said.

"You're not a trash bin anymore!" Billy said. "I'm so happy for you!"

"That really you, old buddy?" Titus said.

"I am, Designation: Whispering," Neal said. "I am also still interfacing wirelessly with the Tower, but I am no longer unable to make use of stairs. I am quite pleased."

"We're pleased for you," Jane said. "Is this a permanent switch?"

"Only until I get him an upgrade," Henry said. "We tested it on one of my older suits of armor, but Neal deserves top-shelf treatment."

Titus stole a glance at Kate, who said nothing. He knew Kate always considered it her fault Neal had to abandon being part of the Tower. She'd never admit it, but seeing him trapped in a small, bucket-sized robot weighed on her. He could see she was biting back a smile.

"Well, come join us, Neal," Doc said. "Everyone should be part of this conversation."

"And that conversation is?" Jane said.

Doc gently nudged the demon hound off his lap and stood up. He took the scrying crystal from Titus.

"We need to decide what to do about Alice," he said.

"I assume letting the kid grow up in peace is not an option," Bedlam said.

"I wish it were," Doc said. "But she's a generationally powerful magical talent. She's on the radar, so to speak. She has begun using her powers at a young age, and, like it or not, received some inadvertent instruction from the Vizier, which means she knows just enough to be a danger to herself."

"There's always us," Jane said. "You're here, Doc. We could take her in."

"Send her an owl. Hogwarts this situation," Emily said.

"It's an option," Doc said. "But she's not ready to be a part of what we do, either."

"I wasn't ready, and I turned out fine," Emily said.

"Debatable," Billy said.

"I'll debate your face, Billy," Emily said.

"I can take her," Lady Dreamless said.

"That's not a bad idea," Natasha said.

"Didn't she almost destroy an entire town because of dream magic?" Titus said.

Titus didn't like the idea, but Lady Dreamless had, they found, been more of a benign spirit than any of them had previously expected. When they disposed of the zombies, they also found that some of King Tears' abominations had not immediately become lifeless in his absence. Some, they discovered to their absolute horror, were still human enough to survive despite their transformation—like Kevin, the poor homeless boy who had attacked Titus. They'd found Kevin's lifeless body in Westwick, but there were several others like him.

Lady Dreamless offered them sanctuary in the Dreamless Lands while her people tried to reverse the damage King Tears had done. Such large-scale metamorphosis would be easier in a place with a lighter grip on normal physics like the Dreamless Lands, Doc explained, and so they planned on sending those victims back with Dreamless when she went home. They were currently being held, comfortably, in the Labyrinth, the defunct superhuman prison Sam's Department of What now used as a base.

Still, sending innocent victims warped by flesh magic was one thing. Sending a very confused kid with the misfortune of having magic in her veins she didn't know how to use felt less humanitarian.

"Great, we're taking advice from a super-villain," Emily said.

"Why is Natasha here, anyway," Kate asked.

Doc cleared his throat.

"She is here," he said, giving Natasha a very pointed look. "Because she is, whether we like it, one of the most skilled magicians alive today, and what happens to the most powerful natural magician of the next generation is something she should have some say in."

"Thank you," Natasha said.

"Also, I don't trust you entirely, and if you know where she's going, then I know you know where she's going, and I don't have to worry about you sneaking around trying to find out where she's gone," Doc said. "I'll know what you know, and I'll sleep better because of it."

"That is less flattering," Natasha said. "But also, the precise level of paranoia I did try to instill in you. So bravo."

"But in all seriousness, hiding her in the Dreamless Lands is not a bad idea," Doc said. "She's already been heavily exposed to dream magic. Which means she's inclined toward using it. Possibly the only place she can't cause widespread destruction with dream magic is in the Dreamless Lands."

"And the reason she was exposed to dream magic is because of my negligence," Lady Dreamless said. "I owe her proper instruction. That is my duty. And her creations will be safe there as well. Her surviving figments. She can bring her guardians there without worry."

"And no one goes to the Dreamless Lands on purpose," Natasha said. Doc started to protest, but she cut him off. "Except you. You are the only lunatic who has ever gone to that madhouse intentionally. She'll be well hidden."

"I don't like it, but I see the logic," Jane said. "But does this mean we'll be taking her from her parents?"

"There are ways she can move back and forth. With guidance," Lady Dreamless said. Because she'll have allies on both sides."

"Great," Billy said. "So, who is going to tell the twelve-year-old she has to run away to fairy land?"

CHAPTER 62:
EVER AND ALWAYS THROUGH THE LOOKING GLASS

Doc watched Alice say goodbye to her parents and thought about how many times he'd taken children from their homes for their own safety.

It wasn't so long ago he pulled a feral Titus from a forest, and Emily from the middle of the street. It felt like yesterday when Jane's powers manifested and she had to leave the Hawkins' farm, and Mr. and Mrs. Hawkins were used to super-powered children. It was for everyone's safety she had to leave the place she'd come to call home.

I do this to keep them safe, and so they can keep the world safe, Doc thought. And yet I always and forever feel like a villain myself when it happens.

Alice's parents were not agreeable, per se, but they understood. They'd seen the empty space where Westwick disappeared. Their daughter came home changed, transformed, older, and stranger. They didn't want her to leave, but they understood.

Doc invited Jane and Emily along for the goodbyes. Emily, with her exuberance, seemed to set everyone at ease, as though she were living proof that one could get caught up in the world of the strange and terrifying and still come out joyful and full of life.

And Jane, well, Jane was who everyone hoped they could be like some day. He could already see Alice taking to her like an older sister.

Lady Dreamless, on the other hand, was more unsettling, but it didn't take a magician to tell there was something more than human about her. As Alice and her parents were saying their tearful goodbyes, Doc found Dreamless staring out in the distance, patting one of the hounds absently.

"I'll miss this world," she said. "I enjoyed it while I was here. It's so vulgar and raw and confused and beautiful."

"It's a little less unpredictable than your world," Doc said.

"No," Lady Dreamless said. "My world is mutable, but yours is… it's feral, Doctor. It fights like hell, in all ways, at all times. It is a dark place, and full of awful things, but there is such will to be better, such drive to make something of every short life that passes through here. You lose that in a plane of whimsy. Whimsy makes you think you have forever, and mutability makes you think nothing cannot be undone. I like the rawness of this place."

"Maybe you'll come back some day," Doc said. "More carefully next time."

"Maybe I will," Dreamless said, taking Doc's hand. "You could come with us. My kingdom could use a great magician."

"This world needs me a little longer," Doc said. "Someone has to mind the store."

He excused himself and approached Alice and her family.

Becca Lapine wiped at her eye.

"None of this feels real, you know," she said.

"I understand," Doc said.

"How will we know if she's okay?" Tony Lapine said. He looked as though he were taking his daughter's departure even worse than Becca.

"That's what I'm here to talk about," Doc said. He withdrew the two mirrors he and Jane had used to communicate before and handed one to Tony. He gave the other to Alice.

"What's this?" she asked.

"Both of you, open the mirror and look inside," Doc said.

The father swore. Alice laughed.

"You can talk through those," Doc said. "There's no battery life to them, you can't wear them out. Use them as often as you need to."

"Magic," Becca said.

"Exactly," Doc said. "And if you need to visit, or anything at all, you know how to call me. I'll help you."

"This feels like a very complicated boarding school," Tony said.

"Or Hogwarts," Alice said. "Only I'll be the only student."

"Homeschooling Hogwarts," Emily chimed in. "Which means you'll probably graduate early."

Alice smiled at Emily, who winked back conspiratorially.

"I'm sorry all this happened," Alice said, looking at each of them in turn. "I didn't mean any of it."

"It wasn't your fault," Jane said. "And now it won't happen again, because you'll be ready."

"It feels like my fault," Alice said.

"Trust me, in this life, everything feels like your fault," Jane said. "That doesn't mean you stop trying to do the right thing."

Doc heard a clanking noise as Sir Teddy walked out of the Lapines' home carrying the last of Alice's bags. He was accompanied by a banged up, but still living, unicorn, who in turn had a small fairy perched on her head.

"Someday, I'll be able to express how weird it's been to have a talking teddy bear, a unicorn, and a fairy living in our house this week," Tony said.

"You get used to it," Doc said.

"Hey," Emily said, throwing an arm around Alice's shoulder. "At least you get to bring your friends with you."

Alice dropped her eyes to the ground.

"Most of them," she said.

"You may be able to bring your shadow back some day," Natasha Grey said. She wore dark sunglasses to hide her glowing, fiery eyes, but otherwise looked more like a CEO than a magician.

"More things I need to make up for," Alice said.

"The guardians you created are incredibly brave, Alice," Doc said. "And when someone creates guardians the way you do, they're always a reflection of the person who made them. You should take comfort in that. If you weren't brave, you wouldn't have such powerful guardians."

The bear puffed up his chest.

"You hear that, Silverhoof? Powerful," he said.

"Yeah," Tony said. "Never going to get used to the talking bear. You know he likes baking shows? Somehow that made it even weirder."

Lady Dreamless stepped forward and took Alice's hand.

"Little wizard," she said. "Are you ready to begin your training? You'll be safe and well-cared for, in a place where the impossible happens every day. I promise you, it is a wonderful place to learn your craft."

"I think I'm ready," Alice said.

"Also, I hope you like dogs," Lady Dreamless said. As if commanded, the two demon hounds each picked up one of Alice's bags in their jaws to carry them.

"Okay," Alice said, taking a deep breath. She sighed, then threw her arms around both of her parents. Doc averted his gaze for a moment to give them privacy.

"If you will, Doctor," Lady Dreamless said. "We'll meet again soon."

"We will," Doc said, producing the planar knife from a sheath on his belt. He concentrated, thinking clearly of the Dreamless Lands, and sliced open a gap in reality. The dogs trotted through, as if happy to be going home. The bear saluted Doc and Jane as he walked by, then led his figment companions into the portal as well. Lastly, Lady Dreamless and Alice stepped through, hand in hand.

Alice never stopped looking back at her parents, eyes locked on them until the portal gently closed.

"We just sent our baby girl to another world," Becca said. "I think I'm going to be sick."

"I think there's a bottle of wine in the fridge," Tony said.

"You, husband, are supposed to be recovering."

"I think watching our kid travel to Narnia through a portal in our back yard is a reasonable excuse to not follow doctor's orders for one day," he said. He held out a hand to Doc, who shook it. "We can call you any time, you say?"

"Always," Doc said.

"This is like sending a kid to college though, right? No panicking the first weekend? Give her time to get comfortable and adjust?" Becca said.

"We could always send you to the Dreamless Lands with her," Natasha said. "But I've spent some time there. It's like living in Disney World full time. I don't recommend it."

"Thanks for…" Tony trailed off.

"It's why we're here," Doc said. "You don't have to thank us."

Eventually, the Lapines went into their house, holding hands and arguing good-naturedly over the bottle of wine. Doc caught them bickering a little bit about how soon they could use the mirror to call Alice.

"I think I need to go visit my folks," Jane said.

"I've been texting my mom this entire time," Emily said. "Can I bug you for a teleportation spell, Doc?"

Doc laughed.

"Of course," he said, opening another, less spectacular portal for Emily to walk through. Jane took off, a streak of flames in the air.

"Just us now," Natasha said.

"You promise you'll leave Alice alone," Doc said.

"Oh, gods, you think I need that kind of trouble?" Natasha said. "I've never even had a pet. I don't want to have charge of some magical savant. I can't handle the mess."

"You're almost convincing right now," Doc said.

"Speaking of convincing," Natasha said. "I have a job for the both of us."

Doc raised an eyebrow.

"You're kidding," he said.

"I wish I were," Lady Grey said. "But our friend King Tears was a necromancer, after all. And I believe he may have done a very necromancer-y thing."

Doc groaned.

"Tell me he didn't," Doc said.

"That arrogant bastard stored his soul in a jar somewhere so he could come back again."

"Nobody wants to come back as a lich," Doc said. "That's so…"

"Gauche?" Natasha said.

"I was going to say medieval," Doc said. "But sure, trashy works too."

"Will you help me find whatever box or jar our least favorite sorcerer stored his soul in?" Natasha said. "I'd like to recycle it before he comes back."

"I suppose we don't have much choice in the matter," Doc said. "No rest for the wicked, is there."

CHAPTER 63: WE'RE ALL INDESTRUCTIBLE, SOMETIMES

Emily and Henry searched a room they'd never seen before with industrial-strength flashlights, coughing at the sand and dust kicked up when they opened the door. Neal stood passively behind them, unbothered by the debris.

"You've really never been in this room before," Emily said, pulling her goggles down to protect her eyes.

"No," Henry said. "Why do you keep asking that?"

"How long was the Tower your team's base of operations?"

"I had my own corporation at the time," Henry said. "I wasn't a bored teenager opening up every door in the base."

"This room looks important," Emily said.

"It really doesn't," Henry replied, aiming his light at a string of cobwebs. "Clearly the place has run for… three generations of superheroes? Without anyone ever coming in here to check the plumbing."

Neal's heavy footfalls stirred up more dust from the floor.

"Odd," he said. "Designation: Coldwall and Designation: Entropy Emily, I have never encountered this room on any of the schematics, but now that I have a location for it, the plans for the Tower do show an unmapped space in this area. It's always been there, but the way it falls between stories has made it somewhat unremarkable."

"There was a hotel like this in Chicago," Emily said. "A serial killer used it to get rid of his victims."

"That's where your brain just went?" Henry said. "Right to serial killers?"

Emily pushed her goggles up dramatically, staring Henry in the eyes.

"What if there's been a serial killer on the ship the whole time," she said.

"Stop," Henry said.

"The calls are coming from inside the house, Henry," Emily said.

"Really?" Henry said. "You went there?"

"I don't hear any calls, Designation: Entropy Emily," Neal said.

"It's a metaphor or something," Emily said. She meandered around the room, kicking pipes that seemed to lead nowhere with her boot. "Ever think this spaceship looks more than a little alive?"

"In some ways, it is, Designation: Entropy," Neal said. "It had a sort of self-repairing system and a rudimentary intelligence I interfaced with, at least until the crash. Both have been offline ever since."

"The ship was alive?" Henry said, incredulous.

"Alive may be inaccurate, Designation: Coldwall," Neal said. "But it was not exactly inert, either."

"Kate killed our spaceship," Emily said.

"I would recommend you not say that out loud in front of Designation: Dancer," Neal said. "It appears to distress her."

"Neal, did you tell Kate she killed our spaceship?" Emily said.

"I sometimes struggle with complex human emotional states," Neal said.

"So do we all, big guy," Emily said.

She noticed a lever on the wall, the size of a slingshot. Curiosity, as it often does, overwhelmed her.

"Hey, I think I found the light switch," she said, flipping it to the "up" position.

The entire ship rumbled.

"Did you just flip a switch we hadn't tested yet?" Henry said.

"Fortune favors the bold," Emily said.

The ship hummed and shook. The ground shifted beneath their feet. Henry, with his bad leg, almost toppled over.

"We have to get to the control room," he said, panic in his eyes.

Together, they bolted from the room, leaving poor Neal clomping after them awkwardly.

***

"I'm thinking once you're back up and running again, I could take you out to the Luminae base," Billy said. He and Bedlam were sitting together in the rearranged rec room, watching a show about misbehaving magical grad students on a tablet.

"Do you have any idea how you'll get me, someone who needs oxygen to survive, all the way out to Saturn?" Bedlam said.

"I have many ideas," Billy said. "I'm not sure if any of them will work, but I have ideas."

"How about we just go somewhere on Earth that doesn't involve fighting power-mad bad guys?" Bedlam said.

"Saturn is really pretty."

"I believe you."

"Look, the way I see it, we never get to be normal, right?" Billy said. "We might as well go all in. Vacation in space. What's more super-heroic than that?"

Bedlam laughed and sank down in the chair.

"Okay, fine, I admit it. I still want to see the alien space station. But only if we can borrow, like a space RV or something."

"I'll see what I can do," Billy said.

The ship shook. Billy and Bedlam stared at each other.

"I don't even want to know," Billy said.

"Neither do I. But…"

"Fine," Billy said, helping her to her feet. "Let's go see what Emily broke."

***

"You're not going back to the City," Titus said.

"I think I need to travel a bit," Kate said. She sat cross-legged on a cot, hair pulled back messily, her gear scattered haphazardly around her.

"Like where?" Titus said.

"My parents used to take me all over when I was little," Kate said. "I was too young to appreciate it. And now I've been on a vengeance kick for… the rest of my miserable life. Maybe it's time to go see Paris or something."

"I think it's a good idea," Titus said.

Kate studied his face, then leaned back.

"Are you not going to ask to come with me?" Kate said.

"I thought this was like, a journey of self-discovery," Titus said. "You don't invite yourself along on a journey of self-discovery."

"Look, I don't know how to be nice. Okay?" Kate said, exasperated. "I thought if I talked about it enough you'd invite yourself with me and we could avoid the awkwardness."

"You expected the self-loathing, depressed, introverted werewolf to just invite himself on your walkabout?" Titus said.

"You remain my one and only weak spot when it comes to assessing a target's behavior," Kate said. "So, do you want to come with me, or not?"

"I'd love to," Titus said.

"I guess Doc learned a lot about magic while he was traveling," Kate said, mumbling the last part.

"You don't have to…" Titus said.

"No, you're right. Someone needs to know these things," Kate said. "Just try not to get weird."

"Weirder."

"You know what I meant," Kate said.

Before Titus could reply, the room shook as if struck by an earthquake. A rumbling hum filled the air.

"I just want one day without a crisis," Titus said. "Just one day."

***

Jane barreled down the hallway from her room, trying to remember where in the Tower Henry and Emily had been doing most of their work. They clearly either fixed or broke something, but from the violent sounds she'd heard a moment ago, she really couldn't tell which they'd successfully done this time.

Then she heard laughing.

She followed the sound, tripping over exposed wiring and knocking a toolbox over along the way. She spotted Kate and Titus at the end of the hall and waved for them to follow, not waiting for them to catch up. Finally, she located the command center, where Henry had been testing the ship's electronics for months.

Emily and Henry were dancing.

Not just dancing, Jane realized. It was some sort of rehearsed dance in perfect imitation of a dance from the *Peanuts* cartoon. Behind them, Neal had sprung into a clunky version of the dance moves Snoopy did famously on Schroeder's piano.

"What are you doing?" Jane said.

"We fixed it!" Henry said.

"To infinity and beyond, baby!" Emily said, grabbing Jane's arms and pulling her into a joyously dumb dance.

"Fixed what?" Jane said.

"We're flying, guys," Billy said, jogging into the room, Bedlam in tow.

"We're airborne again," Henry said. "Neal, can you call up the external cameras?"

The android nodded, and several monitors blinked on, showing an incomplete panorama of the desert outside. They were rising higher and higher, shedding sand like rain. In the distance, the hot desert sun was just dipping into a sunset behind the dunes.

"I never thought the old bird would fly again," Jane said.

Kate and Titus walked in last. The werewolf grinned, shaking his head.

"I knew you could do it, Henry," he said.

"Gotta give Emily this one," Henry said. "She found the missing piece of the puzzle."

"I'm a genius, yo," Emily said. "How many times do I have to tell you guys?"

Kate was quiet for a moment, looking around the room with her usual studious, emotionless expression. But Jane caught just the hint of a smile in her friend's eyes.

"I thought I broke you forever," Kate said, barely a whisper. But Jane heard her.

Nothing around here is broken forever, Jane thought. We're all indestructible. It just takes a little while to get there, sometimes.

EPILOGUE:
ONCE, IN THE CITY

The Tower, as it will always be known even though it was now more of a flying saucer, drifted over the City like a sentinel. The ship looked a bit worse for wear, but its presence, the blinking lights, the soft hum as it floated high above, was reassuring.

The Indestructibles, though, were gathered on the rooftop of Kate's hideout. Doc appeared out of thin air with pizza. Emily floated around serving drinks. It was a viewing party, after all. They wanted to watch the Tower make its circuit above the City it had called home, the sentinel in the sky.

Jane sat in a quiet corner, watching the ship. Billy sat down next to her and handed her a glass.

"You going back to the stars, Billy Case?" Jane asked.

"Not yet," he said. "Dude and I talked. Our place is here, for now."

"It'll be good to have you here," Jane said.

"Yeah," Emily said, butting in as always. "I tried to teach Henry how to play a few FPS games but he's terrible. I need my bro back."

"There are no game consoles on Saturn," Billy said.

"Well then, easy decision, right?" Emily said.

"Also, we're just starting to talk to each other like borderline adults," Bedlam said. She sidled up next to Billy, unconsciously admiring her new right hand. The cybernetics expert Henry matched her up with had provided a complete replacement. It was experimental, but Bedlam told him she was happy to be the guinea pig if his work might help regular people who needed it. Of course, she then had the limb doctored up by one of Agent Black's contacts, saying she wasn't too crazy about being an off-the-shelf cyborg.

"Speaking of people who run off on a regular basis," Billy said. "Hey Titus, are you going to the great white north again?"

Titus made a vaguely vulgar gesture at Billy, then, after scooping a slice of pizza onto a plate, meandered over to join them.

"Nah. Doc and I have some stuff to discuss," he said. "Expand my knowledge base."

"Fine, I'm in," Kate said, rolling her eyes at all of them. "I only really dislike most of you. But you'll never save the world without me."

"I think I'm on the mostly disliked list," Emily said. "But that's okay. I love you, Kate Miller."

Kate started down Emily hard, then reached out and ruffled her neon blue hair.

"I truly can't stand you, Emily," she said.

"Told you," Emily said.

Doc and Henry joined them last. The two older men had been having a quiet conversation away from the group, with Neal dutifully listening in. The android followed them over with a seriousness that teetered on parody.

"You guys look like you have bad news," Jane said. "What's up?"

"Henry figured out something about the Tower we never knew about before," Doc said.

"Even when we were close to your age and always there, we had no idea the Tower's capabilities," Henry said. "I mean, we knew it was more than just a building. We knew it was a spaceship in disguise. But what we didn't know was… well. It's a lot more ship than we thought."

"I knew it was bigger on the inside!" Emily said.

"Tell me it's not a time machine," Titus said.

"Tell me it *is* a time machine," Emily said.

"No, and no," Henry said. "But what we did find is that all this time, it's had what, if my calculations are correct, is an FTL engine."

"That sounds alarming," Jane said.

"We have a *hyperdrive*?" Emily yelled.

"In layman's terms, yes, we have a hyperdrive," Henry said.

"After saving Entropia, I never thought I'd have a better day," Emily said. "I have been proven wrong. Hey, Titus, you know what this means?"

"I don't think I want to know what this means," Titus said.

"It means someday I'll get to actually tell you to 'Punch it, Chewie,'" Emily said.

"I've spent time inside your mind, and I still don't quite understand you," Titus said.

Billy put his hands up.

"So are you saying you could all go to space with me?" he said.

"Theoretically," Henry said.

"Why would we want to go to space?" Kate said.

"I suppose if we ever got bored saving this world, we could

go save others," Titus said.

"Can I propose we shelve that one for a while?" Jane said. "I don't know about you guys, but I kind of want to make sure this world's in one piece before we start traveling the universe."

"Now there's a plan I can get behind," Doc said. "One world at a time."

"One world at a time," Jane said. She looked up at the Tower once more, silently watching from high above. She raised a glass to the starship. "Hey guys? Welcome home."

Also by Matthew Phillion

Novels in the Indestructibles Series – in print and e-book formats

The Indestructibles (Book 1)
The Indestructibles: Breakout (Book 2)
The Entropy of Everything (the Indestructibles Book 3)
Like a Comet (the Indestructibles Book 4)

Tales from the Indestructiverse

Echo and the Sea
Poseidon's Scar

The Indestructibles One-Shots (digital shorts)

The Soloist
Gifted
Blood & Bone
The Monsters We Make
Krampus in the City
Roll for Initiative (an Indestructibles Story) – also available in print

The Dungeon Crawlers Novella Series

The Player's Guide to Dungeon Crawling (The Dungeon Crawlers Book 1)
The Dungeoneer's Bestiary (The Dungeon Crawlers Book 2)
The Ghoul Slayer's Guidebook (The Dungeon Crawlers Book 3)
Lost in Revery: Tales of the Dungeon Crawlers Vol. 1

ABOUT THE AUTHOR

Matthew Phillion is a writer, actor, and film director based in Salem, Massachusetts. He is the author of the Indestructibles Young Adult superhero adventure series, its spinoff series, *Echo and the Sea*, and the RPG-meets-high-fantasy *Dungeon Crawlers* series. A "recovering journalist," he has written on everything from hospital safety to cybersecurity to the opioid crisis.